*In The High Hills Of Burma
Each Must Face The Truth*

DAVID—Famed doctor and great lover
. . . in trouble

MAUREEN—The girl who really loves
him

MICHAEL—Neglectful father, dying of
cancer

ROSE—Voluptuous Eurasian nurse

CARADAY—A man who tries to live by
his ideals

"Good contemporary adventures . . .
well-written, fast-moving, with believ-
able characters"

—PUBLISHERS' WEEKLY

"Characters come alive . . . enjoyable
and extremely diverting"

—BEST SELLERS

"Moves fast . . . exotic adventure . . .
I cou'_____"

—_____ICATE

FORESTS OF THE NIGHT

Jon Cleary

Tiger, tiger, burning bright
In the forests of the night,
What immortal hand or eye
Could frame thy fearful symmetry?

William Blake

POPULAR LIBRARY • NEW YORK

DEDICATION:
For Paul R. Reynolds

Chapter 1

1

"David Alexander Breton!"

As he moved forward in answer to his name, David Breton remembered with dry amusement other Bretons who had been called at court. There had been Gervase Breton, who had spoken French perhaps better than he had spoken English and who, if his memoirs were to be believed, had been a popular man with the ladies at the court of Louis XVI. It had been Gervase who, mistaking a Revolution mob for a pack of irate husbands, had cried out *au secours!* instead of *help!* and had almost died because of his linguistic fluency. Then there had been Charles Breton, who, if *his* memoirs were to be believed, had never taken *nyet* for an answer from the ladies at the court of Alexander I of Russia. Still another Breton, for whom David had been named, who had written no memoirs and who had spoken no foreign languages at all, believing that all foreigners should know how to speak English, had been at the court of a King of Siam. There he had been popular with the concubines, cementing relations between England and Siam in a way that would not have amused Queen Victoria; he had died proudly at the age of ninety-one of venereal disease, and in David's eyes was as much a hero as those other Bretons who had died, perhaps more patriotically but with less panache, on the fields of Waterloo, the Crimea and the Somme. It was that first David who would have looked with the same dry amusement as the present David on the current scene. This was a court of law, not the court of a king, but the Bretons were still involved with women.

David took the oath, then stood waiting to be questioned. There was a quiet arrogance in his stance; taking the oath had not humbled him, as it does so many when they enter the witness box for the first time. He was not a big man, but he gave the impression of being taller than he was; even when relaxed he stood straight, his square jaw with the cleft in it lifted just a little. He was both handsome and distinguished-looking, and his stance suggested that he was well aware of the fact. At first glance one took him for a very well preserved man in his late forties; but his sleek thick hair had been grey since he was twenty-five and he had now just turned forty. If the dark brown eyes looked a little tired, that was because of late nights and not ill-health. The flesh on the strongly boned face was firm and still tanned from the summer; the aquiline nose was a proud beak above the arrogant mouth. Only his air of cynicism, cultivated and certain, suggested the disillusion of middle age.

"Mr. Breton—" Barrington, David's counsel, adjusted his thick horn-rimmed glasses and puckered his thin lips nervously. Why did I engage him? David wondered. He looks like an owl unsure of its own wisdom. "Mr. Breton, would it be true to say that you are one of this country's leading plastic surgeons?"

"The British Medical Association forbids me to advertise," said David, making no attempt to look modest, since he knew he was incapable of it, "but it cannot ask me to contradict your opinion."

There was a ripple of laughter in the court, and Mr. Justice Deansgate looked pained. He looked down out of a face that David, looking at it professionally, estimated would have given him a year's work: hooded eyes, too-large nose, dewlaps that almost hid his high collar. But judges never came to plastic surgeons: justice, unlike truth, was not expected to look beautiful, nor were its practitioners. "Mr. Breton, we appreciate your delicate position, but could you confine yourself to a simple yes or no?"

David bowed his head, then looked back at Barrington. The Indian summer had lingered on through October, and the courtroom was warm and stuffy. David, immaculate in silk shirt, pale blue woolen waistcoat and dark blue flannel suit, could feel the sweat already beginning to start up under his armpits and on his chest. He had always sweated too eas-

6

ily; it had often been an embarrassment to him in the operating theatre. This might be an uncomfortable day. Barrington, also obviously feeling the heat, hitched his gown out from him, as if trying to create a draught. "Never mind, Mr. Breton, I think I have made my point. Now, it has been established that you performed some plastic surgery upon the plaintiff, Mrs. Elinor Beatty."

David glanced into the body of the court, where Elinor Beatty, wrapped in mink and malice, sat beside her husband. She, too, was feeling the heat; her mink stole was flung back over her chair, like the pelt of an animal she had just hunted and shot. A shaft of sunlight, pitiless as the flash of a photographer's bulb, came through a side window and showed plainly the scar on her nose. A strange woman, David thought, one who took a perverse delight in exhibiting what had happened to her because of her vanity. Her natural nose had not been an ugly one, nor had it spoiled the symmetry of the rest of her face. When she had first come to him, he had been attracted to her and he had made the mistake of showing it; when he had realised the character of the woman, predatory and demanding, he had backed away and become strictly professional towards her. He had advised her against surgery, but she had been insistent that she must have a retroussé nose, a Breton nose such as a hundred others of his patients had. She now had a Breton nose, one that was highlighted by a scar that, he mused, would eventually turn her cross-eyed if she continued to pay so much attention to it. He had been willing to settle with her out of court, but she had insisted on parading to the world what his negligence had done to her. It was only when the writ had been issued that he had realised the extent of his blunder in showing interest in her and then backing away. He was going to be made to pay for more than just the scar on her nose.

"Did you advise Mrs. Beatty against the operation?" David said that he had. "Why?"

David glanced at Gorham, Elinor Beatty's counsel, anticipating an objection. But Gorham was doodling with a gold pencil on the brief spread out in front of him; bored and indifferent, he could have been counsel waiting for the next case to be called. David, not accustomed to being ignored, felt a flash of resentment. But he had too much control of himself to show it. He had always prided himself on his control. The successful surgeon and the successful lover, and he was both, never showed their true faces.

7

"I did not feel it was necessary. Mrs. Beatty was already an attractive woman, not needing my help." He bowed in her direction and she gave him a twisted smile in return. Not quite a sneer, he noted. An aristocrat or a factory girl would have given him a full-sized sneer; but Elinor Beatty was middle class right through. It had been another of the things that had made him back away from her. He was a snob, even in bed. "I don't operate just for the sake of collecting a fee."

That sounded smug, he knew, but it couldn't be helped. He had to pay lip service to the myth that doctors were healers first and businessmen only by necessity. He had never thought of himself as anything but a businessman, but one look at the judge had told him such frankness wouldn't pay in this court.

"Why did Mrs. Beatty want the surgery done?"

"She said she wanted it to be a surprise for her husband. Evidently he had admired my handiwork on other women." There was another murmur of laughter in the court. Sitting beside his wife, William Beatty, plum-coloured even to the top of his bald head and considerably older than his wife, looked on the verge of apoplexy. If her husband had been younger and healthier, David thought, none of us would be here in court today. England, like so many countries in Europe, had too many young women married to too many old men. The country was not safe for attractive bachelors like himself.

"Now what happened after the operation?"

David hesitated a moment, but the hesitation did not show as such; to the court he could just have been gathering his facts, trying to put them in chronological order. Without moving his head he looked down into the body of the court, looking for someone who might contradict his story. Louise de Felice was there, sitting with a woman friend. She would not contradict his story; she, like Elinor Beatty, had an apoplectic older husband. She had rung him up only this morning to be reassured that he would not mention her name in court; her sigh of relief had been almost as loud as her gasp of passion on the evening they had been together in her flat. Behind Louise he recognised three women ex-patients; he was pleased to see that none of his handiwork showed on them. He knew what had brought them here: anything for a thrill, any piece of scandal to help fill in their empty days. There was no malice in them: they suffered from the disease of too much time and too little to do: even their operations

8

had been a way of filling in time. Across the aisle and below them, sitting at the Press bench, was Phil Corder, one of the correspondents for a morning newspaper social diary. He was a man who had no time at all: he galloped from luncheons to cocktail parties to balls like a social hyena: the diseased bits of other people's lives were his meat. Pale-faced and lank-haired, shabbily debonair, he stared up at David with insolent derision; *he* would contradict David's story if he knew the real facts; and his expression showed that he suspected that the real facts were not going to be told. Feeling a twinge of unease, David looked away from Corder and only then saw the bland brown face of U Maung Zan.

For a moment he thought a trick of light was working on the face of a stranger, turning it into that of a recognisable friend. He stared, puzzled and hardly able to believe that this was the Burman he hadn't seen in almost twenty years. Then one of the bright black eyes closed in a wink and the brown face split in a wide white smile, a flash of friendliness in the sober atmosphere of the court.

David nodded in reply, then turned his gaze back to Barrington. He felt an even greater unease now that he had seen U Maung Zan. Conscience began to stir like an old and forgotten wound. When he had last known Maung Zan, he would not have committed perjury.

"I left Mrs. Beatty in the care of my theatre sister, Sister Hagen. It was a simple operation and I did not expect any post-op. complications."

"A previous witness, Dr. Quirk, has stated that he considered this a serious operation. Do you disagree with that opinion?"

"Dr. Quirk and I have frequently disagreed. Our opinions have rarely been compatible."

Barrington looked as if he were about to pursue that line of questioning, then changed his mind. "Did you personally tell Sister Hagen where you could be contacted if needed?"

"No." There was no need to say that he had not spoken to Maureen at any time that day, other than to ask for the necessary instruments while he had been operating. Their quarrel had had nothing to do with what had happened to Elinor Beatty. "I left a note with one of the nurses to give to Sister Hagen. I then went to the Royal Automobile Club—"

"That can be substantiated?"

"I believe so." He and Louise had been careful to leave the club separately; but that was one fact he did not want substantiated. "I had to meet an ex-patient who did not turn up."

"Would you care to name that ex-patient?"

"Not unless I am forced to," he said, not making too much effort to sound gallant, underplaying it but making sure the point got across. Although Liz Bismark deserved to have her name divulged. If she had turned up for their date, a perfectly harmless meeting, he would not have gone off with Louise, whom he had met accidentally. He would still have been at the club when Elinor Beatty's hemorrhage had occurred and he could have been at the hospital in time to prevent the damage that had been done. It served him right for making a date with a notoriously unreliable woman. Even when he and Liz had been lovers, she had been unreliable; the only time she had ever been reliable had been in bed. He looked up at the judge and for a moment his mind went off at a tangent: would Deansgate have patience with an unreliable woman, in bed or out of it?

"Your Honour, she is a well-known lady who, I think, would prefer not to have her name divulged here. It would not be in her interests to have it publicised that her renowned beauty is not all her own work."

There was another murmur of laughter in the court; except, David remarked, that Elinor Beatty and his three ex-patients did not laugh. He would have to be careful. Plastic surgery, like castration, was an operation patients did not treat as a joke. He had succumbed to the unforgivable professional sin, laughing at his clients. He looked up again at the judge.

"By all means, Mr. Breton, let us be gallant. Unless plaintiff's counsel—" He looked down at Gorham, who shook his head. "Go on, Mr. Breton."

David hesitated again, looking at Gorham. The latter lolled like a huge madam. His old tattered wig looked like the remains of a cheap permanent wave; a vulgarly huge ring glittered like a badge of office on a fat finger; and his jowls were still dusted with powder. He would be more at home in Bow Street than in this court, David thought. He looked bored and confident, much too confident. David glanced at the Beattys, saw their twin look of smug assurance, as if his evidence would not matter a jot to the final outcome of the case. For the first time David began to feel the nag of worry. He stared at Gorham, trying to answer confidence with confidence, and was piqued when Gorham pointedly looked away, as if he were not interested in David.

"Go on, Mr. Breton," said Barrington, and bit his lips. He, too, looked worried.

"When the lady did not arrive, I then went on to my father's flat——"

"Did Sister Hagen know you would be there?"

"I am sure of it. The information was in the note I left for her."

"Was your father at his flat?"

"Hardly. He is the British Consul in Mandalay." At once David knew he had made another mistake. He saw the hurt look on Barrington's face, and too late he realised he should not attempt to score off his own counsel. His biting tongue was beginning to curl back and bite himself.

"I have a key to the flat and I often go there to work." He didn't try to apologise to Barrington by softening the tone of his voice; when he made mistakes, he put them behind him and tried not to repeat them. It was one of the few characteristics he shared with his father; tolerance, for their own or anyone else's mistakes, had never been a Breton virtue. Michael Breton would read all this in the airmail edition of *The Times*. Cold-looking even in the heat of Mandalay, austere as the army book of regulations that had ruled his life for so long, he would curl a lip and order another pink gin to dispel the taste of his son's disgrace. For a Breton to be in a court at all would be a disgrace in the eyes of Michael Breton; unlike his son, he had never been amused by the peccadillos and pursuits of previous Bretons. Charity had never been one of his failings. "I am less likely to be disturbed at my father's flat than at my own. I am writing a book on plastic surgery."

That was a lie, too. He had notes for the book, but the writing of it was a long way off. "Did Sister Hagen phone you there?"

"No. The first I knew of what had happened to Mrs. Beatty was when I returned to my own flat about eleven-thirty. I rang the hospital and they told me she had had a bad hemorrhage at eight o'clock. I went straight to the hospital, but the damage had been done by then."

"Are you criticising the doctor who had to attend Mrs. Beatty in your absence?"

"Not at all," David said. "But he was not a plastic surgeon. To stop the hemorrhage he had to undo the work I had done. That resulted in the scar Mrs. Beatty now carries. The doctor did his job and did it well. But he was not a plastic surgeon, just as I am not a pediatrician nor an urologist. There are

11

very few doctors who are all-round specialists, just as there are very few lawyers—"

"Judges are lawyers," said Mr. Justice Deansgate. "We are judges, Mrs. Breton, because we aspire to be all-round specialists."

Another mistake, David thought. There was a murmur of laughter from counsel and the court clerks, but this time Deansgate did not look pained; he was not a man to silence his own audience. David looked down at Barrington, but the latter was smiling at the judge. Behind him his junior counsel was also smiling, and across from them Gorham and his junior were enjoying the joke. They are even more of a closed shop than we doctors are, David thought. They were even so sure of themselves that they could afford to laugh at a client. They would argue vehemently against each other in court, but it was all show for the benefit of the clients. Well, he couldn't complain. That was how the world went: one took what one could where one could get it, and never let the taking of it blight one's private conscience. It had been his own credo for the past ten years.

The cross-examination went on, but at last Barrington sat down. Gorham rose slowly from his seat, almost as if he were being pumped up. "Mr. Breton—" His voice suggested that his breath would smell of port wine: it had a dark rich tone to it, the voice of a man always sure of himself. His looks and voice belied his brilliant reputation: he was a sensualist who had not allowed himself to be chilled by the cold logic of law. This man, David thought, would understand what lures another man into a woman's bed. Unfortunately that was not the point they were going to argue.

"Mr. Breton, you are certain that you wrote in your note to Sister Hagen that you would be at your father's flat after going to the Royal Automobile Club?"

"I am sure of it."

"What did you say in the note?"

"How do I know?" David said impatiently, losing control of himself for a moment. Gorham was getting under his skin. "It was a note scribbled in pencil, not a statutory declaration. Can you remember exactly what you wrote in a letter last week, or even yesterday?"

Gorham glanced up at the judge, and Deansgate leaned forward. "Mr. Breton, it is not the practice in this court to allow witnesses to cross-examine counsel. It would no doubt make for a lively illustration of democracy, but the court is concerned with justice, not democracy. It does not feel itself competent to pass opinion on the latter principle."

There was no murmur of laughter this time, but all the legal men in court seemed to sit back with smug looks on their faces: the outsider had been put in his place. David bowed again to the judge and looked back at Gorham. I shall have to watch myself, he thought. This judge is not on my side; and it had been agreed there was to be no jury.

Gorham pushed his wig forward like a man tilting his cap; it would have been a cocksure gesture in a man less majestic. "Mr. Breton, you are also quite sure that you did not hear the phone ring at your father's flat at"—he consulted his notes— "at approximately eight-fifteen on the evening in question?"

"Quite certain."

Gorham looked at David for a long moment, then he nodded. "That will be all, Mr. Breton. I think we have finished with you."

There was no mistaking the contempt in his voice. David flushed, then turned and stepped down from the box. He was suddenly conscious of the fact that he was sweating profusely, but he restrained himself from reaching for a handkerchief to wipe his face. As he set down he glanced back into the body of the court. The Beattys, Louise de Felice, the women ex-patients, were not looking at him; they all seemed to be ignoring him, as if he were already the loser and one not deserving of sympathy. Only two faces were turned towards him: Corder's and U Maung Zan's, the one sharp with malicious amusement, the other bright with friendliness.

"Maureen Margaret Hagen!"

David noticed the stir among the women as Maureen walked to the box. It was the first time any of them had seen her out of her starched white uniform; it was as if they were surprised to find she was a woman like themselves. And a good-looking woman, dammit, David thought; and smiled encouragingly at her as she glanced at him across the court. She didn't return his smile, but her face seemed to tighten. Then she looked at Barrington as the latter rose to question her. He straightened his glasses again and raised his hand as if to smooth down his wig; then abruptly he seemed to give up the idea of trying to look debonair and got down to business. The women in the court sat back, having had their good look at Maureen.

"Miss Hagen, you have been theatre sister to Mr. Breton for three years, that is correct?"

"Yes." Her voice was very low. She put up a hand to push a strand of blonde hair back beneath her small black hat. She wore a black suit that, despite the fullness of the jacket, suggested the full curved body beneath it; David noticed she was wearing no jewelry, not even the pearls he had given her last Christmas. Clothes had always been her one extravagance and he had often chided her for it. She had replied that that was his selfishness coming out again. A man with as many suits as he had was in no position to talk to a woman about wardrobe extravagance; her father, God rest his bitter soul, had had one suit all the time she had known him. As he looked at her now, it struck David that, despite blondes' traditional fondness for black, this was the first time he had seen her in black. He smiled to himself: was she jokingly in mourning for him? He opened the smile to her, trying to set up the current again between them, but again she looked away, refusing the contact.

"Have you always found him a conscientious doctor, interested at all times in his patients' welfare?"

Maureen seemed to hesitate for a moment. Her grey eyes, deep-lidded and heavy-lashed, closed as if in anguish; then abruptly they opened wide, as if a sudden unpleasant thought had startled her. Watching her, David once more felt uneasy, this time more than ever. Maureen was his main defence, but suddenly she looked no more reliable than a stranger called in from the street outside. He took a silk handkerchief from his pocket and mopped his face. He had forgotten the warm stuffiness of the courtroom. He was suffering now the heat of nervousness.

"There have been no complaints about Mr. Breton up till now." Over the past year or two David had been hardly aware of Maureen's American accent. Now, flattened by strain, her voice had almost a nasal twang to it. She hadn't quite travelled all the way from Nebraska, she had not entirely lost the echo of home.

It was Barrington's turn to hesitate. Maureen hadn't phrased her answer quite the way he would have liked. "When Mr. Breton left the hospital, where were you?"

"I am not sure—it was some months ago—" I've never seen her as nervous as this, David thought. Even after their fierce argument that day of the Beatty operation, she had been calm and composed in the theatre immediately afterwards. That had been one of the first things that had attracted him to her, both as a theatre sister and as a woman:

14

her calm, almost urbane way of coping with situations that might have rubbed another woman raw. Like so many Englishmen, he was ignorant of America and Americans; he had been to America once on a fleeting visit and met no one but other doctors. He judged Americans by American tourists, people who were sometimes a little too aggressive because, coming abroad, they felt for the first time a sneaking doubt of their own superiority. It was Maureen who had told him that inferiority, like tooth decay, was something Americans never admitted. She had also told him that if they were sometimes a little too aggressive because of their doubt of themselves, that could be understood even if not forgiven; their aggressiveness was no more unforgivable than the cold disdain of the English, who never doubted themselves when abroad. He had been surprised to find that a woman from Nebraska, ultima Thule to him, a place he had had to look up on a map, should have been so worldly perceptive as to pass an opinion on the English abroad. It was as if an Indian medicine man had passed a sound critical judgement on his own plastic surgery. But Maureen had been full of small surprises and that, also, had been one of the things that had continued to attract him to her. A woman with no surprises made a dull mistress.

"I think I was down in the sisters' quarters," she said, her voice still twanging. "I—I was not feeling well."

"When did you receive Mr. Breton's note?"

"When I came up to check on Mrs. Beatty in her room. The nurse on duty there handed it to me."

"And what did it say?"

Maureen looked at David and in that instant he knew she was going to tell the truth, that she was going to offer him no defence at all. "It said that Mr. Breton would be at the Royal Automobile Club."

"That was all?" Barrington had taken off his thick-rimmed glasses; without them his face looked blank.

"That was all." Her voice rasped: the twang seemed to add a note of finality to what she said. She opened her handbag and fumbled in it. "I still have the note."

Barrington, pained and surprised, looked at David. The look on his face suggested that he was the one who had been betrayed, not David.

David shook his head. The sweat was pouring off him now and all he wanted was to be out of this courtroom. There

15

would be more questions asked, Barrington would put on a show for him, but the case was already over.

He should have known better than to trust a woman who was full of surprises.

2

He waited for her outside the court. He stood behind a pillar, feeling like a private eye in a television film: any moment now he would be asked to move on to make way for the commercial. He saw the Beattys go by, stopping for a moment as the photographers, cameras bared, flung themselves at them; Elinor Beatty flashed a smile, smug as a screen starlet, wearing her scar as if it were an Academy Award. Louise de Felice, sleek, beautiful, and vain, always looking for the reflected image of herself in mirrors, shop windows, the polished paint of her Rolls-Royce, came out into the sunlight wearing dark glasses. The woman with her and the three ex-patients following them also wore dark glasses. They moved together down to the Strand in a blaze of anonymity. David watched them go, smiling to himself, although he felt little humour. He had always laughed at the world and never at himself and that had been another of the things Maureen had found wrong with him.

"Why, if it isn't Mr. Breton! Dodging the sunlight or the limelight?" It was Phil Corder, also keeping to the shadows; he was a night creature and he resented being called upon to work in broad daylight. At least when covering luncheons he was fed.

"Hello, Corder. Going to bury your bone of scandal?" Even though he had been featured regularly in all the gossip columns, he had never courted favour with Corder and his like. He had no time for newspaper reporters: they were vultures or hyenas, some better bred than others but all disreputable and vicious. Corder's mother, a subject for scandal herself, was a film critic on a Sunday newspaper, so he came of good destructive stock. "Is your mother still lauding foreign films she doesn't understand?"

Corder looked at him slyly. "Did the decision upset you?"

I'm stupid, David thought. Trading insults with a hack journalist; why don't I go back and throw tomatoes at the judge? The decision and the judge's comments did upset me, but there is no need to make an exhibition of myself. He leaned on his umbrella and did his best to look unperturbed.

To anyone but Corder, an expert at tearing down façades, the act would have been successful.

Corder shook his head. "Even so, I thought the judge was rather harsh in his opinion, didn't you?"

Go away, David thought. Get lost or drop dead, as Maureen would say. The American language had its uses at times. "Even judges are entitled to their opinions, Corder."

Corder grinned. "Oh, certainly. It is a pity, though, isn't it, that their opinions can cost one money. Two thousand pounds! Deansgate put a high price on Mrs. Beatty's nose."

"That is your comment, Corder, not mine. Don't credit me with it in your column tomorrow morning."

"What may I credit you with?"

"The diplomatic *bon mot*—no comment."

He had seen the last of the photographers disappearing towards Fleet Street, their cameras held like grenade cases and just as explosive. He turned and saw Maureen coming out of the courts with U Maung Zan. Ignoring Corder, he walked quickly across to them.

"I didn't know you two knew each other." He said it almost resentfully.

"I introduced myself to Sister Hagen." U Maung Zan bloomed with cheerfulness: no verdict had gone against him. Then David remembered that Maung Zan had always been cheerful, even when told that he had failed First Year Medicine and would have to sit again. "In Burma one would never do that. The West has certain advantages—but don't quote me."

"Your father asked him to look me up," Maureen said, and David didn't miss the note of accusation in her voice. She knew that he had little time for his father, that he made no attempt to keep in touch with the old man out in Mandalay.

"How are you, David?" Maung Zan said.

"You could have chosen a better day to ask me," David said, then felt ashamed of his rudeness. He smiled at Maung Zan. "Perhaps I could do with a dose of Buddhist resignation. Why are you in London? How long are you here for?"

Then Corder crept in, a hyena picking at the bones of a dead friendship. "Oh, Miss Hagen. Were you pleased with the verdict? Will this make any difference to your relationship with Mr. Breton?"

"Drop dead," said Maureen, and walked away.

"I should quote that one," said David to Corder, and he and Maung Zan followed Maureen.

Maung Zan smiled at both David and Maureen, as if he were blandly insensitive to the tension in the air; but he was not, and David remembered out of the long ago how Maung Zan had always turned a bland face to embarrassment, disappointment, even pain. "I shall see you tomorrow, David. At your flat, perhaps? Goodbye, Sister Hagen. We shall meet again."

He bowed, put his brown trilby squarely on his head as if it were a ceremonial headpiece, buttoned the jacket of the suit that was too large for him, then turned and walked away, leaving them to the chill of their antagonism.

"I'll see you home," David said, and took Maureen's arm.

Gently, firmly, she removed his hand. Her voice was under control now; the twang had gone, Nebraska was once more part of the past. "I don't need you any more, David."

"I'm surprised you admit you ever needed me."

"That has been one of my disadvantages in having anything to do with you. I'm too honest."

"You were too honest there in the court." His voice had regained its old sardonic note; it was better than sounding bitter, made him less vulnerable. "And that note—you didn't tell me you still had it."

"It's the only one you've ever written me. It wasn't a love letter, but it had its sentimental value."

He smiled, appreciating the joke. They had always fenced like this; it was how he had always wanted it. That way he had never been committed to love nor the confessing of it.

"I'll still take you home. Just to show you there are no hard feelings."

She went with him as he led her up towards Lincoln's Inn Fields and his car. She laughed out loud as he removed the parking ticket from the windshield wiper.

"It's not my day," he said, resenting her laughter as much as the ticket. "Two thousand pounds, and now a parking ticket."

"That's British justice." She was still smiling, but it was an effort: whatever happened to David from now on, the joke was still on her. But she was not going to let him know. "You were always telling me about it."

"But they must have seen the badge on the front of the car! I could have been in one of those offices"—he gestured round the square—"attending some stricken solicitor. I assume legal men have heart attacks occasionally."

18

"Lawyers are never stricken in their offices. Who ever heard of an English lawyer dying from working too hard?"

She had regained all her composure now; outwardly she was in high humour. But she was weeping inside, tasting the salt of tears that didn't show. She had wept only once in front of David, after he had made love to her for the first time; and she had learned then that he accepted tears as a weakness, something to be played on. She looked at him as he settled behind the wheel of the car, felt the hateful weakness for him, and looked away again. She should go back to Nebraska, to the farm in the sandhills west of Ogallala and the ghost of her dead father, who had hated all foreigners, including her mother, who had died giving birth to her. Life had been simple there: uncomplicated hate had been the only emotion. She wondered what her father, hard-handed and hard-faced, hard-principled in his hard Lutheran shell, would have thought of David, quite apart from his being a foreigner.

"What are you smiling at?"

"I was thinking of you as a foreigner," she said. "But the English are never foreigners, are they? Not even when they're abroad."

He started up the car. It was a Bristol, with body by Zagato. He was not a fast driver, but he had wanted something different from a Rolls-Royce or Bentley, the usual status symbol of the successful doctor. He was honest enough with himself to admit that the Bristol was a status symbol, but at least it was different. He had never wanted to belong to any mould.

"I wonder what the College will think of today?" Maureen nodded at the plain, stained building of the Royal College of Surgeons as they drove past it. "This may spoil your chances of ever being President."

He glanced sideways at her, looking for malice. But he should have known better: there had never been any malice in her. Much as he wanted to, he could not believe that her testimony in court today had been born out of malice. "Perhaps. But if the Medical Council doesn't call on me, this will all be forgotten in five or six years' time. I couldn't expect to be President before then."

She shook her head. "You're always so sure of yourself, aren't you, David?"

He said nothing, but took the car out into Kingsway, down Aldwych and round Australia House into the Strand. Out of the corner of his eye he saw the posters in the windows: Australia, Land of Opportunity, Land for a New Life. He disliked Australians as much as he disliked Americans; they had the same aggressiveness, the same loudmouthed determination to prove they were right. He drove on along the Strand, turning his back on Australia. A month on the Riviera, that was all he needed to begin a new life.

When he pulled the car up outside her flat in Cornwall Gardens in Kensington, she made no attempt to get out. "No, I'm not asking you up, David. If you've got anything to say, say it here."

"Why did you double-cross me today?"

"I didn't double-cross you, as you put it. I hadn't promised anything."

"You let me believe—"

"No, I didn't let you believe anything, David. Your own insufferable conceit let you believe it. You just couldn't get it into your fat head that a woman who'd let you go to bed with her wouldn't commit perjury for you. You have no sense of sin or shame."

"And you have? About going to bed or about committing perjury?"

"Both. Does that surprise you?"

It did, but he would not tell her so. He had long ago convinced himself that a sense of sin was only a weapon invented by the priests. And shame was only a fit of masochism indulged in by the weak. "You didn't have to commit perjury. All you had to do was not remember."

She sighed, surprised that she felt no anger. Across the road, in the high-railed gardens, four young children played under the proud doting eyes of their young mothers. Had David ever been as innocent as those children? "There's no difference in your eyes, is there? I mean, between the spoken truth and the unspoken lie? Either satisfies your conscience, so long as you're not personally inconvenienced."

"You've lied for me before."

"Not under oath. Only to your ex-patients, the women who wanted to come back for more attention from those sensitive fingers—" The twang came back into her voice. Back in Nebraska, if you could imagine David in Nebraska, she would have hit him with her father's whip. She was full of anger now, the tears starting to her eyes. Behind her, across in the gardens, the children shrieked with glee, twenty years from the pain of love. "I've even lied to Mrs. de Felice for you—"

"So that's it," he said. "You would have kept quiet if you hadn't seen her in court."

"Yes!" The tears came unchecked now; this was their farewell, he couldn't play on her weakness any more. "When I saw her there, I knew whom you'd been with that night. I might have lied for you if it had been one of the others—"

They had fought about Louise de Felice on the morning of Elinor Beatty's operation. He had broken a weekend date with Maureen, told her some lie, to go away with Louise instead; and Maureen, called to the grapevine by some woman whose name he had never learned, had been told about it. He made most of his large income from women and in his leisure moments he needed their company; but they were a curse and while making love to them he made sure he never fell in love with them. He was in love only with himself, Maureen and Louise and several other women had each told him, and they had laughed with bitter amusement when he had taken the remark as a compliment to his own taste.

He drew on his driving gloves. "My dear Maureen—"

She dabbed at her eyes with a handkerchief, angry with him and angry with herself now. "I'm not your dear Maureen, nor am I your Sister Hagen, while I'm at it. You can find another nurse. I've just resigned!"

That shocked him almost as much as her betrayal of him in the witness box. "But, my dear girl—"

"Oh, for God's sake! Don't be so goddam English with me! I've seen you with no clothes on—don't try the stuffed-shirt act on *me*—" She suddenly dropped her voice. The four young children had come to the garden fence; they stood on the other side of the railings, aliens beyond a border where age and experience were the only passport. They looked with wide-eyed frank curiosity at the squabbling grown-ups.

"The crudeness of Nebraska keeps coming out—"

"A little crudeness wouldn't do you any harm. At least it's an honest feeling."

"You've become quite a lecturer in the last half-hour. Is that what you'll do now—become a lecturer on men? Or will you go back to Nebraska and be a farmer's daughter again, marry some crude cowboy and raise a dozen honestly crude kids." He looked across at the children, faces pressed like distorted masks between the railings. "I hope you teach them better manners than those inquisitive brats."

She didn't look at the children, but stared straight ahead.

"No one ever goes back to Nebraska. I wrote to Drucker at the Mayo Clinic and I'm going to work for him."

"When? How soon do you leave?"

"Next week. I'm—" She hesitated for a moment, then looked at him. "I'm going the long way around. I'm going to see your father in Mandalay first."

"My father?" She was full of surprises for him today. "Why do you want to see him?"

She hesitated again, as if she were concealing something. "He sent a message to me through Maung Zan. I—I've been writing to him, David, ever since he came home on leave that time two years ago."

"You never told me."

"You never asked me. You introduced me to him and never even asked me what I thought of him. You never talked about him, ever. So why should I?"

"You were interested enough in him to write to him."

"More than interested. I *liked* him."

"You won't like Mandalay. I was there during the war."

"I'll only be there a few days." She opened the door of the car and got out. "I'll give him your love, David. Or would that embarrass you?"

"It would embarrass both of us. I know my father better than you do."

"Do you? Goodbye, David. I'm sorry for you—and not just for today."

She crossed the pavement and went up the three steps to the front door of the old building in which she had her flat. She had begun to weep again; blinded by tears, she fumbled in her handbag for her key. Then she opened the door and went inside without looking back at him. He stared at the closed door for a moment, then was aware of the four children across the road staring at him. Brats! He was no lover of children, least of all of those who, even if they didn't understand what they saw, were witnesses to his dismissal by a woman he had thought was his for as long as he cared to have her.

He stared back at them as he started up the engine and let in the gears. Then in the moment before he drove off he leaned forward and stuck out his tongue at them. The children stared back at him, then suddenly screamed with delight. He would have liked Maureen to see the gesture, just to prove to her that he wasn't a stuffed shirt. That remark had hurt as much as any other she had made.

U Maung Zan sat sipping his lemonade. David had found the bottle at the back of a cupboard, brought it out and blown the dust off it and poured the lemonade into a glass with a flourish.

"That must be the only vintage lemonade left in London. I should imagine this is the last of a case my mother bought to celebrate the day I was born. She celebrated everything in lemonade. A woman given to passionate living."

Maung Zan had smiled and taken the glass. A Burman who respected the mother's place in a family, he had never grown accustomed to the flippancy of some Westerners when talking about their parents.

"I wanted to get in touch with you last night, Zan, but I didn't know where you were staying."

"The Y.M.C.A. An awfully jolly place. They have special rates for non-Christians," he said with a smile. "And one needs special rates—London is an expensive city now, much more than when I was here last. And my government is frightfully stingy with the foreign currency it allows me."

"You could have come and stayed with me. You didn't have to stay at the Y.M.C.A."

"I didn't know whether you would want me to, David. After all, you never answered any of my letters."

David poured himself a stiff whisky and soda and sat down in the heavy leather chair that was his father's favourite. "I have no excuse, Zan. I've lost touch with a lot of friends. All my own fault."

He could have done with some old friends last night. After he had left Maureen he had stopped by a public phone booth and called his man in his flat in South Audley Street. Dowson had told him that the phone had been ringing constantly and that there were three reporters camped on the front steps.

"I'm afraid you will be in for a very disturbed evening if you come back here, sir. May I suggest you go to a hotel, or perhaps to your father's flat?"

"It's your night off, isn't it, Dowson?"

"That's all right, sir. I'll stay here. Hold the fort, as it were, sir."

"You're promoted, Dowson. You are now a sergeant-major in Breton's Private Army."

"Thank you, sir. Where can I find the—er—general if he is wanted urgently?"

David had to smile, despite his low mood. Dowson was being the perfect gentleman's gentleman, loyal to a fault, trying to say that what had happened today meant no difference to his relationship with his master. "I'll be at my father's flat, Dowson. And thank you."

Later that evening, sitting alone in his father's flat in Queen's Gate he would have been glad of the quiet, correct company of Dowson. Wanting to be neither alone nor have time to think, he had phoned Louise de Felice and asked her to have dinner with him. So coolly that he could not mistake that she was telling him not to call again, she had said she was having dinner with her husband. Then he had called Liz Bismark, and she had been just as cold as Louise and much blunter.

"I read what you said about me in court today, David, even if you spared me mentioning my name. Newspapers publish very full court reports these days, or didn't you know? Public taste or something, or perhaps it's part of the government's broader educational policy. The country is going to the dogs, but we are all terribly well informed. Goodnight, David. If I need a plastic surgeon again, and I probably shall, I'll choose one who has some sympathy for a woman who is losing her looks."

There had been other women he might have called, but he was not accustomed to being rebuffed twice in one night; he did not want to expose himself to a third or even a fourth slap in the face. All at once, for the first time since he had been a student, he had wanted male company. And found to his surprise that none was available. He had no men friends, only acquaintances, and one did not call upon acquaintances to discuss a life that had suddenly begun to crumble at the edges.

That had been the big surprise of yesterday, greater than all the other surprises that had been flung in his face like so much grapeshot. He had never paused to consider, there had been no occasion to do so up till now, that his life was anything but full and complete. He had reputation, money and women: it was all he had ever set out to achieve. For the first time in years he had tasted the acridity of dissatisfaction; later tossing restlessly in his father's bed, there had been the sharper and more frightening taste of self-doubt. What if he alone was not all that he needed? And in his father's bed he remembered the last words his father had said to him when he had been returning to Mandalay two years ago: "I hope you

24

never know loneliness, David. Because if you do, you will never be able to bear it. You've had no training for it."

But his father had been wrong: he *had* had training for it. As a child, as a boy at boarding school, living on one side of the world while his parents lived on the other, in India and Burma, sending letters and cheques as substitutes for love; he had known loneliness long before his father had known it, and long ago he had determined to build a defence against it. And he had been successful, up till now. He had built his defence by making himself dependent on no one. Like the ancient King of the Wood, he had remained forever alert, killing friendship as the king had killed rivals; and now in the night the need for friendship had at last crept up on him, a chink had at last been found in the armour of Rex Nemorensis. It had been his father who had sent him the book on the ancient myths, marking certain passages for him to read. One of the passages marked had been the story of the priest-kings of Nemi, and it had been annotated in the margin: "Never aspire to be king, David. It is a lonely life." David had been fifteen then, and already Michael Breton must have recognised the consuming ambition of the boy. It had been one of several things that had, over the years, kept father and son apart.

"It is good lemonade," said Maung Zan, and David jerked his head up, coming back to the present and the room that still held the echoes of his absent father. "Better than we can get in Burma."

"Why are you back in London?"

"I am buying equipment. I am the Civil Surgeon at the hospital in Sheromere."

"Where's that?"

"On the border of Kachin State and the Shan States. It is a poor town and a poor hospital. Even the mosquito nets are so rotten that the mosquitoes dive right through them."

"How are you getting money, then, to buy equipment?"

"The widow of one of the prewar teak plantation owners died and left us some money. The newspapers, which are still very anti-British, said it was conscience money. I prefer to think it was the sentiment of a woman who still loved Burma."

"My father loves it. Are the Mandalay newspapers against him because he's British?"

"Your father has another handicap besides being British, David. He is a friend of Father Caraday."

25

"Caraday? Who's he?"

"A Roman Catholic missionary at Sheromere. An Australian."

David was not interested in Caraday, but he was interested in the fact that his father was a friend of the missionary. Michael Breton, like his son, had had a deep dislike and distrust of any clergy, particularly the Catholic. "What's made my father such a friend of this priest?"

Maung Zan looked down at his glass. His father had worked for the Bombay-Burma Trading Corporation as a bookkeeper in a teak sawmill, and Maung Zan had grown up speaking English as well as he spoke Burmese. He had the naturally soft high Burmese voice, but in his wilder moments at some of the medical students' parties he had often been as loud and strident as a drunken Welshman or Geordie. David guessed he must be in his mid-forties now, but the years seemed hardly to have touched him. Unless one counted the air of responsibility that David could not remember his ever having worn in the past. He looked particularly sober and responsible right now.

"David, your father is dying."

"Dying?" Despite the fact that he had never been close to his father, rarely gave him a thought unless someone else mentioned his name, he felt a sudden sense of shock. Perhaps it was possible to miss someone one hated as much as to miss someone one loved. He wouldn't know the difference, since he had never loved anyone nor missed them.

"Obviously he hasn't told you."

"We never write, Zan. I saw him for a couple of hours when he was home on leave two years ago. We're not exactly close, Zan. What is it—cancer?"

Maung Zan nodded. "He came to me. I hated to tell him, but he is a man who likes the truth. That was four, no, five months ago. He has another six months at the very most. It is carcinoma of the lung."

"How is he carrying on as Consul?"

"The Embassy know. They have already sent a man up to help him. He takes over from your father as Consul next month."

"Is my father"—he couldn't bring himself to say Father or Dad: that hinted at intimacy, something that had never existed between the two Bretons—"is he coming home?"

"No. He—" Maung Zan looked up, hesitating for a moment. In his bland face there was no sign of accusation: he

26

was only relaying a message: "He said there was nothing to come home for."

David's face was just as bland: he gave no hint that he had got the barbed point of the message. "How is he taking it? The thought of dying, I mean."

"Very calmly."

"He was always a calm man. Cold, I might say."

"No, this is a different calm, David. Father Caraday has had a great influence on him. As he does on everyone. Even me, a Buddhist."

"Has he converted you?"

Maung Zan shook his head, smiling. "He never attempts to convert anyone. That is one of his principal annoyances as far as the *pongyis* are concerned."

"The *pongyis?*"

"The monks. Didn't you know Buddhism is now the state religion? And the *pongyis* have no tolerance for any outside religions. But the government won't listen to them. So the *pongyis* do their best to catch the other religious groups breaking the law, and the other groups, the Christians and Muslims, do their best to do nothing that will cause trouble."

"How then does this Caraday have so much influence if he does nothing?"

"It's the man himself. It's hard to explain, David. All I know is that almost everyone in Sheromere worships him."

"Not my father, I'm sure."

"Why not come out and see for yourself?"

David looked up sharply. "Come out to Burma? Why the hell should I want to go all the way out there?"

"I thought you might like to say goodbye to your father," Maung San said gently. He remembered his love for his own father and the grief he had felt when word had come, while he was here in London, that the old man had been killed by the Japanese. He had never had the opportunity for a final farewell with his father. "I know how estranged you two have been, David. No, he never told me. *You* told me—without meaning to. Not just this morning, but years ago. He would like to see you, David, before he dies."

"Did he tell you that?"

Maung Zan nodded. "He asked me not to tell you. He said it would only embarrass you."

David stood up and walked to the window. The weather had broken abruptly last night and this morning was cold and wet. November had come in with wind and rain; soon everyone would be stumbling through the fogs into December. Rain blurred the window like tears; the houses on the other side of the street quivered as if they were only reflections in water. He would go to the travel agents tomorrow and see about booking for a month on the Riviera. Or perhaps Toremolinos. Or even Marrakesh.

"It would embarrass him, too, Zan. You have no idea of the gulf between us."

"I think I have. But it wouldn't make any difference—at least not to him."

"Are you sure he didn't send you here to ask me to come?"

"Do you want me to say yes? Why, David? To help your pride?" For the first time Maung Zan's voice was tart. He gestured at the newspapers on the floor. "You have no cause for pride this morning."

The newspapers had made a carrion feast of yesterday's proceedings. Leader of the pack, of course, had been Corder. He had written two columns on the case, then mentioned David again in the Diary, quoting David's remark about judges being entitled to their opinions. All the newspapers but *The Times* had published photographs of David; *The Times* had devoted most of its report to the judge's scathing summing-up. The *Daily Mirror* and the *Daily Sketch* had published a full-page photograph of him, as if he ranked with murderers, film stars and drunken playwrights. There were still the *News of the World* and the other Sunday newspapers to come: this was only Thursday.

He had gone out early this morning, bought all the papers and returned through the misery-provoking rain. Letting himself in the front door of the building in which his father had his flat, he had had to stand aside to allow a woman from a neighbouring flat to go out. They had never spoken, but had occasionally nodded whenever they had met on the stairs; this morning she brushed quickly by him, not even glancing at him. Whether she was trying to cut him or trying to avoid embarrassing him, he didn't know. There was just no mistaking the fact that she would rather have not met him.

He had come upstairs, made himself some coffee and toast, and sat down and read the papers as avidly as any teenage pop singer reading his first notices. Only there had been no satisfaction; nor even anger. Only a growing sour sickness, a doubting that was still too dim to have crystallised into any firm shocking realisation. He had sat waiting for phone calls, knowing that some of the women he knew, Louise, Liz, others, knew where he could be found if not at his own flat. But there had been no calls; he was denied even the contact that sarcasm or even abuse would have given him. Then the realisation had come at last. He was utterly alone.

He had sat here in his father's flat, among his father's tastes and memories, so different from his own, and looked at himself for the first time in ten years or more. He had been wise enough to know that this sudden abandonment of him by everyone was not the result of only yesterday; but the knowledge had offered no lift to his spirits nor to his ego. It was no encouragement to know that people had perhaps been trying to break away from him for months, even years. He had been self-sufficient for so long that it was almost like a physical blow to learn that self was not always enough. He had felt the need of someone this morning and there had been no one to turn to. There had been Maureen, of course; he felt sure that if he had called her, she would have responded. But he still had his pride. He wasn't yet reduced to drinking gall.

"Now would be a good time to leave London—" Maung Zan gestured at the papers again.

"I intended to. I was going to—to Amalfi." He picked the name out of the air: he had never been to Amalfi, no one knew him there.

"Whom do you know there?"

"No one." And suddenly he knew that it would be worse there than here in London. There would be company, there always was in places like Amalfi, but he was looking for more than that. But for what? Friendship? Love? He shied away from the first and shut his mind against the second. Whatever it was he needed (needed? It shocked him to find that he *needed* anything), he wouldn't find it in Amalfi.

"Come to Burma, David. The rains have finished. It will be very pleasant there now."

He shook his head. "I couldn't, Zan. Not to stay with my father. Maureen, Sister Hagen, is going out to stay with him."

"Does that matter? He is your father, not hers. You don't need to stay with him all the time. You can come and stay with me in the mountains. It is a good time to be in the mountains now." He looked out the window and shivered. "I love England, but only when the sun is shining. This is no weather for the way you feel now, David."

"Why should you be so concerned for me, Zan? I mean, after so long—I've never written you—" He hesitated, afraid of the answer. "Are you feeling pity for me, Zan?"

Maung Zan shook his head. "Friends don't feel pity, David. Sympathy, yes, but never pity."

Chapter 2

1

David buckled his seat belt as the old Dakota leaned sideways and Mandalay Hill came up in the window. He could see the broad yellow splash of the Irrawaddy, still carrying floodwater from the monsoon, and the green lakes of the rice paddies. Pagodas, like white beehives, dotted the countryside in every direction; religion, he mused, was even more a part of the landscape here than in Rome. He glanced again at Mandalay Hill, rising from the plain like a huge humpbacked beast, its spine a climbing chain of white pagodas.

Across the aisle from him the Kachin woman, who was going through to Putao, put her hand over her eyes, as she had done when the plane had taken off from Rangoon, and sat rigidly in her seat. Beside her the young Roman Catholic nun, apple-cheeked from her leave in Ireland, smiled brightly and in a broad Irish accent tried to comfort the woman in Kachin. Behind them the elderly Chinese couple had taken the seat arm from between them and sat with their huge Alsatian stretched across their laps. At the rear of the plane the drunken Burmese soldier, who had chanted Buddhist prayers for the first hour, had at last fallen asleep. The rest of the interior of the plane was taken up with freight: drums of fuel, pieces of machinery, tires, boxes of ammunition, cases of liquor, bicycles, sewing machines, even a cage full of fowls. When David had seen how the plane was loaded, he had doubted if it would get off the ground, but somehow it had made it. It was an old wartime Dakota and it had probably carried no more mixed cargo then than it carried now.

"Tired?" Maung Zan asked.

David nodded. He was not only tired, but his head was aching. He had stayed only one day in Rangoon, but the heat there had attacked him at once. Each time he had stepped out of his air-conditioned bedroom in the Strand Hotel he had immediately begun to sweat. He had intended visiting the Shwe Dagon pagoda, but the heat had beaten him. With something like awe he had watched five elderly widows, American Express explorers, bustle out into the eye-cracking glare; while he had remained seated beneath a cooling fan in the hotel lobby, sipping a Tom Collins and wondering why he had come all this way to be uncomfortable, unwell and quite possibly unwelcome. His headache was as much due to the thought of the coming reunion with his father as it was to the heat.

"You will find him changed," the Ambassador had said when David had called on him. He was an elderly man who knew the East as well as any man in the Foreign Service, but had one great drawback: exceptionally tall, when he stood straight he towered over the local dignitaries. He had accordingly developed what he called his diplomatic slouch, and after thirty years of slouching he now had a hump on his shoulders. "Your father's one fault was that he never had tolerance."

"It's a family failing, I've been told," David had said.

"It held him back in the Service. Especially out here. An Englishman without tolerance and a certain resignation does not get far in the East. I mean since the war. Before the war, of course, we had it all our own way. It was the locals who had to be resigned in those days. I am afraid they are getting their own back with a vengeance now."

"It must be harder for my father. He was in the Indian Army, you know. I gather that prewar a colonel in India ranked with the lesser Hindu deities."

The Ambassador had discreetly made no comment on that: one often had to be diplomatic even with one's own country-men. They were often the worst, he thought. "Well, your father has changed now. It's this priest Caraday. Can't stand Catholics myself, they're so damned smug—" He realised he had made an undiplomatic remark. "Sorry. Are you a Catholic?"

31

David smiled, letting the Ambassador off the hook: a plastic surgeon also often had to practise diplomacy. "No. I'm a non-practising agnostic."

"Well, I didn't mean to offend. One shouldn't generalise about religion. These Buddhists, for instance—" He caught himself on the verge of another undiplomatic remark. He was near the end of his career: thirty years of steam was coming to a head. "But if one has to have anything to do with clerics, this man Caraday is as good as any. At least he calls a spade a spade, which so many of them don't."

"I didn't think a spade was ever called a spade in diplomatic circles."

"It isn't. That's why we look for the truth among outsiders." The Ambassador smiled and stood up. Then as he shook hands with David his face was abruptly sober. "I think it would be a good idea if you tried to persuade your father to return home with you. I know something about cancer, my wife died of it, and the last weeks can be rather painful. He will at least die more comfortably in London than in Mandalay."

David had just nodded, wondering if his father would find it comfortable to travel home with a son to whom he had never been close.

When he had been called at four o'clock this morning to catch the plane, the headache had been even worse than yesterday. He had sat in the humid darkness of the bus waiting to be driven out to the airport and knew that even the loneliness of Amalfi would have been preferable to this. On the pavement beside the bus a vendor sold hot coffee, turning away while he passed the cups to hawk and spit into the gutter. David would always remember Rangoon as a city where the hawking and spitting of the citizens seemed to drown out the noise of the screeching brakes of the ancient buses. Government buildings carried signs warning people not to spit on the walls; so everyone spat everywhere else. David, a man who wouldn't spit in the ocean, had been about to lean out of the window and tell the coffee seller to move on, when Maung Zan had boarded the bus and sat down beside him, smiling broadly at half-past four in the morning.

"Don't make any uplifting comments," David had said. "I'm in no mood for them."

"Once you're in the air you'll feel better."

But he hadn't, except that in the aircraft there was no hawking and spitting in his ear all the time. And now they were coming down to Mandalay and his headache had, if anything, got even worse.

There had been rain early in the morning and pools of water lay around on the tarmac. The pilot taxied the plane round till he found the deepest pool, then stopped with the door of the plane opposite it. David stepped down and at once his shoes filled with water. Immediately behind him came the Chinese couple with their Alsatian, which jumped into the pool with a huge splash, barking joyfully, and spotted David's linen suit up as far as his collar. He let out a curse and looked round into the bright cheerful face of the young nun. He apologised and she ducked her head and smiled even more brightly. He knew her sort: she was breaking her neck to be a saint. He turned away, doubly embarrassed, and saw his father coming towards him across the tarmac.

"David." Michael Breton put out a hand, and David, laden with camera and small luggage, couldn't find a hand to return the welcome. Michael changed his welcome into an offer of help, taking the camera case. The two Bretons met again without shaking hands, saving each the uncertainty of how much pressure to put into his grip. "Did you have a good trip? Hello, Zan. How was London?"

David had no clear memory of his father's voice, but he was sure it had not been as soft and rough as this when they had last met. He covertly looked at his father while the latter was greeting Maung Zan, and remarked the greyness under the tan. Michael Breton, grey-haired, hawk-faced, bushy-browed, was almost the standard idealised figure of an Indian Army colonel; but the second look told one that he was only a paper silhouette of that figure, that the bark of command would now be only a sigh of regret.

Small talk kept them occupied while they crossed the tarmac and went out into the muddy car-park where the consulate Land Rover stood waiting for them. David was glad now that Maung Zan was with them; and Michael Breton obviously felt the same way. They both talked at and through Maung Zan: it was as if he were suddenly an important person in the lives of both Bretons.

"That man-eater is still loose up in Sheromere, Zan. Five more people killed while you've been away." Michael looked at David, still keeping sentiment at a distance. "The brute has killed thirty-six people so far. Pity I'm not younger. We could have gone out on a shoot together."

"I doubt if I could hit a stuffed tiger at ten feet," David said. "Three seasons running I've been grouse shooting in Scotland and never hit a bird. The R.S.P.C.A. are putting me up for next year's Honours List."

Michael laughed, but kept the laugh under control, as if afraid of hurting his chest. He signalled to the driver of the Land Rover, who came forward and took the luggage and stowed it away. He was a small Gurkha, dressed in khakis and a green beret, his black boots spotless despite the mud that lay around. One cheek was marked by a scar that ran from the corner of his eye down to the corner of his mouth; when he smiled his whole face seemed to crack, like a reflection in a shattered glass. "This is George. He has been with me ever since I first went to Quetta, back in '21."

David looked at the Gurkha. *Forty years: he knows more about my father than I do. We each came into my father's life in the same year, yet this George knows more of his likes and dislikes, his habits, perhaps even what makes him tick, than I'll ever know.* It struck him only then that never once had his father mentioned George, neither in letters nor when he had come home to England on leave. It was as if George belonged to a life that he had never wanted to share with David.

"I've had your room made up, Zan," Michael Breton said. "Fitzgibbons, who is going to replace me, is away up at Myitkyina for a few days. I took it that you would be staying with us till you leave for Sheromere."

Maung Zan looked at David, then back at Michael. *He knows he's the buffer between us,* David thought; *he knows we both need him.* "What about Sister Hagen? Isn't she at the house also?"

Michael looked at David. "I hope you don't mind, David. She couldn't stay at the hotel. There's some cultural mission staying there."

The thought of meeting Maureen again hadn't worried David. Meeting women, mistresses or ex-mistresses, had never embarrassed him. "Maureen would never be happy with a cultural mission. I think she would even prefer me."

Michael smiled, although a little tentatively: he had never had his son's ease with women. "Can't stand intellectual women myself. Your mother was never like that, thank God. Elinor Glyn and Freddie Lonsdale were about her standard. P. G. Wodehouse was mine. What's yours, David? Whom do you read?"

"*The Lancet*, mostly. And detective stories. And whenever I stay at your flat, I often get down one of your Wodehouses."

"You do?" Michael looked pleased, almost grateful. "Had a full set of him till the war broke out. Somehow since then he's seemed a trifle dated. Suppose that happens to all of us eventually."

He turned away and looked out the window of the Land Rover. They were coming into the outskirts of Mandalay; traffic began to clog the road in front of them. David, his head still aching, had put on dark glasses against the glare of the sun. He had been in Mandalay for only three days during the war, after the retreat of the Japanese, and he remembered now how disappointed he had been. He had never been a romantic, but as a boy he had read Kipling, and Kipling's picture of Mandalay had been the only one he had known. He had been disappointed in the town, but he had been cynically pleased to find that Kipling had never been to Mandalay, that the famous images bore no relation to the original. He had been introduced to Kipling by his father, who had thought the writer belonged in the company of Dickens and Shakespeare. David wondered if his father now thought Kipling was as dated as Wodehouse.

"This is my favourite town," said Michael, still looking out the window. Hawks rose in a brown explosion from the middle of the road, and George swung the Land Rover to avoid the dead dog they had been feasting on. A monk gathered up his yellow robe and skipped hastily to one side and glared after them as they went past in a cloud of dust. "I've felt at home here right from the day I arrived. Haven't we, George?"

George nodded, taking the Land Rover between a cyclist who screamed at them and an ox-drawn cart whose driver was sound asleep. "Is all right, sir. I like Sheromere better."

"Father Caraday has been working on you."

"Yes, sir," said George, and grinned broadly.

They drove past the old fort, its crumbling walls reflected in the weed-splintered waters of its moat, then swung abruptly in through a wide gateway and pulled up before a large two-storied house. The house was built of timber, with wide screened verandahs running right round both floors. The Union Jack fluttered from a tall white mast in the middle of a large well-cut lawn. Along the fences were neat gardens, northern roses growing among lusher, tropical bushes; at the side of the house an oak tree raised a brave British umbrella against the dust and heat. Everything was as neat and orderly as in an English park, a contrast to the dirty and neglected town through which they had just driven. The screen doors at the front of the house banged open and two servants, both clad immaculately in white, rushed out and came to an abrupt stop beside the Land Rover. They stood there, stiff and impassive, British butlers under their Indian skins.

"Home," said Michael, and David realised for the first time that he had never heard his father use the term when he had come back to England on leave. This was home to Michael Breton. He got down from the Land Rover, moving slowly like a man conserving the last of a fading energy, and turned as David also got out of the vehicle. "I'm glad you came, David."

David nodded, unable to find words that wouldn't sound brusque. He was not particularly moved by the occasion; he still felt too much of a stranger to his father. But he was not insensitive to atmosphere and he knew that this moment meant something to his father. He had cabled from London that he was coming to Mandalay and had got a cable in reply; both messages had been brief and without sentiment, preparing neither of them for the moment of reunion when it would come. They had survived it without even the slightest friction, but David was still cautious, still too much aware of the years of silence between them. He had long ago given up blaming his father for the gulf between them; he had gone further in life because he had had to go alone. He felt no love nor gratitude towards his father: this was no more than a meeting with a friendly stranger. He would be polite and accommodating, but he was still shy of any closer intimacy.

Then the screen doors opened again and Maureen, cool in yellow linen, came out. "Hello, David—why, who's been throwing mud at you?"

"I'm used to it," said David, but made a joke of it: he hadn't come all this way to continue to fight with her.

She smiled, then looked at Maung Zan. "How was the trip?" There was no trace of the Nebraska twang: everything was under control.

"I do not like air travel," Maung Zan said. "I have an awfully nervous tummy."

"Personally I think it is an uncivilised way of travelling," said David.

"I couldn't agree more," said Michael, leading the way into

the coolness of the house. "One never sees anything but clouds and airports. These days a man can be a world traveller and still be as insular as a country parson. Give me a ship every time."

Well, we agree on the small things, David thought. Reading matter, ways of travel, what else? If they could stay on such harmless topics, perhaps he could get through this visit without too much strain. He was surprised to find that his headache had already begun to lessen. Outside, beyond the screened windows, the heat pressed Mandalay into its flat plain: an alien sun baked an alien land about which he cared nothing. But here in the cool, high-ceilinged room he felt at ease, almost at home. It wasn't home, of course; he had never known what home was; but at least he had a sense of familiarity. Perhaps it was seeing Maureen again, coming towards him with a cup of coffee and a smile, but whatever it was he was glad of it. He was too tired right now to fight for recognition among strangers.

Maureen leaned down as she handed him his coffee. "I'm declaring a truce with you while we're in this house," she said quietly, smiling at him: she could have been offering him a welcoming word of love. "For your father's sake, not yours."

"Father Caraday will be along later," Michael Breton said. "He wants to meet you, David. He was a doctor himself once. He runs the mission up at Sheromere. Remarkable fellow, isn't he, Zan?"

Maung Zan looked at David, then back at Michael. "Remarkable. I'm surprised he hasn't caught the man-eater while I've been away."

"He damned near did, you know. Would have if his beaters hadn't panicked and scattered just at the crucial moment."

"Priest, ex-doctor, tiger hunter," David said. "What else does he do?"

"Works miracles occasionally," said Michael Breton, and began to cough, a man who would need a miracle to stay the death already in his chest.

2

Later, after he had showered and changed, David came back to the living room. Maureen was alone there, reading a copy of *Punch*. "I must be one of the few Americans who find *Punch* funny."

"I'll give you a year's subscription for Christmas. You

might need it at the Mayo Clinic."

"What makes you think I won't have a few laughs there?"

"Perhaps it's the films I've seen. All American doctors take themselves so seriously."

"Did you have to pay excess baggage on your prejudices? I thought you might have left them at home this time." She threw down the magazine and stood up and walked to a heavy Chinese sideboard against one wall. "Drink?" He shook his head. She poured herself a fresh lime and came back and stood in front of him as he dropped into a chair. "David, you and I are finished. That goes for everything—our affair, our partnership in the hospital, yes, even our dislike of each other. It's all over, kaput, finished. In another week we'll be out of each other's lives forever. But for that week we're going to put on a show for your father. He's dying, David—"

"I know," he said testily. "Why do you think I came all the way out here?"

"To be honest, I'm surprised you did. Maybe I've got you wrong, but I think if the Beatty case hadn't turned out the way it did, you'd still be in London."

"You give me no credit for anything, do you?" he said, although he knew she was probably right.

"Give me one good reason why I should." She went across and sat down and picked up *Punch;* she leafed through it, as if determined to find something funny, something to laugh at. "Do you like David Langdon? Or Sprod? Or Searle?"

"I prefer Addams in *The New Yorker.* He draws the sort of women I know."

She looked up and smiled. "That's the old David. I thought you might have lost your touch."

Then there was the sound of a car or truck coming up the gravel drive. It came to a halt with a squeal of brakes, the screen doors slammed, and a deep loud voice yelled, "Anyone home? Where the hell's the British Foreign Office?"

He came into the room, an extraordinarily tall thin man in a bush hat, checked shirt, baggy khaki shorts and sandals. He dropped down on the couch beside Maureen, patted her on the shoulder and looked frankly across at David. "You're Michael's son. I could tell you a mile away. Get me a beer, old girl, will you? I've followed a bus all the way in from Ava, eating its dust all the way. I'm Caraday." He got up, crossed the room, took David's reluctant hand, shook it and put it carefully back in David's lap. "Sorry. I'd forgotten how careful surgeons are of their hands."

David looked down at his hand, then back up at Caraday. "Shake hands with me in a day or two," he said, aware of Maureen watching the two of them closely. "I may be a little less limp than I am now. I haven't come just from Ava, wherever that may be."

Caraday raised a black bushy eyebrow and pushed back his hat. "You're just like your old man, you know. He had the same cold attitude when I first met him, just like an iceworks manager." Then he grinned, showing big strong white teeth. "I'm not really a Wild Colonial Boy. It's an act I put on when I first came here, to impress the locals, and it's been hard to throw off. Priests have got to be good actors. The stage lost some good performers when some of us took the cloth. Thanks, old girl." He took the beer Maureen handed him and raised the glass to David. "Welcome to Burma, Mr. Breton. It's a bastard of a country, but it grows on you."

Then Michael Breton came into the room, followed by Maung Zan. Caraday drained his glass at one gulp, put it down on a nearby table, and threw a long thin arm round Maung Zan's shoulders. He towered over Maung Zan; the latter looked like a small boy under the wing of a giant crane. "Zan, we've missed you up in Sheromere. Did Michael tell you the man-eater has been on the go again? Chewed up five people in three weeks. We could have saved two of them if we hadn't been stuck with that incompetent you left us. He couldn't deliver a baby, let alone save a woman's life. Did you get all your equipment? . . . Good, now maybe the people up there will get some real treatment. He's a good doctor, this cove, you know that, Mr. Breton? He'll be a damned sight better when he gets this new equipment. I don't suppose you have to operate in Harley Street by the light of a Tilley lamp?"

"Not for several years now," David said.

"Old Zan here did three ops. just before he went away by Tilley lamp. The hospital generator had gone on the blink. I've been praying for you every day, Zan, while you've been away, that you'd get the equipment. A Buddhist doesn't mind a few Christian prayers, does he?"

"I shall accept anything I can get," said Maung Zan, twisting his head to smile up at the lanky priest. "Perhaps I can do the same for you some day."

"Okay." Caraday grinned. "But don't tell Pope John, or I might be out on my ear."

This man is at home with all these people, David thought, even with Maureen. He sat looking at the tall thin man as the

39

latter moved restlessly about the room. He had dropped his hat on the floor, as if that were the natural place to hang it. His black hair was thinning on top of his long narrow head, but the hair that grew along his temples was long and thick, badly in need of cutting. His face was narrow and bony, equine-looking, accentuated by the long nose; yet it was not ugly, it suggested rather that it had been on the way to being handsome when something had gone wrong. His mouth was wide and mobile (it had to be, David mused, to allow the flood of words to get out), and his chin was almost aggressively prominent. It was a remarkable face, made even more remarkable by the eyes. They were dark blue, deep set under the heavy brows: at times they looked as black as Maung Zan's, but without his sparkle. They were the eyes of a sad man, unrelated to the laughing voluble mouth; they reflected the laugh, but it was only a reflection, no truer than the laugh seen in a mirror. Father Caraday looked like a priest who had failed to find his own confessor.

"How has everything else been?" Maung Zan asked.

Caraday shook his head. "Shero has been out again. He shot up a convoy last week. Held up two buses the week before."

Michael Breton looked at David. "Shero—that's Kachin for the Tiger—he is an insurgent leader. Quite a troublemaker."

"I thought all Burma's troubles were over, now that they had got rid of us British."

Michael looked embarrassed, as if he felt he should have kept his son informed. "I'm afraid not. The Kachins, the Shans and the Karens, they're all very much active."

"Is this—Shero?—a Kachin?"

Michael looked up at Caraday. The latter shrugged. "No one has ever seen him. He's a very shy character, always wears a mask. His men—and no one knows whether he's got fifty or five hundred—they're a pretty mixed lot. Kachins, Shans, some Chinese."

"No Burmese," said Maung Zan with a smile, and Michael and Caraday laughed.

Maureen said, "Why no Burmese?"

Michael looked at Maung Zan, but it was Caraday who answered. It would be, David thought. I'll bet he's the one who does all the talking even in the confessional. "Sheromere is on the borders of the Kachin State and the Northern Shan State. We have quite a mixture up there. Kachins, Shans, Chinese,

40

Indians, Palaungs. But no Burmese. None, that is, except Zan. They've cut the heads off all the rest."

Maureen shuddered. "You're joking!"

"He's not, my dear," Michael said. "I'm afraid the Burmese are not very popular up there. Nor anywhere in the Shan States, for that matter."

"Then how has Zan kept his head?" David asked.

"I am a friend of Charlie's," said Maung Zan, and though he was smiling, he looked gratefully and admiringly at Caraday. "He is my insurance."

There was a knock at the outside screen doors and a voice said, "May I come in?"

It was not Michael nor the servants who went to the door, but Caraday. Good God, David thought, does this man run everyone's life and home? He looked across at his father, but Michael wore the same admiring look as Maung Zan. It was a shock to find his father, the cold isolated man he remembered from his boyhood, the image that had stayed with him all these years so dependent upon another man.

Caraday came back into the room with a girl. She was a Eurasian and it was hard to tell her age: she could have been eighteen or twenty-eight. She was strikingly beautiful, black-haired and sloe-eyed, the shape of her eyes showing the Oriental side of her parentage. She had the small mouth with the rather full lips David had noted on the women of Burma, but her complexion was lighter than that of the local women. She wore a green Chinese *cheong-sam* that showed off her figure; he noted with satisfaction that her bosom had a Western fulness to it and that her hips, though slim, were not boyish. Out of his wartime days here in Burma he remembered the remark of a brother officer, a man who had spent years in the East: *The mongrel ones are always the best lookers, my boy.*

"Rose, come in," said Caraday, holding her arm and pulling her into the room. God help the Pope if this fellow ever goes to Rome, David thought: *he'll* be the one holding audiences. "Mr. Breton, this is Rose Churchill. She is Zan's theatre sister, A.D.C., bottle-washer and what-have-you up at Sheromere. She's kept your replacement going, you know that, Zan?"

Rose Churchill didn't blush. Poised, almost a little aloof, she offered her hand to David as he rose to greet her. "Maung Zan has often spoken of you, Mr. Breton. He says you were the one who made life bearable for him in his student days."

41

David looked at Maung Zan, who made a pretence of looking away to speak to Maureen. He couldn't remember ever having gone out of his way to help the Burman, and he wondered why Maung Zan should feel so indebted to him. But if Maung Zan wanted to give him credit, he wasn't going to refuse it. He looked back at the girl. "I'm sure he finds life much more bearable with you to help him."

"Watch him, Rose," said Maureen. It was evident from the smiles that passed between the two girls that they had become friends in the week Maureen had been in Mandalay.

"Maureen has warned me about you, Mr. Breton," Rose said, smiling at him now, but still aloof. But he had the feeling that the aloofness was not part of her character. It was part of an act to impress him, an unsophisticated girl trying to be worldly. "And Maung Zan has told me about the extra-curricular anatomy classes you used to hold with the nurses at the hospital."

Maung Zan hooted with laughter, but David was not so sure that the laughter did not hide embarrassment. He could not put his finger on the relationship between Maung Zan and the girl, but it seemed an uneasy one, at least on the part of Maung Zan.

"She is making it all up, David," said Maung Zan, his laughter subsiding. "She is the most frightful fibber. If Father Caraday can ever get her into his confessional, he will be there for a week."

Caraday smiled, but the sadness seemed to deepen in his eyes as he looked at Rose. "There's still hope. We priests never give up."

3

"Just who is Caraday?" David asked.

He and his father were sitting out on the verandah in the early evening. Beyond the wire screening the bats swooped like thrown stones; a gecko lizard clicked away somewhere in the rafters above them. Across the road and beyond the moat, Fort Dufferin had turned rose under the last light of day: dusk brought back some of its romance, blurred both its crumbling walls and the knowledge of its terrible history. It was within its walls that King Thebaw, goaded on by his wife, Supyalat, had massacred most of his relatives. Then during the war it had been Japanese headquarters, and the walls had once again echoed to the screams of those being murdered, tortured or raped. Now it housed the army and the only screams were those of a drunken soldier pursued by the devils in too much rice wine. A mile square, once the pride of kings, it was now no more than a walled army depot. All this David had learned from his father as they had sat out here during the last half-hour. With no buffer between them, still afraid of each other, they had talked about Mandalay, a safe subject. Then David had taken the plunge.

"Caraday?" Michael took out a pipe, stuffed tobacco into it and lit it.

"Should you smoke?"

"You mean my chest?" Michael smiled through the thick smoke that wreathed up past his face, a smile that had no amusement in it. "It doesn't really matter, does it? It is one of the few pleasures I have left."

It was the first mention he had made of his illness, but it was not an invitation to discuss it. He spoke not as if he were afraid of the subject, but as if he felt there was nothing to be gained by speaking of it. He was dying and that was all there was to it.

David backed away from both the subject and the smoke from the pipe. "It doesn't smell like it. What's in that tobacco? Elephant dung?"

"It's tobacco that Charlie Caraday grows up at Sheromere. Does it upset you? I'll put it away—" He went to knock out the pipe.

"No. I've smelt worse." David put a cigarette into his holder and lit it; he sucked in the Turkish smoke, trying to get rid of the other smell. "Who *is* Caraday?"

Michael puffed on his pipe for a few moments. "He's an Australian, as you've no doubt gathered from his accent. He was a doctor in the Australian Army and was sent up here to Burma from Malaya in 1941—to study malaria treatment or something. He was still up here when Japan came into the war. When Rangoon was evacuated he stayed on to look after the wounded. He was captured and spent four years on the Burma Road. After the war he went back to Australia and became a priest. They sent him back here about ten years ago."

"That's all you know about him?"

"That's all." Michael puffed again on his pipe, looking out through the wire screening at Mandalay Hill in the distance, the temples on its summit shining white in the retreating rays of the sun. The garden about the house was already shadowy

43

in the dusk and the traffic out on the road was just a shrill procession of vague shapes. "That, and that he is one of the finest men I know."

"In what way?"

Michael was silent for a moment, as if he had never been asked before to list Caraday's qualities. "He is a very brave man."

"I've met brave men before. Not just physically but morally brave men."

"He is brave in both those senses. He is a charitable man, too. How many men have you met with true charity? Not philanthropic men, but charitable ones. I never knew the meaning of it, David, till I met him."

David didn't bring up the past: he hadn't made the long journey out here to score off his father. He still wasn't sure why he had come, other than to escape from London and the loneliness that he still couldn't quite believe had happened to him. It had been easier to escape than he had imagined; even that knowledge had been almost an insult. When he had rung the hospital and said he was taking no more patients, no on had queried him; it had been almost as if they had expected him to remove himself from the scene. There had been no call to appear before the Medical Council, but there was still time for that: doctors were in no hurry to reprimand one of their own: they were men who had a certain professional charity, he mused.

There had been no embarrassing farewells or explanations as to why he was leaving London; only Dowson, correct as a government official seeing off some foreign dignitary, had come to the airport. He had been in Karachi, drinking flat lemonade out of a dirty glass in the airport lounge, before it had finally come to him that he had come too far to turn back. He was a good liar, but he could think of no good lie to tell Maung Zan, his travelling companion, that he wanted to return to London. And he had not been able to tell him the truth, that the last thing he had wanted at that moment in his life was a reunion with his father. All his life he had progressed in a series of carefully considered steps, but now he had made the mistake that he had seen so many other men make. The bemused step that put them on a plane to begin a journey they didn't want to make, into a bed with a woman who had the perfume of disaster about her, into a life that brought them hell before they deserved it. He would stay here only a week, keep on negatively good terms with his fa-

44

ther, and be gone before hell could catch up with him. There was still time to go to Amalfi.

"He's brought me back into the Church, you know." The sun had gone now and night was rushing across the sky. Michael was a dim figure behind the dusk and the smoke from his pipe. Lights appeared on top of Mandalay Hill: the temples were outlined in electric lights, like cheap dance halls: it was as if someone had hung a string of Woolworth's beads round the neck of Buddha. "I tried Buddhism for a while, but it wasn't what I wanted. I have some Indian friends here, I even went to Muslim services with them. I think I was consciously trying not to be a Catholic again. But in the end the Church won. Its navel cord is strong and long—it never really lets you go."

"I cut it a long time ago. I suspect all priests and parsons. No one gives up the world without a good reason. And no one can tell me these fellows all have the reason of piety. There just isn't that much piety to go round."

"You were always cynical, David. Even as a boy."

David couldn't resist the gibe: it was off his tongue before he realised it: "I didn't think you would have noticed."

"You said more in your letters than you knew. Perhaps you were looking for truth, but took the wrong road." He was silent for a moment, Polonius behind the screen of dusk. "It was my fault, I know that now. It is a little late to ask your forgiveness, but I ask it, anyway."

David was glad of the rapidly gathering darkness. He was embarrassed: he couldn't remember anyone's ever having asked his forgiveness before. This was the reverse of what he had expected: he was not the one being blamed for the lost years. "It is a little late. I don't mean about the forgiveness—that's unimportant. I mean you've left it a little late for us to get to know each other."

"I've thought about that, too." The pipe had gone out; he tapped the bowl on the arm of his chair. A gharry went clattering down the road, the horse's hoofs as hollow-sounding on the macadamised road as the rattling of bones. "It is a pity that a man has to come within sight of his open grave before he begins to regret what he has missed. I was never the soldier I wanted to be, nor the father I should have been."

"You were a colonel. What did you want to be—a general?"

"I wasn't thinking in terms of rank. I was thinking in terms of—respect, if you like. Perhaps even love, I don't know. No one ever really loved me except your mother—and I was never even sure of her."

"I can't comment on that. I knew her no better than I knew you."

"We treated you shamefully, didn't we?" There was no abject penitence about him. He was stating a fact, one in which he had no pride. "Do I sound sentimental, a man wanting to be loved? You've been fortunate. You've been loved, by Maureen."

"Did she tell you that?"

"When I was home in London, yes."

"She never told me. And I doubt if it is true now."

"You mean because of her evidence against you in that case?" It was the only time he had mentioned the Beatty case. "It is your own fault if she doesn't love you now."

David pushed Maureen into the background: she was one complication of his life that was behind him. "Is that what you were looking for all the time you were in the Army—respect or love?"

"Not consciously, no. A soldier doesn't look for such things. If he deliberately seeks those things, then he isn't a leader. But at the end of one's career, one finds oneself hoping—" He was silent again. A breeze stirred the *bho* tree down by the front gates: it was a warm breeze, but he shivered, as if feeling again the cold wind blowing down out of the Khyber Pass, across the sub-continent and the long regretted years. "What do you hope for, David? Are you still ambitious?"

"I think so. I don't hope for love or respect. I'm no country G.P., that's all right for them. Position, I suppose," he said without shame: he couldn't be modest, even with his father. "I'd settle for President of the College of Surgeons."

His father laughed: before it broke up in coughing, it was full of high humour. He lay back in his chair gasping. He took a handkerchief from his pocket and held it to his mouth.

"Can I get you something?" David sensed rather than saw his father shake his head. "You should be more careful."

Michael wiped his mouth and put the handkerchief away. "It is a terrible thing when one has to be careful about laughing." His voice was hoarse, little more than a whisper. "I shouldn't have talked so long. But I've never had the opportunity before—" He stood up, a thin black figure against the lights of Mandalay Hill. "I hope when you get what you want, David, you find it is enough. I'll go and lie down for a while. Dinner is at eight."

"Do we dress?"

A light went on inside the house, throwing Michael's face into relief as he smiled. "This is no longer an outpost of Empire. The natives have no longer to be impressed."

He went into the house, leaving David alone on the verandah. Out on the road some students went by on their bicycles, ringing their bells, singing *God save the Queen* in mocking falsetto voices. The natives were no longer impressed: Britain was gone from Burma, gone without love or respect, at least among the younger Burmans. All at once David felt sorry for his father. He should at least be allowed to die without being jeered at.

"Why don't you come up to Sheromere, Mr. Breton?" Rose Churchill said, beautiful as a rose in the tight vase of her red *cheong-sam*. She had sat beside him on the couch during drinks before dinner, her thigh exposed in the slit of the *cheong-sam*, and despite the heat, his tiredness and the seedy dregs of his morning's headache, he had felt a stir of lust for her. He had recognised now that she was a girl willing to be enjoyed by men, and he wondered if Maung Zan and Caraday had recognised the same thing.

"I've already asked him," said Maung Zan, sprinkling green peppers on his curry. Sweat was pouring out of him; his brown face glistened in the light. He was wearing Burmese dress tonight: a brightly checked *longyi*, or skirt, a black silk tunic and, to show his respect for Michael Breton, his host and the British Consul, a pink *gaung-baung*, the cap with its butterfly wing standing to one side. When he had first come into the living room, David had noted the cap and remarked to himself that here was one native who would never jeer at Michael Breton.

"Maureen is coming up with us tomorrow," Rose said, and David was aware of the mischief in her. She could cause trouble, this girl, and probably had.

David looked across the table at Maureen. "I think I'll stay here with—Father." The word was a little strange on his tongue, like some of the Burmese words he had already picked up.

"Do go, David." Michael looked grey tonight, but he was still a charming host, not throwing his own shadow over other people's lives. "I'm caught up for the next two days, anyway. This cultural mission from India. The local Commissioner has rather made it a command performance for me—he knows I speak Hindustani. We British still have our uses." But he

47

winked at Maung Zan and there was no bitterness about the joke. "I'm coming up there at the end of the week, David, and I can bring you back."

Caraday had been tucking into his curry like a starving man. He had changed into a clean shirt, but had discarded his shorts for what looked like a long divided skirt and David had learned was a pair of Shan trousers. He was the most unpriestly priest David had ever met; but then David had reminded himself that he had met few, if any, missionaries. For all he knew, they could all be as unconventional as this man. To David's way of thinking, a man had to be eccentric even to be a missionary.

"Look—" Caraday swallowed a mouthful of curry. Well, he's spoiled it, David thought: he's just broken a record by staying out of someone else's conversation for five minutes. "Look, travel up with me, David—" David tried to look like Mr. Breton, but Caraday obviously had no time for formality. How soon after meeting the Pope would he be calling him John or Jack? "Zan's Land Rover is going to be pretty full, what with the girls, the luggage and that equipment he brought back. You can squeeze in with me and Moriarty."

"Who's Moriarty?" said David, trying to sound as if he didn't wish to squeeze in with anyone.

"My driver, cook, bottle-washer, altar boy and what-have-you. You can stay with me, too. I've got more room than Zan." He evidently noticed David's reluctance and mistook the reason for it. "Don't worry. I'm not looking for a convert. I've got my quota this year. All I want is someone to natter to." Then he smiled, and David noticed again how his face seemed to be split into a contradiction: the mouth opened wide, the teeth shining whitely, but the eyes were still dark with sadness. "And frankly, I'd like to have you stay with me, David."

David could be rude without effort, but he found it hard to be churlish. Everyone but Maureen, and she had said nothing, appeared to be pushing him up into the mountains to Sheromere, and there seemed no way out but by being churlish. And it did seem foolish to come all this way and see nothing but Rangoon and Mandalay. What was it his father had said about the insular-minded traveller of today? "All right, I'll be glad to come."

"Good," said Caraday, going back to his curry. "We'll get away about seven. Better be on the road before the gendarmes are out and about."

48

"The gendarmes? You mean the police?" It was the first time since they had sat down that Maureen had spoken. She had been unusually quiet this evening. For the first time, listening to the others talk among themselves, she had realised that she was the stranger here. Even David seemed to have settled in now. "Why do we have to avoid them?"

Caraday had a mouthful of curry, giving someone else an opportunity to answer the question. Maung Zan said, "If the police know of any strangers, such as yourselves, making the trip up the Sheromere road, they try to insist on giving you an escort. And an escort is the last thing one wants. The dacoits or the insurgents, whoever happens to be out at the time, shoot up the escorts from ambush. So everyone tries to avoid the safe passage that the police try to give them."

Maureen shuddered. "This sounds like Nebraska in the 1880's. You didn't mention all this when you invited me up to Sheromere."

Caraday had swallowed his mouthful of curry. "You'll be all right. By and large, they leave Europeans alone, especially women."

"I think I shall travel with the women, then," David said. "When danger threatens, look for the nearest woman's skirts."

"I'll be wearing pants tomorrow," Maureen said. "Better try Rose."

"I'll be in trousers, too," Rose said, but she was not brushing him off as Maureen had.

"So you're stuck with me," said Caraday, grinning.

"Have you ever been held up?" David asked.

"Half a dozen times," said Caraday. "Usually by mistake. They just look annoyed and wave me on. Missionaries are pretty poor pickings."

"I am surprised at all this strife you talk of," David said. "Doesn't Burma boast of being one of the strictly neutral countries? Evidently neutrality doesn't begin at home."

Everyone was silent and David realised they were all looking at Maung Zan. The latter was not smiling as he answered David: "My country still has a long way to go and a lot to learn. Perhaps we are a little superior, some have called us arrogant, in telling other nations how to run their lives. But that is only natural, David. The British spent a long time telling us what to do."

David knew he had made a mistake. Although highly critical of other nations and nationals when they did not come up to his standards on certain matters, he had never been particularly nationalistic nor even patriotic himself. If anyone wanted to criticise Britain or the British, he would irritate them by perversely encouraging them. It had been another of the matters for argument with Maureen. He would begin by criticising the Americans, she would retaliate with the criticism of the British, he would agree with her and in the end she would finish up criticising him for not being more patriotic. Maureen had left the United States, but she still saluted the Stars and Stripes; the Fourth of July was as important to her as her birthday. He had put that down to the overcompensating patriotism of some expatriates; he had never been out of England long enough to have had to prove his Englishness. He could not remember Maung Zan waving the Burmese flag when he had last known him. But then, of course, there had been no Burmese flag: the Union Jack had waved over Burma in those days. He looked at Maung Zan, a patriot, with new interest.

"I'm sorry, Zan. I didn't mean to offend."

Maung Zan was still sober-faced as he looked across the table at David; then he smiled and winked, the old Maung Zan. "I'm even more critical of our government than you are. But that's part of the wages of independence. We only get sensitive when someone else thinks he's entitled to criticise us."

"Just like Australians," said Caraday. "And we've been independent for sixty years."

"And Americans," said Maureen. "After nearly three hundred years, we don't like people to find fault with us."

"I suppose we Britons were the same once," Michael said.

"I doubt it," Maureen said, and for the first time, like a spark of the old contact between them, smiled across at David.

"Oh, I think so," said Michael, not missing the look that had passed across the table. "I'm told that when the bombing during the war exposed an old Roman wall in London, there was an inscription on it: *Abite, Romani.*"

"What does that mean?" Rose asked.

"Romans, go home," said David, and looked along at his father and smiled. He could never remember his father displaying a sense of humour before. But that hadn't meant his father didn't have a sense of humour. It was only further evidence of the gap between the two of them, the ignorance each had of the other.

Later, just before going to bed, David went out into the

garden for a final cigarette. Caraday had driven Rose back to the Mandalay hospital, where she was staying. Michael, Maung Zan and Maureen had gone to their rooms, and the lights had been switched off in the living section of the house. Somewhere further down the road there was a chanting, prayers or a hymn. First there would be a single voice, nasal and high-pitched, almost like the speeded-up cawing of a crow, then a host of voices would come in in reply. There would be silence for a moment, a gong would be struck, then the single voice would begin again. David had no idea what was the occasion nor did he care. He had always had the ability to turn a deaf ear.

His deaf ear must have been working perfectly, because Maureen was standing beside him before he heard her. "May I have a cigarette?" He gave her one, snapped his lighter for her, then waited for her to say something. He had nothing to say to her. As she had said, they were finished; he was not even sure that he wanted to begin again. He was tired beyond caring; loneliness had become a refuge. "David, don't come up to Sheromere with us tomorrow."

"My dear girl—" She let that pass: it was a hollow phrase now, anyway. "I shan't bother you in Sheromere or anywhere else. I got your message today. We are finished. I should like to say I am sorry, but right now I couldn't care less."

In the darkness he couldn't tell whether she flushed or not. But her voice was calm, under control. "I am not thinking of you and me. I am thinking of you and Father Caraday. You don't like him, David—"

"You haven't heard me say a word against the man."

"You don't have to. The curl of your lip can be seen a mile away."

"Your eyesight is too good. Unfortunately you don't seem to be able to read as well as you can see. If you have seen my lip curling today, it has been because of some of the vile food my father serves his guests."

"You just don't appreciate good curry, that's all."

"Perhaps. But I class eating as a pleasure, not a form of masochism. Eating curry is like trying to give oneself a massage with a file."

"Well, anyway—" Maureen knew this had often been how their conversations had gone. She would attack him on one subject and before she knew how it had happened, he had steered her on to another subject and was arguing with her

51

on that. "I didn't come out here to argue with you about curry. I came out to ask you not to come up to Sheromere with Father Caraday."

"Why?"

"Because I've found out since I've been here that Father Caraday is the one prop your father has left in the world. I don't want to see you try to knock that prop out from under him."

She'll never stop being an American, he thought: always rushing in to offer aid. Once she had wanted to protect him, till she had found he didn't need protection. Now she was protecting his father, being a good American Samaritan. "Why don't you stay out here and join Father Caraday? Be a Sister of Mercy?"

"I'm a Lutheran. Or I was."

"A Lutheran on the side of a Catholic priest? There must be spinning in the graveyard in Wittenberg."

"At least we're Christians. I don't believe you've ever had a Christian thought in your life."

"That's a typically Christian un-Christian remark, if I may sound paradoxical. What sort of thoughts do you think Buddhists and Jews and Muslims have?" He dropped his cigarette on to the gravel of the path and trod it out. Down the road the single high-pitched voice was rasping away at the night; perhaps all the others had gone home, leaving him to plead for them with the gods. Then abruptly the other voices chimed in, fresh and loud: they sounded as if they could go on all night. "I am not going to try and chop Caraday down, Maureen. Hard as it may be for you to believe, I, too, would like to see my father die in peace. I had my fingers crossed when I took the Hippocratic oath and I've always charged fees as high as I thought I could get. But I was never a sadist nor—with the exception of our friend Mrs. Beatty—a negligent doctor. I've always tried to ease pain, not inflict it." He saw her silhouette stiffen. "Don't say it. I am speaking professionally, not about my private life."

"This is your private life."

"Only partly. I am taking over my father as a patient."

She felt deflated. All she could say was, "I don't believe you."

"Twenty-four hours ago I should not have believed myself. But now—" He looked back at the dark house; his father lay there within sight of his open grave. It was not frightening, he had seen enough of death; but it was disturbing, he had

52

never seen the death of anyone close to him. His mother had died in India while he had been at school in England; he had never known his grandparents, dead before he was born. He had known only the deaths of strangers, and he had always been too cold and detached to be affected by them. "Zan says he thinks my father has six months. I don't think he has that long. He'll be dead in three months at the most."

"Are you going to stay out here that long?" Her voice twanged a little with incredulity: now she *knew* he was lying.

"Probably not," he said, deflating her again with his frankness. "I'll try and persuade him to come back to England with me."

"What if he won't go?"

He had no answer to that. He hadn't entirely bridged the gulf between himself and his father; he was not going to be the one to make all the effort. "I can't do any more than ask him. I'm too old to start learning how to plead with anyone."

"You're never too old for that," she said, ten years younger than he but sure of what she knew. "You'll find that out some day."

Chapter 3

1

"I am Patrick Dublin Moriarty," said the Indian, putting out his hand. He was short and plump, his handsome face marred by the cast in one eye. He was dressed in a purple-and-brown checked *longyi*, a red shirt and a faded green-and-yellow striped cricket blazer; at seven o'clock in the morning he was hard on the eyes, a peacock whose feathers were tatty at the edges. "Roman Catholic."

"Breton," said David, then added, "Agnostic."

But the Indian's handshake had been swift and he had already turned back to loading the jeep before David had described himself. David looked at Caraday. "Do you teach all your converts to label themselves like that?"

"No," said Caraday, grinning. This morning he was in shorts again and wore the battered slouch hat. The hat had a hole in the crown, as if a rat had gnawed at it, but the *puggaree* was new and of bright purple silk. "When Moriarty came to me ten years ago, he introduced himself the same way. Out here in the East people aren't ashamed of their religion. That's all it amounts to."

The sun had not yet broken through the overcast and the morning was still cool. But David still carried with him the effect of yesterday's heat: he still had his headache, although it was milder this morning. "If I come to stay with you, Caraday, don't let us discuss religion."

54

"Okay, we'll talk medicine. But you'll have to forgive me if I'm a little rusty."

"I'm the same way about religion. Completely corroded."

The Land Rover and the jeep were loaded and it was time to leave for Sheromere. Maung Zan, Maureen and Rose got into the Land Rover, waved goodbye to Michael Breton as he stood on the steps of the house, and went off down the drive. David looked at his father. "Are you sure you don't mind my going?"

"Are you prepared to suffer three days of culture?" They had achieved some degree of intimacy: they could joke with each other.

David shook his head, smiling in reply. "I'll see you up at Sheromere at the week end. Take care of yourself."

Between two other men it would have been a casual phrase given in farewell. But both David and Michael recognised it as something more. It had come unbidden to David's lips, an involuntary moment of regard for his father, and Michael accepted the sincerity behind it. "I'll take care. Good luck."

David climbed into the jeep beside Caraday, who was driving. Moriarty, smoking a thick cheroot, lolled on the bedrolls in the back, like a rajah come down in the world. Caraday let in the gears with a clash, they went down the drive at speed and swung out in front of a bus, which had to brake sharply to avoid them.

"Bloody terrible drivers," said Caraday, stirring the gear lever with sublime disregard for the gear box; the jeep moaned and screamed like a dying beast. "They never give way."

Mist was rising from the moat: the fort was a pink castle on a cloud. The streets of Mandalay were already busy. "When you're poor," said Caraday, "you spend as much time as you can making a living." The noise clamoured at them even above the rattling and thumping of the jeep. Horns hooted, bells rang, voices shouted, dogs barked; buses and trucks charged out of the dust, and cyclists glided away from them at the last moment, like matadors avoiding the bull. A white-coated policeman, stone-faced but also baby-faced, taking himself too seriously because he was new to the job, stood at an intersection trying to control the confusion. He waved on a bus and it came forward with a rush, then pulled up with a sudden jerk that raised a babel of yells and screams from its passengers. A humpbacked cow, oblivious of the policeman and his efforts at traffic control, instinctively certain that it must not be killed, ambled placidly across the road.

"Bloody cows and dogs—" said Caraday. "Buddhists won't kill any living thing, but more people are killed in trucks and buses that crack up because their drivers have tried to avoid the cows and dogs—" He shook his head. "I have great arguments with the head *pongyi* up at Sheromere. I maintain Buddhism is an egocentric religion, that's why it appeals to so many Western self-styled intellectuals, and he asks me what sort of religion is Christianity that it maintains that human life is worth more than any other life. *That's* egocentricity, he claims."

"Christian religion is the best," said Moriarty, holding his cheroot aloft. "Especially the Catholic. I am a Catholic."

"You've got your message across, Patrick," said Caraday, winking at David. "You've done enough proselytizing for today."

"I do not understand the word you use. Is it a Catholic word?"

"No, it's an old Australian aboriginal word. I'll teach you the language one day."

"A man can never have too much education," said Moriarty. "I take it you are educated, Mr. Breton?"

"I thought I was, but perhaps I'm not." David looked at Caraday, who smiled and winked again.

A crowd of boys in purple *longyis* flashed by on their bicycles, skimming along like a flock of bright birds. "High school students," said Caraday. "Tomorrow's demonstrators. That's the thing you notice these days—the demonstrators are much younger. Or I'm older. Perhaps older people only demonstrate when they're hungry. Can you remember the Depression?"

"Barely," David said. "And you forget, I was a soldier's son then. Soldiers are never out of work, especially in depression times."

Caraday looked sideways at him, and the jeep plunged recklessly on its own way. "It's a long time since I met a true cynic. I'm going to enjoy your company, David."

"Not if you're going to drive like this. We are about two seconds from disaster."

Caraday looked back at the road, wrenched the wheel and the jeep scraped along the side of a heavy truck, whose driver called down every *nat* in heaven on the heads of foreigners.

"Thanks," said Caraday, unruffled. "That's the closest I've been for some time."

"It was a pleasure," said David.

They were fencing with each other, with David playing a passive defensive role. He had always shied away from friendship offered too readily: it savoured of salesmanship, the other man selling himself too much. David turned away, preferring the dust and dirt of Mandalay to the smile of the priest.

They were heading out of town now. Garbage lay in heaps beside the road; pi-dogs scavenged like large rats amidst the refuse. Kites wheeled in the sky, waiting for the dogs to be gone; somehow the filth of the place stretched up to them, so that they seemed to dirty the sky. The overcast had suddenly gone—everything had a suddenness about it here: dawn, night, storm clouds that rose up with the swiftness of an atomic explosion—and the sun blazed down fiercely. The rice fields stretched away on either side of them now like a green still lake: men stood up to their necks in it, only their wide circular hats showing: from a distance they looked like giant brown water lilies. A flock of egrets floated down, a snow flurry out of the brassy sky, melting and disappearing into the green lake of rice. The dirt and dust of the town were behind them now, the speeding jeep creating its own cooling wind, and David settled down to enjoy the ride.

It wasn't long before they began to climb, the air becoming noticeably cooler. Caraday drove with complete disregard of the rules of the road; the local drivers seemed to do the same. Cars, jeeps and buses drove straight at each other; at the last moment they swung aside, the drivers smiling at each other, having lived till they met another vehicle coming towards them. Several times David was chilled by more than the cooling air of the hills into which they were climbing.

"What's the accident rate in Burma?" He hung on desperately as Caraday took the jeep round a corner on the wrong side, blowing his horn and trusting in God.

"Pretty high." They were going downhill now, the jeep gathering speed. Caraday had to shout against the noise of the wind. "Most of the trucks and buses are wartime stuff. Some of them have been over the side half a dozen times. This jeep, for instance. I've hauled it up from the bottom of a gully twice and re-built it."

"Who was driving it when it went over?"

"I was," yelled Caraday, and David could well believe it.

The Land Rover had gone on well ahead of them. They stopped for morning tea at a small Chinese café in one of the villages and were told that the Doctor from Sheromere and the two women had gone through about ten minutes before.

"I should have told Zan to stay closer to us." Caraday looked worried as he got back into the jeep. "The dacoits killed a Burmese Baptist preacher last week. They're likely to kill another Burmese while they're in the mood."

"Are we in dacoit country now?" They had left the village behind. Jungle stretched away on either side of them, thick and solid as a green cliff-face. An army could be hidden there, David thought. Something moved and he turned quickly to look back as they sped past. But it was only a buffalo moving slowly out of the bushes to cross the road.

"Scared?" Caraday said. "Don't be ashamed to say so. I'm never easy-minded when I come up this road. Yes, we're in the dacoit country. And the insurgent country, too. Once you pass that village back there, you're shoving your neck out."

"What about the women?"

"They'll be all right."

"Not if Zan gets his head chopped off. Maureen isn't used to that. I understand the Indians in Nebraska have been tame for a long time."

"I am Indian," said Moriarty, coming awake from his doze on the lumpy bedrolls. With his lids closed, the cast eye hidden, he had looked remarkably handsome. "Are the Indians in Nebraska Roman Catholic?"

But before David could find an answer to that, Caraday abruptly slowed the jeep and brought it to a halt. He leaned out, listening. "Thought I heard rifle shots." Even as he spoke there were two sharp cracks from somewhere up round the bend ahead of them. He looked at David. "Do you want to get out?"

"What are you going to do?"

"I'm going on. I may be able to help."

There was no bravado about the man. It was his vocation to help; he could have been a mechanic going to repair a broken-down car. Then David remembered that Caraday had been a doctor before he had become a priest; his whole adult life had been dedicated to aiding others. *Dedicated* was a word David himself suspected; but at least Caraday sounded sincere. "What about Moriarty?"

58

"He always goes with me," said Caraday, and looked back at Moriarty, who nodded.

"Always? You mean this has happened before?"

"Half a dozen times, perhaps more. I'm always running into ambushed convoys. Well, are you coming or not?" He sounded impatient.

"I'll come," David said.

Caraday said, "I thought you would," let in the gears and they went slowly up the road. David himself had not been so sure that he would stay in the jeep; if there had been only strangers up ahead, he felt sure he would have got out and waited down the road. He had never made any pretensions to heroism, although he liked to think he was not cowardly. It would have been cowardly to get out of the jeep and remain back down the road, knowing that Maung Zan, Maureen and Rose were in danger up round the bend they were now approaching.

He sat up straight, his stomach tightening, as the jeep labouring against the climb, came up to the bend in the road. He was sweating, feeling it break all over him, and his hand was clenched tightly on the grip bar in front of him. He glanced sideways at Caraday, but the latter was staring straight ahead, no expression at all on his face. Then David noticed that Caraday's lips were moving slightly.

"Are you praying?"

"What else?" said Caraday, and took the jeep up round the bend and pulled up behind the Land Rover and the two buses.

The leading bus had run off the side of the road into a ditch and was canted over, the pile of freight and luggage on top spilling off to lie around in the thick bushes beside the road. The second bus was stopped at an angle across the road, both front tires burst and its windows shattered. The Land Rover was in the middle of the road immediately behind it and didn't appear to have been damaged at all. The passengers stood in a line at the side of the road, and two men with Sten guns stood at the back of the Land Rover waiting for the jeep to come up to them.

As soon as the jeep pulled up the two men ran up on either side of it and shoved their guns at David and Caraday. David felt the barrel ram into his ribs and did his best not to flinch. One of the men said something in the language that David now knew was Kachin, and David looked at Caraday.

59

"I nominate you as spokesman." He had always laughed at the Englishman in fiction and films who was so cool and casual in the face of danger. He felt neither cool nor casual, but downright frightened; yet he found it helped to control his fear by putting up a cool front.

Caraday looked at him for a moment, then turned to the man who was menacing him with the gun. He said something in Kachin, the man barked something in reply, and Caraday looked at David and Moriarty. "They want us up with the others. And don't try anything, David. These blokes are always looking for an excuse to shoot off their guns."

"What are they?" The three of them walked up the road ahead of the two gunmen. "Dacoits or insurgents?"

"Insurgents. I recognise these two—they're a couple of Shero's men." One of the men prodded Caraday in the back at the mention of Shero's name. "Better keep quiet for a while."

They came up past the buses and David saw the bloodstains on the steps of the second bus. Then relief flooded through him. He had not realised how much he had been wishing (or praying, like Caraday?) that Maung Zan and the two women were unharmed. He saw them standing among the bus passengers, and his relief was so great that he smiled and almost waved at them. Along either side of the road were some thirty or forty men, all armed; others were searching the buses and the freight that had spilled from the wrecked bus. Then beyond the passengers David saw the six figures in the middle of the dusty road, strewn there like so many bags of rice.

He heard Caraday swear, then the priest had quickened his step and moved forward towards the people, four men and two women, lying in the road. One of the gunmen jumped forward, raising his gun threateningly, but Caraday ignored him and walked on. There was a moment of tension; David expected the scene to rip apart like torn silk. All the guns came up, aimed at the tall thin man walking towards the wounded and the dead. Maung Zan moved closer to Maureen and Rose, as if to protect them from any bullets that might fly. The line of bus passengers tightened together, as if each individual fear had congealed into the one mass of terror. An idiot boy stood to one side, grinning vacantly at the raised gun; and a baby in a woman's arms began to whimper. David sucked in his breath and beside him he heard Moriarty whispering in prayer.

Then a voice rang out from the bushes on a bank beside the road. "Father Caraday! Stop!"

Caraday stopped and looked up towards the bushes. "Shero?"

"Stay where you are, Father. My men haven't searched those people yet to see if they are armed."

"Tell them to get on with it, then!" Caraday spoke with the blunt voice of command; it was as if he were in charge of the hold-up. "Some of these people may be dying. Perhaps I can do something for them."

The voice behind the bushes said something in Kachin and one of the gunmen moved forward. He turned over the wounded and the dead, handling them roughly; they were nothing to him, part of a day's work. He came to the last man, who lay with his face in the dust of the road, blood gushing from a wound in the back of his neck; the man's red turban had come unfurled and had spread out about his head; he lay on a flat pillow of bright red cloth and blood. The gunman turned him over with his foot, then suddenly dropped beside the man, snatching at the man's belt. He stood up, holding aloft an old long-barreled pistol. He said something to the hidden leader, then turned back to the dying man. He slung his Sten gun over his shoulder and whipped a short ugly sword from his belt. As he raised it, Caraday suddenly stepped forward and grabbed the gunman's arm.

"Let him be!"

The two men strained against each other, but Caraday was too tall and too strong: the arm with the sword remained poised rigidly in the air. David involuntarily made a half-step forward; he pulled up with a jerk as the barrel of the Sten gun was rammed into his back. No one else had moved: it was like a film which had jammed in the projector. David was aware of the frieze of passengers standing along the side of the road, of the gunmen, even those in the bus, all turned now towards the middle of the road, their guns all aimed at Caraday. He saw a vine fall from a tree, a tic against the corner of his eye, and now he could hear the water gasping and bubbling in the radiator of one of the buses. Everything had the unreality of a dream, except that the gun jammed in his back was real.

Then there was a movement in the bushes up on the bank and a man stepped out. He was a good thirty yards from David and standing high up on the bank; but David saw that

61

he was taller than the men he commanded. He was dressed in some sort of green uniform; it looked like American jungle battle-dress. He held a Sten gun in the crook of one arm, and a slouch hat dangled by its chinstrap from the barrel of the gun. His head and face were covered by a green hood in which eyeholes had been cut. He had evidently put it on just before stepping out from the bushes, because his voice now had a muffled note to it that it hadn't had before.

"Let my man go, Father, or I'll have you shot!"

"You can't shoot me without shooting him." There was a note of strain in Caraday's voice, but he still held the gunman's sword arm in a firm grip. "Tell him to let this man die in peace."

"He is only a Burmese." The voice behind the mask was coldly sneering. "He will die, anyway. My man wants to help him on his way. He is being merciful."

"Don't joke, Shero. He's a Burmese, but he's also a man, a human being."

"Do you know him?"

"I know none of them. They are all strangers to me."

"What if he is not a Christian?" David could imagine the sardonic smile behind the mask. "Will you waste your blessing on a Buddhist?"

"A blessing is never lost on any man," Caraday said. "Not if he is in need of it."

There was silence for a moment. A flock of green parakeets whipped across the road and the insurgent leader turned his head and watched them disappear into the trees. When he turned back he looked relaxed and almost careless. He gave the impression of giving in to Caraday, yet without losing face or control of the situation. His attitude had the confidence of a true leader, one utterly sure of himself.

"Let go my man, Father," he said almost conversationally. "He won't use his sword."

Caraday continued to stand for a moment, and David thought he was going to disobey the insurgent leader. Then he stepped back, letting go of the arm of the man with the sword. The latter turned quickly, looking back up at Shero, who said something to him in Kachin. The man hesitated, then he turned back, spat at Caraday's feet and sauntered back to join his colleagues. At once Caraday dropped down on his knees beside the wounded man.

"Is there anything we can do?" Maung Zan called.

"Nothing." Caraday stood up. "He's dead now."

"You didn't bless him," mocked Shero. He hadn't moved since he had stepped out from behind the bushes; he controlled the whole scene from the elevation of the bank like a film or stage director. There was everything here: tragedy, melodrama and the comedy of the idiot boy now relieving himself behind the screen of gunmen.

"I was too late," Caraday said. "Where he is now, he is blessed or cursed forever." He looked about him at the other wounded passengers, then back at Shero. "These other people could do with some attention." He gestured at Maung Zan, then at David. "This man is a doctor, too. Let them attend to them."

Shero seemed to look at David for the first time. "You are English?" David nodded. "Have you come to work here?"

"Just on a visit," said David.

"A tourist? Sightseeing?"

David looked around at the dead and wounded, then back at Shero: he did not feel quite so afraid now. "You could call it that."

Shero nodded and laughed behind the mask. Then, almost negligently, he said, "Go ahead," and turned and barked something at his men. At once half of them slung their guns over their shoulders and ran to the two buses, the Land Rover, and the jeep. They began to ransack all the vehicles, throwing cushions out into the roadway, ripping open bedrolls, smashing suitcases and boxes open with their swords.

David, moving forward as Maung Zan did, stopped and looked back at the jeep. "Come on, David," Maung Zan said. "There is nothing we can do."

"Do they have to be so destructive?"

Maung Zan shrugged and glanced up at the figure of the insurgent leader. "I can never understand why he lets them do this. You would think a rebel leader would do his best to gain the goodwill of the local people. But he never seems to care."

Maung Zan was attending to a man whose elbow had been shattered by a bullet. David, a few feet away, was trying to examine the wound of a woman who had been hit in the breast. Despite her weakness, she kept clutching at her blouse front, trying to prevent him from exposing her. He looked up at Caraday, who stood above him. "Are they always as modest as this? Can't you tell her I'm a doctor?"

Caraday said something to the woman in Kachin, but she continued to clutch at her blouse. "It's no use. These people are among the most modest on earth. I've seen Zan having to give them injections by shoving the needle into their behinds through their *longyis*." He looked up at Shero. "Shero!"

The insurgent leader had been watching his men loot the vehicles: one could almost imagine the indulgent smile behind the mask, like a parent watching children at play. He turned his head slowly as Caraday called to him. Then he said impatiently, "What is the matter now?"

"Let the two women"—Caraday waved toward Maureen and Rose—"help us. This woman won't let the doctor touch her."

Shero looked at Maureen and Rose, then after a moment he nodded. The two women came forward and knelt down beside the wounded woman. She stared at them for a moment, still holding tightly to her blouse, then looked back at David, glaring fiercely at him. He stood up and moved on to attend to a man who had blood running from a head wound. Rose said something in Kachin and slowly the wounded woman relaxed. In a moment she was letting Maureen and Rose attend to her.

"Why do you bother, Father Caraday?" Shero suddenly said. "These aren't your people."

That's a good question, David thought. He continued to work on the wounded man beside whom he knelt, but he was waiting for Caraday's answer. He felt no relation to the man lying beside him, the blood seeping gently from the wound along the temple; he knew the man would be dead within the hour, a stranger whose name he would never know. Why bother? he thought; but went on with the pretence of trying to save the man who he knew was beyond saving.

"Are they yours?" said Caraday, and moved his hands at the dead and wounded lying about him. He's got him there, David thought, and looked up with something like admiration at the tall skinny priest. He had always admired a man who was good in argument.

Shero nodded, and again one could imagine the smile behind the mask. "You're like all the rest of the priests, Father. Always answer a question with a question."

"It's the easy way out," said Caraday, and suddenly sounded weary, almost exhausted. "Some day I'll have an answer for you, Shero."

"How's that woman?" David looked at Maureen.

"The bullet has lodged up under the clavicle." They were

64

professionals, working as a team again, on a road six thousand miles and a world away from Harley Street. For the second time in two minutes David found himself admiring someone, as he looked at Maureen, calm and matter-of-fact despite the shock and tension of the last ten minutes. "She will have to be operated on."

"She'll be the first to have the new instruments used on her," said Maung Zan.

Then the gunmen were coming back from the vehicles, burdened down with what they had stolen. David saw a man go by carrying his camera, his leather-pouched shaving kit and the new suede shoes he had bought the day before leaving London. He stood up, a protest on the tip of his tongue, but Maung Zan was beside him.

"Let him go, David. They will only shoot you if you try to take it from them."

"But they're taking your new instruments!" Two men went by carrying between them the black box that contained some of the equipment Maung Zan had brought back from England with him.

Maung Zan shrugged: once again David noticed that the bland face showed no emotion. "We'll have to find another benefactor."

"Why don't you ask them to let you keep that box?" Maureen and Rose had made the wounded woman comfortable and now stood beside David and Maung Zan. "What good is it to them?"

"They can sell it over the border in China," Maung Zan said. "It is no use, Sister Hagen. These people never give anything back."

The last of the looters went by, and Caraday, who had been standing almost as if in a daze, suddenly stepped forward and snatched the small cardboard suitcase out of the man's hands. The man snarled, spun round and swung up his gun, screeching something in Kachin. Caraday stood with the suitcase held against his chest, as if he expected some protection from the thin battered cardboard.

"You're not having this!" He leaned forward, snarling, too: both faces were contorted with anger. "You can have everything else, you're not taking this!"

Again everyone had stopped and turned back towards the priest. At Caraday's feet the wounded woman tried to roll away, as if trying to get out of the way of the dead priest as he fell. David pushed Maureen and Rose behind him, edging back out of the line of fire. Maung Zan stayed where he was, looking earnestly and pleadingly at Caraday.

"Let him have it, Charlie. You can get another one."

"Not for weeks! I'm keeping this—they've never tried to take it before!" He spun round, still leaning forward, still snarling. "Shero! Tell this man I'm keeping this!"

"What is it?" Shero made his first move, a step towards the edge of the bank. He sounded impatient, a little edgy, as if he had had enough of Caraday and his rebellion. David remembered something he had read about rebel leaders: that they admired another rebel only when he didn't cross their path. He wondered if it had been in one of the books his father had sent him, parental advice annotated in a margin.

"It's my pyx—and my vestments—I need them for saying Mass!" Caraday moved forward, stood at the foot of the bank staring up at Shero; the gunman moved forward at the same time, his Sten gun shoved deep into the skinny back. They stood there below the insurgent leader, like plaintiffs before a judge.

"What good is it to him, Shero? He'll wear the vestments for a joke—chew the bread of the Host and spit it out—"

"The pyx is made of silver, isn't it? He is only a poor man, you know—"

"I could kill him!" Maureen suddenly hissed, and David felt her arm tense under his restraining hand. "What's behind that mask—a beast of some sort?"

"Shero," said Rose, and David looked at her with surprise; she was staring up at the insurgent leader with something like awe on her face. "The Tiger. Cruel—and beautiful—"

"Cruel is the word." Maureen hadn't looked at Rose; she was still staring fiercely at Shero. "But at least a tiger shows its face, doesn't it?"

Caraday was still clutching his case. "A few kyats' worth of silver, that's all, Shero. But I'm not going to give it up. You'll have to kill me to take it from me." There was no snarling now: the deep voice was calm, almost a whisper: everyone, even the idiot boy, seemed to lean forward to hear what he said. "I mean it, Shero. You'll have to kill me."

"Are you tempting me or threatening me?" Shero's voice, too, was a whisper. Among the passengers a child whimpered and was instantly hushed: no one wanted to miss a word of what was said, even though Shero and Caraday were speaking in English and most of the passengers didn't understand a word of it. David stood outside the scene, his hand still on Maureen's arm, hardly able to believe that he was here on this jungle road, that he was about to witness the possible murder of a man in cold blood.

"Not tempting you, Shero." The kites had already begun to swing in the sky above the road, waiting to take possession of the dead, waiting on the dying and those about to die. "I am not allowed to believe in suicide. But I'm in earnest, believe me. I'll die before I'll let you take this away from me."

Why? David thought, angry with the priest for his stupid defiance, his throwing away of his own life. Why not give up the pyx and the vestments? The Church will go on; it can survive a few Sundays without Mass being said. Give it to him! he thought, trying to will the priest into submission. Give it to him before he kills us all!

Then Shero said, straightening up and laughing behind the mask, "Keep it, Father. Who knows? Some day this man may want to ask something of you."

"Or even you," said Caraday, and David noticed that the priest offered no thanks for being spared. "Even you may some day ask something of me."

"Or even me," said Shero, and the mask bubbled with his laughter. Then abruptly the laughter died, he barked an order, and so swiftly it was almost incredible the gunmen were suddenly gone. The bushes stirred, settled into place, and there was only the huddled line of passengers beside the vehicles and the limp figures lying in the middle of the road. One of the kites swooped down, Moriarty turned and chased it, swearing at it, and the idiot boy giggled. Then everyone relaxed and began moving around. The drivers of the buses went to their vehicles to see what could be done with them. The passengers began sorting over their baggage to see what had been left by the gunmen, some of the women breaking into tears as they discovered some treasured possession had been taken. And the relatives and friends of the dead and wounded came forward to offer comfort that their faces said they knew was too late.

Caraday was still standing at the foot of the bank, staring up at where Shero had disappeared into the jungle. Maung Zan moved forward and touched his arm. "They've gone, Charlie. They won't be back."

Caraday turned, still holding the cheap battered suitcase against his chest. "I'm sorry, Zan. I should have asked them for your equipment—" He looked past Maung Zan at the

67

wounded. Then he put the suitcase behind him, as if ashamed of it. "I'm sorry, Zan. Forgive me."

"There's nothing to forgive," said Maung Zan, and David knew he was not just being kind: he respected the strength of another man's faith, something David couldn't bring himself to do.

2

"But why?" David asked. "Why risk your life, perhaps all our lives, for what was in that suitcase?"

Caraday, standing beneath a fly-speckled portrait of the Virgin Mary, poured beer into a glass as if it were sacramental wine. He turned and offered the drink to David. "Sorry it isn't whisky or gin—they're too damned expensive in this neck of the woods. Why did I stand up to Shero?" He sat down in the ancient cane chair, a sad caricature of a bishop's throne. He sipped his beer while he stared out through the open window at the cliff-face on the other side of the river. Somewhere at the back of the house Moriarty was banging pots and pans and singing a hymn in a flat nasal voice. Caraday cocked his head to one side. "I'm sorry I taught Moriarty those hymns. Some of them are pretty banal, aren't they? I often wonder if the Lord is a music lover."

"We were talking about Shero and you," said David, sipping his beer. It was not good beer, but then he had never been a beer drinker at all.

"It wasn't just what was in the suitcase—although I wouldn't have slept too easily, thinking of what that thug might have done with the pyx. I saw how far the Japs could go in the way of desecration during the war. I wasn't a priest then, but I still remember being sick at the things I saw them do."

"I'm no believer in religion, but I understand how you felt. I saw some of our own chaps using Buddhist temples as latrines, thinking it was a great joke."

Caraday looked up sharply. "Were you out here during the war?"

"Only the last few months," David said, and wondered if he had been mistaken: had there been a flash of fear in the other man's eyes? "I saw very little real action."

"Don't be apologetic about it." David hadn't meant to sound apologetic, but he said nothing. The war for him had never been anything but a damnable interruption to the ordered course of his life. He had not seen his father during the whole course of the war and, thinking back now, perhaps that had been just as well. In those days Michael Breton, not yet possessed of tolerance nor charity, a dedicated colonel of Gurkhas, might have done his best to have had his son court-martialled for such an attitude.

"Only fools enjoy war," Caraday said, and David wondered if his father and the priest had ever discussed their respective parts in the war.

"You tried to start a war this morning."

Caraday nodded and looked out the window again. They had come on from the scene of the hold-up and had been here at the mission bungalow half an hour now. The surviving wounded had somehow been packed into the Land Rover and brought on to Sheromere; they were now in the hospital, but Maung Zan did not expect all of them to survive the night. The Deputy Commissioner and the police had been told of the hold-up, and a convoy of three jeeps, crowded with armed policemen, had gone racing back down the road, putting on a show but expecting no results. Maureen and Rose, the former now suffering some reaction from what she had seen this morning and the latter as calm as if returning from a picnic, had been settled in at the hospital's nurses' quarters. Then Caraday and David had come on with Moriarty in the jeep to the mission.

The mission stood in the middle of a small meadow beneath a steep tangled hill. Below it two rivers met in a brown whirlpool, then went rushing on in wild skeins of white water over rocks to ease out into a broad placid stream just above Sheromere, a mile below the mission. Opposite the mission a three-hundred-foot cliff rose sheer from the river; eagles hovered above it like a thin brown nimbus. Behind the cliff ridges ran steeply up to a towering peak, the top of which was now cloaked in rain mist.

"That's the Mountain With No Name," Caraday had said as they came up the road towards the mission, skirting the river. "No one has ever climbed it. It is supposed to be the home of the local *nats*."

"You mean spirits, ghosts?" Caraday nodded. "Have you ever tried to climb it?"

"No," Caraday had said. "Why should I?"

"I thought that was how missionaries always worked. Get rid of the other fellow's ghosts, prove that what he believes in doesn't exist."

"Only fanatics work like that and they usually finish up

being killed. I'm no fanatic and neither are most missionaries."

Moriarty had got down and opened a gate and Caraday had driven the jeep into the meadow that was the mission compound. The mission itself consisted of the main bungalow, two or three huts at the rear, a large store shed and the church: a red brick structure that looked as if it had been transplanted intact from an inner suburb of any Midland city. One expected a tramcar to go rattling by its door, and looked for the Working Men's Club that should have been close by.

"Built by my predecessor," Caraday had said as they had driven by it. "He came from Leeds and should never have left it. He used to say Mass once a year that Leeds United would win the Football Association Cup."

"He was human at least."

"Priests are," Caraday had said. "Too many people forget it."

David had been shown to his room in the bungalow, a room that, like the rest of the house, seemed stacked with the miscellany of years. Books, magazines, records, newspapers were piled against the walls like so much surplus furniture; guns, spears, bows stood in every corner, making the bungalow an arsenal; battered suitcases, bedrolls, even a golf bag full of rusted clubs, waited like forgotten luggage in a railway luggage room. David wondered if Caraday had kept the odd collection as tangible memories, as some sort of protection against the loneliness that must occasionally assail any intelligent man here on the edge of this wilderness. He had paused for a moment, trying to remember all the contents of his own flat, and had been surprised at how little he could recall to mind. He had prided himself on some of his possessions, and now they did not even provide him with memories. Every time he stopped to think he was becoming more and more aware of the wilderness that had surrounded him in London, the capital of his life.

Now Caraday took another drink from his beer and said, "Shero runs this district. The people are scared of him and so are the authorities. And the *pongyis*, too. Everywhere else the *pongyis* thumb their noses at everyone, even the government. But not here in Sheromere. When Shero says something, they bow down."

"And you don't?"

"I can't afford to. Once I knuckle under to him, I'm a goner."

70

"A goner?"

"Gone. Finished." Caraday grinned, and for a moment the sad eyes were as full of humour as the wide mouth. "The Aussie slang still sticks to my tongue. It's a taste of home, I suppose."

David tried the taste of home on his own tongue, but there was none. "Why can't you afford to knuckle under to Shero?"

"These people around here depend on me." He looked down at his glass for a moment, then looked directly up at David. "You are a confident man, David—"

"Thanks," said David drily. "Do you mean confident or conceited?"

"Probably both," said Caraday with no apology. "But I never criticise a man who has confidence in himself. I don't know that I do have confidence in myself, but I am confident that these people here depend on me."

"Aren't priests supposed to have humility?"

"They are also supposed to face the truth. And the truth is, I'm the one that the people in Sheromere look to for some sort of leadership."

"Why you?"

Caraday shrugged. "The Deputy Commissioner is a weak no-hoper. All he wants is to keep his chair warm and not offend Rangoon. The head *pongyi*—well, up here in the mountains the *pongyis* don't have quite the influence they have down in Mandalay and Rangoon. And the head bloke here has enough trouble keeping the young *pongyis* in hand. The young *pongyis* are a very ambitious lot and they're not too careful how they go about things. The yellow robe used to be respected once, but today it hides a lot of thugs, parasites and men who are using it to promote their own ends. Not just here, but all over Burma. You'll find a lot of very devout Buddhists who would like to see the monks cleaned up. The old man *pongyi* up at the monastery has just about given up. All he wants now is to die."

"So that leaves you?"

Caraday nodded. "That leaves me."

"You sound conceited enough to be a medieval Pope."

"Some of the conceited Popes did a lot of good. They may not have been pietists, but they were good politicians."

"That, of course, is what a good many of us have against the Church. It is more political than religious. Are you hoping to turn this part of Burma into a Catholic state?"

Caraday shook his head, drained his glass and stood up.

71

He went to the door, shouted to Moriarty to bring another bottle, then turned back. "Every year I get ticked off by my bishop for not increasing my congregation. Last year I got exactly two converts and lost three. I do my best to collect souls for the Lord, but I find it hard to get past the fact of their physical suffering. I'm still too much a doctor, no matter how poor I am at that."

"Do you want to be the leader of these people against Shero? Is that what you consider your vocation?"

"Of course not!" Caraday spoke almost too sharply, too loudly. I've touched him on a raw spot, David thought: he is afraid that it might be the truth. Could a priest fail because he was more concerned for people than for souls? "All I want to do is to help them. Haven't you ever wanted to help someone?" It was almost a plea: tell me I'm right in what I'm doing.

"No," said David truthfully, and felt a perverse cruel desire to laugh at the shock on the priest's face.

Then Moriarty appeared in the doorway with a bottle of beer. "Father, a woman is at the back door. She wishes to talk with you."

Caraday excused himself and went out of the room. Moriarty looked at David. "You wish more beer, Mr. Breton?"

"No, thanks." He looked at the Indian, noticing again how the squint spoiled the man's looks. He wondered if Elinor Beatty had yet gone cross-eyed, squinting at the scar on her nose. "Moriarty, were you frightened today when Father Caraday defied Shero?"

Moriarty nodded vogorously. "Oh yes. Yes, indeed, I was very frightened."

"For yourself or for Father Caraday?"

"Why, for myself! Shero had only to lift his finger and his men would have shot us all. All but Father Caraday, that is."

"And why not Father Caraday?"

Moriarty shrugged and opened his eyes wide: the cast eye, showing more of the white, seemed larger than the good eye. "I do not know. One cannot imagine Father Caraday being shot."

"He's not immortal, Moriarty."

Moriarty shrugged again. He was full of Gallic gestures, and David was to learn later that he had been brought up on a French mission at Pondicherry. "Who knows, Mr. Breton? You have no idea of the dangers he has survived."

He put the bottle of beer on a table and went out. David got up and began to wander about the room. Out at the back of the house he could hear the murmur of voices, Caraday's and a woman's, speaking in Kachin. What had the woman come to ask Caraday? Charity? Blessing? Or perhaps to have him rub off some of his immortality on her? They have put you on a pedestal, Caraday. How will the bishop like *that*?

A table stood in one corner piled high with books. Many of them showed Caraday's calling: a Bible, tattered at the edges as if rats had gnawed at it; books on the saints, on martyrs, on missionaries, coated with mould, as if they had not been opened in years; books by Catholic philosophers, all showing the same neglect. Scattered among them were other books that looked as if they had had more use: detective thrillers, books on cricket, a volume on famous churches. The table looked like a jumble lot in a sale, the castaways of a dead man's library. David picked over the books, his finicky fingers barely touching the mouldy pages as he flicked them over. Back down the road, at the scene of the hold-up, he had been aware of the smell of the jungle pressing in on each side of the road; it was here in this room, in these books, thick and sweet and dead. These were part of the jungle of Caraday's life: he had turned his back on them, given up trying to battle with their cultivation. Thomas Aquinas, Augustine, Agatha Christie had achieved a certain level: all had been discarded by Caraday. David turned over the books, wondering again why the priest cluttered his house like this; a neat and orderly man himself, he could not understand why anyone should collect unwanted rubbish. Then, beneath a copy of Gerard's *Hunted Priest*, green with mould and eaten by rats, he came upon the photograph in its rusted metal frame.

The man was much younger and in uniform, but it was Caraday: the long equine face, not so thin then, and the wide smiling mouth, the big teeth parted as if even before the camera he could not stop talking. But something was missing. David picked up the photograph, peering at this soldier of twenty years ago: where did the resemblance end to the priest of today? Then he saw it: the eyes. In 1940 or '41, whenever the photograph had been taken, Caraday had laughed with his eyes as well as his mouth. He had not yet experienced the pain or grief, whatever it was, that had brought the sadness to them.

There was a knock at the door of the room that led directly

73

on to the front verandah. David turned, the photograph still in his hand, as Rose Churchill opened the screen door and came into the room. She was still dressed in the khaki slacks and shirt she had worn on the journey up from Mandalay, but there were now clips holding her slacks tight round her ankles.

"I cycled up," she said, noticing the direction of his gaze. "Where is Father Caraday?"

"Out the back with one of his parishioners. Is there anything I can do?"

"Not unless you can administer the last rites. One of the wounded is dying." Then she saw the photograph in his hand. "Oh, is that you?"

He turned it towards her. "I found it under this pile of books."

She took the photograph from him and turned it towards the light of the window. "He was much happier in those days."

He was surprised. "You've noticed it, too?"

"Of course. He laughs a lot, but it is for the benefit of others, I think. He is an awfully sad man at heart."

He looked at her with new interest. Up till now he had seen her only as a beautiful woman possessed of that extra appeal that women of mixed blood so often have for men: the in-between colour, the different slant to the eyes, that were like visible marks of the lust in which most of them had been conceived, as if the daughter must be of the same easy virtue as the mother. But there was more to Rose Churchill than mischief and flirting promise. "Has he ever told you why?"

"We have never talked about it. And I wouldn't dare ask him."

"Ask him what?" Caraday had come into the room, smiling at Rose as at a child; David almost expected him to put out a hand and pat her head. Then he saw the photograph still in her hand and, with a gasp something like a cry of pain, the smile was gone. He snatched the photograph from her. "Where did you find that?"

"I found it," David said mildly, and motioned towards the table. "I was just looking through your books—"

"You had no business going through my things!"

"Steady on, Caraday. I had no intention of going through your things, as you call it—What's the matter, Rose?"

Rose was holding a finger from which blood was oozing. "It's nothing. I caught it on the picture frame—"

Caraday turned away from David and moved towards Rose, instantly all contrition. "Rose, I'm sorry! Oh, what a clumsy bastard I am! We must get something on it—the frame is rusty—"

"Please, Father." She seemed embarrassed by his solicitude. "I'm going back to the hospital—I'll attend to it there." She sucked on the finger. "Maung Zan wants you—one of the wounded men is dying—he is a Catholic—"

"I'll get my things. But you're sure that finger is all right?" He was more concerned about her than about the dying man waiting to be prepared for eternity. "I'd never forgive myself, Rose, if it turned septic." He looked at David, all animosity forgotten: the clash of a moment ago might never have occurred. "You have to watch every small scratch in this climate."

Seconds before David had been full of anger at Caraday. All his initial dislike of the man had come back with a rush, plus the reaction to being spoken to so curtly and accusingly. Hard words had been in his mouth, ready to be spoken, when he had seen the blood oozing from Rose's finger and the tears of pain in her eyes. Now the anger was gone, dissipated like a child's fury in the sudden change of face of Caraday; again David felt himself placed at a disadvantage, made to appear churlish if he didn't respond to the priest's abrupt friendliness. "We'd better get down to the hospital," he said brusquely, not able to adapt himself immediately: even encounters with difficult patients had never prepared him for the chameleonlike behaviour of Caraday. "You're more in need as a priest than as a doctor."

Caraday looked at him and for a moment David thought their argument might begin again. But Caraday only smiled. "I'll have to watch myself. I'll be teaching kangaroos how to hop next."

He went out of the room to get the suitcase for which he had so recently risked his life, the battered cardboard container that held the food for a dying man's last journey: the Viaticum that, had Caraday not clung to it, might now be just chewed bread, spat out and lying in the mud of a mountain track. It was as if he had known, back there on the road at the hold-up, that the contents of the suitcase were even then needed for a man who believed in their efficacy. The bishop will be pleased, David thought sardonically: he is about to pass another soul into Heaven.

The three of them rode down to the hospital, Rose on her bicycle, Caraday on his and David on Moriarty's. "I never use the jeep around here," Caraday said. "We have to economise on petrol. We whites are the poor ones now in Burma."

Rose went along to the dispensary to have her finger treated, and Maung Zan took Caraday and David into the main building of the hospital. "We have fifty beds," Maung Zan told David. "Sometimes it is enough, other times—" He shrugged. "We had a cholera epidemic last year. We had to pick our way among the patients as they slept on the floor."

"He and Rose got four hours' sleep in three days," Caraday said, hurrying ahead of them, tapping the foot of each bed as he passed and saying something in Kachin to the patients, who would smile in reply and struggle to sit up. "And not a word of thanks from Rangoon."

"You got no more sleep than we did," Maung Zan said. But Caraday was now too far ahead of them down the ward to hear. He arrived at the screened bed at the end of the ward and disappeared behind it like a man rushing into hiding. Maung Zan looked at David, then the two of them walked on past the screened bed and out into Maung Zan's tiny cluttered office at the end of the building. "When Charlie wasn't helping me as a doctor, he was working as a priest. We didn't have enough serum to inoculate everyone and he wouldn't let me use some on him. At one stage I thought we had lost him —he went down with cholera, but somehow he managed to pull through."

David sat down in the torn canvas chair across the table from Maung Zan. He looked about the room, at the broken screen on the window, the battered and rusty filing cabinet that he recognised as old British Army stock, the mildewed out-of-date medical library on the shelves along one wall. "Is this the best they can give you, Zan?"

Maung Zan's face seemed to close up. "I told you, David. My country still has an awful lot to learn."

"How long does it want to learn elementary things like health administration?" David said. "Dammit, Zan, why do all new countries put up the excuse about wanting time to learn? Learn politics and diplomacy, yes, but not how to run hospitals. You can lay a lot of faults at the door of us British, but we did teach you ordinary day-to-day administration, local government, stuff like that."

"The war wrecked our country. We suffered more than any other country in Asia."

"The war's been over for sixteen years, Zan. How long do you expect to hang on to that for an excuse?"

Maung Zan watched the green lizard that ran down the wall like a long drop of oil. There was no cheerfulness in his face now: he was no relation to the man who had sat in the flat in London and told David it would be very pleasant now in Burma. Then he looked back at David, his black eyes sombre. "You're right, old chap. But if ever I said such a thing—" He drew his finger across his throat. "Do you know why I didn't have enough serum when the cholera epidemic was here? The government had appealed for serum all over the world, and it got it at once. Some of it was flown here within twenty-four hours, from England, America, Australia, everywhere. And then it was kept in Customs for almost three weeks waiting to be cleared."

"Kept in Customs?"

Maung Zan nodded. "Oh, the newspapers found out about it and created a terrible stink. But it was too late then. The worst of the cholera outbreak was over. People died who might have been saved, but whom could we blame?"

"Surely someone was to blame?"

Maung Zan shrugged. "Have you heard of Parkinson's Law? It operates here, too, you know. It is one lesson we have learned more quickly than any other from the West. I am not in favour of army control, that way leads to dictatorship, but a couple of years ago the Army took over Burma and ran it awfully well. The streets were cleaned up, everyone had to do an honest day's work, people with authority had to assume some responsibility—things began to work. After six months they gave the country back to the government. And now it is just as bad as ever." He watched the lizard as it climbed the wall again. "I don't want the British back, no decent man wants to see his own flag exchanged for that of another country, but sometimes—"

A boy of about twelve, dressed in checked *longyi* and a starched white shirt, came in and handed Maung Zan a note. He stared at David with bright eyes and a wide smile while Maung Zan read the note: there was no shyness about him, he was sure of his place here in the hospital. "All right, Karim Naung," Maung Zan said. "I shall come in ten minutes."

The boy ducked his head in a quick bow and was gone. Maung Zan had slumped back in his chair and was staring at the door through which the boy had disappeared. Crows were cawing mournfully in the chestnut tree outside the window, and back in the ward someone was crying in long gulping sighs. Under his hand on the desk were some papers marked *Urgent;* but what was the use of urgency in a land where all the clocks showed a different time? He was tired and dispirited, back here only a day and already half-defeated. In London it had been so easy to forget the battle.

"Karim Naung wants to be a doctor. His father is an *oozie,* an elephant driver, on one of the teak plantations down near Bhamo. I found him there and brought him in here. If the older people had that boy's enthusiasm and ambition, this country could be magnificent. But they haven't, at least the majority haven't. They call us the Irish of the East, but we're worse than the Irish."

"What does Karim Naung do here?" David asked.

"He is our messenger boy. If I or my assistant or any of the nurses is wanted, he runs around looking for us." He smiled, but David noticed that the smile was not cheerful but sour. "We have no internal communication system. That is my own personal ambition for this hospital. Amplifiers all round the place that shout my name whenever I am wanted. Conceited, eh? And foolish. I could wish for more useful things, but I know I have no chance of getting them, none at all. So I wish for foolish things." He gestured at the old-style upright telephone on his desk. "That is the only telephone in the hospital. Everything comes through that—medical calls, kitchen calls, messages for the patients, even Rose's boy friends ask me to make dates with her for them." As if on cue the phone rang and Maung Zan picked it up. He spoke in Kachin for a minute or two, then hung up. "That was the stationmaster. Our week's fish supply hasn't arrived. The dacoits blew up a bridge down the line and derailed the train." He sat up in his chair and his smile brightened: it was almost as if the bad news had acted as a tonic. "It was never like this in the old days in London, was it, old chap?"

"I can't ever remember dacoits on the Bakerloo Line." David recognised that Maung Zan had closed the conversation on the shortcomings of the hospital at Sheromere. He appreciated Maung Zan's sensitivity to criticism from an outsider, but he wondered how much Maung Zan had done to try and improve matters. The short walk through the hospital had shown him how sadly dilapidated the place was: the mosquito nets as rotten as Maung Zan had said, the iron beds

78

chipped of their paint and turning rusty, the blankets torn and frayed. To a man as fastidious as David, it was difficult to reconcile the thought of a doctor with such conditions. He stood up, all at once depressed by the tiny cluttered office and the shabby run-down buildings of which it was the nerve centre. "I'll look round while I wait for Caraday."

"How long are you going to stay up here, David?"

"A few days. When my father comes up at the weekend, I'll go back with him."

"Were you glad to see him again?"

David hesitated, then said truthfully, "Yes."

"You're glad you came?"

"I didn't say that." He turned back at the door. Behind Maung Zan he saw a large cockroach disappear behind the medical books on the shelves; the volume on *Public Hygiene* looked as if it had been gnawed by rats. "Don't expect too much of me, Zan. It is not easy to adopt a father at forty. Not even when he is one's own."

He went out of the hospital grounds and walked down towards the town, walking with the aimlessness of a man who, for the first time in years, found himself with nothing to do. He had even lost the habit of strolling; he had to make a conscious effort to keep himself from striding along briskly. Though the monsoon season had finished, all the cloud had not yet gone from these northern skies; the mountains beyond the river, the border with China, were crowned with towering clouds that looked to have more substance than the ranges below them. The air was much cooler up here than down in Mandalay, and David began to wish he had brought a sweater with him from the mission. He passed a woman, bright with orange beads, who looked at him out of the corners of her eyes, turned away to hawk and spit, then looked back at him over her shoulder with the frank curiosity of a child. He was not accustomed to being stared at, but it didn't disturb him. Whatever else had happened to him since his arrival in Burma, his hide was still as thick as ever. As Maureen had said, an Englishman never felt a foreigner. He looked back at the woman, smiling at her as he might have at a child, had he had the habit of smiling at children, and when he turned round to continue his walk Maureen was blocking his path.

"Looking for conquests even here?"

"Sheath your hatpin," he said. "I'm in no mood for sticking games."

"You're not enjoying Sheromere?"

"Are you?"

"When I look at you, David, I wonder how the British Empire was ever built."

"I understand it was built by Scotsmen. The English stayed at home in the City and collected the dividends."

"If they were like you, I'm sure they did. Don't you find it just a little bit encouraging to know that you can put up with some discomfort when you have to?"

"Masochism has never been one of my vices. Let's go for a walk." Without demurring, smiling in quiet amusement at him, she fell in beside him and they began to walk down towards the town. "Have you had a good look at the hospital? Do you think Maung Zan finds it encouraging to know that he can put up with such conditions?"

"Maybe he can't do any better. You've been used to the best all your medical life, David. You can't seem to realise that some people, most people, have to go through life putting up with fifth or sixth best." She looked away for a moment towards the distant mountains. "Coming out here to Burma has, in a way, reminded me of home. My father had to battle the way these people do. He was a little better off than they are, but he never knew what it was to have the best."

"Are you getting sentimental about your father? You know, you amuse me. You couldn't stand your own father, yet you gave me lectures on how I should treat mine."

"If a person waited till she was perfect before setting an example, examples would never be set. Even the best of saints must have had a flaw or two."

"I've never thought of you as a saint. Somehow I can't see you in a niche in some church. You don't have the figure for it."

"You've changed the subject again."

"Have I?" But now they were in the midst of the bazaar crowd and any further chance of conversation was lost. He reached back for her hand and, again without demurring, she gave it to him. The crowd pressed about them, curious but friendly; European strangers were a rarity here in Sheromere. A woman offered a bunch of flowers from her basket; David took them, paid for them and offered them to Maureen; the crowd beamed as if wanting to share in the compliment to the beautiful white woman. A man held up two monkey skulls, but Maureen shook her head, smiling; the man and the crowd joined in the joke when she pointed out she had no place to wear them. Two Buddhist nuns in their pale salmon-pink robes, sexless-looking with their shaven heads, crept round the edge of the crowd. They carried their black bowls on their heads like beggars' crowns; in a land of monks they were second-class citizens. They peered from the corners of their eyes at Maureen, allowing themselves the small sin of envy. She looked at them and smiled, but they turned away and hurried on, dedicated to being ignored.

"I wonder how you would look with your head shaved," David said.

"Have you noticed that the nuns here have no standing at all?"

"That's the way it is in most religions, isn't it? In the eyes of God all men are created equal, excepting women."

"Are you on our side?"

"No." Then he smiled. "I almost said I was on God's side."

They came out of the crush of the crowd, past the line of women sitting beside the large flat bowls of dried fish, and Maureen, uttering a cry of disgust, suddenly pressed against David. He put his arm round her and looked after the diseased pi-dog as it crawled away on three legs, the whole of its rump one huge festering sore.

"Why don't they kill creatures like that?" Maureen said.

"Buddhists kill nothing. It's part of their religion."

"They kill only people, you mean."

"You mean Shero and his men this morning?" He shrugged, taking his arm from round her. The small intimacy had embarrassed neither of them. They were no longer lovers, but both still had the memory of closer and more passionate embraces. "Perhaps Shero is not a Buddhist. He struck me as a man who believes only in himself."

"You would have recognised him, then," she said, but she was smiling and the barb was a gentle one. They were at ease with each other again now, drawn together by the fact of being the only strangers here in this alien crowd.

They turned to retrace their path through the bazaar, and Maureen grabbed David's arm. "Look! Over there by that dentist's office!"

David looked across the heads of the crowd at the open store with its dentist's chair prominently displayed and the huge dental chart hung over its wide doorway. "Imagine the dentists in Wimpole Street advertising like that. Look at that ghastly grin—"

"Not *that!* The man, I mean—the one talking to the woman—he's one of Shero's men!"

"You're imagining things, my dear girl. All these people look alike—" The crowd parted for a moment and he saw his new brown suède shoes on the feet of the man. "God, you're right!"

Then the crowd suddenly thickened about them again. Before they could move towards the dentist's shop, the man and the woman turned and disappeared down a narrow alley beside the shop. David took Maureen's arm and moved ahead of her, pushing a way for them through the crowd. They came to the dentist's shop and an old Chinese, almost blind behind thick-lensed glasses, came out and smiled invitingly at them, forceps at the ready in his wrinkled brown claw.

"Trouble with your teeth, sir?" Above him the huge sign grinned wickedly. "I do first-class extractions, sir. And gold fillings."

But David was looking down the length of the alley, at the crowd that choked it like a turgid stream, that had drowned the man and woman who had plunged into it seconds before. He wondered if it would be worthwhile trying to find the man now or whether he should go back to the hospital and start his search from there.

"Did you recognise the woman he was with?"

"I didn't even look at her—her back was to me. Why?"

"It was Rose Churchill," he said.

Chapter 4

1

"We're going to have to organise another hunt for that tiger," Caraday said. "He tried to jump another woman this morning, but fortunately she got away."

David kept to windward of Caraday as the two of them wheeled their bicycles back up the hill towards the mission. Caraday had lit his pipe and even the mountain air was foul with the smell of the tobacco he used.

"What about the man you went down to see?"

"He died with the Host on his tongue. A good way to die."

"No propaganda, please. Where will you bury him?"

"Up at the mission. I have quite a cemetery there."

"Keeping score with crosses, eh? The bishop must be pleased when he sees a new one."

Caraday blew a cloud of smoke. "Don't you find your cynicism a bit of a burden at times? You appear to me as a man who has to *work* at disbelieving."

"If I do, then it's work I enjoy. Stop proselytizing, Caraday. Stick to your natives."

"You think of your father as a native?" Then Caraday blew a gust of smoke and said, "I'm sorry, I shouldn't have said that. Back to the subject of the tiger. Would you like to come on a hunt with me?"

"Just the two of us? No, thank you. I also work at being a coward."

Caraday grinned, the smile reaching his eyes this time. "No, there'll be half a dozen of us. Some of the locals will come with me if I ask them. It's safe enough if you're careful."

"I don't have a gun."

"I have four or five."

"Does the bishop know?"

Caraday grinned again. "He often comes up here and goes out shooting duck with me. He's Irish and a terrible shot, but he's a trier. They threw him out of the I.R.A. because he wasted so many bullets. So he joined the Church."

David laughed, suddenly warming to the priest. "I think you're a terrible liar, Caraday. Who gives you absolution?"

"The bishop," said Caraday, and grinned again, his teeth bright in a sudden flash of sunlight that speared through the clouds and surrounded them as they walked in the middle of the road.

"Do you patronise any of the dentists here in Sheromere?"

"Yes, I go to Ho Sang, an old Chinaman."

"An old man with thick-lensed glasses, has a shop in the bazaar?"

"Did you meet him?" David shook his head. "He has been here for years, came out of China early in the 1930's. At one time he was the only dentist in Sheromere, but now there are a dozen. All the young blokes have taken the business away from him. Their wrists are stronger for extractions."

"How does he live then?"

"Have you ever seen a poor Chinese—outside of China, I mean? Ho Sang socked his money away while he was making it. He owns one of the local tea factories."

"Does he know Rose?"

"I guess he knows everyone, he's been here so long." Caraday walked a few yards in silence, then looked at David. "Why do you ask?"

"No reason. I just thought I saw her coming out of his place this morning." He had cautioned Maureen not to say anything about Rose and the man she had been with this morning. He did not want to get Rose into any trouble if her meeting with the man had been innocent. "Is Rose half-Chinese?"

Caraday puffed on his pipe for a few more yards. "I suppose she could be. There's some Chinese heritage there."

"What do you know about Rose? I mean, where does she come from?"

Caraday took his pipe out of his mouth, knocked it out on the bar of the bicycle and looked at David. "What's your interest in Rose? I gather you're a ladies' man, Breton—"

There was no mistaking the sudden coolness in his voice, the use of the formal *Breton*. "I assure you I have no intention of practising as a ladies' man up here." They passed a cluster of bamboo huts. He looked in, saw the dirt floor and the sleeping mat spread out on it. "I like to sin in comfort, Caraday. So set your mind at rest about my designs on Rose. Though, between you and me, I think she would be well able to look after herself. Maung Zan tells me she doesn't lack for boy friends, even up here."

"I wish she would give up the others for Maung Zan." Caraday was looking straight up the road ahead of him. He seemed to have forgotten that a moment ago he had been on the verge of conflict with David. "He is in love with her."

They had reached a level stretch of road and each of them swung on to his bicycle, Caraday balancing his suitcase on the handlebars. They skirted half a dozen buffalo, shining with black mud as they climbed out of a wallow beside the road, and pedalled briskly up towards the mission. The clouds had gone all at once, and the eagles were clear against the blue sky above the cliff on the other side of the river. Beyond the cliff the mountain, its cloak of rain mist gone now, stood out as a black-green mass of jungle-matted ridges; if the *nats* lived there, David thought, they were safe from disturbance. It would be an ideal retreat for *nats*, dacoits and insurgents.

Another buffalo ambled by, a small boy lying spread-eagled on its back as if on a rock. Caraday shouted a greeting at the boy, and the latter slid off the buffalo, waved and shouted in reply, his face split in a grin like an over-ripe fruit, then scrambled back on to the plodding heedless beast.

"Can you remember when you were that young?" Caraday said, wobbling dangerously as he looked back at the boy. "I lived in the bush when I was a kid. Still would, I suppose, if I were home now. My family run sheep up on the Monaro— you know anything about Australia?" David shook his head. "Well, the Monaro is getting up towards the mountain country, down in the south-east. Breed some of the best merinos in Australia up there."

"Getting back to Rose—" It amused David to think that this priest had the same conversational trick as he himself.

They could talk for days and never get to the point of a subject. "What do you know about her?"

"Practically nothing," Caraday said irritably. "She's an orphan, she's about twenty-one, and she hasn't lived in Sheromere all her life. That's all I know about her. When you've been here in the East a little longer, you'll find that life is much easier for you if you don't know too much about the people you mix with."

"That's a negative attitude for a missionary, isn't it?"

"Why are you so interested in Rose, anyway?" They had reached the mission bungalow and dismounted. "Don't you English always pride yourselves on how you respect each other's privacy?"

David could see that Caraday was going to tell him nothing about Rose. He was not tempted to tell Caraday that he had seen Rose talking to one of the insurgents. All his life he had done his best to avoid the complications of other people's circumstances, and now would be the worst time to break that habit. If Rose was involved with any one or all of the insurgents, her reasons were no concern of his. "We English are just as curious as anyone else. Why do you think the *News of the World* sells so many copies?"

Caraday grinned, his good humour once more suddenly restored. "I guess you're right. But why do you English perpetuate so many myths about yourselves?"

"You sound like Maureen."

"A sensible girl, that. I'm no great admirer of the American women I've met out here, but she's all right."

"You have some prejudices, I'm glad to see. It may not be long before we find ourselves on common ground."

"I live in hopes. You have no idea how incompatible your father and I were when we first met. He thought Kipling had helped write the Bible. Took me quite a while to cure him of that delusion."

David went up into the bungalow ahead of Caraday and straight to his room. He did not want to pursue any talk of his father; he was still feeling his way there. He lay down on his bed, while he heard Caraday go out to the kitchen to ask Moriarty what was for supper tonight. He grimaced when he heard Moriarty say there would be curry and rice, but he knew he would have to eat it or starve. They had had curry and rice for lunch with Maung Zan at the hospital. He was a long way from London and the Mirabelle and a choice of dishes.

He was a long way from London period, as Maureen would say. There was still no sense of being astray; he was not yet yearning for the security of the familiar. London had been glad to be rid of him for a while and he was surprised to find that he was glad to be rid of it. He knew the feeling wouldn't continue, that eventually he would heed the call of Piccadilly, but for the time being he was content where he was. No, perhaps not content. Resigned. Resignation was a new frame of mind for him, but it was not disagreeable. He would just have to watch that the state of mind did not become permanent. Resignation was the refuge of the forlorn. And he was not that far gone yet.

He dozed off, and when he woke it was almost six o'clock. Caraday stood in the doorway of his bedroom. "I'm going across to the church. I have to say my Office."

"I thought that was a morning duty."

"A bloke in my job fits things in when he can. The only punctual item in my schedule is supper. That's seven-thirty."

"I'll be on time."

"Amuse yourself while I'm gone. I have to milk the cows, too." Then he turned back, his long face sober and stiff with the effort of what he was about to say. "Mooch around as much as you like. I mean, if you want to read any of my books, play any of the records. I'm sorry about jumping down your throat this morning. I know you weren't trying to pry. It's just—well, a priest has to put some things behind him. He doesn't like to be reminded of them. See you later."

And he was swiftly gone, leaving David to wonder what had happened to Caraday in his army career that he did not want to be reminded of it.

David rose, showered and changed again, went out, got Moriarty's bicycle and rode down again to the hospital. He parked the bicycle against the trunk of a jacaranda tree and went looking for Rose. He found her coming out of the long ward, taking off a bloodstained tunic, which she handed to one of the ward attendants. She took a heavy Chinese bracelet from the pocket of the tunic and put it round her wrist.

"Hello, David. We have just had another tiger victim brought in. A small boy."

"How is he?"

"He will live, unless there is a delayed shock reaction. The tiger must feel frustrated tonight. He didn't get the woman this morning and now he's missed the boy. Did you want to see me or Maung Zan?"

"You."

"Why?"

"I don't know. Perhaps to talk about tigers." He watched carefully for any reaction, but she either ignored or had not caught his innuendo. She led him across to a small bungalow that was almost hidden by large rhododendrons and had a cherry tree at each corner. A narrow verandah ran along the front of the bungalow and five small rooms faced on to this. She opened the door of an end room and waved him in.

"These are the nurses' quarters."

"In English hospitals the nurses aren't allowed to entertain men in their rooms."

She closed the door behind her, smiling quietly at him. "I don't think I should like English hospitals."

He sat down in the one chair in the room, a wooden chair with a canvas back. "Do you do much entertaining?"

"I am not answering that. Maureen has warned me that you are a man who takes advantage of everything a girl tells you."

"You and Maureen seem to have discussed me quite a lot. Which is her room?"

"The one at the other end of the verandah. Why? Are you afraid of her finding you here?" She took off the bracelet and washed her hands in a bowl on a small side table. Then she combed her hair before the mirror in the large old-fashioned wardrobe and put on more lipstick. She looked at herself with childish satisfaction while he watched her with concealed amusement. Then she went to a small closet and poured two glasses of lime juice. He took the one she offered him and watched her as she curled herself up on the bed, balancing her own drink on the flat smoothness of her lap. She had changed from the khaki slacks she had worn this morning to a yellow *cheong-sam*. Her thigh was exposed through the long slit in the gown and again he felt the warming stir of desire. But then amusement overcame desire: the coquetry in her face was too obvious. This, he thought, was how clerks in Clapham got themselves into trouble, seduced by schoolgirls.

"This isn't the first nurse's bedroom you've been in," she said.

"Maureen didn't tell you *that*."

"No, but I guessed. You've been in her bedroom many times, haven't you?"

"I may not be a gentleman, Rose, but I practise gentlemanly habits. One of them is never to tell on a lady. But you tell me something. What do you know about Shero?"

She had been about to drink from her glass. He noticed the momentary staying of her hand before she put the glass to her lips; then she drank slowly and with too much obvious enjoyment. "Ah, lime is awfully good, the best drink there is for this climate. I've tried everything else," she said almost boastfully: she was like a schoolgirl making a daisy chain of her vices, "but I've always come back to lime juices."

"Let's come back to Shero. What do you know about him?"

"No more than anyone else. Why?"

He leaned back in his chair, sipping on his own drink: he did not want to appear too much the cross-examiner. "I saw you talking to one of his men today. One who was in the hold-up down the road, one who stole my shoes and was wearing them."

She giggled, but recovered at once. "Me?" She set the glass down on the small table beside the bed. He saw the three paperback novels there, all with lurid covers. He was beginning to realise that this girl lived in a dream world of escape. But why? Why, with her looks and intelligence, did she remain here in this isolated mountain town? "Oh no, you didn't see me, David! I haven't been out of the hospital all day—"

"You must have a twin then. She was wearing the same clothes you had on when you came up to the mission this morning."

She saw her mistake. "Oh yes, I did leave the hospital—but that was the only time!" She sat up, swinging her legs over the side of the bed. The *cheong-sam* slid up, exposing the creamy smoothness of her thigh still further. She saw the direction of his gaze and once more he was the target of the too-obvious coquetry: "You're just like Maureen said—you have a roving eye."

"It is very good for the oculomotor nerve. It is one of the few exercises I indulge in."

She giggled. "It is a pity you aren't going to stay long, David. I think you'd be awfully good fun."

He noted the English prep school phrase; Maung Zan had the same habit of speech. He had noticed the same phrases always on the ends of the tongues of Indian doctors he had met in London; and he remembered a coal-black Ghanaian who had found everything "absolutely wizard." The British had been kicked out of India and Burma and were being kicked out of Africa, but there were still people in those countries who tried to identify themselves with the British, tried with their pathetic secondhand slang to show that they were not as native as the masses who made up the new India or the new Burma or the new What's-its-name. Rose had more excuse than most: she was trying to identify herself with her anonymous British father. But the phrase still sounded strange coming out of a face that was as much Oriental as Occidental. It had the same ridiculous air of farce as when he had seen West End actors, disguised with cigars and horn-rimmed glasses, trying to sound like Americans. Maureen had been amused at that, and now he was amused. He smiled, and she mistook the reason for the smile. She stood up and came across to his chair. For a moment he thought she was going to sit in his lap; but she wasn't *that* obvious in her coquetry.

"There are so few interesting men around here."

He looked up at her, still smiling. "What about Shero?"

But she didn't take the bait. "I wouldn't know what he looked like."

"What about Maung Zan?"

She shrugged. "He's too wrapped up in his damned hospital. You can't make love with a man who's always got a syringe in his hand."

"You don't sound like a dedicated nurse."

"Oh, I'm not! I find it frightfully boring most of the time. But what can a girl do? I have to work. I mean, it's the hospital or the bazaar."

"Why don't you go down to Rangoon?"

She turned away and walked to the window at the rear of the room and looked out through the worn bamboo blind. It was dark outside now and he knew she could see nothing, but she made a pretence of being interested in something. "There's an old horned owl comes down every night and sits in one of the cherry trees. Did you know about those cherry trees? When the Japanese came here during the war, they raped all the nurses but one. She was here in the bungalow, in this very room, and the Japanese let her be, because of the cherry trees at the corners of the bungalow. The cherry tree is sort of divine to the Japanese, did you know that?"

"Did the nurse spend all the war in this bungalow?"

"Oh no, she came out after two days. She was nearly starved by then."

"What happened to her?"

"Oh, they raped her."

"Not under the cherry trees, I hope. Were you here during the war?"

"No, I didn't come up here till two years ago."

"Why did you come?"

"Maung Zan asked me to come back. I was studying to be a nurse, down in Rangoon."

"Asked you to come *back*?"

"I was here for a year about five or six years ago. I was living with my grandfather, but I ran away."

"Who is your grandfather?"

"Ho Sang, the dentist."

David wondered why Caraday hadn't mentioned that fact when he was talking about Ho Sang. "Where is your mother?"

"She died when I was born. She was like me. She ran away to Rangoon when she was young."

"Who brought you up—Ho Sang?"

She shook her head. "He didn't find me till I was fourteen. I was brought up by more people than I can remember. The Burmese love children, even a half-caste orphan like I was. But I was always being passed from one family to another. It was during the occupation and sometimes the head of a family disappeared without any warning and the woman would be left trying to find food for her children. I was always the extra one, so I'd be passed on. I can remember once, for a month or two, I don't know how long, I was looked after by Japanese nurses at one of the hospitals. That was when I ate best of all, I suppose."

"You did well to survive," he said, looking at her with new interest now. There was evidently more fibre to her than he had supposed. She was a romantic and a coquette, but that perhaps was better than being a bitter grasping shrew. He thought of Louise de Felice, who would one day be a bitter shrew because she had everything and had no dreams left.

"You forget I am part Chinese," she said. "The Chinese have a talent for survival."

"You still haven't told me why you don't go back to Rangoon."

She picked up the Chinese bracelet and put it on her wrist again. "Because I'm a Eurasian. It isn't a good thing to have white blood in countries that have just got rid of the whites. Oh, you're not a social outcast, although you do find the women resenting you because your skin is whiter than theirs.

The women are always the worst. I don't know whether they envy you or not. All I know is, they manage to make you feel awfully uncomfortable."

"What about the men?"

"Oh, the men are very interested in you. I could have had a dozen men." She didn't say it boastfully, but with bitterness, the first trace of it he had noticed in her. "But what is the good of being some man's mistress if he can never take you anywhere?"

He looked at his watch: it was almost seven-thirty, time for supper. He stood up. There wasn't time now to ask her all the questions that crowded his mind. He walked to the door and opened it. "Father Caraday is waiting supper for me. But I'll be back tomorrow, Rose. If half of what you've told me is true, you're the most interesting girl I've met in a long time." He smiled. "I remember that Maung Zan said you were a terrible fibber."

She came to the door and stood close to him. "Maung Zan knows nothing about me," she said, and leaned forward and kissed him full on the lips. He returned the kiss, but didn't put his arm round her. She could turn out to be another Elinor Beatty, and he was too far from home for that sort of involvement again. She drew back from him. "You're not very responsive, are you?"

He gestured at his watch. "Father Caraday is waiting."

"Don't keep him waiting then. He is one of my favourite people, an awfully nice chap." She opened the door wide. "Do you spend all your time with him asking him questions?"

"Goodnight," he said, smiling again. "If you should see that man of Shero's again, ask him to return my shoes. But more important, ask him to return Maung Zan's medical equipment. After seeing the hospital, I'm sure he needs it."

"That was exactly what I was doing," she said, and shut the door in his face.

2

"You've got lipstick on your mouth," Caraday said, "if you don't mind my mentioning it."

"Not at all," said David, wiping his lips with the threadbare napkin.

"Have you made up with Maureen?"

"In a way," David said, fibbing like Rose, taking the way out that had been, consciously or otherwise, offered to him.

He was not quite certain that Caraday hadn't guessed where he had been. But he was not going to get involved in an argument with him over Rose. He had made it a practice never to argue with another man about a woman. That way led to involvement with fathers, brothers, husbands, and rival lovers, and an affair became too complicated. To argue with a priest over a woman could lead to complications too complex to imagine.

"Did you see Rose?" Caraday said, as if he had guessed the trend of David's thoughts.

"Fleetingly," said David, trying to concentrate on the curried goat and finding it difficult. Moriarty, he guessed, must be among the world's worst cooks. He looked up and Moriarty was standing beside him with a bowl of the curry.

"More, Mr. Breton? Only Indians can make good curry, you know. It is one of our natural talents, like hockey and love-making." He looked at Caraday. "I speak only in the national sense, Father. Personally, I am a good Catholic celibate. Are you a celibate, Mr. Breton?"

"At present, yes," said David. "But curry acts on me like a love potion, so I shan't have any more."

Moriarty looked surprised. "Curry a love potion? I had not heard of that. Perhaps I should cut down the curry, Father?"

"We'll see," Caraday said, and Moriarty went out of the room shaking his head. "I don't blame you, David. He is a terrible cook, but I haven't the heart to tell him."

David pushed the plate away from him. "You have a soft heart and a hard stomach. Certainly harder than mine."

"He also makes an atrocious dessert. He is the only man I know who can make a rock-hard blanc-mange."

They were smiling at each other and the atmosphere between them was relaxed and friendly. I don't trust this man, David was thinking, yet I like him. He has all the marks of a Fifth Columnist, he has designs on what he likes to call my soul, yet I like him. One has to watch these priests, they were the original Fifth Column long before the term became fashionable—

"What's amusing?" Caraday asked, consigning the last of his curry to his hardened stomach.

"I was thinking that Moriarty's curry could be used as a sort of Fifth Column." I'm a practised liar, David thought. Rose is just a beginner compared to me. What about Caraday? Do priests have to stick to the truth all the time or does the Church allow them a certain number of lies? "Fifth Column. One no longer hears that phrase. It rather dates one, doesn't it?"

Caraday rang the small bell beside him and Moriarty brought in the dessert. It was blanc-mange, rock-hard. When Moriarty had gone outside again, Caraday said, "If you can't eat it, you'd better give it to me. I noticed how hurt he looked when he saw you hadn't eaten all your curry. Were you in the Spanish Civil War?"

With an effort David swallowed a piece of the blanc-mange. "I was too young. It was just ending before I realised what it was all about."

"A soldier's son?" Caraday raised an eyebrow.

"Perhaps that was why. The last thing I was interested in was a war."

"I almost went to Spain to fight. I was packed and ready to go when my mother suddenly took ill. I think it was the thought of what I was going to do that put her to bed. Then, somehow, all my idealism died and by the time my mother was better, I'd forgotten all about it."

"I'm not political-minded, but was there any idealism in wanting to fight for Franco?"

"Oh, I wasn't going to fight for Franco. That was the bit that made my mother ill." Caraday was swallowing the blank-mange as if it were crepes Suzette. "I was going to fight for the Republic."

"Does the bishop know of that part of your past?"

Caraday grinned. The sadness seemed to have lifted from his eyes; he seemed to be enjoying the conversation and companionship of David. "He knows. Even though he's an Irishman, and the Irish and Spanish Catholics are pretty much alike, he has no time for the Spanish Church."

"Are all missionaries as radical as you and your bishop?"

"You going to finish your blanc-mange?" David shook his head and pushed his plate across to Caraday. The latter took it, scraped off the blanc-mange on to his own plate and handed back David's empty plate. "Missionaries aren't radicals, David. But we aren't reactionaries, either. If we appear more broad-minded than priests back home, it's only because we have to be broad-minded to survive. Not only in the moral sense but in the physical sense, too. Do you think I can apply suburban standards to these people around here? We all come out here with our bags full of piety and what-have-you, on fire to save souls, to fill up Heaven with ex-Buddhists, ex-Muslims, ex-Hindus, ex-What-have-you, but after a few years the zeal wears off. There are some of us who have given up trying to save souls, that is, as the primary aim, and are trying to save people."

"Have you?"

Caraday toyed with the blanc-mange, then suddenly pushed it away. He put his elbows on the table and rested his chin on his clasped hands. The sadness had clouded his eyes again. "I don't know. We are supposed to go home every seven years and each time we go home we do some soul-searching, our own souls, that is. I've talked about this with some of the other blokes and most of us feel the same way about it. We come back with renewed zeal, promises to God and the Superior-General and all that, but it soon wears off. Except with the saints, and there are very few of us who are that. I've been home only once. I'm not due to go again for another four years. God knows what I'll be like by then."

"Does it worry you?"

"Of course. It's my profession or vocation, call it what you like. Wouldn't it worry you as a doctor if you found you were not interested in curing people?"

Moriarty came into the room with the bowl of blanc-mange. "Ah, Mr. Breton, you enjoyed your blanc-mange? Would you care for some more?"

David shook his head. "But it was delicious, Moriarty."

"It is my own special recipe. Indians are very good makers of blanc-mange. We learned it from the British, you know." Then he saw the blanc-mange on Caraday's plate. His bad eye seemed to squint more with hurt surprise. "Father, you haven't eaten your share! Is there something wrong with it?"

"No, Moriarty," said Caraday, and looked across at David who was hiding a smile behind his napkin. "I'm just tired to-night, that's all. Too tired to eat."

Moriarty murmured sympathetically, picked up the plates and took them outside. David said, "I was wondering earlier if the Church ever allowed you chaps some divergence from the truth."

"I'm a practised liar. In small things, that is," he added, but not before David had seen the sudden cloud, almost like a grimace of pain, pass swiftly across the long face.

David was practised, too—in hurting people. It was the long-engrained habit rather than any malice of the moment that made him say, "Were you lying by default when you neglected to mention that Ho Sang is Rose's grandfather?"

Caraday looked up. His face tightened, and he looked

more on the defensive than at any time since David had met him.

"Who told you that?"

"She did."

"Was that her lipstick on your mouth?"

"No," David lied, not wanting the conversation turned. "Why didn't you tell me he was her grandfather? The way she spoke, it doesn't seem to be any secret."

"Why are you so interested in Rose?"

David hesitated, then he said, "I wasn't going to tell you this. I saw her this morning down in the bazaar talking to one of Shero's men."

"You were seeing things." His voice was snappish.

David shook his head. "He was wearing my new shoes, for one thing. For another, Rose has admitted it. She said she was asking him to return Maung Zan's equipment. Perhaps she was, but I was intrigued, and still am, as to how she made her contact with this fellow."

Caraday lay back in his chair. It was not a relaxed movement, but rather one of a man stretching his legs before getting ready to run. He looked fidgetty, angry and sad all at the same time. "All right, Ho Sang is her grandfather. I don't know why I didn't tell you, except—well, Ho Sang has contacts, too, with Shero. I've known for some time that Rose has contacts with him, too, although I don't believe she's ever met Shero himself. I've kept quiet about it, because I reckon it's her business. And Ho Sang's, too. Shero has a lot of sympathisers in these mountains."

"He won't keep them if he goes on killing people the way he did this morning."

Caraday slumped still further in his chair; it was as if he had given up the idea of running. "I can't understand him. Shooting up army and police convoys, yes. But not innocent people. Murder never won anyone any sympathy."

"How long has Shero been operating round here?"

"About two years. That is, with his own band of men. He may have been around here before that, working under someone else."

"Would Ho Sang be helping him actively?"

Caraday got up, went to the mantelpiece and found his pipe among the clutter there, returned to the table and lit it. The smell of the tobacco soon filled the whole room. "I don't know. Perhaps, but I don't think so. I've known Ho Sang ever since I first came here, but I've never got to know him well."

96

"The inscrutable Chinese, eh?" David said, and Caraday shrugged. "How well have you got to know Rose?"

"Better than I know Ho Sang. But that doesn't mean I understand her. A priest is no better equipped, no, he's worse equipped, than any other man to understand a woman." He looked at David. "Are you going to try to understand Rose?"

"What I don't understand is why you should be so concerned as to whether I do or not."

"I'm concerned about all the people around here. But particularly Rose. You're not really interested in her, David. You don't want to take a half-caste girl from the mountains back to London."

"Nothing was further from my mind! Good God, does a little mild interest in a woman always mean marriage in your eyes? I thought you were more sophisticated than that. Is that the only tobacco you have?"

"I'm afraid so. Does it annoy you?" He got up and tapped out the bowl of the pipe in the fireplace. "I'm not sophisticated, David. Crude tobacco tastes, crude moral outlook. I'm simpler than you give me credit for."

"I'll send you some Dunhill mixture when I get back to London. You need educating."

"Perhaps I do. Perhaps I've been too long in these mountains. Perhaps I should never have come here at all." Standing by the fireplace, he looked down at David. "Do me a favour, David. Don't ask too many questions of Rose about her contact with Shero. Let it be her own business."

"It might lead her into more trouble than just having a man from London take a little interest in her."

"Maybe. But at least she will be involved with her own people in her own country."

"Which was more than her mother was," said David with a moment of insight.

"Things might have been easier for Rose if her mother and father, whoever they were, had kept that in mind."

"Meaning it would have been better if she had never been born? Isn't that against the Church's teaching?"

Caraday nodded, his eyes black now with sadness. "I just don't like to see people destined for unhappiness. And I'm afraid that is all Rose has ahead of her."

Later David lay in his bed and listened to the night sounds outside. He had expected to go to sleep as soon as he had lain down, but the bed had proved to be lumpy and hard; he had not noticed it this afternoon, but he had been more tired then than he was now. As he had tossed and turned, wondering if he should split open the mattress to see if it was stuffed with old blanc-mange, sleep had gone further and further away from him. At the end of half an hour he was wide awake, irritable and wondering once more why he was subjecting himself to this discomfort. He had heard Caraday moving round in his room across the hall, then at last the bungalow had been silent. Now, an hour after coming to bed, he was listening to the noises outside.

He got up, wrapped a blanket about himself against the cold night air, went to the window and looked out through the rusted wire netting. There was bright moonlight outside and he could see the clear outline of the church further across the meadow. Two shadows crossed the meadow close to the ground and he guessed they were a couple of the half dozen dogs he had seen about the mission, dogs that were better fed and much healthier-looking than those he had seen down in Sheromere. A bird cried, one of the dogs barked, and from somewhere up in the hills behind the mission there came the sawing of a leopard, a sound that would be identified for him later by Caraday. Behind the sounds there was the soft rumble of the river at the confluence, like faraway thunder.

David pulled the blanket tightly about him. Amalfi would have been better than this, he thought. At least there there would have been no loneliness of the flesh; I should have had more than just a blanket to keep me warm. And the women in Amalfi would not have worried about becoming involved with a man from another country; love-making in Amalfi was an international sport, an intertwining of limbs and not of lives. Here I am lonely in every possible way, he thought. Nothing here touches me. I am not one for dirt roads, jungle-clad hills, the sound of animals in the night. He longed suddenly for the sound of a taxi horn, the screech of tires, the rumble of the Underground heard in the stillness of early morning: *they* were his sounds. Those, and the murmur of a woman's voice, any woman who was beautiful, practised and not intent upon involvement. He would never surrender to love, the vice that possessed Caraday.

He saw the third dark shape cross the meadow, larger than the two that had gone before. It came out from behind the screen of bamboo that fenced the hill end of the meadow, moving slowly but with deliberate purpose. It stopped for a moment, its head raised as if it were aware that someone was

98

watching it. It had begun to move again before David realised that the dark shape was that of a tiger, lighter now that it had moved out of the shadow of the bamboo and into the bright glare of the meadow.

He dropped the blanket, turned and raced out of his room, calling for Caraday. The latter, still fully dressed, opened his door as David reached it.

"A tiger! He's out in the meadow!"

"He's after the cows!" Caraday pushed past David and went quickly into the front room. David, following him, saw him pick up a gun and some shells. "Stay on the verandah. I might pick you off instead of him."

He slipped the shells into the barrels of the rifle, opened the front door and stepped quietly out on to the verandah. He went silently down off the verandah, the rifle held at the ready before him, and ran swiftly down the path that led to the meadow, running as noiselessly as his shadow that followed him. He moved like a man who has been trained to kill, David thought. What has he been besides doctor and priest?

David shivered as the night air bit into him, but he did not want to go back for his blanket. He moved to the end of the verandah to watch Caraday. It was still bright moonlight and everything stood out in sharp relief. There was the mass of the hills against the starred sky, the angular shape of the church, the gently waving frieze of bamboo, the huge dark bell of the *bho* tree, and the blue-green lake of the meadow. And the tiger, now close to the ground, moving down towards the restless cows in the small yard in one corner of the meadow.

Caraday was running down one side of the meadow, keeping close to the rough fence that enclosed it. He was fifty yards short of the tiger, when suddenly it raised its head and looked in his direction. David guessed that Caraday in that moment realised he would get no closer to the tiger. He saw Caraday stop, raise the rifle to his shoulder, then the shot echoed and re-echoed round the surrounding hills. A second shot rang out, but the tiger had already turned and was bounding swiftly across the meadow towards the bamboo from behind which it had appeared. In a moment it had gone from sight against the blackness of the hill.

Caraday began to walk slowly back towards the bungalow as the dogs began to bark furiously and lights went on in the huts down the road from the mission. As Caraday reached the steps up to the verandah, Moriarty came running round the corner of the house from his hut at the rear.

"It's all right, Moriarty," Caraday said. "It was a tiger. He's gone now."

Moriarty blessed himself rather elaborately. He makes a ceremony of everything, David thought. "A tiger down here! He has never been so close before!"

"Probably frustration," Caraday said. "I don't know if it was the man-eater, but chances are it was. We'll check the pug marks in the morning," he said to David. "The man-eater has a scar on one of his forepads."

"Will he be back tonight?"

"I shouldn't think so. But we'll go looking for him tomorrow— What's the matter?"

"Up there, on the other side of the river." David pointed. "There's a fire, a big one."

Caraday and Moriarty turned. On a distant ridge flames burned brightly against the night sky, taking the light from the lower stars.

"It looks like Mong Na," said Caraday. "If it is, the villagers there must be wondering what they've done to annoy the *nats*." He looked up at David at the top of the steps. "Last month Shero and his men held up every shopkeeper in Mong Na and took all their cash. And now—" He looked back at the blaze on the distant ridge. "No village deserves that sort of bad luck twice in a month. I'll go out there tomorrow."

"I thought we were going to hunt the tiger," David said. "You're trying to do too much, Caraday. You were a doctor. You ought to remember that a man can only do one operation successfully at a time."

"Perhaps you're right," said Caraday, and came up the steps on to the verandah. "All right, we'll go after the tiger tomorrow. Have you ever hunted tiger before?"

"No," said David. "I've never hunted anything. Except women."

"Only you will know if there is any difference," Caraday said. "I'll ask you tomorrow night when we get back."

Chapter 5

1

"What did you find out from Rose?" Maureen said. "I know you paid her a visit last night."

"I found out she is Ho Sang's granddaughter. The old dentist yesterday, remember? And she admitted she had been talking to that fellow who stole my shoes."

"Those shoes."

"It is my personal grudge against the man. Although it must give him a certain distinction around here. Whoever heard of a brigand wearing a pair of Peal shoes?"

"I've met some well-shod brigands in the City of London."

"Who is the cynic now?" He smiled. Then he tapped the large box that lay open on the table before them. "But Rose has now proved she has a contact with Shero. She told me she was asking for this box of equipment to be returned, and here it is."

He and Maureen were working at a table that had been set up outside the dispensary, under the shade of a *bho* tree. He had cycled down with Caraday to the hospital after breakfast. They had been aware of the air of excitement as soon as they had dismounted outside Maung Zan's office; then they had seen the nurses and attendants grouped round the box outside the dispensary door. Maung Zan and Maureen had come out of the office as they had parked their bicycles against the wall.

"It was on the doorstep this morning," Maung Zan had said when Caraday had jerked his head towards the box.

"No one knows who brought it back?" Caraday asked, and David, watching him, saw that the priest all at once looked strained, almost nervous.

"No, it was there when the day staff came on duty."

"Just like a foundling box," Maureen said.

"Not quite," said David, still watching Caraday. The priest, he knew, was avoiding his eye. "It belonged here in the first place. It just hadn't arrived, that was all."

There was a constraint on all of them. None of them had mentioned Rose, but it had struck David at once that all of them, even Maung Zan, knew who had been responsible for the return of the medical equipment. They were like children keeping up the pretence of Santa Claus in front of each other. "Well, it is back," said Maung Zan. "That is the important thing. I just hope it is all there and none of it is broken."

"David and I will check it for you," Maureen said. "We've got nothing to do."

"I may even find my shoes," said David.

But his shoes were not in the box. The equipment itself had not been touched, was still in its paper wrappings. David and Maureen went through it methodically, checking each item against the list Maung Zan had given them. "It's little enough," David said, "yet Zan had to come all the way to England to get it. It hardly seems worth the trouble." He looked across at the hospital ward, at the broken netting over the windows, the unpainted walls, the vulture sitting on the gable like a macabre weathercock. Then he saw the building that was the out-patients' clinic and the long line of people waiting outside it with a cheerful patience that suddenly, and for the first time in longer than he could remember, made him feel ashamed. He said, more to himself than to Maureen, "No, perhaps it is worth the trouble."

Maureen looked at him, but checked any expression of her surprise. "Some day they may have a good hospital here," she said carefully, afraid that any wrong word might just as suddenly douse the spark of charity that had flickered in him. Then she saw Rose coming towards them from the ward, wearing a large, peasant's bamboo hat against the glassy dazzle of the sun. "Are you going to say anything to Rose about the return of the box?"

"I think she should have a vote of thanks," he said, and smiled at Rose as she came up to them under the shade of the tree. "I see your friend returned the box when you asked him."

"Not my friend." Under the wide shallow plate of her hat her face was bland: this morning, he thought, she is going to be inscrutably Oriental. "Just someone I was able to talk to."

"Well, whoever he was, I'm sure Maung Zan is grateful to you," Maureen said.

"Maung Zan doesn't know." For a moment the blandness of her face cracked. She looked at David. "Unless someone told him."

"No one told him. But from what I remember of Zan in our student days, he was a very good guesser." David unwrapped a scalpel and stepped out from the shade to examine it against the sunlight. Two small boys crept close to look at the glittering blade; he flashed it at them and they scampered away. He came back into the shade of the tree, his eyes watering from even the moment's exposure to the stabbing glitter of the sun.

"You shouldn't have done that," Maureen said. "You might have frightened them."

"Boys in these mountains grow up with the knife," he said. "Isn't that right, Rose?"

"You seem to have learned an awful lot since you came up here," Rose said. "Is he always as quick as this, Maureen?"

Maureen looked at both of them, then decided not to take sides. She had convinced herself that she was finished with David, but now all at once she trusted him more than she trusted Rose. At least she knew how *far* she could trust him, which was more than she knew about Rose. She was saved from replying by the arrival of Caraday.

He came in under the umbrella of the tree, stopping for a moment to knock out his pipe on his boot. He looked up at the tree. "Buddha knew what he was about when he chose a tree like this to sit under."

"There are other trees that throw a deeper shade," Rose said.

"But none that have leaves shaped like the human heart."

"What about the Lombardy poplar?" said Maureen, full of surprises again: even though she was a farm girl, David had never heard her show any interest in nature.

"Now that I come to think of it," David said, "my man at home has a rubber plant in the kitchen. It has a heart-shaped leaf."

"I'm surrounded by botanists," said Caraday, looking sur-

103

prised. "I concede defeat. Then I wonder why Buddha did choose the *bho* tree."

"Perhaps it was just convenient," David said. "You theologians are always clashing your symbols."

"A very pretty pun." Caraday smiled, but the smile was only fleeting. It was obvious he had not come across to them to discuss trees. He looked at David. "That was Mong Na that was burnt out last night. Every shop and hut."

"Shero's men?" David asked, and watched Rose without looking directly at her. But she showed no reaction: her Chinese mother was working well in her this morning. She still wore the hat and when she tilted her head forward its wide brim sometimes hid her eyes.

Caraday nodded, his long face dark and sad again. He was facing facts now, not symbols: facts that he knew must have shattered a few human hearts in Mong Na. "I can't understand it. Just pure vandalism, that's all it was. The sort of thing the dacoits would do."

"Perhaps he is a dacoit," David said, watching Rose: there was still no change in her expression. "Who said he was an insurgent?"

"He put out a proclamation. Rose remembers it, don't you, Rose? He said he was fighting for the independence of the Shan States."

"I thought Sheromere was in Kachin State," David said.

"You have learned a lot, haven't you?" Rose's expression was still bland, but her voice had a rasp to it. What twang of home comes out in her when she is upset, David wondered, East or West? "But you haven't learned that up here boundaries don't mean much."

"She's right," said Caraday quickly. It was as if he sensed the antagonism between David and Rose, and wanted to be on her side. "You can't draw a boundary line up and down a mountain range. Even the frontier gets lost sometimes." He nodded towards the distant mountains to the east. "In the monsoon, when the police and Army stay in the towns, even China runs into Burma."

"And insurgency runs into dacoity," David said. "Shero looks to me like a man at home in both occupations." He put away the last of the equipment and closed the lid of the box. "But I suppose we should be thankful for his returning this. I only wish he had returned my shoes. You might ask that chap next time you see him, Rose."

The blandness of her expression broke for just a moment

before she turned and walked stiffly away towards the nurses' bungalow. Maureen looked after her, suddenly softening towards her, not liking to see another woman hurt. "You didn't have to be quite so blunt with her, David."

"I'm discovering a set of principles I never before realised I had," he said. "I find it goes against my grain to traffic with murderers. That's what Rose is doing. Isn't she, Caraday?" he said, and looked cruelly at the priest. He saw the look of pain pass across Caraday's face, but it was too late to undo the hurt: the barb, fired out of habit, had gone home.

"It's time we went home for lunch," was all that Caraday said.

Going up the hill towards the mission on the bicycles, Caraday said, "I see hope for you, David. There's a crack in the cynicism. Your newly discovered principles, I mean."

He has forgiven me for that remark about Rose, David thought. A month ago he would have resented forgiveness: it was a virtue that he had always looked upon as belittling the forgiven as much as it enlarged the forgiver. Now, unaccountably, he felt better for Caraday's magnanimity. "Don't be optimistic," he said, still unable to throw away his defences completely. "Once I move away from here, those principles can be put back in mothballs. One has little to do with murderers in W.1."

"W.1.?"

"London. A postal zone. Where I live."

"How *do* you live?" They were both up on their pedals now, pushing against the grade. The fierce sunlight fell on them almost as a physical blow; they rode above the black corpses of their shadows. David waited till they were up over the rise and on the flat stretch that led up to the mission. The seat of the bicycle was beginning to cut into his crotch. He wondered if Moriarty, a good Catholic, looked upon the bicycle as an instrument of penance. Five Our Fathers and five times round the mission on the bicycle.

"I don't know what standards you have other than those up there." He nodded towards the mission. The church, red and angular, looked as incongruous as a London bus in the bright glare of the meadow and against the brilliant green of the hills behind it. "I do have a man who can cook. Curry and blanc-mange are not his idea of a banquet."

"I'm sorry about that."

"Don't apologise. I just admire you for being able to put up with it."

"Admire me? Watch yourself, David. Yesterday you didn't even understand me."

"Did I say that?"

"No, but it was written all over you, like a huge question mark."

"I still don't understand you."

Caraday dismounted and opened the gate into the meadow. He leaned on the gate as David cycled through. Behind him the cows grazed in the meadow, the tiger of last night forgotten. "Some day you may, David. In the meantime I'm beginning to understand you. We're going hunting that tiger this afternoon. I have a theory that each of us, all of his life, is hunting a tiger, his own particular tiger. Do you agree?"

"You don't expect me to answer that straight off. A bicycle seat is not my idea of a philosopher's chair. The crotch has generated some explosive ideas, but not one that is aching like mine."

Caraday laughed, closed the gate and remounted his bicycle. "I think your particular tiger is love. No, not crotch love, but real love. You're afraid of it, aren't you?"

"You aren't luring me into any confessional." David eased himself forward on the seat again. "What is your own tiger?"

Caraday's long horse's face was suddenly blank in the white glare that blazed up from the track on which they rode. He pedalled ahead of David, a long thin figure, a man of pipe arms and pipe legs on the thin frame of the bicycle, his noon shadow just a moving dark line in the dust. His voice came back as if out of a throat choked with the heat and dust of years. "I have a dozen."

2

In the middle of the afternoon they went hunting the tiger. The three of them, David, Caraday and Moriarty, left the mission and started on the long walk up the track that led to the village of Mali Ga. The two white men each carried a gun, Caraday a Mannlicher and David a Springfield, and Moriarty carried sandwiches and two thermos bottles in a fringed, brightly patterned native bag.

"Are you sure you want to come?" Caraday had said to David as he had handed him the rifle. "It'll be a bit grim and uncomfortable if we have to sit up all night."

David had reached a stage in his relationship with Caraday where he felt himself challenged by the attitudes of the other man. He had been challenged in the past, by other doctors, by women, by his absent father; but those invitations to competition had somehow been different, had been simpler and more direct than these implied doubts of himself. To his own surprise he found himself wanting to accept the challenge.

"I'll be all right. It so happens that I went to a school that included discomfort as part of its curriculum."

"A school for soldier's sons? I know the sort. Some church schools are like that. Make a uniform of the hair-shirt. I went to one like it."

"And you liked it so much you've worn the hair-shirt ever since?"

Caraday shook his head. "For a while after I left school I wallowed in luxury—and enjoyed it, too. I am not an ascetic by nature."

"Then why do you stay on in this hermitage?"

"Hunting tigers," said Caraday, grinning, but his face and eyes were dead behind the smile: he was not going to tell David anything further. "But about today's tiger. We've had some luck. He killed a sambhar stag this morning up near Mali Ga, but the villagers disturbed him before he could carry off the kill. We'll use it to bait him back."

"He must be a rather rabid beast by now. Four frustrations in two days."

"There must be something wrong with him. He's either an old man feeling his age, or he's partially crippled. Tigers usually don't turn man-eater if they're still active enough to kill game."

"Do you think that is why Shero is now burning down villages? Is he crippled, too?"

"One thing at a time. Remember?" Caraday had said almost curtly. "We're after the man-eater today."

Now they were on the track three miles from the mission and still climbing. It was not a road for either jeeps or bicycles; beneath the thick overhanging trees the monsoon mud had not yet dried out. Occasionally they passed a buffalo cart lurching along, moving at a rate that suggested it would reach its destination only in time to avoid the next monsoon. The track angled its way gradually up the side of a steep ridge, passing through evergreen jungle. Trees, coiled tightly about by climbing plants, came to the very edge of the track; when the wall of trees broke for a moment, it was replaced by thick whispering walls of tall bamboo. Rhododendrons grew in thick profusion and there were other trees and

107

bushes that looked familiar to David. Monkeys chattered in the trees above them, but kept out of sight. A thick vine uncoiled itself from a small tree and slid away into the undergrowth; David was past it before he realised with a shock that he had come close to a python. Then somewhere down the ridge below them there was a fierce chattering and calling.

"Gibbons," said Caraday, looking back at David. "There must be something down there. A leopard. Or maybe our mate."

David just nodded. He was breathing heavily and he could feel a fluttering in his legs as he pushed up the slippery slope. He had developed a stitch, but had become accustomed to it; it was lost among all his other aches and pains. He pushed stubbornly on, at the same time cursing himself for this stubbornness: what was he trying to prove with this stupidity? He was not interested in the tiger, nor was he much disturbed by the number of people it had killed. So many victims, so many statistics: they meant no more than the number of traffic victims on a Bank Holiday. He might feel differently if he saw a victim, but so far he had only heard of what the tiger had done. If a victim were brought to him as a patient, he would do his best to save him or her. But this climbing hills to hunt the tiger—this was taking prevention to the extreme. Even the British Medical Association didn't expect this of its members.

Caraday stopped again and looked back at him. "How are you going?"

"Wondering why I'm here."

"I told you, the country grows on you," said Caraday, and turned and walked on before David could think up an answer to that one.

"Walking is good for the soul," said Moriarty, plodding steadily through the mud, a dead cheroot stuck out like a black tusk from the corner of his mouth.

"Father Caraday tell you that?" David said, and Moriarty nodded. "I thought so. He probably sees a religious purpose behind even a bowel action."

Caraday, without turning round, raised a hand in acknowledgement.

They reached Mali Ga when the sun was still some height above the western ranges. The village was no more than a collection of huts strung along the spine of a ridge. Gardens, fenced with bamboo, stood on either side of the track at the entrance to the village.

"Opium poppies," Caraday said as they passed the gardens.

"Opium? Haven't you tried to talk them out of that?"

Caraday gestured at the wilderness of mountains that stretched away on all sides; the village lay like a piece of flotsam on the crest of one wave in a wild green ocean. "What escape would you try if you lived up here? If you couldn't read, didn't know any other life but this?"

"Does the bishop know about your tolerance of opium?"

Caraday shook his head, grinning. "There aren't any Christians in this village. These are pretty primitive Buddhists. They go all out for the worship of *nats*."

The villagers came running out of their huts to meet the newcomers. Each man came forward to greet Caraday, David and Moriarty in turn, shaking hands in the Kachin way of showing friendship and respect, his own right wrist gripped by his left hand. It was evident from their warm reception of Caraday that he was almost on a level with their *nats*.

David sat down on a stool outside a hut while Caraday talked to the men. He was almost sick with fatigue, but he did his best not to show it. Both Caraday and Moriarty looked unaffected by the climb; one would have thought that they had driven up from the mission. Caraday stood among the small turbaned hillmen, talking to them all at once, more voluble than any or all of them; he was asking for information on the tiger, but David wondered how the villagers were managing to get in their answers. The hillmen were an animated group, their weather-beaten faces continually alive with expression; after a while David was aware that a consistent expression was one of admiration for Caraday, the look of children who have unlimited trust in an adult. Is that why he stays on here? David wondered, remembering yesterday's conversation. Does he crave esteem such as he gets from these simple hillmen? Oh, Caraday, he thought, are you a clay idol, an all too human *nat*?

Caraday turned to him. "The stag's carcase is half a mile down the ridge. They've covered it over with branches and there are three men guarding it. We'll go down, stake out our positions before it gets dark, then we'll grab a bite to eat." He looked up at the sky. "It will be a full moon tonight, no cloud, so we may get a sight of him."

David dragged himself to his feet and followed Caraday, Moriarty and three of the villagers through the village and down a track that cut at an angle down the side of the ridge. As he walked through the village, women and children came to the doors of the huts to stare and smile at him. He looked in behind them, at the primitive conditions in which they lived: how could people look so cheerful and contented in such poverty? A bamboo hut, rush mats on a dirt floor, a few sticks of furniture; portraits of Aung San and U Nu looked down from the bamboo walls in sober contemplation of how some of their countrymen still had to live. Independence means nothing to these people, he thought; freedom means nothing to a man who has never known that he was a slave. I wonder if these people would cheer or jeer my father, the British Consul. The women and children stood with their backs to their private poverty, giving him the gift of their smiles. An old woman came forward and pressed some small bananas into his hands. She said something in Kachin out of a toothless mouth and he looked towards Caraday, who had stopped a few yards ahead of him.

"What did she say?"

"She said that they are in your debt for what you are about to do to the tiger."

"I am not about to do anything to the tiger. I shall just sit all night and wait for you to do it."

"Do you want me to tell her that?" Caraday's tone was kindly: David realised the priest was not trying to score off him.

He looked down at the woman standing beside him, her brown wrinkled face soft with gratitude beneath its head-piece of bright red beads. It came to him all at once that he was important to this woman. He had been important to other women, to Liz Bismark and others who had clung to him in their vanity, depending upon him to save what beauty they still had; but they had never been as grateful as this woman was, they had expunged their debt with cheques, they had thanked him with their bodies and not their hearts. The toothless, wrinkled face smiled and he caught a glimpse of beauty that would never need a knife to repair it. Humility lay like salt on his tongue.

"No," he said. "Just tell her thank you."

They went down the track, past the steep fields of hill rice, and came to a fork in the path. At the junction a split bamboo had been driven into the ground, and several sharpened sticks were wedged into it.

"That's a signpost for the tiger," Caraday explained. "Notice that all the sticks are pointing away from the village? If he's an intelligent tiger, the villagers believe he'll get the hint that he's not wanted up at Mali Ga."

They went on down the lower track and came to the clump of bamboo and low lantana scrub where the three men stood guarding the branch-covered carcase of the sambhar stag. Caraday, acting like a man who had done this a score of times, scouted the ground and chose his sites. He came back to David.

"The tiger is lying up further down the ridge." He pointed to a large canebrake half a mile along the ridge. "That means he probably has ideas about coming back for his kill. It's a pity there aren't some trees around here for us to climb into. I always feel safer up a tree." He looked about him, then back at David. "I'll be up there behind that bamboo with Moriarty. You'd better get up there beneath that rock outcrop, behind that lantana."

"I was hoping Moriarty and I might have had the chance to discuss Catholicism. It may be a long night."

Caraday grinned. "No, I may need Moriarty. He's a good man on a tiger hunt. I'll have one of the villagers stay with you. You might be glad of his company, even if you can't chat with him."

"Will the tiger come down here if he knows we're here?"

"No. But I'm banking on his not knowing we're here. I'll send the rest of these blokes back to the village, getting them to make as much noise as they can as they go. Tigers can't count. If we keep quiet enough, he'll think we've all gone. How do you feel about using that rifle?"

"Quietly unconfident."

"Let me shoot first then. If you do have to take a shot, take your time and make sure you're on target. Don't go spraying bullets around like a garden spray, otherwise you might wing me or Moriarty."

"The bishop would never give me absolution for *that*."

David took some sandwiches and one of the thermos bottles and joined one of the hillmen behind the lantana scrub and below the outcrop of rock where Caraday had directed him. He sat down, feeling the earth damp and thick with leaf mould beneath him, and leaned back against the rock. The

111

rock had been exposed to the sun all day, but it was already now cold in the evening air. David offered a sandwich to the man beside him, but the latter smiled and shook his head. He was a young man, no more than twenty, David guessed, dressed in a ragged sort of dark blue tunic and wearing a faded red turban from which two pieces of bamboo stuck up like featherless quills. A braided strap, slung crosswise across his chest from one shoulder, carried a bamboo scabbard from which protruded the heavy handle of a long knife. He was squatted on the ground with his knees drawn up in front of him, and on his knees rested his crossbow, a weapon that looked as if it could drive its arrows through a tree. He was shy of David, smiling tentatively each time David looked at him, but there was an air of calm purposefulness about him that comforted David. He is used to hunting tigers, David thought. I wonder how he would feel sitting in ambush in the wilds of Mayfair. Does *he* wonder what I'm doing here?

Somewhere down in the narrow valley below the ridge a bird made a call. It was like the call of a cuckoo, and the Kachin must have seen the puzzled look on David's face.

"Koel," he whispered, and with his fingers imitated the movement of a bird's beak.

The sun had now gone down and the mountains to the east had lost their rose tint. David had never been particularly conscious of nature and its wonders: the seasons for him had always been no more than a change of wardrobe. He had seen sunsets on the snow peaks around Klosters, the moon shimmering on the water at Antibes: both sights had been no more than pleasant backgrounds to the more sensual delights he had been enjoying while on holiday at those places.

The young man spread a hand towards the surrounding mountains and said something in Kachin. David did not need to know the language to understand that the hillman was speaking with pride of his country, was describing it as beautiful. The ridges stretched away into the distance like green waves; smoke from the villages along their crests curled up like blue spume. Mist was already forming in the narrow valleys, unreal as ectoplasm: the *nats* would roam the hills tonight. Far away to the right, down by Sheromere, the river caught a last flash of light: it shone for a moment like a green glacier. The air was still, taut as a bowstring from ridge to ridge: sounds came easily on it to brush against the ear: the cuckoo call of the koel, the sawing of a leopard, the boom of a buffalo, and far away, like the silence of high places begin-

112

ning to splinter, the faint thin tinkling of a bell. Behind the ridges, far, far away, was the last and highest range of mountains, part of China, their peaks outlined by a ragged ribbon of snow. And above it all was the sky, clear and unblemished, its purity pointed by the diamond glitter of the stars that were now beginning to appear.

"Beautiful," David said softly, and the Kachin nodded and smiled, as if he recognised another man who appreciated what nature had to offer. David smiled back, thinking: You are too trusting, dear boy, you would never survive where I come from. You are safer here, even with the tigers.

3

The tiger came in the early morning.

It had been a long night and David had dozed off several times. The moon had been full and the track where the dead stag lay had been clearly illuminated all night. Once they heard the tiger roar, the sound carrying from the canebrake half a mile away as if amplified; perhaps it was warning off some other beast on its way to examine the dead stag. In any case, no other animals came up the track, and they sat all through the night while nothing happened. Just before dawn David dozed off again, the koel, which had been calling all night, still calling in his sleep like some mocking bird of death, echoing in the caves of his mind till he moaned and cried out, and sat up to find the young villager resting a comforting hand on his shoulder, looking at him with troubled eyes. He shook his head and tried to smile reassuringly at the hillman, still feeling afraid and not knowing what had frightened him. It was as if an omen had been thrust upon him, except that he did not believe in omens.

The sun came up out of China; not across the bay, as Kipling had said, but out of the mountains; and there was another sound, the belling of a sambhar stag. The sound, deep and beautiful and unearthly, came up out of the surf of mist that filled the valley below; it was as if the sambhar were echoing the last belling of the stag on the path before it had been killed. The sound still hung in the air, dying away like a faint defiance, as the tiger came into view far down the path.

David had no idea of the comparative size of tigers, but he guessed from the soft hiss of the man beside him that this beast was a big one. He came up the path in the morning sun, walking without hurry in a world of his own, the mist shining behind and below him. David lifted the binoculars

113

Caraday had lent him and focussed them on the tiger. He saw that the tiger was favouring its right front leg and he remembered Caraday's guess that the beast had turned man-eater because of some permanent injury. A pheasant suddenly rose from a screen of bamboo, a bolt of red plunging down into the mist below, and the tiger stopped, its head raised. He looks magnificent, David thought. For the first time he had some feeling about the tiger: it was a shock to realise that he would regret the coming death of the tiger. He looked at the Kachin beside him, but the latter this morning was no lover of nature and its beasts: he was already fitting an arrow into his crossbow, his eyes narrowed and full of hatred for the tiger. David put down the binoculars and picked up the Springfield. He glanced up to his left, but there was no sign of Caraday or Moriarty. The ambush was perfect. I wonder if Shero plans them this way, he thought.

A hundred yards short of the kill, the tiger suddenly left the path. It was as if he suspected that there might be an ambush set up for him around the dead stag. He was coming back for his kill, but he was coming with all the caution and cunning of a tiger that had learned, from experience, that man was different from other animals. The Kachin hissed again, this time with anger and frustration, but there was nothing to do but go on waiting. This man and his fathers, David thought, have been waiting a thousand years for tigers. I'm tired of waiting, I want to get up and walk out on to the path, warn the tiger, but I can't. Whether I like it or not, I am on this man's side.

He eased his cramped legs out in front of him, then slowly drew back his feet till his knees were high enough to act as a rest for his elbows as he put the rifle to his shoulder. It was years since he had fired a rifle as heavy as the Springfield and he hoped its recoil would not be too severe. It was a beautifully kept gun, oiled and shining, but it was an old one and David wondered how it had found its way here to these remote mountains. Despite the chill of the morning he had begun to sweat, and all at once he hoped that the tiger would not appear again.

Then the hillman slowly raised his bow, and David saw the tiger coming down the shallow watercourse between his own position and that of Caraday. He came still cautiously, the big head held low, beautiful in the slow liquid rhythm of his movement, silent as the mist. The sun came up over the ridge, struck down into the watercourse, and there he was, yellow and black and huge, a perfect target. David froze, waiting for the crash of the Mannlicher. But no shot came, and suddenly he knew that Caraday was at the wrong angle to get in his shot.

Oh God, he thought, it's up to me and our friend with the crossbow. The tiger came on, and he raised the Springfield, sighting along the barrel, feeling the sweat running from him, feeling his hands beginning to shake with nervousness. *Now*, he thought, and squeezed the trigger as the tiger came down with one last quick bound on to the path. The shot rang out, and another from the Mannlicher, like a louder, heavier echo; but the tiger had not dropped by its kill, had not even been hit. It spun in the mud of the track, roaring, then came in great bounding leaps up towards David and to his right. The Kachin, snarling like a beast himself, stood up and fired his crossbow, but he had moved too quickly and the arrow whipped over the tiger's back and into the bushes. David rose on one knee, swung up the rifle and brought it round to bear on the tiger as it flashed by him no more than twenty feet away. He saw the blur of yellow and black, and he squeezed his finger. And nothing happened. The tiger went away up into the bamboo above them crashing its way through; David lowered the Springfield, his quivering nervous fingers still clamped round the trigger guard. He felt sick, as if the scalpel had slipped in his hand and he had just killed a patient. Except that he had killed nothing, and that had been his sole reason for being here, to kill the tiger.

Caraday and Moriarty came clambering up the slope. "What happened, David? Why didn't you get your second shot in? You had him, man—" Then Caraday stopped, saw the strain and self-disgust on David's face. "Well, it couldn't be helped. Anyone can make a blue on his first tiger hunt. We'd had to wait too long, that was all."

David stood up, the sour taste of vomit in his mouth. Sweat was pouring from him now, and he shivered, as if in the beginning of fever. His fingers had stiffened and he took them slowly away from the trigger guard. "I'm sorry, Caraday. I panicked." He looked at the Kachin, but the young man's face was stiff and sober: the silent camaraderie of the long night's wait had gone, blasted by the shot that hadn't been fired. "Tell him I'm sorry."

Caraday looked at David for a long moment, then he turned to the young hillman. He spoke to him in Kachin, and when he had finished the young man smiled and turned to

115

David and put a hand on David's arm. "What did you say to him?" David said.

"I told him this was your first tiger hunt. I said that there were no tigers where you came from, that you would do better next time."

"Do we have to lie to him?" David said angrily. "You know there isn't going to be a next time."

But he looked at the hillman and returned his smile: once more he had been trapped into appearing churlish if he was to be honest. This young man and the old woman in the village yesterday evening had reached out, even though strangers, and marked him with their belief in him. It was some sort of faith, a minor reflection of the faith that had them believe in *nats*, that held Caraday to his God. It was trust pure and simple, something that had never happened to him before. This man believed in him, or more truly, believed what Caraday had said about him. I can't hurt him, he thought, and put down his rifle and shook the man's hand in the Kachin style, left hand on right wrist.

Then Moriarty said, "Now we shall go home and I shall make curry and blanc-mange."

Chapter 6

1

Maung Zan and Maureen came up to the mission to see how the tiger hunt had gone. Caraday and David had just finished eating, curry without the blanc-mange, when they heard the Land Rover coming up the road across the meadow.

"What are you going to tell them?" David said. "The truth?"

"Do you want me to?" Caraday began to fill his pipe.

"I'm not asking favours. I'm as disgusted as you are with myself. I've always prided myself on my control. Then to do a stupid, panicky thing like that—"

"To coin a cliché, none of us is perfect." Caraday lit his pipe. "Have you ever looked before for imperfections in yourself?"

"Of course not. I've been aware of some, but I've never *looked* for them. I leave that for soul-searchers like you. Let's go outside. That damned pipe smells like hell."

"Maybe I should use it some time at my Sunday sermons." Caraday got up and followed David out on to the verandah. The Land Rover had almost reached the bungalow. "I'm just going to say that luck was against us. I was just as much to blame as you, for not guessing which way the tiger would approach us."

David had been prepared to face Maung Zan and Maureen and accept the blame for the tiger's escape, even to accept

117

the shame of confessing that he had panicked. But now, unaccountably, he was grateful for Caraday's offer of a way out. A trace of cynicism still remained as he thought: I've been given absolution; but all at once his self-respect had become important to him. He turned his face into the thick suffocating smoke of Caraday's pipe and said, "Thank you."

"You may be able to do something for me some day." Caraday went down the steps to greet Maung Zan and Maureen as they got out of the Land Rover.

"We heard the bad news," Maung Zan said. "Jolly hard luck."

David looked with surprise at Caraday, and the priest said, "News travels fast in these mountains. Bush telegraph, grapevine, what-have-you."

"What did you hear?" David was suddenly cautious.

"Just that the tiger got away. How did it happen?"

"He was too cunning and quick for us," said Caraday.

Maureen looked at David, and he waited for her to make some facetious remark. But all she said was, "Did you enjoy it?"

"It was an experience," he said carefully.

She sensed that he was holding something back: three years of intimacy with him had sharpened her perception of him. But she didn't pursue her curiosity: that would only mean further involvement with him. "A tiger rug would have looked fine in South Audley Street. Perhaps you'll get another chance before you go back."

"Perhaps," he said, and didn't look at Caraday.

"I had a phone call from your father," Maung Zan said. "He is coming up from Mandalay this evening. He didn't sound well. Or perhaps it was a bad line."

"He shouldn't go gallivanting around the countryside," Caraday said, sounding more than usually concerned. "Why doesn't he take things quietly?"

"Perhaps he found culture more wearing than a trip up here," David said.

Maureen had been rummaging in the back of the Land Rover and now she came out with a fishing rod and a dilapidated net. "I'm going fishing," she said in answer to David's raised eyebrows. "Maung Zan says there is good fishing in the river."

"Whenever were you a fisherwoman, except in argument?" David said.

"Years ago." She was checking the line and the reel; she

118

was clumsy at it, but traces of experience remained in her hands. "Bass, trout, crappies, bluegills. Other kids and I, we used to catch them all. Wall-eyed pike, too. I remember once —oh, never mind. The thing is, I used to love fishing." But she didn't say why: she didn't have to tell them that it had been one way of escaping the atmosphere of home.

"You can catch mahseer here," Caraday said, grinning approvingly at Maureen; it was almost as if he had noticed her for the first time. "Fifty-, sixty-pounders. You'll need a stronger line than that, though. I'll lend you mine."

"No, give it to David. He's coming down with me."

"I am?"

"Yes," said Maureen, and then he guessed from the tone of her voice that she was telling him he had to come with her. "We'll catch something for your father's supper tonight. Does he like fish?"

"How would I know?"

"He loves it," said Caraday, and went inside to get his tackle and basket.

David looked at Maung Zan. "Did my father say why he was coming up this evening? He wasn't due till tomorrow or Saturday."

Maung Zan shook his head. "Perhaps he feels he should not be wasting what time he has left, down in Mandalay. Seeing you again, David, meant a great deal to him. He told me so."

"Seeing him meant more to me than I had expected." David was surprised at his own confession: he had never been one to give confidences before. He saw Maureen watching him, but he turned away as Caraday came out with the tackle and a basket that looked as if it had been used to carry bricks instead of fish. He took the tackle from Caraday and said, "Who's going to cook the fish? Not Moriarty, I hope."

"I'm going to cook it," Maureen said. "We're all having dinner at the hospital tonight. Provided, of course, that we catch some fish."

Down by the river David and Maureen chose their spots and cast their lines. David was a rank novice, and Maureen had to show him how to handle the rod; but his hands were nimble and strong, and he was a quick learner. He had rolled his trousers up above his knees and Maureen, who was wearing jeans, had done the same. The water, monsoon-dark and ice-cold, went past their legs in long silver daggers under the bright hot sun. They were fishing above the confluence and

119

the water here was not quite so swift. Below them a tree trunk stuck up out of the river like a black skeleton; the tip of one long limb wore a faded red turban, the banner of some boy's daring. Across the river the cliff rose sheer, throwing back the sunlight from its glittering wall; it was a hundred yards away, but it seemed to tower right over them. High above it, as if on an invisible carousel, the eagles whirled slowly. There was no sound but that of the river.

"Tiger hunting. Fishing. Next thing, I shall be bird-watching." David had made a lucky cast with his first throw, and the line floated well out and downstream from him.

"I never thought of you as the huntin', shootin' and fishin' type, but you don't look so out of place at that. When I get home, I'll have Abercrombie and Fitch put you on their mailing list."

"My respects to Mr. Abercrombie and Mr. Fitch, whoever they may be, and they know what they can do with their mailing list. Why did you drag me down here?"

"Maung Zan wanted to talk to Father Caraday about that village that was burned down—Mong Na?" They spoke quietly to each other across the stretch of water that divided them. She had been told that the river was alive with fish and she was intent on catching some. Whether she caught a fish or not, as soon as she had stepped into the water, had cast her line, she had captured something: a memory of child-hood, one of the few pictures of home that had been worth keeping all these years. "Evidently Shero went too far the night before last. The people are turning against him."

"What does Zan want Caraday to do?"

"I don't know. I gather that everyone just depends on him. They expect something of him."

"They have no right to!" His voice rose angrily; she looked at him reproachfully and he dropped it to a whisper again. This is bloody ridiculous, he thought: straining my throat so a few fish won't be disturbed. "These people, they're always shoving their trust on to someone! They give it away, like measles or a cold. What right have they got to expect any-thing of Caraday? He's not God or one of their *nats*."

"What's got into you?" Maureen said lightly. She could see that he was disturbed, but this was no place for an argument. She felt a certain happiness standing here in the cold water of the river: a vague and brittle happiness, to be sure, but one that she did not want destroyed just yet. She turned her back on him, giving her attention to her line. "Father Caraday can look after himself. Perhaps he *likes* having people believe in him. Perhaps that is what keeps him going up here."

She may be right, he thought. She has put it in another, less cynical way from the way I put it the other night, but perhaps that is the answer. I am not really concerned for Caraday, to be truthful. I resent only that the old woman and the young hillman had begun to believe in me, had begun to infect me with their trust. "Take no notice of me," he said. "I'm tired. I got little sleep last night."

"You could take that at one time. I've seen you operate after being up all night at a party."

"Age is catching up with me. I'm suffering from precocious senility. Or perhaps hunting tigers is more wearing on the nerves," he said, tempted to tell her how he had failed. Then the line went tight, almost jerking him off his feet. "My God, I've hooked a *nat* or something!"

It was only later that he would recall that he had never seen Maureen so excited. She was on the periphery of his sight, so that he never once looked at her directly, but he would remember clearly how she acted. She was yelling at him what to do, telling him to play the fish, to let out his line, to hold it; she still held her own rod, but she was waving it round like a whip, urging him on. He heard all her instructions, but heeded none of them, too excited himself to worry about doing the right or wrong thing. He acted by instinct. The reel spun with a shriek as the line whipped out; fortunately the fish turned back before the line had reached its limit. They could see the fish now, threshing in the middle of the river; it came back towards them and David rapidly wound in. It was a big fish, a mahseer, a twenty- to thirty-pounder, and he was going to die hard. And suddenly, remembering how he had lost the tiger, David wanted this fish very much.

They fought for a long time, the man and the fish. David had no idea how long the battle went on. But he did not panic: he was in control of himself and the fish all the time. His hands had been grazed and gashed by the reel and line, but he was unaware of any pain. Caraday, Maung Zan and Moriarty, attracted by Maureen's shouts, had come down to the river bank; but David did not see them come and, when he finally landed the fish, had no idea how long they had been there. He walked backwards into the shallows, slowly pulling the exhausted fish towards him, and at last sat down, the fish still on the line, and only then saw the blood on his hands.

Maureen took the rod from him and Caraday went down into the water to bring the mahseer ashore. Maung Zan and Moriarty stood on the bank, beaming with pleasure, almost with triumph, as if they had shared in David's victory over the fish.

Maureen threw an arm round his neck and kissed him on the cheek: it was an impulsive gesture, without embarrassment for either of them. "You were wonderful! We must do this again!"

He looked up at her. "Where?"

But then Caraday came ashore dragging the still-writhing fish. "Take him up and clean him, Moriarty."

"How shall I cook him?" Moriarty said. "He will make very good machchi curry."

David looked up with a mixture of horror and despair, but Maureen had already staked her claim to the fish. "No, Moriarty, he's mine. I'm taking him back to the hospital. We are going to have mahseer *à l'américaine*."

"Never heard of it," David said.

"Neither have I," said Maureen. "But we Americans are nothing if not adventurous."

"They invented frozen foods," David said to Caraday, who was grinning at the exchange between the two of them. "An adventure that set the world's palate back a thousand years." Maureen went to say something and he waved a warning hand at her. "Remember, there's a priest present. None of that crude Nebraskan dialect."

Maureen looked at Caraday and Maung Zan. "Fancy an Englishman criticising another country's taste in food! Any palate that rhapsodises about Brussels sprouts—"

Caraday, still grinning at both of them, said, "You'd better let Zan look at those hands, David. We don't want them infected."

"Your father would have been proud of you today," Maung Zan said. "He is an awfully keen fisherman, you know. That was how I first introduced him to Charlie."

2

"I used to fish for mahseer up in the Punjab." Michael Breton put tobacco in his pipe, went to light it, then for the first time seemed to realise what he was about to do. He put

122

the pipe back on the table beside his plate. "It never tasted as good as this, Maureen."

"The best meal I've had since landing in Burma," David said. "But don't tell Moriarty."

"Eh? Oh no, of course not." Caraday was looking at Michael, as he had been through most of the meal. He had been remarkably quiet and had paid little attention to the conversation that had gone on round the table. He answered David without looking at him, still keeping his eyes on Michael. "You'd better have an early night, Michael. You look washed out after your trip."

Michael and George, the Gurkha, had arrived in the consulate Land Rover late in the afternoon. As soon as he had stepped down from the Land Rover at the mission bungalow steps, both David and Caraday had noticed the change in him. In the few short days since they had last seen him in Mandalay, he seemed to have aged ten years. He was greyer, thinner and the straightness had gone out of his back: it was hard to imagine that he had ever barked an order, had ever had an air of command. He has reached his open grave, had been David's first thought: it is only a step away.

"This trip up here must be getting longer." Michael had evidently noticed the look of concern on both men's faces. He was getting in early, forestalling any awkward questions. "Even George was saying it tires him more than it used to. Didn't you, George?" But he didn't give the Gurkha time to answer. "Hallo, David. What happened to your hands?"

"A little bout with a mahseer."

"Really? I didn't know you fished. Why, if I'd known—"

He is talking too much, David had thought as the afternoon turned into evening and they had at last gone down to the hospital for dinner in the staff dining quarters. He is going to talk himself into his grave, if he doesn't watch out, just to stop us discussing what has happened to him since we saw him last.

When they had reached the hospital and Maung Zan, Maureen and Rose came out to meet them, David had looked at them closely as they had greeted Michael, to see if their reaction was one of shock, as his and Caraday's had been. It was. None of them said anything, but their expressions, even those on the usually bland faces of Maung Zan and Rose, gave them away. Even the way they avoided mentioning Michael's health at all only pointed up their shock.

"Perhaps I had better retire early," Michael said now. He

put the pipe away in his pocket. His hands were shaking a little, the hands of an old and very sick man. "I am a little worn out. I wanted to talk to you, David, about the tiger hunt, but we'll have to leave it till tomorrow. I wish I had come up here yesterday. I could have come with you. We've shot some fine tigers together, haven't we, Charlie?"

"There'll be more," Caraday said, and David saw the charity in the lie.

He was doubly glad that his father had not been here to go up to Mali Ga with them. He was sure that the long climb to the ridge where the tiger had lain up would have killed his father. He was just as certain that, if his father had survived the climb, he would not have been able to bear the shame of his son's panic at the moment of truth with the tiger. Having lived the life he had for so long, he found his test of a man in that man's reaction to danger, his disciplining of those weaknesses that a soldier must never admit. David had no desire to be looked upon as a hero by his father; heroes, he knew, were often only separated from cowards by a stronger will to survive, which was another form of cowardice in itself. But it had suddenly become important to him that his father should not be hurt. It was not something as positive as wanting his father's respect; it was more that, even though negatively, he should pay his own respects to his father's peace of mind. David did not know the extent of his father's peace of mind, nor indeed if he had any at all. But the old man, dying as he was, deserved every consideration.

He took his father out to the Land Rover and handed him over to George. The Gurkha knew that his colonel was dying: he fussed with him as he would have with a sick child. "He spoils me," Michael said as David closed the door of the vehicle. "He always has. When your mother died, he took me over. Didn't you, George?"

The Gurkha's dark face was hardly visible in the dim light from the dashboard. "I have been very happy, sir."

"Some day you must go back to Nepal, George. He has never been home, David. We should all go home eventually, don't you think?" He coughed and put a handkerchief to his mouth. When he took it away, George had started up the engine. "Goodnight, David. I'm sorry we didn't go on that tiger hunt together. We appear to have left it too late for a lot of things."

David stood and watched the Land Rover go down the drive, past the tamarind and cherry trees, and swing up the road towards the mission. The moon was not yet up and the night was almost black in the valley. The Land Rover's beam of headlamps probed its way up the road; the sound of the engine came back as a deep growl. Then the vehicle had gone over the crest of the rise, and there was only silence and blackness. The silence and blackness of the grave.

"I don't think we should even let him go back to Mandalay," Caraday said behind him. "I've been talking about him with Zan. He's almost dead on his feet, don't you reckon?"

"We can do nothing, that's the frustrating thing!" He lost control of himself again for a moment; his voice rose angrily, as it had this afternoon down at the river. "Three of us doctors, and you a priest, besides, and we can do nothing! No wonder people don't believe in God."

"God never promised immortality to anyone, David. You can't say there is no God just because people die." There was no argumentative tone to his voice; he was stating a fact in which he believed. And David knew he was right, and nodded agreement. "You know why he has suddenly got worse, don't you? He has been waiting and hoping for months to see you, and now—"

"I had hoped I hadn't disappointed him too much."

"You haven't disappointed him. In fact, he feels he's disappointed you. He told me so this afternoon."

"Does he take you into his confidence on everything? You have that advantage of me."

"Don't resent me, David. Maung Zan and I are all he has had these past few years. Oh, and George, too. But we weren't enough. I was the one who persuaded him he should try to see you before he died."

"Why?"

"Because I think I'd guessed what was wrong with him. What is wrong with you now, David. All his life he'd fought involvement with people—even with your mother, I fear. You are much like that, aren't you?"

"Go on. We're talking about him."

"Point taken. I'll mind my own business. But I couldn't mind my own business about him. Because I was involved with him, you see?" He looked up in the direction of the mission. He mentioned nothing of love, but his meaning was clear. "It took me months to break him down, to get him to admit that what he wanted most was to see you again."

"Well, I'm grateful to you," David said slowly. "But I don't know that it has achieved much, if it just hurried him into his grave."

"A quick happy death is better than a lingering sad one. And he is happy now."

"He sounds more sad to me. Full of regrets."

"There is room for regrets even in a happy man. Who do you think knows the full measure of happiness—the innocent kid or the laughing man who once knew tears? Your father has had his share of tears. He's happy enough now. And the credit is yours."

"I feel spurious, an impostor. Or have you already recognised that?"

"You are judging yourself by what you may have been before you came out to Burma."

"I haven't changed. Not that quickly."

"Maybe not. But you are faced with a different set of circumstances from anything you've experienced before, so how do you know you haven't changed? You have a certain honesty about yourself, David. I guess any true cynic does. If he doesn't, then he is not a true cynic. Just another impostor. No, since you've been out here, you haven't acted the impostor. Maybe for the first time you've been your real self."·

David smiled in the darkness. "Metamorphosis is a talent I've never laid claim to. Since Dr. Jekyll and Mr. Hyde, the B.M.A. has frowned on the practice."

"There's more hide than Hyde in you. If I may return yesterday's pun." He had been smoking his pipe and its foul smoke had kept the mosquitoes away from them. Now he knocked out the pipe on his boot and at once the mosquitoes came down on them. "Ho Sang has invited us all down for some rice wine. Do you want to come?"

David couldn't see Caraday's face in the darkness. "The point is, do you want me to come?"

"Rose brought the invitation. You were specifically included."

3

Ho Sang ushered them in under the dental charts, past the dentures on trays in the glass cases: the whole shop offered a grinning welcome. He took them into a large living room with a bank of windows that looked out across a garden to the river and the mountains beyond, dim under the rising moon. "I like to look back at China," he said to David, blinking at him behind his thick-lensed glasses.

"You see nothing of China at night," Rose said.

"The memory doesn't need daylight," Ho Sang said. "Is that not so, Mr. Breton?"

"Most of Mr. Breton's memories are night-time ones, anyway," said Maureen, and mockingly returned David's bow.

"Those are the best," said Ho Sang, and smiled at Caraday. "Forgive me, Charlie. We shouldn't discuss such things in front of you."

Caraday was not embarrassed. "What are we drinking to-night? Shao hsing or kaoliang?"

"Do you know our drinks, Mr. Breton?" Ho Sang asked.

"I know nothing of Chinese food or drink at all. I once ate chop suey—"

Rose, who had been arranging plates of savouries on a table against one wall, wrinkled her nose. "You have just lost face in the eyes of Grandfather. No self-respecting Chinese would eat chop suey." She came forward with a plate and stood in front of David. There was a confidence about her to-night, a return of the poise that she had had when he had first met her down in Mandalay. It was as if she had made up her mind that her contact with Shero and his men was her own business and no one else's. "Try these. P'i tan, preserved eggs. They are known as 'thousand-year eggs.' Very good for the memory."

"That is one of her fibs," Maung Zan laughed, but Rose gave him a cool look and moved on with the plate of eggs. Maung Zan looked after her, his face suddenly sober again: love clouded his face like an expression of pain.

Ho Sang came forward with a tray of glasses. "That is shao hsing, yellow rice wine. This is kaoliang."

"Watch the kaoliang," said Maung Zan, turning back from watching Rose; he was smiling again, bland once more to pain. "Charlie calls it the fillet drink. It removes the bones from your legs in awfully quick time."

Caraday was stretched out in a chair, as much at home here as everywhere else David had seen him. "I'll have tea, Ho Sang. You don't get very good tea up here," he said to David, "but I have my reputation to think of. I don't want you carrying me home over your shoulder."

David had taken a glass of the yellow rice wine and was doing his best not to show that he did not like it. It was warm and had the taste of a rough medium-dry sherry, never a fa-vourite drink of his; the kaoliang or even tea would have been preferable to this. Rose had gone out to make tea, and David sat down beside Caraday. Ho Sang, having served Maureen and Maung Zan, came back and sat on a stool near the two men. "I should like to bring in tea to serve my guests," he said. "But owning a tea factory here, I have to make a show of local loyalty."

"Why isn't the local tea any good?" David asked.

"There are no tea plantations or estates here. The villagers have their own small gardens and we buy from them. And they will not trim their trees. They pick only the bottom leaves, never the top leaves, which is the best tea."

"Why not the top leaves?"

"The *nats* of their ancestors live in the tops of the trees. We have our local problems, haven't we, Charlie?" The thick lenses of his glasses were just pools of light, and there was no expression on the wrinkled yellow old face. David glanced at the priest, but his long dark face was just as expressionless. Yet David felt that Ho Sang's harmless-sounding remark had another meaning behind it. "For the outsider, living here is not as simple as it looks."

"You consider yourself an outsider?" David said. "I understood you came here in the 1930's."

"A Chinese is always an outsider, wherever he is. There are third- and fourth-generation Chinese living in London, but do you think of them as Englishmen? Why should the people here think of me as one of them? After all, twenty-five years is but a tick of the clock in the history of these people."

David looked at Caraday. "Are you an outsider, too?"

"Of course."

"He is less of an outsider than I am," Ho Sang said.

David didn't comment further on that. "Have you no desire to go back to China, Ho Sang?"

The old man smiled. "Of course. But what place is there for an old man like me in the new China?" Rose came back into the room with Caraday's tea. Ho Sang looked up at her. "Rose is all I have. And she would never come back to China with me."

"Never," she said. "It would be even worse there for me than in Rangoon. Or even London."

Ho Sang watched her as she crossed the room to join Maung Zan and Maureen. Then he looked at Caraday. "It is a pity she rebels so much against her white blood. But there is not enough Chinese blood in her for her to be philosophical about it. But then her mother was a rebel, pure and simple."

128

"What will happen to her when you are gone?" David said.

"I am depending on Charlie," the old man said, but the priest had his face turned away, was looking across the room at Rose.

"I have to go, too, some time," he said without turning round. "Maung Zan is our only hope."

David took a sip of the wine and tried to avoid making a face. The room was warm, and heavy with the smell of joss sticks, although he could see none. He was tired now, feeling the effects of having had little sleep last night. "What about Shero?" he said, and a moment later could have bitten his tongue. It had been a careless remark, coming out of a mind that was half-asleep, out of the old habit of fencing with people. Caraday seemed to stiffen without moving and Ho Sang turned the blank searchlights of his glasses on David.

"What about Shero, Mr. Breton?"

It was too late to back out now. "I understand that Rose has quite a lot of admiration for Shero. She told me so herself," he said, only half-lying: he remembered the look on her face the day of the hold-up.

"She can get nowhere with Shero," Caraday said flatly. "We'd see to that."

"She is a young impressionable girl," Ho Sang said, and looked across the room at Rose. She sat grouped round a low table with Maureen and Maung Zan. She and Maureen were talking, and Maung Zan sat just gazing at Rose. Occasionally she would smile at him, but it was a smile turned on and off like a light: he was one of her many admirers and she was giving him just enough attention to keep him interested. "She already has contact with Shero through one of his men, but I frown on it. Unfortunately the old family discipline doesn't mean anything to today's children. In China—no, from what I hear, even in China today the parents and grandparents have no say." He looked back at David. "There is nothing I can do about it, but one doesn't favour one's grandchild having anything to do with a bandit."

"A bandit? I thought he was an insurgent."

"So he is," Caraday said emphatically.

"No, Charlie." The old man's voice was bitter. "We have been fooling ourselves for too long. He is a dacoit, nothing more, nothing less."

"You have always been harsh in your judgements," Caraday said, but there was no argument in him.

"Not always," said Ho Sang.

129

David had the feeling the two men had forgotten him. *He* was the outsider now. He put down the glass of rice wine; he had drunk enough not to offend Ho Sang's hospitality. "Does Rose think of him as a dacoit?"

"Why don't you ask her?" Caraday said angrily; then seemed to regain control of himself. "No, leave her be. I think what happened the night before last up at Mong Na upset her. One of her boy friends comes from there. His father owned one of the shops that was robbed a month ago."

"A Shan boy?"

"A Chinese boy," Ho Sang said. "All the shops in Mong Na are owned by Chinese.".

"Was that why Shero burned down all the shops? Does he hate the Chinese?"

"Who knows?" Ho Sang said, staring out of blank glass eyes; but David was certain that he did know.

Then Rose came towards them again, bringing more savouries. David shook his head. "One 'thousand-year egg' was enough for my memory. I am likely to go to bed and dream of my ante-natal period." He smiled up at her, declaring a truce. "You look beautiful tonight, Rose. I don't know how you remain safe in Sheromere."

"I sleep beneath the cherry tree," she said, smiling back at him: she responded to flattery like a child. "Remember?"

Caraday put his hand over his eyes and for a moment looked as if he were about to weep. Then he took his hand away: there were no tears, but his eyes were almost black, dull and sad. Why does he involve himself with people so much? David thought. My father, Rose, the villagers of Mali Ga, of Mong Na: does he think he is Christ, carrying the burden of the world? That was the trouble with priests: they all wanted to march up Calvary. They advised charity, but they used it for their own ends: it was a key to Heaven. David felt the early resentment of the priest, the distrust that made him suspect Caraday's every gesture. His expressions of love were as elaborate as Moriarty's expressions of Catholicism: he sold himself too much.

"Hunting tigers?" he said softly but viciously.

Caraday looked blank for a moment, then he shrugged. He looked at Ho Sang and Rose. "It's a small joke we have."

"You have come to know each other very well if you are already exchanging jokes," Ho Sang said.

"Oh, we're coming to know each other very well," Caraday said, getting to his feet. "Aren't we, David?"

Chapter 7

1

In the morning Michael did not get up for breakfast. David went in to see him. "You look much better than you did last night."

Michael sat propped up against pillows. Moriarty had brought him a breakfast tray: porridge, toast, marmalade; but he had barely touched it. "I have no appetite. I've had this same breakfast all my life. Am I too old to start craving something exotic to begin my day? Caviar instead of marmalade on my toast?"

"You have no taste left at all, have you?"

He looked up and shook his head. "None, David. Or rather, there is just one taste—" He twisted his mouth.

"I'm going down to see Zan about taking some X-rays of you."

"Why bother? Who wants pictures to tell him something he already knows?" He coughed and almost upset the tray. David took it away from him and put it on a chair.

"We'll have a look, anyway."

"You're the doctor, as the saying goes." He put up a thin claw and pushed back the thick grey hair. His pyjama top was undone and showed the white shrunken chest. It suddenly occurred to David that he had never seen his father any other way but fully and impeccably dressed, his hair sleekly brushed and his face smoothly shaved, always ready for inspection. Michael now rubbed his palm against the grey bristle on his chin, but seemed unaware of it. He had become careless of his appearance; there was no inspection beyond the grave. "You are a good doctor, aren't you, David? I should have liked to see you at work. We never did see each other at work, did we?"

"I was never interested in soldiering, you know that." Outside in the meadow a boy was shouting at the cows as he brought them down for milking. It was going to be another hot day: already the dew was drying on the grass.

"No." There was no resentment in the soft rough voice. "Neither was your mother, did you know that?"

David was surprised. "Why on earth did she stay out here then? You said something the other night down in Mandalay —that you were never even certain that she loved you. What did you mean by that?"

"It was my own fault. She did love me, but I never let her tell me so. But I think she was frightened of me, too. Oh, I never beat her or anything like that. I never pulled rank on her at home." He smiled, enjoying the small joke. That is all he has left now, David thought: small jokes, the tired smile instead of the full-bellied laugh. But even in his young days he could not imagine his father's ever having been a hearty laugher. "No, I just kept her at a distance, that was all. The worst thing that a man can do to the woman he loves. And I did love her, but never admitted it. Not the way a woman wants it to be admitted."

"How do you know what a woman wants? Aren't I supposed to be the womaniser in this family?"

Michael smiled again. "Since I gave up Wodehouse, I've been reading the memoirs of some of our ancestors. Very interesting. Very informative. Have you read them?"

"Yes. But I don't admire men who write about their conquests. Lovers and generals, they both should keep their mouths shut. One never hears of them writing about their defeats."

"Perhaps. But I had to seek my education somewhere. I was too old to go out and seek it in the field."

David suddenly laughed, thinking of his father doing his field study with women like Louise de Felice and Liz Bismark and, yes, Elinor Beatty. "I think perhaps you adopted the safest course. Your education may be sketchy, but at least you avoided being hurt."

"Have you been hurt, David?"

"No."

Michael recognised that he should not have asked that question. At least on David's part, father and son had not yet reached that stage of confidence. He said lightly, making another small joke, "I am an expert on military manuals, but unfortunately there doesn't appear to be a Clausewitz on the war between the sexes."

"There are a dozen experts on the subject, all contradictory. In the end one finds that one's own approach is the best."

"And what is your approach?"

"It differs with every woman. That's the secret of it."

"It is just like jungle warfare then?" He shook his head. "What a pity I never knew."

David raised an eyebrow. "You mean you'd have liked to be a Punjabi rake?"

Michael didn't smile: the small joke was over. "No, not really. There was only ever one woman for me, your mother. I just made the mistake of never telling her."

David stood up. He felt he had reached the limit of confidence with his father for this morning; he felt almost as if he had crept into his parents' bedroom, caught them in the act of love. "I'll get George."

He went outside, found George and told him to go and see that Colonel Breton was washed, shaved and dressed, ready to go down to the hospital in half an hour's time.

"The colonel is sick, sir?"

"Very sick, George. Didn't you know?"

"Yes, sir, I knew." His eyes flickered towards the bedroom window behind David. "I was hoping, sir, that I would die first—"

"It will be a long time before you die, George." Across the meadow the white crosses in the cemetery flashed like teeth: the last laugh lay there waiting for them all. "I hope you don't talk like this to my father?"

"Oh no, sir!" George stood at attention, as if he were answering some charge of military misconduct. "The colonel and me, we never talk of such things. Especially not now, sir." He looked towards the bungalow, then back at David. His face quivered for a moment: the scar on his cheek twitched like a lizard on brown earth. "The colonel is a good man, sir. He does not deserve to die like this."

"He is a very good man. And none of us deserves to die like this." But God's mercy was not something one discussed with a Gurkha; he did not even know what was George's religion. He saw Caraday coming towards them. "All right, George. See to the colonel, will you?"

The Gurkha saluted smartly and turned away. David's hand was halfway to his forehead in a return salute before he realised what he was doing. Clumsily he turned the gesture into one of smoothing down his hair, but it didn't fool Caraday. "I'll have to catch you the same way some time. Have you making the Sign of the Cross before you know what you're doing."

"Then it wouldn't mean anything, would it? Or are you priests satisfied with just the gestures?"

Caraday noticed the sharpness in David's tone. He looked towards the bungalow, then back at David. "How does he look this morning?"

"Better than last night, but still rather grim. I'm taking him down for some X-rays. Does Zan have an X-ray technician?"

"He does them himself, with Rose. But why do you want X-rays? The picture is clear enough, isn't it?"

"That's what he said." David nodded towards the bungalow. *Father* was still an uncomfortable word on the tongue. He was like a linguist who had occasional moments of fluency. But today was not one of his days. "But I'd still like to see some X-rays. I'm a doctor, Caraday, not a priest. I like to see proof."

"Or are you looking for hope? Priests do that, you know. No, go ahead," he said, as if not wanting to rub David any further with argument. "We'll take him down to the hospital. Maung Zan was going to go out to Mong Na with me this morning, but I'll go on my own."

"What are you going out there for?"

Caraday hesitated a moment. "Because it looks as if we shall have to do something about Shero."

"Who's we?"

"Sheromere itself. The D.C. doesn't want to bring in the Army. They'll take over and that means he'll just be a figurehead. He's not much more now, but at least he can make a pretence."

"Wouldn't it be a good thing to bring in the Army? Zan told me it did a good job of running the country a couple of years ago."

"It did. But isolated army units—they're not a good thing. They get arrogant, start to run the towns and villages as if they're some sort of occupation force. I've seen it happen where the Army has finished up more unpopular than the dacoits. I'm on the D.C.'s side in this. If we can do without the Army, well and good."

"Can you do without it?"

"We can give it a burl." Then he grinned. "Give it a try."

"Thanks. I sometimes find Australian as difficult to understand as Kachin. So what are you going to do about Mong Na?"

"See if I can make contact with Shero first."

"You don't need to go all the way out there. Why not get Rose to make the contact for you?"

"I want to leave her out of it," Caraday said sharply. He looked hard at David, recognising now that the latter had retreated to the cool antagonism of their first meeting. "What's the matter with you today? I thought you'd lost that chip on your shoulder."

"The chip on the shoulder turned to sawdust long before I met you, Caraday. If I appear critical, it's because I wonder just a little at all this talk of doing something about Shero. You seemed determined last night to think of him only as an insurgent, not as a dacoit. This morning you want to drive all the way out to Mong Na on what looks like a wild-goose chase, when your best chance of getting in touch with Shero is right here in Sheromere. You'll excuse me if I think the D.C. is not the only pretender around here."

Caraday flushed with anger. "I'm sorry I asked you up here, Breton—"

"I'll leave any time."

"Not till your father goes, anyway. I don't want him upset by any Donnybrook between you and me." He looked towards the bungalow, then back at David. "There's no pretence about *that*. I don't want him upset."

"Neither do I. We're going back to Mandalay on Sunday morning, so you and I can—make a pretence, shall we say?—till then. In the meantime—"

"In the meantime I'm going out to Mong Na." But his voice sounded vague. It was as if he admitted the pretence: he was playing blind man's buff in a country that he knew like the back of his hand. David felt that Caraday could put out his hand and make contact with Shero any time he liked.

2

"I'm going back to Mandalay with you and your father," Maureen said. "It's time I was getting home. Dr. Drucker won't wait for me indefinitely."

They were sitting on the verandah of the nurses' bungalow. Michael had been X-rayed and now he was across in Maung Zan's office having morning tea. Tea at ten-thirty and at four was an English custom Maung Zan still kept up: it gave him dignity, established his caste: his assistant drank only beer, his breath always reeking of it. He had tried to teach the hospital cook how to make crumpets, but the effort had not been successful. So soggy and crumbling biscuits were served with the tea; and another pretence, David had thought, was kept up. He and Maureen, never tea drinkers, had escaped from the office and come across to sit on the verandah while they waited for Rose to bring the X-ray plates.

"When are you going back to London?" Maureen said.

"I don't know. The way my father looks now—" London was part of another world, hardly rememberable this morning. The "thousand-year egg" last night hadn't worked at all, it had been another of Rose's fibs. He looked at Maureen, wondering how much of Nebraska she remembered. "You know, dear girl, when it comes time to actually say goodbye to you, I don't think I shall be able to believe it."

"Oh, you'll believe it all right," she said, nodding her head emphatically. "That is *one* good thing about air travel. Farewells are abrupt and final."

"Unless the plane is delayed. Then they can be agonising."

"Not for you and me, old boy." Her voice was light. She put a hand on his as he sat beside her. She felt safe: she could trust herself with him now. "Don't worry, David. I shan't make it hard for you."

He smiled at her assurance; *she* was now making it easy for *him*. "Are we going to keep in touch?"

"No. You were never a letter writer and I don't expect you to start now."

"Do you still have that note I wrote you about Mrs. Beatty?"

"Tied with ribbon and put away in my—what was that box maidens once used to have? My hope chest?" She looked down towards the road, where children ran up and down, trying to send kites aloft on the almost breezeless air, and remembered the children in Cornwall Gardens. Were these boys down on the road as innocent as those children had been? At what age did children here in the East know the pain of love? One boy suddenly screamed with delight as his kite shot up into the air and hung in the sky like a bright red bird. "No, David, I haven't got it at all. I burned it that day

136

of the court action. After I left you, when you drove me home that day, I went straight upstairs and burned it."

"A feeling of guilt perhaps?" But the barb had only a feather touch to it. He could see Rose coming towards them with the X-ray plates, and what had happened in London was no longer important.

"No. I just didn't want any reminders of you at all, that was all. I thought that was our goodbye."

"And it wasn't. So don't rely on that plane leaving on time." He stood up as Rose came up on to the verandah. "Have you shown them to Maung Zan?"

"No. I thought you would like to see them first." Rose handed him the plates. "I didn't think Maung Zan should see them, not while your father is in the office with him."

"As bad as that?" He took the plates and held them up to the light. Maureen stood behind him, peering over his shoulder. He studied them carefully, looked at Maureen, then at Rose. "I wouldn't want my father to see these."

"I thought not," Rose said.

"Looks like a military spread." Maureen took the plates from David and looked at them again. "It must be agony for him even to breathe."

"I'll talk it over with Zan. From the look of these, I don't think he should even go back to Mandalay. Down there, with the humidity—it's not worth it. He'd be dead in a week."

"How long if he stays up here?" Rose said.

"A fortnight perhaps."

"Is it worth operating?" Maureen said.

"Not from what Zan has already told me."

"How are you going to keep him from going back to Mandalay? You'll have to tell him the truth."

"The spoken truth or the unspoken lie," he said, but there was no spite in his voice. "Which do you think is called for now?"

"It's up to you," she said. "But I'm glad it isn't me who has to make the choice."

He took the plates from her and went off through the glare of the morning towards Maung Zan's office. Beyond him, down on the road, the red kite suddenly dived towards the earth and caught in the branches of the tamarind tree by the gate; it looked more than ever like a bird, even more so than in the sky, trembling among the branches as the boy who had been flying it tugged desperately on its string. David stopped, and for a moment Maureen thought he was going down to help the boy free the kite. Then he went on, and she knew he hadn't even seen the boy. He had stopped to look at the X-ray plates again, as if to convince himself that what he saw there was the truth, was what he had to tell his father.

"Poor David," Rose said.

"Yes." Love, admiration, resentment had often been expressed for David; she could not remember a woman's ever having expressed sympathy for him before. But Rose was right: it was *poor David*. Then she said, "And poor Michael, too."

"Oh, of course," Rose said. But it was evident that her sympathy for Michael was an afterthought. She's not interested in men, Maureen thought, except those who can give her love, money or escape from here. She suddenly felt sympathy, too, for Rose—no, more than sympathy: pity. But Rose was not one who would accept pity. She was half-Chinese, she was a girl who would fight against losing face. And to accept pity was to lose face.

"I must go," Rose said. "It's time for Maung Zan to do the morning rounds." Then she said, only a hint of wistfulness in her voice: her face was still bland: "It must have been fun working with David. I mean, no drudgery of doing hospital rounds. Just working with him in the theatre, being with him all the time."

Don't envy me, Rose, she thought. There's no future in it. It wasn't fun, believe me. It was heartache all the way. But all she said was, "Oh, it was all right. But I'm looking forward to the change. Things will be different at the Mayo."

"Yes, I suppose so," Rose said, and again there was the hint of wistfulness in her voice. London, Rochester, anywhere would be fun for her: anywhere so long as it was out of Burma. "Well, I'd better go."

She went off towards the ward block. Across the stretch of badly cut lawn Maureen saw David, Maung Zan and Michael come out and stand by the consulate Land Rover. Maung Zan helped Michael into the Land Rover, and David came across towards Maureen. As she watched him come towards her, his tanned face sober and drawn, his eyes squinted against the glare, his grey hair looking almost white in the bright sunlight, all the old love came back into her in a flood and she almost cried out with the pain of it. Oh God, however could I have fooled myself? It had been fun: even the heartache had been something to treasure: it was better than loneliness, better than nothing at all. Which was what she would have when she got to Rochester.

"What did you tell him?" she said.

He looked back at the Land Rover, then back at her. "The truth."

"Did it hurt him?"

"It hurt both of us." Oh, now is the time to tell him I still love him. Now is when he needs me. The words were in her mouth, when he said, "I'm taking him back to the mission. He is going to stay there, not here at the hospital. Then I have to go out to Mong Na. Caraday has wrecked the jeep or something."

"Is he hurt?" The words forced themselves out past the ones she wanted to say but couldn't.

"That man is indestructible," he said. And she thought: That is more than I am. But all she said was, "I'm glad you told your father the truth. It's always best in the end."

"Is it?" he said.

Chapter 8

1

David left his father with George at the mission bungalow. "See that the colonel sits quietly, George."

"You don't have to worry." Michael sat back carefully in the old cane chair on the verandah. "I don't like the thought of what you've told me, but I'm not a fool. I don't want to prove I'm as hale as I ever was." George had gone into the bungalow to get a drink for the colonel. Michael coughed, hid a grimace of pain behind his hand, then after a moment drew his hand away and looked down towards the river. He seemed to have forgotten David. He sat in a grey stillness of his own, completely removed from the bright dazzle of the day; it was impossible to tell whether he was empty of thought or paralysed by a hemorrhage of emotion. Then a look of hopelessness crossed the thin grey face; then that, too, was hidden by the hand; hopelessness was as shameful as fear to the professional soldier. He took the hand away again and looked up at David. "You'd better go out and get Charlie. Are you going to tell him what you've told me?"

"I'll have to, shan't I? You can't stay on here without telling him why. In any case, he'd guess after the first day or two. Consuls don't desert their posts without a reason, do they? I'm afraid I don't know much about consuls."

Michael smiled: unintentionally, it was a caricature of a smile, another grimace sketched on the thin grey face. "Consuls have a very strict sense of duty. A lot of tripe is written about drunken, irresponsible consuls, but it isn't true. Some of us may be drunks and a good many of us may be bumblers, but we're never irresponsible." Then suddenly the smile died and he said, "I'm sorry, David. I didn't mean—"

David looked blank for a moment. Then he remembered. London was even further away than he had realised: he had already begun to forget Elinor Beatty. "It's all right. I know I was irresponsible in that case. I've never denied it to myself, no matter what I said in court."

"I'm glad of that, David. Perjury is bad enough, but being dishonest with oneself is both criminal and foolish. I learned that only after your mother died." He looked up, the hand across his face again. "Better go out and get Charlie."

Driving out to Mong Na—"You can't get lost," Maung Zan had said. "Once you cross the ferry, there is only the one road."—David had gone several miles before he noticed that the peasants, when they passed him, saluted him instead of waving as they had done when he had travelled with Caraday. They stopped, their faces opened in a salvo of smiles, and the men's hands came up in sketchy salutes. Puzzled, he saluted back; then he caught sight of the small Union Jack flying from the near-side front mudguard. At the top of a rise he jerked the Land Rover to a halt. He got out, walked round to the front of the vehicle and almost angrily jerked the flag out of its holder. He threw it on to the back seat, got in and drove on. As Caraday had said, he was not an impostor. He did not want the salutes that were due his father as the Queen's Consul. Then it suddenly occurred to him that no salutes were due, that the British flag was a foreign flag here.

He was still thinking about the matter when he drew up on the road above the wrecked jeep. Moriarty, who had been sitting on a log surrounded by a crowd of curious adults and children, came out into the middle of the road and waved him down.

"Mr. Breton, it is splendid to see you!"

"What happened?" David asked as he got out of the Land Rover. "And where's Father Caraday?"

"He is up at Mong Na. Ah, the accident! Father Caraday tried to avoid a stupid bloody cow—" He's talking like Caraday, David thought: here's an impostor, if ever I saw one. "These Buddhists and their bloody sacred animals—" Moriarty looked about him, secure and superior in his Christianity and his foreign language. "We missed the bloody cow, but

141

the jeep has no brakes—" He gestured with a shrug of his shoulders, a Gallic impostor now.

"No brakes? It seems to me that the cow was not the only stupid thing on the road." Then irrelevantly he said, "Do you speak French, Moriarty?"

Moriarty looked blank for a moment. Then he went off into a gabble of French, looking around at the peasants as he did so. But they were unimpressed: all foreign languages were the same language to them.

David cut him short. "I'll go and get Father Caraday. Do you want to come?"

"No, I shall stay here." Moriarty looked around him again. He is so bloody superior, David thought. How has he managed to remain alive up here? "They will steal the jeep if I don't watch them."

David walked to the edge of the road and looked down to where the jeep rested on its side against a tree fifty feet below him. "You were lucky that tree was there."

"The Lord looks after us," said Moriarty piously; and David wanted to laugh out aloud. If this man ever makes Heaven, he'll turn it into hell for the rest of them there. He is a religious snob, the worst kind of snob there is. Moriarty held up his rosary beads for all the crowd to see; he was like a woman showing off a diamond necklace. "I have already said fifteen decades as thanks."

"Attaboy," said David.

He went back to the Land Rover, got in and drove on up to Mong Na. He came round a bend in the road and there was the village in front of him, a long stretch of blackened waste along the top of the ridge. The charred frames of some huts still stood, like pen-and-ink drawings against the sky beyond. He drove the length of the one and only street, taking his time as he looked at the results of Shero's vengeance or whatever it had been. He saw the occasional stone chimney still standing, like a black pagoda; the pi-dogs scratching among the debris, less hideous because their sores were covered with soot; the undamaged chair standing in the ruins of a house like an invitation to sit and contemplate the disaster that had hit its occupants. Then he came to the end of the street, where the villagers had put up rough bamboo shelters.

Caraday detached himself from a group of men and women and came towards him. "Did you see Moriarty?"

"He's all right. The Lord is looking after him."

Caraday looked at him, but said nothing. Instead he turned back to the villagers and said something in Kachin. David looked about him at the villagers, surprised at the number of Chinese among them; less than half of them appeared to be Kachins or Shans. Then he noticed another thing. Although there was no definite line of division, the Chinese and the Kachins were not standing together in the one large group. The crowd was made up of several groups, all close together; but no Kachins and Chinese stood together. David had the sudden feeling that these people made up the population of Mong Na, but that was all. It was not a village that had been destroyed here, only a collection of huts and stores.

At last Caraday turned back to David. "Well, shall we have a go at getting the jeep back up on the road?"

"What about Shero? Did you learn anything?"

Caraday brushed by him. "I'll tell you later," he muttered, and moved on to put his arm about the shoulders of a Kachin villager and walk with him towards the Land Rover. David hesitated, then followed him.

"This is Karim Gam." Caraday seemed to know the names of everyone he met in these hills. The man smiled as Caraday said his name, as if the priest had granted him a personal favour. "He'll get us a rope and a couple of his mates. Then we'll see how we go." He slapped Karim Gam on the back and the villager went off at a run up the street. Caraday looked along the street, then back at David. "Shero did a good job, eh?"

"Did you learn anything about him?" David repeated.

"Later. Some of these Chinese speak English." Caraday put out his hand as the villagers began to move past him. He stood there beside the Land Rover, like a priest outside his church on Sunday; he shook hands with all of them, yet David was sure that none of them belonged to his congregation. David himself had his own hand grabbed, and the next moment he, too, was shaking hands as the villagers filed past.

"What am I supposed to be? Your curate or the visiting bishop?"

"Oh, play the bishop," said Caraday, grinning. "You would never have made a curate."

Then Karim Gam came running back with a thick rope coiled over his shoulder. He and two other Kachins scrambled into the back of the Land Rover, David and Caraday got in the front, and they drove out of the village to the accompaniment of shouts and waves. At the end of the street a

143

group of children lined up and saluted, their faces split like over-ripe melons by their bright cheeky smiles.

"They go in for saluting a lot up here," David said. "All the way up they've been flinging salutes at me as if I were the British Raj himself."

"The British are still welcome up here. Maung Zan will tell you—if the British ever came back here, these hillmen would run out the red carpet."

"Zan doesn't think we will come back, does he?"

"Of course not. You British have one talent all the other empire builders never had—you know when to get out."

"There are a lot of people at home who wouldn't agree with you, who think we should still be here and in India and all the other places we've vacated. People who think the winds of change are nothing more than a seasonal breeze, that everything will blow over and go back to being just what it was before—backward regions waiting for the civilising influence of Englishmen."

"It was a good phrase of Macmillan's, the winds of change. But it doesn't apply everywhere. Here in Burma the wind of change is what we'd call a willy-willy in Australia. The breeze goes round and round, stirring up the dust, then after a while everything settles back and we're back where we started. These people have lived at their own pace for too long. They're not like the blacks in Africa—they have a long history and they are well aware of it. And the man at the top makes a difference. U Nu is a rare bird today—a national leader who's more interested in moral values than material ones. I wish there were a few more like him."

"I'm afraid that in the Western world, moral values don't get too many votes. We've been voting through our pockets too long." He glanced over his shoulder at the three men in the back seat, all of whom broke into smiles as soon as they saw him looking at them. "These chaps speak English?"

"No," said Caraday. "About Shero, you mean? Well, it is going to be harder than I thought. There's a three-way split back there in Mong Na. I've suspected it for some time, but now it's come out in the open."

"Three-way?"

"The Kachins are all for going after Shero, catching up with him and trying to have a showdown."

"How would they go?"

"Pretty well, I think. These fellers know how to fight. And

144

they're pretty cranky this time. If they got on to Shero, they'd cut him up for curry."

David wrinkled his nose. "Don't mention curry. What about the Chinese—they make up the other two lines of thinking?"

Caraday nodded. "It's pretty common knowledge up here in the hills, but you never read anything about it in the papers down in Rangoon and Mandalay—there's a lot of infiltration from China in these hill villages. Some of them are genuine refugees, but a good many of them are Red plants. There's a definite pattern to the infiltration, they are in the towns and villages down the Burma Road and the Ledo Road. And that puts this area right in their path."

"Doesn't the government do something about all this?"

"What can it do? It can't prove anything. In this sort of country, who knows where who comes from?" He gestured at the jungle-tangled ranges that looked as if they stretched to the very edge of the world. "And the government is supposed to be on friendly terms with China. The Chinese Embassy is the hardest-working embassy in Rangoon, always offering help, scholarships, cultural exchanges, what-have-you. This is one of the few countries in the world where the Yanks and the Russians find themselves looking with the same suspicious eye on the same customer."

"So you mean there are some Red Chinese here in Mong Na and they don't want to stir up trouble, for fear the Army will move in? That's one line of thought. What's the other?"

"The other ones have me tricked a bit. I don't know whether they're genuinely neutral, whether they want to be absorbed into Burma and just stay out of trouble, or whether some of them are KMT supporters and there's some pressure being applied."

"KMT? Has this part of the world started reducing everything to initials, too? What the hell's that?"

Caraday grinned. "The Kuomintang, Chiang Kai-shek's crowd. Back in 1950 the last of the Kuomintang—"

"Righto, call it the KMT. But don't start referring to J.C., or I'll write the bishop."

"That's one thing I've noticed about you. Blasphemy is not one of your failings."

"Back to the KMT," said David.

Caraday grinned again. The bitterness of their early morning encounter at the mission was forgotten. Once more they were two men who found pleasure and some sort of comfort in their fencing with each other. "Well, the last of the KMT divisions was kicked out of China in 1950 and came across from Yunnan down into Kengtung—that's further south, down by the Laos and Thai borders. It was a dirty business, went on for quite a while. They were getting money and supplies from somewhere, and it looked like it was the Americans who were giving it to them. The Burmans naturally weren't happy about having a foreign army camped on their territory —after all, they'd just got rid of the British. Eventually they took it to the UN—the United Nations"—he grinned—"and Chiang Kai-shek's crowd was supposed to evacuate the whole mob. But they never did. There're still six or eight thousand KMT troops down in Kengtung, only now they're dacoits, not soldiers, and it's the Burmans who suffer, not the Red Chinese."

"So how are they involved with Mong Na?"

"One of the Chinese took me aside this morning and had a word in my ear. I don't know whether he was giving me advice or a warning. But he suggested that Shero might be one of the KMT crowd who'd moved up here."

"Do you think that's likely?"

"I don't know," Caraday said after a moment. "It's hard to know where his sympathies lie. That is, if he has any."

"Exactly," said David. "If he has any."

Caraday looked back at the Kachin men in the back, all of whom smiled at him, then he looked back at David. "What would you do to him if you were in the party that caught him?"

"Shoot him on the spot."

"That's lynch law. Is that the fashion in English law these days?"

"Do you think lynching is too good for him? Or not good enough?"

"I hope I'm never in a position to have to pass that judgement," said Caraday, then they had come to the spot where the jeep had gone off the road.

Moriarty came towards them, his rosary beads still dangling from his hands. "I have thanked the Lord for our miraculous escape, Father."

"Break it down, Moriarty," said Caraday. "The Lord doesn't waste miracles on the likes of you and me. If we hadn't hit that tree, we'd have hit another one. There's enough of them."

Moriarty looked chastened and disappointed: it would have been an honour to have had a miracle happen to oneself. He put his beads away. "You are too humble, Father—"

"Let's see what we can do about this jeep," Caraday said impatiently, and went sliding down the slope towards the wrecked jeep.

Moriarty looked at David. "Don't you think it was a miracle, Mr. Breton?"

"I've had no experience of miracles," David said. "But as I understand it, the Church is not very much in favour of them."

Moriarty nodded sadly. "True, Mr. Breton. It almost makes you think the Church is not on the side of the Lord."

"That's an argument that's been levelled against the Church on other grounds," David said, and slid down the slope towards the wrecked jeep, leaving Moriarty looking bewildered.

"That wasn't fair," said Caraday, who had evidently heard the conversation. "If you want argument about the Church, pick on me. Poor old Moriarty's no advocate."

"I'm sorry," David said. "But he rather gets under my skin with all his piety. He's rather like those chaps who wave streamers in one's face on Boat Race Day. How's the jeep?"

"No worse than it's been before." Caraday inspected the jeep. "We'll be able to patch it up again."

"You might try fitting brakes to it this time."

"That's an idea," said Caraday, grinning once more. "Otherwise the day will come when we'll need a miracle. And frankly, I don't think there are any miracles set aside for my use."

"You may need one to get this Shero business cleaned up."

"He'd never grant me one for that particular bit of business," Caraday said, and turned away before David could ask him what he meant. "Moriarty, have them throw down the rope!"

It took them almost an hour to get the jeep back up on the road. Twice the rope broke and twice the jeep plunged down the slope into the same tree again. David and Caraday took turns driving the Land Rover as it attempted to pull the jeep up on to the road; while one was driving, the other was down the slope pushing and pulling with Moriarty and the three villagers. By the time the jeep was up on the road David was exhausted, his shirt and trousers torn and black with mud, and the cuts on his hands opened and bleeding again.

"You're a worker," Caraday said appreciatively. "Thanks."

"A pleasure, dear boy."

They smiled at each other, their intermittent antagonism forgotten. A simple task, calling for sweat and effort, had united them for a moment. They both turned and the villagers, even Moriarty, were smiling, pleased at the job done.

Caraday walked across to the jeep and inspected it again. "It'll run, but just. We'll haul it back to Mong Na. You can stay with it, Moriarty, and I'll come out tomorrow with a truck and we'll take it back to Sheromere."

"Oh, but I can't stay here, Father!" Moriarty exclaimed, his squinted eye seeming to roll round in its socket. "Who will cook dinner for you tonight?"

Caraday looked at David without a smile, then back at Moriarty. "That's a hardship we'll have to put up with, Moriarty. But we'll manage somehow."

2

"How's your father?"

They were driving back to Sheromere, bumping down the narrow road past the buffalo-drawn carts on their way down to the weekly bazaar. "He's very weak—do you mind if I call you Charlie?"

"I was hoping you'd get round to it some time. I've never liked this English habit of calling people by their surname. Too formal." He looked at David, then at himself, at their torn and mud-caked clothes. "And right now we look anything but formal."

David nodded, but didn't smile. What he had to say couldn't be said with a smile on the face. "Well, he has about a week, two weeks at the most, to live. The plates showed a military spread. I don't want him to go back to Mandalay, Charlie."

"I don't think he should. Mandalay is no place for any man to die in."

"I didn't leave him in the hospital with Zan, but took him back up to the mission. May he stay there?"

"Of course. It's little enough to see that a man dies in some sort of comfort—though God knows, I'd hardly call the bungalow comfortable. What are you going to do?"

"Stay on. Is that okay with you?"

"Of course. I'm glad you were able to make it out here, David," he said. "He will die in peace now, no matter how much physical pain he may have."

148

"He won't have much of that. I'll put him under sedation as soon as it gets really bad."

"You won't have any ideas about mercy killing?" Caraday looked at him sharply.

"I haven't thought about it at all," David said, and hoped that he would not have to.

"I had to think about it several times during the war." Caraday had relaxed again. "My religion was all against it, but I was tempted. It's a hell of a decision to make, when you see a man screaming with pain and know he has no chance of surviving. Especially when you don't have any sedations to give him."

"What did you do?"

"Shut my ears and prayed for him. And, God forgive me, sometimes it seemed a pretty negative approach."

They came down the long steep slope to the ferry. Here the river ran down a narrow gorge between two high ridges. Thick jungle covered the ridges, growing right down to the water's edge. A cluster of three bamboo huts stood beside the road, their interiors dark and dank as caves. The ferryman's wife, tiny and wizened and sour-tempered, stood at a table outside one of the huts, collecting the fare for the crossing and selling flat lemonade and greasy rice cakes.

"Want something to eat?" Caraday said as David brought the Land Rover to a halt behind two trucks and half a dozen carts. "We shan't be back home in time for lunch."

David glanced at the cakes under the moving net of flies. "I think I'll make this a day of fast and abstinence."

He went down to the river and squatted down to wash the mud and blood from his hands. Beside him a young girl sat on her haunches in the water, rubbing laundry on a smooth black rock. She didn't look at him, but kept her face hidden behind the huge plate of her hat. The women here in these hills had no coquetry, he thought: he wondered what they would think of Rose and her flirting.

Caraday came down with two cakes and a bottle of lemonade. "As you remarked once before, I have a strong stomach. Back home we call it an aboriginal's gut. Takes in anything."

"Don't you ever get a yearning for even a day or a week of soft living?"

"Of course. I told you, I'm not an ascetic by nature." They walked up and sat down on logs beside the rough landing stage. The ferry was coming back from the other side of the river, slant-wise to the current as it strained against the rope

149

that held it to the main cable that ran from bank to bank. The buffalo drivers on their carts and the passengers on the two trucks smiled and spoke to Caraday as he moved up among them, and he returned their greetings with a familiarity that established his place among them. Caraday finished the lemonade, burped, and gave the bottle to a small boy, who rushed back up to the huts with it. "I wouldn't suffer if I had to put up with some soft living. My mother was a wonderful cook—most Australian countrywomen are—and I grew up on good food. Except when I was away at boarding school —*that* cured me of any hidden urges towards asceticism that I might have had. My people were not the sort who had to scratch a living from the bush—we always had more than enough money to go round."

"You're not one of those rich boys who threw up everything when he saw the light? I've always suspected those stories. They sound too much like propaganda."

"You mean Francis Xavier, Philip Neri, the rest of them? You shouldn't be so cynical, David. People do have ideals, you know. Oh, I don't mean I'm in their class. I didn't suddenly give up luxury—though it's stretching it to call it that. Let's call it comfort. I didn't give it up all of a sudden. You forget I had four years as a prisoner of the Japs. That was quite a period of conditioning."

"Why *did* you become a priest? It's something that has always puzzled me—why a man or woman gives up the world. Do you do it out of a feeling of insecurity?"

Caraday threw away the last half of his second rice cake. "I suppose some do come into the religious life because they feel insecure in the outside world. No one will ever try to tell you that all the religious of the world took their vows for love of God alone."

"Did you?"

The ferry swung in against the landing. The first truck, stacked high with freight, eased its way down from the road on to the ramp. The driver revved the engine, took his foot off the clutch, and the truck lurched up on to the landing stage and across on to the ferry like a tank aimed at destruction. It pulled within inches of the far end of the ferry and two men leapt to shove blocks under its wheels. The driver got out, saw how close he had come to plunging into the river, and threw back his head and roared with laughter. Everyone joined in the laughter: the joke was on the river.

"Happy people, aren't they?" Caraday said.

"You're not happy."

Caraday looked sideways at him. "That has nothing to do with God. No, I'm not happy. But it's not because I chose the wrong vocation or anything like that. But we're not going to talk about that," he said bluntly, and his long face closed up, like a book snapped shut.

"All right," David said patiently. "But you still haven't told me why you joined the priesthood. Why anyone joins it."

"I can't tell you why *anyone* joins it," Caraday said almost angrily. "Everyone joins it for his own reasons. I joined it—well, out of gratitude, perhaps. Or because I'd become accustomed to God. I don't know, to tell you the truth. All I know is that once I'd taken the step, I knew I'd done the right thing. I still think so." The ferry was ready to go back across the river, taking the truck and two buffalo carts and a dozen or more people. It went out into the stream, held precariously, it seemed, by its rope as the current swung it downstream. The huge pulley screamed like a wounded bird as it flew over Caraday's head on the long cable. "It was God who kept me going while I was in the bag. Others got by on their own strength, but I found I needed Him. I'd always been what the pamphlets like to call 'a good Catholic'—though, to tell you the truth, I don't exactly know what a good Catholic is— so I was prepared for depending on Him."

"I know what you mean. When I was at school"—David's mouth twisted at the memory—"it was pumped into us day after day that one couldn't get along without God. Those priests took all the dignity out of man himself. I couldn't forgive them for that."

"Well, I was luckier than you. We had an enlightened old head brother—I went to a Marist school—who taught us the love of God, not the fear of Him. Well, anyway, when the Japs grabbed us"—he stopped for a moment, and a look of shock passed over the long dark face: it was as if he had not thought of the war in a long time, and now the memory of it was like a sudden spasm of illness. He looked at David. "It was grim, David. Absolutely bloody. Not what they did to me personally. I got off pretty lightly, I was a doctor and they never knew when they might need me. But what they did to the others— Not just for a day or two, or for a couple of months, but all the time right up till we were released. Torture, beatings, what-have-you—" He spat into the river, as if the taste of the years was like vomit. "Tell you the truth, there were times when I doubted if there was a God. You say

151

the priests at your school took the dignity out of man. You should have seen what the Japs did here. They reduced our poor beggars to animals. I used to lie down at night sometimes and cry at the degradation I'd seen during the day. You wondered how men could survive such treatment. And then, all of a sudden, a man would stand up on his hind legs and say something—sometimes a yell of defiance in language that would have him gaoled for obscenity back home, but that sounded like a song to us. Or sometimes it would be nothing more than a joke, and a pretty weak joke at that. But"—the sad eyes shone for a moment with what looked like a glaze of tears "—whatever it was, it was beautiful. It was man getting up out of the muck heap, getting off his knees, proving that no matter what the Japs did to degrade the human race, man still had dignity. And after a while it came to me that that dignity came from God. Not in a sudden blaze of light or anything like that. Just gradually, the way you acquire an education in science or mathematics or law. I acquired an education in the love of God."

"You got it the hard way." David had long ago convinced himself that he had no capacity for belief in anything but the material. Abstractions, such as the love of God, were beyond him. "But I still don't see why you wanted to become a priest. It seems logical to me that one can love God without having to take vows about it."

Caraday was silent for a while, watching a giant butterfly as it fluttered like a bright purple leaf just above the water. Behind him the buffalo drivers and the passengers on the second truck waited patiently for the ferry to come back. A boy had taken a pair of stilts from one of the carts and was walking up and down the road like a giggling stork, followed by a flock of younger children. The yellow river, shining like brass where the sun caught it, spun by like the endless coil of time itself.

"You shouldn't ask me, David. Whenever a man does anything out of the ordinary, that calls for some sort of sacrifice by everyday standards, whatever reason he gives sounds priggish. There's a malady of suspicion in the world today that makes it difficult for a man to sound genuine about his reasons for doing anything. I got into the habit of helping people during the war, of *wanting* to help them, and God was all part of it. You can say He gave me the strength or whatever you like, but He was also *part* of it. When the war was over it just seemed the natural thing to do, to go on being partners with Him." He stood up, hitching up his torn shorts, straightening the battered hat on his head. God chooses strange partners, David thought, then smiled inwardly at his own snobbery. "You are the wrong man to explain all this to, David. Cynics are empty vessels, without doubts or beliefs. I'd stand a better chance with a man full of doubts."

"Sorry I can't oblige. My doubts went out of me at the same time as my beliefs, in the one purgative action."

"A hollow man. Don't you sometimes feel sorry for yourself?"

It was David's turn to smile. "Never. So I suppose that gives me some standing in the eyes of God, does it? He can't have much time for people who feel sorry for themselves."

"You know," said Caraday, "you aren't quite as hollow as you think you are."

At last it was their turn to cross by the ferry. They bumped off the landing stage on the other side of the river and began to climb up out of the gorge. The jungle hung on the steep cliffs like thick curtains on a wall; occasionally patches of limestone rock showed through like exposed masonry. The jungle came to the edge of the road: the Land Rover drove by within a few feet of green impenetrable mystery.

"This would be just the place for another of Shero's ambushes," David said, and felt the tightening in his stomach again as he said it.

"Relax. Shero never holds up a single car or truck, unless he knows it's carrying money. We're not going to be lucky enough to meet him this way."

"Lucky? I'm not looking forward to meeting him again."

"My mistake. I thought you were."

David looked at him in surprise. "What on earth gave you that idea?"

"Your curiosity about him. You're the one who's been accusing me that I'm not determined enough about bringing him in."

"I think perhaps you are now. But you weren't, not last night at Ho Sang's." .

"Why do you think he should be brought in? He's no concern of yours. You'll be gone from here in a week or two. Do you have a belief or two, after all? Belief in the law?"

"I don't believe in murder, if that's what you mean. And no matter how you look at him, Shero is a murderer."

153

"I'm afraid so," said Caraday after a moment, and there was no mistaking the reluctance in his voice.

3

When they returned to the mission there was mail waiting for them. Pleasure lit up Caraday's face as he saw it: he had not entirely cut the link with home. He was a priest, a partner of God, as he had claimed; but he was still son and brother to the family back in Australia. Blood might not be as thick as faith, but it had its claim on him still.

"There's mail for you, too, Michael, sent up from the consulate." Caraday was undoing the string that held the bundle of mail together. "Looks like all official stuff."

"That's all I get," Michael said, but there was no bitterness in his voice. He had been sitting out on the verandah when they had arrived back, dressed as neatly as ever but still looking grey and forlorn, like some forgotten old man waiting for death and final oblivion on the verandah of some institution. It had hurt David to see his father in such a light, but he had masked his pity behind a casual greeting. Michael, almost as if he had stood off and looked at himself, had seen how far he had come from the ramrod-straight colonel of the parade ground, had brushed quickly over the moment before any comment could be made on how he looked or felt. The bundle of mail had been lying in his lap and he had picked it up and tossed it to Caraday.

"And my subscription notice for the Army and Navy," he said, holding up a letter. "I think I can forget that one. Do you belong to a club, David?"

"The R.A.C. and White's. And several night clubs that you've never heard of." Caraday had gone inside with his mail and father and son were left alone on the verandah.

"I haven't been in a night club since—good God, it must have been 1927 or '8. I was home on leave with your mother. Why, it was when we took you back to England to school. It was our last night and we went to some club in Mayfair. It was run by some notorious woman, Kate Someone-or-other."

"Kate Mayrick."

"Did you know her?" Then Michael smiled. "How could you? You were only six or seven at the time."

"I'm an authority on the history of night clubs. What's that?" His father was holding up a letter.

"It's a letter for you. Care of the consulate."

David took it and looked at it curiously. He didn't recognise the handwriting on the envelope. Was it a letter from some woman—Liz, Louise, perhaps even Elinor Beatty firing a final arrow from a distance? But it was from none of them. It was from Phillips, a fellow surgeon: ". . . and the Council has decided not to pursue the matter any further. So why not come back? Burma may be interesting, but if you'll forgive my saying it, old boy, it is not your sort of territory—there can be no demand for Breton noses out there. Talk has already died down, but it could begin again if you stay away too long."

Phillips had always been the type who made other people's business his own. *Talk had already died down* . . . but Phillips' would have been one of the liveliest tongues while the talk had still gone on. The important thing, however, was that the Medical Council was not going to take any action against him. He had been secretly afraid that it might. He knew that it would not pass any judgement on him that would seriously affect his career; a stiff censure would probably have been its extreme sentence. But its action, no matter how mild, would have gone against him in the future. The Royal College of Surgeons did not elect as its presidents doctors who had gone against the principles of the profession. So he was at least thankful to Phillips for passing on that piece of information, for putting his mind at rest.

"Bad news?" Michael asked.

"Eh? Oh, no. No." He looked down at his father, and once again London was a long way away. "Just a chap envying me my holiday out here, advising me to stay as long as I could."

"And will you?"

"Of course. I've needed this break."

It was as if each of them stood on either side of the open grave, ignoring the body that would soon be lowered into it. Now that death was certain, they were not going to mention it at all.

As if satisfied that David was not going to desert him, Michael picked up the rest of his mail. "A Christmas card from your mother's cousin. A little early, don't you think?" He opened the card, looked at it with no expression on his face at all, then quite suddenly began to laugh. It was a horrible laugh, bitter and hollow: it was full of mockery, coming strangely from the mouth of the tolerant, patient man who had been sitting here a moment ago. Then the laugh just as suddenly turned to a cough and he huddled over, his breath coming in great rasping gasps. At last the coughing subsided and he sat back, his face ashen, his mouth loose as he moaned quietly with pain.

David shook his head, shaken and upset. "You'll have to be more careful. Nothing is funny if it racks you like that."

Michael nodded, his eyes dark with tears of pain and laughter. He held up the card and croaked, "It's for last Christmas. Look at the date."

Caraday had come out on to the verandah when he heard Michael coughing. "Oh, you're lucky to get your mail at all up here. They arrested the postmaster a couple of months ago. He was dumping the mail in the river, after he'd steamed the stamps off the letters."

"Used stamps?" David said. "What good would they be to him?"

"These were outgoing letters. He'd steam the stamps off before the letters were franked, then sell them again. I noticed once or twice that some stamps I bought were pretty tatty, but I didn't wake up to what he was up to. He'd sell the same stamps half a dozen times and pocket the money. The bloke who bought a stamp last, when it was too far gone to steam off the envelope, was the one who got his letter posted."

"But why would he dump incoming mail in the river?"

"Probably reckoned that if the people here got no answer, they'd think they were being ignored and go on writing letters demanding to know why. And so they'd go on buying stamps."

He and David had been talking to each other above Michael's head, discreetly ignoring him. The screen of small talk gave him an opportunity to regain his breath and his composure. Now he sat back and smiled up at them. "I shouldn't be surprised if the British Post Office had its own little troubles when it first started. One can't expect a tradition of service to spring up overnight."

"You're too tolerant of these beggars," David said.

"Perhaps," said Michael, still smiling, all the mockery gone now. It was difficult to know whether he had been laughing at life or fate or the hand of God; but for a moment it seemed he had been like his son, empty of hope or belief. "But I was intolerant for so long, it is almost a pleasure now to smile upon a few peccadillos."

David looked at Caraday. "You've taught him this toler-

156

ance. The Staff College at Quetta would have you shot for subversive propaganda."

They were all smiling at each other, the ugly moment of Michael's pain now past. There was an air of camaraderie amongst them: David and Caraday could have been brother officers of Michael, men who had shared years of the same life with him.

"I think I could do with a drink," Caraday said.

"I brought up a couple of bottles of whisky and a couple of bottles of gin," Michael said. "George put them out in the kitchen. I forgot all about them."

"I shan't say you shouldn't have done it," Caraday said, "because I'm damn glad you did. I think I might get drunk tonight, then phone up the bishop in the morning and ask for absolution."

He went inside and David said, "Has he ever got drunk? I shouldn't blame him if he did once in a while."

"He's got merry once or twice. But never out of despair, if that's what you mean. It was always to celebrate something, a birthday, something like that."

"What's he planning to celebrate this evening?"

But before Michael could answer, they saw Maureen coming up the road on a bicycle. She jumped off and stood the bicycle against the post at the bottom of the steps and came up on to the verandah. She was puffing slightly, her face shining with perspiration, her bosom rising and falling beneath her shirt. "Phew! And women actually *pay* to do that at beauty salons! They must be nuts." She flopped down in a chair and fanned her face with a handkerchief. "I'd give my eyeteeth for a nice long cold gin-and-tonic—"

Caraday came out with three glasses on a tray and David took one of them. "You owe me your eyeteeth," he said, handing the glass to Maureen. He looked at his father. "I'll get you another."

When he came back with the second gin-and-tonic, Caraday said, "Maureen has come up to cook dinner for us."

"I heard you'd left Moriarty out at Mong Na," she said. "I'm glad of the chance to *do* something. I can't remember when I've had so much time on my hands. I could help them down at the hospital, I suppose, but I don't know if they'd welcome an outsider."

"Better to leave them alone," Caraday said. "Zan is a bit nationalistic when it comes to running his hospital. He wants to make a go of it on his own."

"He let you help during the cholera epidemic, didn't he?" David said.

"I offered my help, but he said no at first. It was Rose who eventually came up and asked me to go down and help. Zan was almost out on his feet by then."

"Did he resent your help?"

"Oh, no. It was just that he wouldn't *ask* me to help. We think Zan is pretty Westernised, but he's still very much a Burman. He's a bit of a bumbler, like most Burmans, never caring about details, always willing to put things off till tomorrow, but he *is* a trier. He reckons the Burmans will get nowhere unless the Burmans do it themselves, and I think he's right. They don't always go about it in the right way, but some of them here are trying. And Zan is one of them. So I never butt in down at the hospital unless he asks me."

"Does he ever ask?" David said.

"Occasionally, since the cholera business. I know a bit more than he does about tropical diseases—that was what I was doing before the war and I've kept up to date as far as I could—and once or twice he's asked my advice."

"He's not likely to need any plastic surgery advice up here," David said, "so I'm not likely to offend him by volunteering any."

"There's plenty of opportunity for plastic surgery up here," Caraday said. "People with malformed features, others who have been cut up by the Japs or dacoits, a few who had been mauled by tigers. But plastic surgery is the sort of luxury these people don't even dream about, because they don't know such a thing is possible. A woman up here is smashed up in accident, or scarred by a knife, or hit by a bullet, and that's it—she's lost her beauty for life. The women here are vain, like women everywhere"—he grinned at Maureen, who raised her glass to him—"but they don't have the money to spend on their vanity. You could never peddle a Breton nose up here, David."

David looked up, startled: it was almost as if Caraday had read Phillips' letter. "Where did you hear of the Breton nose?"

"Oh, Michael sends me up copies of *The Times*. And Zan gets *The Lancet*."

"I must do some reading about you some day," David said. "What would you be in—*The Ecclesiastical Quarterly?*"

The good humour of the three men continued right through dinner. Maureen ate with them—"just to show I have confidence in my own cooking." She had made a ragoût of goat, and though David did not think it was entirely successful, it was a change from curry. Her dessert was deep-dish apple pie, and even though it was made with tinned apples it was a great improvement on blanc-mange. When the meal was over George came in to clear the dishes away, and Maureen stood up.

"Don't go, Maureen." Caraday was well on the way to being merry: the bishop looked like getting a phone call in the morning. "It's Saturday night, party night."

"Stag party night." Maureen had been well aware of the good feeling among the three men. She knew that if she stayed on, it would not be long before she would be the outsider. It warmed her to see how David had settled in with his father and Caraday, and she would dearly have loved to stay on, just sitting outside the circle of the men watching them and listening to them. She was the sort of woman who preferred the company of men to that of women, who would have enjoyed having brothers when she was young. To her it seemed that there was always much more give and take among men, and tonight there had been a lot of give and take among David, Caraday and Michael. "You can all let your hair down."

"I'll take you back to the hospital," David said. "Can't have you take the risk of being mauled by the tiger. I don't want to have to perform plastic surgery on you."

They put the bicycle in the back of the Land Rover and he drove her down to the hospital. The lights went out in the wards as he drew up outside the nurses' quarters. He switched off the engine and the headlamps. "Are you going to ask me in?"

"No. They're expecting you back at the mission. You can't walk out on their party now."

"I know. But I had to escape for a while. It depresses me. My father sitting there doing his best to ignore the fact that he'll be dead in a week or so, and Caraday being merry and bright and getting drunk, as if he's holding the wake in advance."

"Poor David," she said for the second time that day, and put a hand on his. He looked at her, suspecting sarcasm, but the pressure of her fingers had sincerity in it. "You're changing, you know."

"Oh, for God's sake!" he said irritably, and drew his hand away from under hers. "You sound just like Caraday. He says

159

I'm changing, too. You make out that I was some sort of ogre, incapable of a little human feeling."

"Weren't you?"

He said nothing for a moment, staring out through the windscreen at the moon coming up like a bland yellow face out of China. "Was I really as bad as that?"

"Ever since I've known you, David, you've never made anything easy for anyone. You were a well-dressed, cultured son-of-a-bitch, but you *were* a son-of-a-bitch."

"You couldn't have thought I was too bad."

"Never trust a woman's judgement—remember how often you used to tell me that? In bed or out of it, you were always telling me that a woman's opinion could never be trusted. I never made the comment in those days, but in a way you were passing judgement on yourself. Because, after all, in those days you were the top of my Hit Parade, my Family Favourite, my Lover Boy, whatever you liked to call yourself. Oh, I knew you were right, all right. I mean about not trusting a woman's judgement. But what woman ever trusts to judgement when she falls in love? What man does, for that matter? Except you, of course, you son-of-a-bitch." Abruptly she began to cry, all her good feeling for the evening gone. She went to get out, but he reached across and held the door shut. "Let me out!"

"Not just yet. Look—" She had taken him by surprise. He was not exactly sure how he wanted to treat her, what he wanted to say to her. He only knew that he did not want to say goodnight to her on this note. He had the feeling that the rest of the night was going to be bad enough without the added bitterness of another quarrel with her. "Dear girl—"

"Oh, to hell with your 'dear girl'! That's you English all over—full of words that never mean anything! I'm not your 'dear girl.' I never was—"

He tried again: this was not the time for another of their transatlantic arguments. "Maureen, look—I may have been what you've described me as, but it was not my ambition to be one."

"Oh, what an argument!" She had dried her tears and now sat facing him; she was ready to fight with him all night. "Do you think that excuses you—because it wasn't your *ambition* to be a son-of-a-bitch?"

"I wish you wouldn't keep using that expression," he said with a touch of his old hauteur.

"What would you prefer—swine, cad, bounder? Take your

pick. I'm bilingual, I can describe you in English or American."

He sat back. He didn't have to hold her in the Land Rover now. The way she was now, he might eventually have to *put* her out. "All right, forget it. Goodnight."

"Oh, you're not getting rid of me like that!"

All at once he started to laugh. It was a relief, like the release effect of a valve; there was little amusement in it, it was more like a sudden collapse of physical tension. He laughed quietly, sitting there in the darkness of the vehicle, aware of the occasional moan of pain in the darkened ward across the lawn, aware all at once and for the first time of the sigh of death behind the laughter, of the skull behind the mask of the face. As a doctor he was a familiar of death, but he had remained untouched by it: professionalism had allowed no room for compassion, he had been no more than a craftsman working on the machine of the human body. He tried to remember if he had ever been moved by the death of a patient, and couldn't. He knew that early in his career he must have felt *something* when someone under his care had died: a sense of waste, perhaps, that a young man or young woman should die before their promise was fulfilled; but no faces came back out of the past, he felt no sense of loss; despite what Donne had said, he had not been diminished by any man's death. And for the last ten years there had been no deaths at all. Once or twice he had been called in to help save a patient's life, but usually a plastic surgeon's work began when the patient was on the way back to recovery. And there had certainly been no life-or-death crises with the women who had come for Breton noses.

"What are you laughing at?"

He looked at Maureen, wondering for a moment what had started him laughing. "Oh, it was you! One moment you're struggling to get out of here, the next you accuse me of trying to get rid of you. My dear girl—sorry, I take that back—"

Then she, too, sat back and began to laugh. This was a repetition of the past; so often had their scenes ended like this. Her own laughter had often been forced, and tonight it was the same: she was putting up the defences again, she had almost given herself away. She would have to get away from here quickly. Already she could see the old roundabout starting up again, herself the only rider.

"You'll never change, David—"

161

"A minute ago you said I *was* changing."

"Maybe you are. I don't know. But you'll never change towards women. Every girl will always be 'dear girl' to you. I suppose it's something. Back home it's 'honey' or 'baby,' and they're worse than 'dear girl.' I don't think I could ever be any man's 'honey' or 'baby.' "

"Good luck at the Mayo, then. If Drucker calls you 'baby,' let me know and I'll report him to the A.M.A."

"I'll need luck at the Mayo," she said, no longer laughing. "Which reminds me—I'll have to see about catching the bus back to Mandalay tomorrow, now that you and your father are not going back."

"You won't go by bus," he said, suddenly concerned for her. "You stand too much risk of being shot up by our friend Shero. George and I shall drive you back. We can stay the night in Mandalay, put you on the plane and come back here Monday."

She wanted to stay till Michael's end came; but she knew that might also mean the end of herself. "Well, if it's not too much trouble—"

He went to say "My dear girl," but stopped himself. The phrase lay too readily on his tongue: it was like some patent medicine in a cabinet brought out as a sedative. He felt he was pushing her off to America, but she so obviously wanted to go. He was piqued to think that she was looking forward to working with Drucker. The American was a good surgeon, but not as good as himself. Even in the privacy of his mind, he did not indulge in false modesty. "Maureen, it's no trouble. I'd never forgive myself if something happened to you on the way down to Mandalay. And I mean that, dear girl." The phrase slipped out, despite his intention, but it didn't sound so insincere this time.

She remarked the old endearment, but she said nothing. She leaned across, kissed him on the cheek. She was aware of the smell of him, so different from that of the old David: no smell of talc, of after-shave lotion, of the specially prepared oil that he used on his grey hair. He had never been lacking in masculinity, but she preferred the smell of him now.

"Goodnight, David. You're a son-of-a-bitch, but you're the nicest one I know." The horned owl hooted in the cherry tree as she got out of the Land Rover. She started, then giggled at her own nervousness. "There used to be a barn owl back home—"

"You seem to be thinking a lot of home lately."

"Maybe it's because I've had so much time to think. The last three years have been pretty hectic. There was never much time for thinking—which, maybe, was just as well." Her face was serious for a moment, then she smiled at him as she closed the door of the vehicle. "These past few days I've been having a few nips of nostalgia, getting secretly drunk. There's always something worth remembering, even from the worst of times."

Then she was gone under the shadow of the cherry tree. He heard her footsteps on the verandah of the nurses' bungalow, her door opened and closed, and a moment later the light went on in her room. He sat for a while, wanting to follow her, suddenly wanting some comfort from her: he knew no one else who could offer it to him.

Then Rose was standing right beside his elbow. "Maureen didn't ask you in, David?"

He had been about to switch on the engine, but now he sat back. "How long have you been there, Rose?"

"I've just come across from the wards. I haven't been eavesdropping, if that's what you mean. Would you like to come in for a nightcap?"

"Lime juice? It's not my drink."

"You can sit and watch me."

For a moment he was tempted: anything to delay going back to the mission. But the coquetry was once again too obvious; he had learned long ago to be wary of the woman who was too easy. He switched on the engine. "Some other time, Rose."

He saw a shadow of temper pass swiftly across her face: she was not so bland that she could accept a rebuff from a man. But she recovered almost instantly. "Goodnight, David. We'll get together some time yet."

He drove slowly back up the hill to the mission through the soft Burma night. I'm an ex-son-of-a-bitch, he thought, despite what Maureen says. But he had no new identity, and he needed one. One that could deal with tragedy and an impending sense of loss. One that would recognise for whom the bell tolled. . . .

Then as he stopped at the mission gate, he heard the bell tolling in the church tower.

4

He drove swiftly across the meadow and up to the bungalow. He switched off the engine, jumped out of the Land

163

Rover and ran up the stairs into the house. Michael sat stiffly in his chair, still as if dead, pain and horror making a grotesque mask of his face. David reached him in a couple of strides.

"Are you all right? Where's Charlie?"

Michael blinked as if trying to get some focus back into his gaze, then he looked up at David. "David, where have you been? I couldn't hold him—I hadn't the strength—"

"Is he across in the church?" Michael nodded. "You sure you're all right?" Again Michael nodded. "Stay here. Don't try to follow me. I'll be back in a minute."

He went out of the house on the run, down the steps and across the meadow towards the church. The church bell was still being rung, wildly and without rhythm. Lights were coming on in the huts down the road, as they had the night Caraday had shot at the tiger. As soon as he saw them, David ran even faster. Without being clear as to his purpose, he knew he had to reach Caraday before the villagers did.

When he was halfway across the meadow, he heard the singing beneath the wild jangling of the bell. Caraday had a good bass voice, the sort that any choirmaster would welcome: but he was not singing hymns tonight. David could not distinguish the words, but the song had a rollicking rhythm to it that he had never heard in hymns. As he got to the door of the church, which stood wide open, he caught a line of the song: " '. . . or else you may turn outlaw, like the Wild Colonial Boy.' "

He went up into the dim interior of the church. He saw the small red glow of the altar lamp, like a drop of blood suspended in the air. Moonlight slanted down through the large painted window high above the altar; the mission hadn't been able to run to the expense of a stained glass window; the Crucifixion had a wild surrealistic look to it in cheap water paints that had run as the rain had dribbled in. A centre aisle ran up to the altar, flanked on either side by rough wooden benches. There were no cushions or kneeling steps: one knelt on the rough concrete floor to pray. A fashionable congregation would have had its faith tested here.

Despite the dimness of the church, David had no trouble finding Caraday. The priest was at the rear of the church, swinging on the bell-rope, still singing: " '. . . and that's the way they captured him, the Wild Colonial Boy!' "

His voice rose to a final wobbling note, then abruptly stopped. He slumped forward on the rope, the bell gave a last sharp clang, then he slid down on to the floor. Silence rushed back into the church; David had the feeling he was standing in a vacuum. He moved forward towards the fallen priest.

Caraday lay face down on the floor, his arms flung wide in the attitude of the Crucifixion. David knelt down and put a hand on Caraday's shoulder. Only then did he feel the silent weeping in the tall thin body.

"Charlie—" His voice was low: he was talking to a sick patient.

Caraday shuddered, then abruptly turned his head and looked up. David was shocked at the man's face; it was racked with pain, as if he had suffered some terrible injury. The dark, nearly black eyes stared up at David, not seeing him; a whole life lay behind the film that clouded them, a life that was the man's secret. The flesh, too, had turned dark, hanging from the bones like crepe; the mouth, usually so mobile, was no more than a dark gash in the dark skull. He is alone, David thought: I am not even here for him.

With some difficulty he lifted the priest, who didn't complain or struggle, and hung him over his shoulder. Caraday was still weeping, the dreadful weeping of a man beyond hope. David, moving as quickly as he was able, went to the door and looked out. In the bright moonlight he saw the first of the peasants coming up the road from the huts, just beyond the gate to the meadow. He stepped out, closed the door behind him, then hurried across the meadow towards the bungalow, Caraday hung like a sack across his shoulder. Down by the gate the peasants stopped, seeing the huge humpbacked creature hurrying through the moonlight. They stopped dead, fear a gate that they could never pass through, then turned and went running back down the road to the safety of their huts, certain that one of the *nats* had come down out of the hills and rung the bell in the mission church.

David reached the bungalow, went up the steps and straight to Caraday's room. He laid the now unconscious priest down on his bed and pulled the blankets up over him. Then he went out to Michael. "What brought that on?"

Michael was still grey, huddled in his chair as if beaten there by the storm of what he had witnessed. His own coming death had all at once looked blacker and more unbearable, his resignation swept away by the flood of Caraday's despair and hopelessness. "One moment he was sitting there humming some old songs, songs he said he had known as a boy, then all of a sudden he jumped up and raced out of the room—"

"He got drunk suddenly, like that?"

"I don't think he's drunk, David. Not the way one usually thinks of people being drunk." He gestured at the bottle on the table. "I've seen him drink twice as much as that and still be as sober as a judge. Or a bishop." But the last remark was not meant as a joke: he was beyond humour this evening. His voice was bare of emotion; he could not trust himself to speak, to give emphasis to a word, for fear that he, too, would break. And for the sake of his son, he did not want that to happen. The discipline of years, the stiff upper lip that was the butt of so many jokes, that he knew must often have been satirised by his son, now saved the evening for both of them.

He stood up. "I shouldn't mention this to him in the morning. Unless he does."

"I'm not entirely tactless," David said with some tartness. This was the second time tonight he had to defend himself.

"I'm sorry, David. It was tactless of me to suggest that you were. Tomorrow is Sunday. I wonder if Charlie will be in a condition to say Mass."

"Not till after he's phoned the bishop," David said. "No matter what we may think, he's going to crave absolution in the morning."

Chapter 9

1

David was sitting out on the verandah, drinking the coffee George had brought him and watching the mist rise from the river, when he saw Karim Naung cycling up the road from the gate. He was pedalling furiously, head bent over the handlebars; and David smiled at the boy's effort to impress as a speedy messenger. He had probably lingered all the way up from the hospital and now, having seen David sitting on the verandah, was putting on a grandstand finish. He skidded to a stop at the foot of the steps and fell off the bicycle. He picked himself up, held the bicycle against his hip while he greeted David with both palms pressed together, then he said, "U Maung Zan wants Father Caraday quick."

"Father Caraday is saying Mass." David looked at his watch and made a guess: all he could remember about the Masses at school was that they had usually lasted an hour. "He won't be out for at least another ten minutes."

Karim Naung frowned. The boy has a sense of responsibility, David thought: that at least gives him a future in this country. "U Maung Zan said he wanted the father quick, at once."

"Did he say what for?" The boy shook his head, surprised: messenger boys were not taken into the confidence of hospital doctors. "Is someone down at the hospital dying?"

167

"I do not know, sir. U Maung Zan just said he wanted the father quick."

David stood up. "All right, Karim Naung. Go back to U Maung Zan and tell him that Father Caraday will be down at once."

Karim Naung got on his bicycle, wobbled the first few yards, then gathered speed and went off down the road. David went down the steps and walked across the meadow towards the church. The cows stood in one corner of the meadow, waiting to be brought up for milking; a calf ran away from David as he approached it, like a frightened child. David looked around for the bull that had sired the calf, but could see none. Perhaps it was a papal bull sent round regularly to all the missions' herds: he giggled quietly at the joke. He felt lightheaded this morning from lack of sleep. He wondered if Caraday, too, was lightheaded this morning. Although the priest, to be sure, would not be in the mood for jokes.

He had not spoken to Caraday this morning. The priest had risen early and David, who had slept only fitfully during the night and woken at dawn, had heard him moving quietly about his room. Then Caraday had gone out of the house and David, rising and going to the window of his room, had seen the priest going down the road on his bicycle. It had not been difficult to guess where he was headed: to the hospital, to use Maung Zan's phone to call the bishop.

Caraday had not come back to the house for breakfast. David, breakfasting on the verandah, had seen him come back up the road and go into the church. That was more than two hours ago and Caraday had not emerged since. Michael, looking grey and weak, his eyes red from lack of sleep, had come out on to the verandah and David had offered him breakfast.

"No, I'm going to Communion." He was dressed in suit, collar and tie, wearing his Sunday best as if he were going to Mass at Brompton Oratory back home. He looked across towards the church. "That is, if Charlie is saying Mass."

"I think he will be. He went down into Sheromere very early and I'd bet it was to ring the bishop, wherever he is."

"Down in Bhamo," Michael said absently, still looking across towards the church. "I hope he got on to him. Phone connections are not good up here." The bell had begun to ring, slowly and rhythmically this morning, and people were coming up the road and down the tracks from the hills in answer to its summons. Michael looked at David, half-apologetically, as if he felt he shouldn't ask the question: "I don't suppose you'll be coming to Mass?"

David shook his head. "It would be hypocritical if I did. And it might be embarrassing to Charlie. It would look as if I'd just come to see how he conducted himself on the altar after a wild night."

"That's a charitable view," Michael said, and for a moment the tension went out of his face. He hesitated, then he put his hand on his son's shoulder. "Charlie would appreciate it. His whole life is based on the charitable view. He would be less susceptible if he were more selfish."

Then, as if embarrassed by the gesture of touching his son, he turned away and went quickly down the steps and across towards the church. He walked stiffly upright, as if going out on some parade ground to inspect the troops, his stick swinging at his side; but it was an effort for him to do so, and as he got further and further away from David, the latter could see the stiffness going out of the old man's back. As he disappeared into the church, Michael looked small and bent over, a man burdened by more than the weight of his years.

Now as David himself approached the church he could hear the tinkling of the Communion bell. The door of the church was wide open and birds flew in and out. There was the sound of coughing and the scraping of feet; a child whimpered and was quickly hushed. He went up the steps and stood at the open door. The church was not crowded, but there was a bigger congregation than he had expected. The heads of those in the rear seats turned to look at him; feeling conspicuous, he moved inside the door. A tin bowl nailed to the wall held holy water; his hand went out to it automatically, a reflex action from years past; then he dropped his hand quickly. Angry with himself for no clear reason, he moved across to stand in a corner at the rear of the church, beside the bell-rope and almost on the spot where he had picked up Caraday last night. He was standing there when Caraday turned, the chalice held before him, and looked out at the congregation.

". . . *Domine, non sum dignus*—" Then he saw David and stopped. The altar boy, a lad of about twelve, deputising, David guessed, for the absent Moriarty, rang the bell and waited to ring it again. His head was bent, but after a moment he raised it, looking up to see what was delaying the priest. People were already coming up the aisle to the altar rail; they had stopped and knelt down, waiting for the second and third bells to be rung. They, too, now looked up, wondering why the priest had suddenly become silent. Caraday stared across the church at David, a mixed look of agony and anger on his face.

Only then did David realise where he was standing. He thinks I've come back to taunt him about last night, he thought; and abruptly he moved forward and away from the bell-rope. He knelt down in the rear seat, his head bent and his hands folded in the old, almost forgotten clasp of prayer. He had forgotten all his prayers, but that did not matter. He was kneeling here, not out of adoration of the Host in the chalice, but out of charity towards Caraday. He heard the bell ring twice more, but Caraday's voice was inaudible; then there was once more the shuffle of feet. He looked up and saw that Caraday was now at the altar rails, head bent, intent on laying God on the tongues of the believers.

Then Michael was moving slowly down the aisle to the altar, head also bent, the stiffness gone from his back, moving with the almost reluctant step of a man who knew he would soon be beyond the need of sacraments. He knelt down and Caraday came to him, the chalice glinting like a globe of light in his hand as sunlight struck through the window behind the altar. Caraday turned, blocking out the ray of light; for a moment both Michael and the chalice were in the shadow of Caraday's body. Then the priest took the wafer from the chalice and laid it on the dying man's tongue.

David watched it all without passion or memory. His body had gone through the actions of long ago: the movement of the hand towards the holy water, the kneeling in the pew, the clasping of the hands in the attitude of prayer: he was like the old soldier who goes back to the barracks, handles the gun with familiar ease, but has forgotten how to kill. His mind was a blank: God was a stranger, not even recognisable as a wafer of bread. He could only envy the comfort it seemed to give his father.

Caraday went back up the altar steps. The last of the communicants returned to their seats, lips pursed with piety, eyes downcast in temporary humility. The birds swept in and out, like small dark cherubs busy with the affairs of God: the government of souls went on round the clock: David wondered if there was a bureaucracy in Heaven, taking itself seriously like bureaucracies everywhere. The non-communicants sat up, getting the kinks out of their knees and out of their consciences, satisfied that they had done their duty for another week. In a few minutes Mass was over. David waited while the people filed out, then moved up to where Caraday stood beside the altar taking off his chasuble. Michael was still kneeling in his pew, his head still bent in prayer.

"Zan wants to see you. He sent his messenger boy up. It's urgent."

"Someone dying?" Caraday folded his altar garments and put them away in a small cupboard in a recess at the side of the altar. The garments were faded and frayed: Caraday put on his Sunday best to worship God, but it was a poor man's Sunday best, no better than the clothes worn by the peasant congregation.

"I don't know." David was speaking in little more than a whisper: even the voice acted in a reflex way. But his mind still had no memories or regrets: the Mass hadn't touched him in that way. "I'll come with you."

As they went down the aisle David stopped beside his father. "I'm going down with Charlie to the hospital. We shan't be long."

Michael looked up, blinking as if coming awake. He had been a long way from here: lost in dreams of the past or nightmares of the future, it was difficult to tell. He nodded, looking up at both of them. "I'll stay here awhile. You don't need me to go with you, do you?"

The offer was pathetic, the gesture of an old man who was reluctant to face the fact that he could no longer be of any use to anyone. "No," said Caraday gently. "I'll be back in time to have breakfast with you."

He and David went across to the bungalow and collected their bicycles. Caraday brought his battered suitcase with him. "Just in case," he said. "It may be some poor beggar who needs the last rites."

"When it comes time to administer them to my father, don't call me in, will you?"

"Why not?"

They were cycling down to the gate, the morning breeze fresh on their faces. Some boys, free from the restraint of church, were running down towards the river, trailing kites behind them that swooped and soared in the air; the boys' shouts came back as shrill unintelligible cries, heightening the effect that it was birds plunging in the sky, trying to escape the strings that held them. "I saw it happen once, my first year in a hospital. It horrified me, if you must know. It

171

seemed to me that the priest was conducting the funeral service with the patient still alive and looking on."

"Did the patient look horrified?"

David got down to open the gate. "No," he said as Caraday cycled through. He closed the gate and remounted his bicycle. "What's that got to do with it?"

"Everything. He was the one in need of that last blessing. Not you bystanders. No, it's a question of belief again, David. You just can't bring yourself to believe that a lot of people find solace in God. The thought of meeting Him face to face is not as horrifying to them as it is to you. Some people welcome the thought. I think your father will."

"What about you?"

"If I'm prepared and in the right moral condition, yes, I'll welcome Him." He pedalled for a few yards, then looked at David. "I shouldn't have welcomed Him last night, if that's what you mean. Who was it brought me across and put me to bed, you or George?"

"Me."

They caught up with the last of the parishioners on their way home from Mass. It was a small group, a family of father and mother and four young children. They all waved and smiled at Caraday and David. Once again David felt as if he were standing in for the bishop, sharing in the villagers' respect and affection for Caraday. He was suddenly glad that he had managed to get Caraday across to the bungalow last night before any of the villagers had arrived at the church.

"Did anyone else see me in the church? I dimly remember going in there, I think I was singing, and then I began hauling on the bell-rope—" He looked at David for confirmation.

"You were making a hell of a din. It woke up the people down here—" They were passing the huts at the top of the rise that led down to Sheromere. Children rushed out and ran along beside them, laughing and shouting: the two men rode like royalty through the collection of huts. "But I got you out and across to the bungalow before they got as far as the church."

"Thanks." Caraday swung the bicycle to avoid a too-enthusiastic child that had scampered across the road in front of him. Then he swung back beside David. "Did I do any gabbling?"

"You were singing, that was all. Something about the Wild Colonial Boy."

A smile creased Caraday's face for a moment, reaching

even the eyes. "That was always a favourite of mine, even as a kid. And that was all I said?"

"Yes." A few yards of silence, then: "What did you tell the bishop this morning?"

"Just that I'd got drunk." He smiled again, almost laughing out aloud now. If he had any remorse for last night, he had put it behind him or was keeping it secret. "It was a bad line to Bhamo and I had to shout so he could hear me. Talk about the privacy of the confessional! Have you ever said an Act of Contrition at the top of your voice?"

"Hardly," said David. "That must be like making love at the top of your voice."

"Could be," Caraday said, then they had swung into the driveway of the hospital. "Here we are. I reckon I must have woken every patient in the wards when I was on Zan's phone. That's probably what he wants to see me about. Someone is complaining about being woken by the recital of another man's sins."

2

"A fellow named Karim Gam came in from Mong Na with a message for you," Maung Zan said. "I've sent him over to the kitchen to get something to eat. He rode in on a bicycle. It is an awfully hard ride."

"What was the message?" Caraday asked.

"Someone out at Mong Na tried to blind Moriarty," Maung Zan said expressionlessly. "They put out his good eye."

Caraday had been about to sit down, but now he straightened up and let out a terrible roar of rage. It was like the cry of an animal; David could imagine that a tiger would roar like this as a trap snapped on its leg. Caraday turned and blundered about the room; it was almost as if his own eyes had been put out. "Why? Why, why? Why Moriarty?"

Maung Zan's expression had cracked. There was pain on his face now at the sight of the pain experienced by his friend. "I don't know, Charlie. Karim Gam found him this morning. They heard him scream, but they didn't see anyone. Neither did he, I gather. They put out his eye while he was asleep."

"Only one eye?" David said.

"His good one. They didn't touch the one with the squint."

"What did they use?"

"A knife."

Caraday was leaning against the wall of Maung Zan's office,

173

staring unseeingly out the window. He was breathing heavily, as if trying to keep back a torrent of words that he knew were not fit for a priest's tongue: his face was working, the muscles moving like lizards beneath the dark skin. "It was Shero," he said at last, his voice no more than a whisper.

"We don't know that, Charlie," Maung Zan said.

"It was Shero, I tell you!" he roared, and beat his fist against the window frame. The rusted wire screening split away from the frame as he hit it, but he didn't seem to notice. He turned round, tall and thin and terrible against the early morning glare beyond the window. "Moriarty never did him any harm—"

The phone rang, the bell jangling against the nerves in the tense atmosphere of the tiny room. Maung Zan picked it up. He said something in Kachin, listened for a moment, said something again in Kachin and angrily thumped the phone back on his desk. "What a time to ring! Some teacher from the high school, wanting to make a date with Rose!"

"She has another date she can make," Caraday said, turning towards the door. "Where is she?"

"Across in her room, I think. It is her day off." Maung Zan followed Caraday to the door and held his arm; beside the tall thin priest he looked like a small boy trying to restrain his father from a rash act. "Leave her be, Charlie. She had nothing to do with this—she is awfully fond of Moriarty—"

"I didn't say she did have anything to do with it!" He pulled his arm free of Maung Zan's hand and strode out of the office.

Maung Zan turned to David. "Can't you do something to stop him, David?"

"Stop him what?"

"He'll go looking for Shero, get himself killed. There is no love lost between the two of them. Shero would have killed him long ago, if Charlie hadn't had such influence with the people here."

"If he kills Charlie now, won't the people rise up and kill Shero?"

"Probably. Some of them would, but the rest—I don't know. But who wants to sacrifice Charlie for that end? Charlie alive is worth more to this community than Shero dead. People need a leader, David, and Charlie is the leader here in Sheromere. He holds no title or anything like that, and he has to watch himself that he doesn't antagonise the government by trying to take things over, but he is the leader, all right.

174

The D.C., the head *pongyi*, no one ever goes to them when something is wrong around here. They go to Charlie." He looked down at his desk, tried to make some order out of the disorder of papers that lay there, then swept them all into one heap and looked up. "I go to him, too. Without him, I don't think I could have kept going here."

David shook his head and said irritably, "How can one man become so indispensable?"

"He is not indispensable, David. No one suggests that. We'd survive without him, if we had to. But so long as we can have him, we want him."

David sighed. "*You* asked me to come out here, Zan. It was supposed to be an escape for me from London and a reconciliation with my father. That was all. But since I've been here I seem to have done nothing but become involved with Caraday."

"Everyone is involved with him in some way or other, David. But it is worse for him. He is involved with everyone, and he is only one man."

David had no answer to that. He was in strange territory; involvement was something he himself had avoided like a disease. It *was* a disease: it could kill as easily as cholera. Especially in such a situation as was confronting Caraday now. He sighed again: he should have gone to Amalfi. "I'll try and stop him," he said, and went out of the office and across towards the nurses' bungalow.

Caraday and Maureen were on the verandah. "I don't know where she is," Maureen was saying. "Maybe she has just gone down to the bazaar. You're wrong, Father. Why should she try to avoid you?"

"She's found out about Moriarty." Caraday turned as David came up on to the verandah. "She's found out from Karim Gam and she's buzzed off because she knew I'd be looking for her—"

"I don't think so," David said quietly. "Here she comes now."

She was coming towards them up the drive, her face hidden by her wide bamboo hat. She was wearing a green silk *cheong-sam*, and the heavy Chinese bracelet dangled from her wrist. She's dressed up for so early in the morning, David thought: I wonder whom she has a date with today. Caraday leapt down off the verandah and almost ran towards her. Maureen went to follow him, but David held her arm. "No, this is between themselves—"

"But he's wrong about her," Maureen said. "He's almost blaming her for what has happened to Moriarty. Poor Moriarty," she said, and shook her head as if fighting back tears.

"Poor Moriarty," David agreed, and suddenly left her just as she was about to say something else. He went down the drive towards Caraday and Rose. "Charlie—"

"Leave us alone for a moment, David—"

"No," said David sharply, and caught the priest's arm and swung him round. A flush of anger darkened Caraday's face, but David didn't give him time to speak. "Listen to me! All you're thinking about now is revenge. When was that part of a priest's make-up? All you're thinking about is Shero—but what about Moriarty? He's out at Mong Na, God knows what agony he's going through, and you haven't given him a thought—all you're intent on is revenging him. Our first concern is Moriarty himself—he needs medical care more than he needs revenge. I'm going up to get the Land Rover—I'll be back in ten minutes." Rose had been standing silently, face expressionless beneath the deep shade of her hat. "You be ready to come with us, Rose. Better get Maureen, too—" He looked back at Maureen, who still stood on the verandah. "Bring a medical kit. And you'd better bring your suitcase"— he looked back at Caraday—"just in case it's needed. If you do need it, then it will be time to start thinking of revenge."

Caraday was standing with a stunned look on his face, as if David had held up a mirror to him and he had been faced with some truth he had forgotten. He said nothing as David spoke to him, and David didn't wait for an answer. He turned and went quickly across to Maung Zan, who stood at his office door. "Can you run me up to the mission to get the Land Rover?"

"No," Maung Zan said. "You can take the hospital Land Rover out to Mong Na. You'd be in trouble if it got down to Mandalay that the British Consulate was involved in this."

"Involvement, involvement, that's all I bloody well hear!"

"You've led a sheltered life, David," Maung Zan said without sarcasm. "You'll find that most of the world suffers from involvement in some way or other. Take the hospital Land Rover. I'll see that a bed is ready for Moriarty when you bring him in."

"Can you send someone up to tell my father where we've gone?"

"I'll go myself. I haven't spent as much time with him as I should have."

176

David put out a hand and squeezed the other's shoulder; he was not aware of the fact that it was a gesture he had not made in years. "Thanks, dear boy."

"Don't mention it, old chap." The old friendship had been fully rekindled: they spoke and acted as they had twenty years ago as students.

David and the others were on their way in less than five minutes. David drove, Caraday sat beside him, and Rose, Maureen and Karim Gam sat in the back seat. They drove in a silence that was almost painful to three of them. David had something to occupy him as he drove the Land Rover at speed along the rough winding road, and Karim Gam was wrapped in his own shyness as he sat beside the two women. The vehicle could have been full of strangers.

On their left the river had settled down to its steady pace all the way down to Rangoon and the sea; thick and dark from the monsoon rains, it was almost sensual in its movement under the bright shine of the sun. Then the river swung away from them, the road climbed, and a little later they were coming down into the gorge to join the river again and cross it by the ferry. The ferry was on the other side of the river and they would have some time to wait for it. Caraday was still sitting silently in the front seat, seemingly unaware of the others. David nodded to the two women, and the two of them got out and followed him down to the water's edge.

"Rose," David said, "have you had any word about what's happened to Moriarty?"

"Only what Father Caraday told me." The bracelet on her wrist jingled as she moved her hands nervously. She had taken off her hat and in the brassy glare of the sun she looked unusually pale. "Do you think I would have anything to do with a horrible thing like that?"

"Rose, I'm not accusing you of having anything to do with it," David said patiently. "I'm just asking if there was anything you had heard. We don't even know if it was Shero's men who did it, that's what I'm getting at." He nodded back towards the Land Rover. "I'm trying to save Father Caraday from committing suicide. That's what he'll be doing if he goes hunting Shero on his own. Can you find out for us if Shero really did do it?"

"And if he did?" Maureen interrupted. "How are you going to stop Father Caraday then?"

"I don't know." David felt suddenly weary, the lack of sleep last night all at once catching up with him. It was as if

177

he were in the middle of a long difficult operation which he knew now could be hopeless: the patient was going to die anyway. He might just as well leave the patient and go away and lie down and sleep. "But if he's going to commit suicide, it's better he do it for some purpose."

"Father Caraday may not commit suicide, but he is going to destroy himself eventually," Rose said. "Sad men always do."

David watched her in surprise as she got up and went back up towards the Land Rover. "Where did she pick up that little observation?"

"I don't know," said Maureen, looking after Rose with the same puzzled surprise. "Unless Confucius said it."

"More likely Charlie Chan. I don't think Rose has ever read a serious book in her life."

"She could get her opinions from Ho Sang. Or from Shero."

"What do you mean by that?" he said suspiciously.

"I wonder if she spent last night with him. She was out all night, David. I thought you would have guessed that when you saw how she was dressed."

"I wondered why she was wearing a silk *cheong-sam* and a bracelet at breakfast time. How do you know she was out last night, though?"

"When Karim Gam came in with the message, I was in Maung Zan's office. I went across to the bungalow to tell Rose. She wasn't there and her bed hadn't been slept in."

"Does Maung Zan know?"

"I think he guessed it somehow. She really gives that man the run-around, doesn't she?"

He didn't comment on that. "What about Caraday—did you tell him?"

"Of course not. I think he'd blow his top if he knew. In any case, it's none of his business where she spent last night. It's none of our business, either."

"That remains to be seen," he said.

The ferry was coming back across the river and they went up towards the Land Rover. Caraday had been talking with Karim Gam. He turned now as David and Maureen got into the Land Rover; he seemed to be ignoring Rose. "One of the Chinese gave some first aid to Moriarty." He was still on the defensive: this was his answer, half an hour late, to David's accusation that he had neglected Moriarty's welfare for the

178

thought of revenge. "They're very good at that sort of thing."

"Why didn't they bring him into Sheromere?"

"It's only the Chinese who own trucks out in Mong Na," Caraday said. "They wouldn't risk bringing him in for fear of being held up by Shero, for fear of being accused of taking sides."

"The Chinese in Mong Na seem to make a social habit of fence-sitting," David said.

"The Chinese are the Jews of the East," said Caraday. "When they are out of China, they often have to fence-sit to stay alive. Only the size of China itself and its nearness to all these small countries has prevented any pogroms. The Jews were never lucky enough to have a giant homeland. Nobody out here loves the Chinese. Am I right, Rose?" He looked at her at last.

She hesitated, not because she had any doubts but because she seemed reluctant to voice the truth. "It's true. Even Ho Sang. People respect him, but nobody loves him. He is still an outsider," she said bitterly, and one knew that she felt as much sympathy for herself as for Ho Sang. I wonder if that is why she is attracted to Shero, David thought: he, too, is an outsider.

The ferry had berthed and David took the Land Rover down on to the landing stage and on to the ferry. In a moment or two the ferryman had let go the ropes and they were swinging out against the current. The ferryman, all bone and sinew, his legs bowed from years of pushing against the huge oar by which he steered the ferry, stared impassively and without curiosity at his passengers. His whole life was bounded by the two banks of the river; it was almost as if the river itself was the sole reason for his existence. I wonder if he has managed to escape involvement, David thought.

"What about these factions you told me about among the Chinese in Mong Na?" David asked. "Will they stick together against the Burmans?"

Caraday nodded. "Like glue. Don't the whites stick together in Africa?"

"I wouldn't know. Africa is an even darker continent to me than it is to most people."

"I'd forgotten how narrow your interests are." Caraday seemed to be out of his slough of depression now. The old rasping note of mild antagonism was back in his voice. We're back where we started, David thought. "To put the analogy closer to home, don't you doctors stick together?"

"Naturally," said David, not letting him get away with it completely. "Just like you priests."

"All right," said Maureen from the back seat. "If you two want to fight, wait till there are no ladies present. Right, Rose?" She looked at Rose, who hesitated, then smiled. Beside her Karim Gam also broke into a smile, although he had no idea what the conversation was about. Maureen looked back at the two men in the front seat. "There is enough strife in this country without religion and medicine putting on the gloves."

Her voice had just the right tone of lightness. Everyone smiled, and the air of friction went out the window with the river breeze. Then the ferry was bumping against the landing stage on the other side of the river, and five minutes later they were climbing out of the gorge towards Mong Na.

Moriarty was in Karim Gam's hut. As soon as the Land Rover drove into the village, the villagers converged on it. As David and the others alighted outside the rough hut that had been built to replace Karim Gam's burnt-out house, they were swamped in a tight press of people. But again David noticed that the Chinese and the Kachins did not mingle.

"Come in with me, David," Caraday said. "There'll only be room for two of us."

The hut was small and crude: a roof of rusted galvanised iron that had been blackened by fire, walls of bamboo, an open doorway whose door was a piece of bagging. The interior held only the necessities of furniture: a rough table, some stools, rush mats laid on the dirt floor as beds. In one corner stood an upturned box holding a collection of photographs in cheap, smoke-blackened frames: Karim Gam and his wife smiled on their wedding day with all the brash hopefulness of youth: hope and the photographs were all they had managed to salvage from the fire that had destroyed their house.

Moriarty lay on one of the rush mats, a blanket thrown over him, his head resting on his own rolled-up cricket blazer. David noticed that the green and yellow stripes were now smeared with red: Moriarty had added the badge of his own blood. Caraday dropped on one knee beside the wounded man. "We've come to take you back to the hospital, Moriarty."

Moriarty's wounded eye had been bandaged, roughly but adequately. He opened his other eye and David was surprised to see that the squint had gone; then he remembered that this often happened, that a squint would correct itself

180

when a good eye was shielded. And Moriarty's good eye had been shielded in the most permanent way. "Father—" Moriarty's voice was no more than a whisper. His hand fumbled under the blanket and when it came out David saw the rosary beads twined round the brown fingers. "All night—praying—a miracle I did not die—"

"Yes," said Caraday, and David felt like an intruder. He did not know whether Caraday believed in such jiggery-pokery, but he felt embarrassed by being a witness to such a belief. This was like something from the old books of myths and legends that his father had sent him: the beating of drums to drive away the evil spirits, the burning of bundles of hemlock, caper spurge, rosemary and sloe to expel the witches. But if the superstition of prayer had brought Moriarty comfort, had indeed enabled him to survive the night, it was not his place to sneer. He would just rather have not seen an intelligent man like Caraday accept the belief.

Caraday looked up. "Do you want to look at the eye or shall I?"

David knelt down. "There's nothing to stop both of us looking at it. Undo the bandage."

Moriarty moaned as Caraday lifted his head and began to take off the bandage. The wound, when exposed, was an ugly one: whoever had handled the knife hadn't been concerned with neatness. The eyeball was still in the socket, but it would never again be of any use to Moriarty. "I'll give him a shot," David said, rising. "The trip back will be too rough on him, otherwise. He'd go out of his head with the pain."

He went out to the Land Rover to get the medical kit Rose had brought. The crowd pressed about him as he measured the morphine into the needle; it held the same fascination for them as if he held a cobra in his hand. He felt a shadow fall across him and looked up into the belly of a boy towering on stilts above him. Maureen pushed her way through the crowd. She grabbed the stilts and looked between them, like a woman looking out through the wooden struts of a gate. "How is he?"

"Pretty bad. We can't save the eye." Rose had struggled through the crowd to stand behind Maureen. "Rose, you had better find out if Shero did have anything to do with this. I'm feeling like Father Caraday now."

"You're not going hunting Shero!" In her surprise Maureen almost wrenched the stilts out from beneath the boy. He yelled and wobbled above her. She looked up at him, said,

"Shut up, kid," then looked back at David. "You're not going after him!"

"No. But someone's got to go after him. The police or the Army."

"It's none of your business, David." Rose was torn with emotion, every expression showing on her face like a splash on water; she was not her mother's daughter this morning, the Oriental side of her had lost out for the time being. "Let these people make up their own minds."

"Do you think you can trust them to? Moriarty was asleep when his eye was put out. Who was it told Shero's men which was Moriarty's good eye?"

"You keep saying it was Shero and his men." Rose, too, grasped one of the stilts; the boy above them was anchored. "What if it was one of these people here?"

"It could have been," David said, remembering Moriarty's arrogance towards the local villagers. "But I think some traitor here just put the finger on Moriarty, that was all. If these people here had actually done the deed, they wouldn't have left him here in the village. He'd have been taken out along the road and dumped in the bushes. No, I'm sure it was done by Shero. The fact that they didn't kill Moriarty is some sort of message or warning." He looked around at the crowd. All the faces had the same blank look; it was hard to tell if anyone had understood what he was saying. Surprisingly, he did not care; anger had made him reckless of whatever danger there might be in talking. He *was* angry: that was the real surprise. "These people couldn't care less, Rose. Moriarty is an outsider, Rose, just like you and me. It's the outsiders who have to look after the outsiders. Which is why I'm going to the police as soon as we get back to Sheromere. If you won't help me, then damn well don't! But some day you may be looking for an outsider to help you, too."

He went back into the hut: the crowd parted in front of him as he advanced on it with the needle held like a gun. "This is going to ease your pain, Moriarty," Caraday said, and rolled up the wounded man's sleeve.

"A miracle I'm alive—" murmured Moriarty, head turned away from the needle; the fingers of the hand clutched the beads as the needle went in. "A miracle—"

They put him in the back of the Land Rover and drove out of Mong Na, chased to the end of the street by curious children. Caraday had said something in Kachin to Karim Gam just before getting into the Land Rover, and the Kachin had shaken his head. Now David said, "What did you say to Karim Gam?"

"I asked him if anyone in Mong Na had done that to Moriarty. He said no. He would know if anyone had."

"So it was Shero," David said. "Although I still think there is a traitor in Mong Na." And he explained his theory to Caraday.

Caraday nodded. "But he's not the man I want." He looked back at Rose. His voice was quiet; if he was still angry, his anger was now under control. "Get in touch with Shero, Rose. Tell him I want the man who blinded Moriarty sent in to be handed over to the police."

"Do you think he will do that?" David said.

"No," said Caraday. "But I've got to try every way first before I go hunting him myself. A priest is allowed to kill tigers, but not men."

Behind him David heard Rose begin to weep, but he didn't turn to ask her the reason. He was sure now that she had known what had happened to Moriarty long before she had returned to the hospital this morning.

3

Maung Zan operated on Moriarty to repair the wound, but the eye was damaged beyond repair; the eyeball was removed and Moriarty was left with an empty socket that might later take a glass eye. It was an operation that required skill, and David was surprised at Maung Zan's competency; somehow he had expected that Maung Zan's skill at surgery would be no better than his rather poor skill at administration. David and Caraday, Maureen and Rose assisted at the operation; the rest of the staff crowded in as best they could to watch. Moriarty, when he recovered, would be flattered and pleased to know that he had been the most important patient the hospital had ever had.

"He'll be a mess to look at when it's healed," Maung Zan said. "But I can't help that. He needs a plastic surgeon now."

"It's too early for that," David said, feeling that Maung Zan was unfairly trying to put him in a spot. "And I'll be gone by the time he's ready for it. A pity," he said, looking down at the still form on the table; he suddenly felt a warm regard for the Indian with his conceited Catholicism and his atrocious cooking. "I'd like to help him."

Caraday looked at him, but said nothing. He peeled off his gloves and cap and led the way out of the small, stiflingly hot theatre. Rose and Maureen stayed behind to supervise the removal of Moriarty to a ward; the three men, after washing up, went on to Maung Zan's office. Maung Zan produced a bottle of lemonade from a drawer in his desk. "All I can offer is lemonade." He smiled at David. "Not even vintage stuff, like your mother's."

"My palate has undergone such abuse since I've been here, lemonade may not taste so bad after all."

"Well, you won't have to put up with blanc-mange again for a while," Caraday said, taking the drink Maung Zan poured for him. "But then neither will I." He took a swift drink from his glass, as if he were trying to wash away more than the remembered taste of rock-hard blanc-mange.

"You'll have to find another cook for a while," Maung Zan said. "Unless you'd like to come down here and eat with me."

"I may do that. Unless——" Caraday looked at David. "When is Maureen leaving?"

"I intended taking her down this afternoon to Mandalay. I don't know if she has changed her mind about leaving."

"Why should she?" Maung Zan said.

David shrugged. "Yes, why should she? But unless she has changed, Maureen is not the sort of woman to walk out in the middle of something. And we are in the middle of something —exactly what, I don't know, but your friend Shero has the answer to it."

"What about you, old chap?" Maung Zan was savouring his lemonade as if it were vintage wine. "Do you want to leave?"

"I'd leave tomorrow if it were not for my father. None of this is any concern of mine." He took one mouthful of the lemonade, then put the glass on the bookshelf by which he stood: beside it was a copy of Brookes and Alyea's *Poisons*. He would never have a sweet palate, no matter how much abuse it took. "This affair isn't going to end suddenly, not unless you get off your behinds and do something about it. Shero will still be here in a year's, two years' time, still doing whatever he wants to do, still holding up buses and convoys, still murdering people. Yes, and still putting people's eyes out."

"You're convinced now that he did it?" Caraday said.

"I'm convinced."

"Well, what's your suggestion for putting a stop to him?"

"Get the Army in. Hunting Shero isn't like hunting that other tiger we went after. Crossbows won't do any good against Sten guns. You're only risking the lives of the villagers if you ask them to help you bring him in."

Caraday tossed off the last of his lemonade, put the glass down on Maung Zan's desk and belched. "Pardon. I shouldn't drink like that. I try to imagine that everything I drink is whisky. Wishful drinking," he said with a grin, looking at David. "All I get is gas, not pleasure. About the Army. I don't know if it is worth it, do you, Zan?"

"Nobody wants the Army if they can do without them," Maung Zan said. "It's the same in any country, I should think. Soldiers have a habit of acting like conquerors, even in their own countries."

David remembered what Caraday had said about the Army. It was the same in England, he guessed: garrison towns there never seemed to welcome their role. "So what will you do?"

"Be like Moriarty," said Caraday, only half-joking. "Pray for a miracle."

"I noticed you didn't deny him his claim to a miracle for being kept alive last night."

"Would you have?"

"Perhaps not. But what if he keeps talking about it when he's fully recovered?"

"It'll be an advertisement for the Church," said Caraday, refusing to be drawn. "Unlike doctors, we're allowed to advertise."

When they went outside Maureen called to David from the verandah of the nurses' bungalow. He went across to her. "Do you want to leave for Mandalay this afternoon?"

"I don't know. I feel as if I'm walking out in the middle of something."

"That's what I told them."

"Do you think I should go?" He didn't answer. She took the plunge, hating herself for her weakness: "Do you want me to go?"

"No," he said at last, and she could have wept, mistaking his selfishness for kindness. He was tired from last night's lack of sleep, and his head had begun to ache; the sunlight bounced up from the ground, searing his eyes. He felt sick and lonely, feeling the same loneliness he had experienced that night in London after the Beatty case. "If you could stay another week—"

"I'll write to Drucker," she said eagerly; she had to hold

herself back from reaching for his hand. "He'll understand. I'll tell him about your father—and there's Moriarty to be looked after—" She was looking for excuses to stay, collecting patients like a poundkeeper collecting dogs.

"Will you come up and cook for us?" He recognised her eagerness to stay, was now afraid that she might go too far. He was not ready for love, or whatever it was that had kept them together for three years. He tried on the old sardonic air, like a suit of chain mail: "Or wouldn't that look good in a letter to Drucker? 'Please excuse me for further week. Have taken job as cook.'"

She smiled. She was not going to be drawn into an argument; she knew this was all part of the old act, she had seen it so often. She changed the subject, using the same defence that he had taught her: "Did you tell Father Caraday and Maung Zan about Rose not being here last night?" He looked past her along the verandah, and she said, "It's all right. She went out somewhere as soon as we'd moved Moriarty to the ward."

"Where's she gone?"

"I don't know. Maybe to pay another visit to Shero."

"Do you think that was where she was last night?"

"I'm sure of it. What I'd like to know is whether that was the first time or whether she's been seeing him all along. Did you tell them?" she repeated, nodding across to where Caraday and Maung Zan stood by the office door.

"No. I may tell Caraday later, when we're alone. But I wasn't going to tell both of them. Better to hurt one man than two."

"They both have a lot of time for her, haven't they? No, more than time—love, I guess. More than she deserves," she said with a trace of bitterness, and thought with irony of her own position: she loved David more than he deserved. But at least he wasn't a traitor to her: that much she could be thankful for.

"Much more than she deserves," he said, blind like a man to the imbalance of their own relationship. "Well, are you coming up to the mission?"

"How would you like goat paprika tonight?"

"Anything but curry."

Chapter 10

1

When they drove back up to the mission, they found that George had put Michael to bed. The Gurkha, looking worried, came out on to the verandah as the hospital Land Rover drew up at the steps.

"The colonel was very sick, sir," he said to David. "I had to order him to go to bed. Me, an amaldar, ordering a colonel to go to bed! But I had to do it, sir. He is so sick."

"You did the right thing, George. This is not the Army. You were in charge of the colonel."

"It is not the way it should be, sir." The scar on the Gurkha's face twitched like a wound that was about to open.

David patted the Gurkha's arm reassuringly, went to say something and could think only of empty platitudes, and went on into the bungalow.

Michael lay flat in his bed, his head resting on a thin pillow. One look at him told David that it was now only a matter of hours before his father would be dead. Already he felt a sense of loss: for his father himself, for all the wasted years, even for his mother, whom he now hardly remembered. He sat down in a chair beside the bed and Michael turned his head.

"How is Moriarty?"

"You don't want to hear about it."

"But I *do*." In the last twenty-four hours all the flesh

187

seemed to have left his face; grey skin and grey hair covered the skull that rolled in denial on the pillow. "Are you afraid I'll be upset by what has happened to someone else? They didn't kill him, did they?"

"No. They blinded him in his good eye."

"Zan came up to see me after you'd gone out to Mong Na. He gave me another dose of morphine. He told me what they had done, but he wasn't sure if Moriarty was still alive. Why are some men so cruel?" He looked out the window, about to leave life and puzzled now why so many men should want to spoil it. He had forgotten that all his own life he had led a career that was dedicated to killing: killing in the interests of justice or of peace, but killing nevertheless. He is not going to die happy, David thought, despite what Caraday has said. He is going to die in pain, not all of it pain from the cancer. God damn it, he thought angrily, he's been infected by Caraday: now *he's* worrying about human nature.

"Perhaps soon you'll know the reason," he said.

The grey skull rolled to look back at him. "You mean when I'm dead? Do you think there will be enlightenment on the other side?"

"I don't know. I don't think about the other side, as you call it."

"I wish you would, David." Then he shook his head almost imperceptibly. "No, I shouldn't say that. I shouldn't be lying here asking you to come back to the Church. Not now, when I'm so close to dying. That's blackmail."

"Then don't ask, because you'd only get a disappointing answer. I'm sorry, Father." The word came easily now. "I just haven't capacity for belief in that sort of thing. A vessel with a hole in the bottom doesn't hold water."

Michael smiled, a ghastly grimace. "You sound as if you are quoting from a parable."

"No," he said, returning the smile, knowing his own must also be a grimace because he could feel it working on his face. "Actually, it's an old Carthaginian proverb. Remember Frazer's *Golden Bough*, you sent it to me when I was a boy?"

"It wasn't in that," Michael said, still smiling. "But I'm glad you remember the book. Perhaps I should read it again myself some day. It explains quite a deal why men behave as they do." Then he looked up. "But there won't be time, will there? I mean, to read it."

David shook his head. "I told you the truth when I showed you those X-ray plates. Do you want me to keep on repeating

188

it? The truth can hurt him who tells it as well as him who hears it. That's another old Carthaginian proverb."

"Proverbs and sayings always cancel each other out, haven't you discovered that? There's one from Browning, I think it was—'Truth never hurts the teller.' "

"I was never keen on Browning. He was too much the optimist for me."

"Well, truth may hurt the teller, but optimism never did. Disappointment hurts, but never optimism."

"One is the shadow of the other. Another old Carthaginian proverb."

Michael smiled. "Tell Charlie I'd like to see him, would you?"

David went out of the room, told Caraday that Michael wanted to see him, then went out on to the verandah. Maureen was still there. Caraday had poured her a drink and she sat in one of the old cane chairs, gazing out at the mountain across the river.

"What's the name of that mountain?"

"It hasn't any name. That's what it's called—the Mountain With No Name. It probably has a Kachin name that sounds much more euphonious, but that's what it means in English."

"English often falls down, doesn't it? Back home there are a lot of beautiful Indian names. Put them into English and they sound as banal as a pop song. How's your father?" she said abruptly.

He went back into the living room, poured himself a stiff whisky and came out on to the verandah again. He drank before answering her. The whisky took a variety of tastes out of his mouth: the taste of beginning grief, Maung Zan's lemonade, the anger at what had been done to Moriarty. It seemed that he had almost run the gamut of taste today.

"A day or so at the most," he said.

She was silent for a moment, looking down at the river. "Do you think Father Caraday would mind if a woman moved into his house? I'll come up and nurse your father."

"I can do it," he said, but he was grateful for her offer.

"No, a woman is better than a man at a time like this." Again she was silent, then she looked at him. "I'm sorry, David. I mean, that he has to die now, just when you've become father and son again."

"So am I," he said slowly, aware again of the taste of grief. It was a new taste to him, one that, perversely, he almost enjoyed: it was like a new drug that was having a cauterizing

189

effect on an old wound: it hurt, but he knew it was doing him some good, though how, he was not sure. He took another drink of his whisky. "I'm sorry for you, to. That things were as bad for you in your family."

Surprise opened up her face like a flower. "That's one of the nicest things you've ever said to me." She stood up, standing close to him but not daring to touch him. There was a fragility about their relationship at this moment that she knew could be destroyed by a wrong word or a wrong gesture. "I think we were both unlucky when we were young. But I'm glad, really glad, that one of us managed to see the other side of family life. Now I'd better go in and start dinner," and she went quickly inside the house before he could see the tears that were already shining in her eyes.

David continued to sit on the verandah. Down by the river a monk was walking back along the bank towards Sheromere. His yellow robe was the one bright patch of colour in the green and grey of the landscape; the sun struck through his umbrella so that he seemed to wear a huge bright orange halo. He walked in a world all his own, and David for the moment envied him his isolation. Then he realised that the monk's isolation was only an illusion. He would go back to the monastery and be trapped by the webs of other people's lives just as surely as the most gregarious person in the most crowded city in the world. If there was one thing he had learned in his week here in Burma it was that true isolation, non-involvement with others, was not possible. It was ironic that he should have come to this realisation in a country where the state religion had as one of its principles the renunciation of the world. He would talk that one over with Caraday some time.

It was a good half-hour before Caraday came out on to the verandah. He brought a whisky with him, and sank down into one of the chairs with a heavy sigh. He tasted his whisky, then said, "He wanted me to hear his confession."

"What would he have to confess? What sins has he committed since he went to Communion this morning?"

"I've been listening to the sins of his lifetime." He put his hand over his eyes and bent his head. "I'm going to miss him, David."

"So am I," said David, making his own confession. "I've never been one for turning the clock back, but I'd do it now if I could." Caraday looked up from beneath his hand, but before the priest could say anything, David forestalled him.

Not wanting to expose any more of himself, he exposed Rose: "Did you know Rose was out all last night, that she didn't sleep at the hospital?"

But it was no secret after all: "I guessed it when I first spoke to her this morning. Women don't dress the way she was dressed so early in the day."

"You're observant for a priest. But you're canny, too. Why didn't you say something?"

"For the same reason you didn't. And Maureen, too, I suppose. *And* Zan. We're all trying to protect Rose."

"From what?"

Caraday took another drink. "From herself? I don't know, to tell you the truth. But how we do it by not admitting what she has already done, I don't know."

"You'll have to face her with it sooner or later. I think she knew about Moriarty long before you told her this morning."

"I'm sure of that, too. When I went down the drive to her this morning at the hospital, she was waiting for me to jump on her before I'd even opened my mouth. That was when I knew she'd been with Shero all night, and not one of her other boy friends."

David shook his head, cynically amused for the moment. "Dear boy, you could spend a long session in the confessional with her."

"I have no more chance of getting her into the confessional than I have of getting you there."

"A good yardstick," said David, giving him no encouragement. "All right, what are you going to do about Rose? One of you will have to do something. You or Ho Sang or Zan. You can't all sit still with your tongues tied."

Caraday nodded. "But do I do it now or wait till—" He nodded back at the wall behind him. "How long do you give him?"

"What's my father got to do with it? You're procrastinating again, looking for a way out."

Caraday offered no denial. He took another drink, then said, "How long do you give him?"

David slumped down in his chair. Rose was Caraday's problem: why should he concern himself with her? He looked down towards the river, at the cliff-face opposite shining like steel in the direct light from the lowering sun. The monk was now almost out of sight, going down the river bank towards Sheromere: he was just a tiny yellow mote in the eye as it looked at the grey-green landscape. "It's just a guess, I don't know how strong is his will to live, but I'd say twenty-four hours, perhaps a little longer."

"I'll wait till then," Caraday said, and it was impossible to tell whether he was determined to get to the bottom of Rose's contact with Shero or whether he was relieved that he had been able to put it off again. He stood up. "I'd better go and milk the cows."

David watched him walk across the meadow towards the cows, calling to them in his deep voice in what sounded like a parody of cowboys at roundup. Then it came to David that this was how Caraday had looked and acted back home—on the range? Well, whatever it was called—in Australia. He had never lost the look and the air of an outdoors man, and David wondered if he had ever regretted leaving home. Life back on the Monaro could never have been as complicated as life here in the Kachin hills.

Maureen came out on to the verandah. "Have you ever peeled potatoes?"

"Often," he said, taking the dish of potatoes she handed him. "When I got my first dermatome, I used to practise on potatoes with it. For a while there, I was making my own potato crisps."

She smiled, picturing him at work on a potato with a dermatome, the instrument surgeons used for slicing skin grafts. "That was before I knew you. You never offered me potato crisps when I came to your flat."

"What did I offer you?"

But she just smiled and went back inside the house. This was no time for bringing up the omissions of the past.

2

Dinner that evening had none of the gaiety of last night's meal. So much had happened today that David found it hard to believe that only twenty-four hours had elapsed since the meal at which there had been such good humour and good fellowship. He and Caraday sat opposite each other at the table and Maureen sat at its head. "I feel like a Mother Superior," she said, then looked quickly at Caraday, wondering if she had offended him. Like most women, she was never quite sure how far one could go in joking with clerics.

But he just smiled at her. "No Mother Superior could ever cook like this."

"Have you got a service tonight?" David asked. "I find it hard to keep remembering that this is Sunday."

"I don't have night services. I wouldn't feel much satisfaction in having spread the Word if on the way home some of my parishioners ran into Shero or the man-eater. I am not a night-shift priest, except in case of emergency." He half-turned his head as if to look towards the door and the bedroom beyond where Michael lay, then thought better of it. But from that moment the meal became a melancholy affair, unrelieved even by the excellence of Maureen's cooking.

When the meal was over and George had cleared the dishes away, Maureen said, "Father Caraday, you have a spare room out back. Would you mind if I moved up here till —" She nodded towards the door. "He'll need a nurse from now on."

"Of course. I'll get George to make up the bed for you."

He got up and went out to the kitchen, and Maureen looked at David. "Will you drive me down to the hospital to get my nightie and my toothbrush?"

"I think it might be an idea if we took shifts. Is four hours apiece too long for you?"

"I've done longer. You forget I haven't always been a surgical nurse."

"My dear girl—" Then he stopped, smiling at her. "No, I must get out of that habit."

She stood up, pausing behind him as she moved towards the door. She put her hand on his shoulder, making an effort to be casual and light. "You'll never be able to change, David. All the women of the world will be your dear girls, forever and ever. You are not the sort of man who would ever be owned by a woman."

"And that's a bad thing in the eyes of an American woman, isn't it?" His own tone was light and casual.

Her hand remained resting on his shoulder. "You have been reading libel written by foreigners. English foreigners."

"No, actually I heard it from an American. A doctor who came to London for a conference. He talked very dully about the evils of socialised medicine, forgetting we know more about it than he did, but very interestingly about the evils of American femocracy, about which we knew nothing." He stood up and her hand dropped from his shoulder. " 'My dear girl' is a phrase I think I shall always keep reserved for you. In twenty-five years' time, when I come to lecture at the Mayo—"

"As the President of the R.C.S.?"

"Naturally," he said, returning her smile. "When I meet the matron in charge—"

"Who will be me."

"Naturally. I shall greet her with 'My dear girl.'"

"You'll still be a son-of-a-bitch," she said, smiling, but wanting to weep. Faced all at once with the empty years ahead, she almost surrendered completely. He could have her on any terms he liked. She was one American woman who would never vote for a femocracy. She believed in the dictatorship of the male. Or anyway, one male. She was saved from slavery by the return of Caraday to the room.

"Your room is all ready," he said. "I've left some religious pictures on the walls, but they aren't meant as propaganda. They just cover the holes."

"Isn't that what holy pictures are for?" David said. "Covering the holes in one's faith?"

Caraday shook his head, smiling at Maureen, taking her as an ally against the cynic. "Cynicism is a form of faith in itself, although he doesn't recognise that. I wonder what pictures cover the holes in his disbelief."

"Pictures of himself," said Maureen, and David bowed to her. This was the old Maureen, the one he knew and could trust. Trust? Well, perhaps not. He had trusted her that day in court and she had spat in his eye. But all that seemed a long time ago, something in another life, something done to him by another woman with the same name as this woman smiling at him now as she walked by him out of the room.

"I'll see how Father is," he said. "I may need to get some things from Zan, just in case."

Maureen walked out and down to the Land Rover, parked at the corner of the bungalow. She got in and sat there in the darkness of the vehicle. She could feel the chill coming up from the river, and she shivered; she wound up the windows, shutting out the cold and the sounds of the night. Suddenly, out of the past, there came back just such another night as this. It had been colder, she remembered the snow flurries in the light of the neon signs, but she had been waiting like this for another man, her father. It had been a Saturday night and they had driven into Ogallala to do their weekly shopping. Their last call had been at the liquor store to buy her father's weekly bottle of rye. He bought only a bottle at a time and when he got home would mark the bottle off into sixths. He would drink a portion each night from Monday through Saturday; Sunday was his dry day. Eric Hagen had got out of the old beat-up truck and gone into the liquor store, and she had sat there in the unheated truck cabin, shivering with cold and something like fear, waiting for him to come out and to tell him that she was leaving home. She remembered the snowflakes falling like glowing cinders against the red of the neon sign, and the shadowy shapes of the men outlined against the misted windows of the liquor store. The windows of the truck had been rolled up and there had been no sound; and as she had waited everything but the glowing neon sign had been blotted out as the snow had begun to thicken. Everything had become unreal, she had had the feeling of sitting alone in a silent dream world; then her father had come out and got into the truck, and everything had become real again and even more frightening than any dream.

She had told him bluntly and in few words, because she could not trust herself to talk too much, that she was going away, leaving home for good. He had said nothing till they were almost home, twelve miles out along the highway. Then all he said was, "Why?"

She could not bring herself to tell him that she hated him and that that was why she was leaving him. Cruelty had never been part of her make-up: if it had been, she would not have chosen the profession which was the secondary reason she was leaving home: "I want to be a nurse."

"You can be a nurse at the county hospital. They always got a place for a willin' girl."

She shook her head. "No, I want better training than that. In a city hospital."

"Where you want to go? Omaha? 'Tain't far. You can come home weekends."

Omaha was too close: she had already decided even then that she would never come home again. The break was going to be clean: it was the only way. "No, I'll go to Chicago. Maybe even New York."

"A girl can git into trouble in them places. You can be mighty unhappy in a big city."

"I'll be all right," she had said. They had turned off the highway, were driving up through the thickly falling snow towards the farmhouse that had never held any happiness for her.

"I'll miss you," he had said, but there had been no love in his voice: he would miss her hands, her capacity for work, not her.

"Yes," she had said, and had left it at that. She could not bring herself to lie, to say that she would miss him.

She had left home on the following Wednesday, and by then he had drunk the full bottle of rye. There had been no outburst of temper such as she had been used to and had expected. He had gone about his work with a sort of sullen resignation; it was almost as if he had been expecting her to leave him. On the Wednesday he had driven her into Ogallala to put her aboard the train for Omaha and points east: she would make up her mind when she got to Omaha whether she would go to Chicago or New York. At that time she had never dreamed that points east would some day include London and now even Burma.

Her father had shaken her by the hand and wished her goodbye and good luck, as if he were no more than a friendly neighbour. There had been no one else to say farewell to her; she had told no one she was going. She had had friends, girls with whom she had gone to high school, boys she had gone to dances with and one whom she had allowed to make love to her, but she had not been able to bring herself to say goodbye to them. She had expected that saying goodbye to her father would be trial enough; but he had made it easy for her by being stiff and formal and unemotional. He had stood back as the train had begun to draw out, and that had been her last memory of him: a dark figure standing in the middle of the white expanse of the snow-covered depot, getting smaller and smaller till at last he was gone into the white oblivion of the falling snow. She had sat back in her seat and cried, not because she loved him and would miss him, but because he had robbed her of the happiness of the family life she had seen in other homes.

She had written him half a dozen letters, but he had never answered. Then one of her high school friends, with whom she had corresponded intermittently, had written to say that her father was dead. She had been in London then, and he was already buried before she had got the letter. It had been a cold January day and she had gone out of her flat in Cornwall Gardens and walked up to the park. She had walked there for an hour, trying to feel some grief because she thought she should, but there had been none; at last, shivering and cold, she had gone back to the warmth and comfort of her flat. David had come that night, but she had not told him of her father's death. By then she had known of the estrangement between David and his father, and she was in no mood for any of his sardonic comments on parents. She would not speak ill of the dead, no matter how little love she had had for them.

She shivered now in the cold of the Land Rover, waiting for David to come out and drive her down to the hospital. In a day or two she would have to say another farewell, one that she did not want to say, one that she would have to say not out of hate but out of love. Too much love. She wanted to be a slave, but she would have to cast her vote for femocracy. She was going to be mighty unhappy either way, but at least saying farewell would give her another chance. Points east might bring her another man whom she could love.

As David came out of the bungalow, a young Chinese boy on a bicycle came up the road. He jumped off the bicycle and as Maureen wound down the window she heard him say something in Kachin to David. The latter shook his head, turned round and called to Caraday. The priest came out on to the verandah.

"Looks like another messenger," David said, indicating the Chinese boy.

Caraday came down the steps and spoke in Kachin to the boy. Then he turned to David. "I'll come down with you. Ho Sang wants to see me."

"Has he got something on Shero?"

"I don't know. But *something* is wrong. He's never sent up for me before."

Good, thought Maureen. Perhaps I'll have an excuse to stay even a few more days.

3

They drove down into Sheromere. The stores were still open and people sat in their yellow interiors, grouped about glowing charcoal braziers. They passed the Chinese gambling shop and the opium den; men stood outside each with the same hopeful look of escape on their faces. A procession came along the main street, headed by children banging cymbals and youths doing parodies of dances.

"There's to be a *katein* tomorrow," Caraday said. "That's the annual gift-giving to the *pongyis*. They have these processions to show their neighbours what they're giving." The Chinese boy, riding down with them, said something in Kachin and Caraday nodded. "The people are giving twice as much this year, hoping that prayers will be said to keep Shero and the man-eater quiet for the coming year."

"Are the *pongyis* for or against Shero?"

"The old ones are against him. The young ones—well, a lot of them are opportunists. Their price for prayers will be pretty high."

"You sound a little bigoted, Father," Maureen said. "It's not like you."

"No, I'm not bigoted. Even Buddhists around here will tell you that it is only a minority of the *pongyis* today who are really devout. Buddhism is like any other religion—in practice it's nowhere near as perfect as its believers try to make it sound in theory. That goes for my Church, too, I'm quite ready to admit. The trouble with Buddhism is that entering a monastery doesn't mean a permanent sacrifice—you can enter it for only a few months, for a year, two years, any time you like. Kids from up here go down to Rangoon or Mandalay as students, shave their heads and put on the yellow robe and get free board and lodgings, but they are no more *pongyis* than you are, David. The yellow robe gets a lot of abuse in this country, unfortunately. Sometimes it is even used as a hiding place by thieves and murderers. The old *pongyis* know, but they say nothing. They just pray that the offenders will be converted. They never are, of course."

"The bishop wouldn't like to hear you say that," David said, driving carefully through the badly lit streets. "Priests are supposed to believe in the efficacy of prayer, aren't they?"

"I've done my share of praying for the conversion of thieves and murderers," Caraday said. "I haven't seen it work yet."

"And it won't," said David. "That's why I think you should get the Army in."

Then they were drawing up outside Ho Sang's store. The huge dental chart above the entrance was lit up by a light at either end of the store front: the big teeth snarled or smiled a welcome, depending on one's attitude towards Ho Sang. Caraday and the Chinese boy got out, and the latter went round to get his bicycle out of the back of the Land Rover.

"Don't wait for me," Caraday said. "Go on to the hospital, then pick me up on the way back."

"I'd like to hear what message Ho Sang has for you," David said.

"I'll tell you. I promise."

David let in the gears and drove on. Maureen looked sideways at him, puzzled by the relationship between the two men. "You shouldn't ride him so hard."

"He needs it. He's like a man with a tumor. He'll be better off without it, but he's afraid of the operation."

"What caused this tumor?"

"I wish I knew. It's a pity we can't X-ray a man's mind."

"I'm glad we can't," she said. "A man is entitled to his secrets."

They reached the hospital and David took the Land Rover up the drive and pulled up outside the nurses' bungalow. He switched off the engine and got out with Maureen. The light was on in Rose's room, but as soon as they stepped up on to the verandah the light went out. Maureen looked at David, but said nothing. She went into her room and he waited on the verandah, looking along towards Rose's closed door. Did she have someone in the room with her? Had Shero ever come down here to the hospital and spent the night with her? She was someone else with a secret.

Maureen came out with a small airline bag. "I've got all I want." She noticed the direction of his gaze. "Leave her alone."

"My dear girl—" he said defensively: it was his stock phrase whenever she admonished or criticised him. Then he smiled, put his arm about her shoulder and stepped down off the verandah with her. As he opened the door of the Land Rover for her, Maung Zan came across from his office.

"I wanted to see you," David said. "May I borrow that kit I took out to Mong Na this morning?"

In the yellow light of the headlamps, Maung Zan looked tired and wan. "Has Michael got worse?"

"It's only a matter of hours. There's not much I can do, but I'd like some more morphine on hand. There's none up at the house."

"I know. I brought it back with me today. I saw how ill he looked. I was afraid—"

"Of suicide?" David shook his head. "I don't think so. You forget how strong a Catholic he is now. He's looking forward to Heaven. He wouldn't want to spoil his chances of getting there."

"Must you always be so cynical?" Maureen said angrily.

David looked at her patiently. "My dear girl, I was not being cynical. I was stating a fact." He turned back to Maung Zan. "In any case, he would probably need a massive dose to kill him now. He must have a tolerance for it, you've been dosing him so long."

"Yes." Maung Zan turned and called out in Kachin. The

small boy, Karim Naung, appeared out of the shadows like a silent Puck. Maung Zan spoke to him and the boy went off at a run, shaming them with his enthusiasm and making him feel old and hopeless. Maung Zan said, "If there is anything I can do—"

"Nothing," David said. "You have enough on your hands now. How is Moriarty?"

Maung Zan smiled, but it was a tired smile: even humour was a trial of strength for him tonight. "Number One Patient. He has two distinctions. One, he was singled out for some sort of vengeance by Shero, although he doesn't know why. Two, he survived, and that means he has figured in a miracle. He will be up and walking about tomorrow. He's awfully keen to tell everyone what happened to him. He has already told everyone here in the hospital. Tomorrow he will want to go outside and publicly exhibit himself."

"Will you let him?" Maureen asked.

Maung Zan shrugged. "Why not? If it speeds his recovery, what harm is there? Conceit and vanity have their uses."

"You are starting to sound like David. Cynical."

Maung Zan looked up at David and smiled. "Are you flattered, old chap?"

"No. Annoyed. Who will notice me if there is another cynic trying to steal my limelight? I have my vanity, too."

"I can vouch for that," said Maureen. "I'll give you a reference on that any time you ask, dear boy."

Then Karim Naung came running back with the medical kit. He handed it to David, who took it, then put out a hand and patted the boy on the head. Karim Naung looked startled, then ducked quickly away. He stood for a moment poised on one foot, then he darted off into the shadows. David stared after him in puzzlement.

"What the devil—"

"You shouldn't have touched him on the head," Maung Zan said. "That's infra dig, old chap. Burmans don't touch each other like Westerners do. Especially on the head."

David looked back at the nurses' bungalow, at Rose's still darkened window. "Rose was wrong. I haven't learned very much at all since I've been out here."

"Perhaps it would have been better if you had learned nothing at all." Maung Zan was looking in the same direction as David. Down on the road the *katein* procession went past, banging its cymbals and drums: it could never offer enough gifts, enough prayers could never be said to grant him his wish. In the yellow glow of the headlamps his face was a

200

mask of anguish. He will never be a cynic, Maureen thought: he is too susceptible to pain. It seemed to require a physical effort for him to drag his gaze away from where Rose sat or lay hiding in the darkness of her room. He said abruptly, as if he had only just come out to meet them: "The man-eater killed another man today."

David recognised the need for a change of topic. "Whereabouts this time?"

"Near a village called Arahzup. That's on the other side of the river, almost opposite the mission."

"I'll tell Charlie. He needs a tiger. Perhaps he'll settle for that one."

They said goodnight to Maung Zan and got into the Land Rover. As they drove down the drive, Maureen looked back. The light had gone on again in Rose's room. She saw Maung Zan hesitate, then he went up on to the verandah of the bungalow and walked along towards Rose's room. The Land Rover had turned out of the drive and into the road before he reached Rose's door. She was glad. She did not want to be a witness, even at a distance, to the door's not being opened to his knock.

Caraday and Ho Sang were waiting for them outside the dentist shop. The *katein* procession went by, a long noisy dragon of gaiety; but the faces of the old Chinese and the priest remained closed up: they reflected none of the townsfolk's celebration. Several of the youths came out of the procession and circled round the two men in a dance; but they recognised the mood of the two foreigners and soon moved on. David, driving the Land Rover slowly past the edge of the procession, wondered what would be the mood of the people if they knew of Rose's contact with Shero. Would they forget their gifts and offer Rose herself as some sort of sacrifice? These people were Buddhists, they killed no living thing, but their patience and principles must run out some time.

As David brought the Land Rover to a halt, Caraday jumped quickly into the rear seat. Ho Sang closed the door after him and stood looking in, the passing torches of the procession making swirling pools of yellow fire of his thick glasses.

"Try not to think too much about it, Charlie." He looked apologetically at David and Maureen. "I have just given him bad news. It was necessary. Better to learn it from me than from someone else."

"What was it, Charlie?" David looked over his shoulder at

Caraday, who was slumped in one corner of the rear seat. He held his unlit pipe between his hands and he was working it round and round, like a man with a gun trying to find the courage to shoot himself. "You promised to tell me, remember?"

Caraday's voice was dull and mechanical: "Rose *was* with Shero last night. It was Shero who ordered Moriarty's eye to be put out. He did it because he thought I'd left Moriarty behind in Mong Na as a spy."

"Charlie." Ho Sang's voice was patient and kind. He spoke with the voice of a man who had seen more sadness than all of them put together. He had seen famine and flood, seen a thousand people die a lingering death from starvation; he knew that life could always hold something worse, that the ultimate pain was never reached till death. "Charlie, do not blame yourself."

"It was my fault!" Caraday burst out. He sat up, clutching the pipe: he looked as if he were about to drive the stem of it into his temple. "I shouldn't have left him there! Everything I do turns into disaster for someone else!"

David wrenched himself round in his seat. Maureen, sitting beside him, thought he was going to hurl himself at Caraday. "For God's sake, Caraday! Stop beating your breast so bloody hard! It was no more your fault than it was mine or Maureen's or even Moriarty's himself. All you are looking for is a cross to carry up Calvary. You'd be more help, be a better Christian, if you like to call it that, if you went out looking for Shero, got the Army to track him down and kill him, instead of sitting there chanting *mea culpa* and looking for some place where you can hang from a cross in public. You're no better than Moriarty—you're making an exhibition of your charity, just as he does of his piety!"

Caraday looked away, out of the window of the Land Rover. He slumped back in his seat, as if David had dealt him a physical blow. The *katein* procession came back, its torches throwing shadows that danced across his stiff and bony face like spasms of pain.

"David, you have no right to say such things—" Maureen said.

"No, he's right." Caraday's voice was once more dull and mechanical. The voice of the confessional, David thought, calming down now. Both sides of the confessional: the priest and the sinner. "He's right. *Mea culpa* is no answer to anything."

Chapter 11

1

Michael died as the sun came up over the Mountain With No Name. He sank into a coma just after midnight and after that it was only a question of how long before he died. The three of them, David, Maureen and Caraday, sat by his bed, each wrapped in the cocoon of his own thoughts. It was a quiet farewell to Michael; grief in this room was a silent emotion. Maureen got up once and went out and made coffee; but even the passing of the cups brought no small talk. Once they heard the sawing of a leopard up on the hill behind the mission, and Caraday raised his head automatically, like an old hunter; but there was no recognition in his eyes of the sound he had heard, and a moment later he dropped his head again. A nerve twitched in Michael's temple, as if he, too, had heard the sound; but it was the echo of a sound he had heard forty years before, that of another leopard in another land, and the tremor in the temple was the reflex of an action performed by a young man a long way from death and decay. Only David saw the movement of the nerve, but he knew the strange way a body could act of its own accord, and it gave him no hope. Michael's mind, the essence of the man, was already dead.

David sat in the uncomfortable wooden chair saying goodbye to his father through the long slow hours of the night. The electric light hanging from the ceiling had been turned off, and a small kerosene lamp burned on a chest of drawers against one wall, throwing just enough light to illuminate the bed and enough shadows to darken the shabby bareness of the rest of the room. The light is kind to him, David thought: it hides the meanness of where he spent his last night on earth. Then he remembered that his father had never been concerned with the grandeur nor even the comfort of a place. Austerity had been the keynote of Michael's life for as long as David could remember. It came back to him now with a certain wry amusement that, as a boy, he had often felt that his father had chosen his school for him because it had a certain resemblance to the austerity and discomfort of barracks. He had resented his father in those days, and gradually the resentment had grown like a weed into hate. But there was none of that now, neither resentment nor hate, only a sense of loss, of love that had come too late. In the dimness of the room, sitting well back in the shadows as if to hide his confession, he finally admitted to love.

As the first tide of daylight began to wash up into the sky beyond the window, Caraday looked across at David. "I'd like to anoint him now, David. Is that all right?"

David nodded. "But I'd rather not watch." He stood up and went to the door. "I wish I could help you with a prayer or two, but I can't. I'll leave it to you to speak for me."

He went out on to the verandah. The light was increasing in the sky and the stars had begun to pale and die like snow crystals before the heat of the not yet risen sun. The mist was rising from the river, climbing up the face of the cliff opposite. There was an utter stillness to everything that only seemed to accentuate the coming death within the bungalow, as if the whole valley were waiting for Michael's last breath. David's boots scraped on some gravel on the verandah floor and the sound was like the rasp of a file against the eardrum. He stood still, almost at attention, trying to retain the silence, as if it were some sort of comfort he needed.

Then there was the crunch of boots on the gravel path and George came round the corner of the bungalow. He saluted. "How is the colonel, sir?"

"He will be dead this morning, George." It was blunt, but he knew that the Gurkha would not understand any sympathetic evasions. "But what are you doing up so early?"

"I have not been to bed, sir. I knew this was the colonel's last night—" He did not explain how he had known and David did not ask him. "I have been waiting in case I was needed, sir."

All his life David had fought sentiment: it was the disease the cynic feared most. Now he felt a rush of regard and affection for the small tough Gurkha who had spent the night standing guard over his colonel who was already beyond protection. "The colonel would want me to thank you, George."

The Gurkha bowed his head and looked away for a moment. When he looked back his face was expressionless, but before he could say anything, Maureen came out on to the verandah. The sun came up over the mountain, striking directly into her face, so that her eyes were shut for the moment as she said, "He is dead, David. Just a moment ago."

David looked down at George. "You'll be needed now, George. We'll bury the colonel today, over there." He nodded towards the small cemetery beyond the meadow: in the morning light the crosses shone like icicles, cold as death itself. "Later, when the town is awake, go down to Sheromere and order a coffin. They may have one, or one may have to be made, but we shall want it this morning, you understand? Nothing fancy," he said, remembering his father's passion for austerity. "The colonel wouldn't like that."

George saluted, turned on his heel and went away with a crunch of gravel along the path and round the corner of the bungalow. Maureen said, "Did you have to be quite so abrupt with him?"

"He understands orders. He's been taking them all his life. At a time like this, the less his routine is upset, the better he'll be." He looked at her, saw for the first time the tears on her cheeks. "I'm trying to be kind to him, dear girl."

She nodded. "I know. It's just that—Oh, David!" She turned towards him, laid her face against his chest and wept. He stood with his arms round her, his mind churning but no clear thought emerging, feeling the sobs that shook her as something within his own body, wanting to weep but unable to squeeze tears out of ducts that had been dry too long. His grief was no less than hers for the lack of tears. His loss, he knew, was greater. He wanted to weep, not just for the death of his father, but for all the wasted years.

Caraday came to the door. "Do you want to see him, David? I'll go down and get Zan to come up—he'll have to certify the death. We'll bury him today. In this climate—"

"I know," David said, saving Caraday the embarrassment of speaking of Michael's body as if it were a piece of fruit or meat that would not keep. "I've already told George to get us a coffin."

"You would like him buried here, wouldn't you?"

"I think that's what *he'd* like."

He went past Caraday into the bungalow and down to the room where Michael lay beyond pain, love or regret. He lay ready for the last inspection, arms stiffly at his side. His eyelids, nostrils, ears and lips glistened with the oil with which Caraday had anointed him. Looking at his father, David got the same impression that all dead persons gave him, that the lifeless body was considerably smaller than the living man had been. Michael Breton had lost all his air of authority. He was no longer a colonel of Gurkhas, nor even an amaldar: he was just a ranker in the regiment of the dead.

Maung Zan came up just before breakfast to certify the death. He came back again in mid-morning for the funeral, wearing his best suit and a black *gaung-baung*. There was no Requiem Mass. "What's the point?" Caraday had said to David. "Although it's not me who should say that. But who'd be at the Mass? A Lutheran, an agnostic, a Buddhist, a Taoist, Rose—" He shrugged. "And George—I haven't asked him what his religion is. There'd be only two Catholics at the Mass, your father and me. I think he deserves more than a farce like that." But when Maung Zan came up for the funeral he brought another Catholic with him: Moriarty.

Looking more Indian than ever beneath the turban of his bandages, Moriarty got shakily down from the hospital Land Rover. "I came to pay my respects," he said to David. "I am an Indian who always had respect for the English, Mr. Breton."

Don't spoil it, David thought, and felt sorry for the Indian who would never learn to moderate his emotions. "Thank you, Moriarty."

Moriarty glanced at the plain unvarnished coffin sticking out of the back of the consulate Land Rover. He blessed himself elaborately and looked back at David. "A pity a miracle could not have spared your father, Mr. Breton. When someone as unworthy as myself is granted one—"

"That's enough!" Caraday snapped. He was wearing his surplice and in the breeze that came up from the river it fluttered about his long thin frame. He looked as if he were about to say something else to Moriarty, then he seemed to think better of it and turned away. "All right, George. Drive slowly, and we'll walk behind."

The Gurkha saluted, got into the Land Rover, started up the engine and began his colonel's last journey. The mourners fell in behind the slowly moving vehicle. David walked just behind Caraday. Feeling self-conscious here in these wild hills, he had got out his suit and donned it with a collar and tie; he had been glad he had, when he saw that Maung Zan had also dressed for the occasion. Behind David were Maureen and Rose, Maung Zan and Ho Sang, and at the rear Moriarty walking alone. It was a motley procession for a man who had marched at the head of a regiment, a poor cortege for a man who, had he died earlier and in another land, would have been given a military funeral, been buried to the roll of drums, the crash of rifles and the farewell from a lone bugle.

Rose, wearing a black rice silk coat buttoned to her throat, had not spoken to anyone when she had come up from the town with Ho Sang in a jeep taxi. She walked now with eyes downcast, remote from the others. There was no air of sympathy about her; she was here because it was expected of her. As they reached the grave, she lifted her head and glanced at David; but as soon as she saw him looking at her, she dropped her gaze again. She was ready to flee at any moment, and this morning he had no desire to stop her.

The grave had been dug by two men from the mission staff and now they stood by to lower the coffin into the ground. Over by the fence that divided the cemetery from the meadow, a line of peasants stood, curious but not wanting to intrude. There was very little privacy in the East as Westerners understood it, but these simple hill people did respect the privacy of grief. A caravan of buffalo-drawn carts came down the road skirting the meadow, but didn't stop; the drivers stared across at the group standing round the open grave, but none of them halted his cart. The sun blazed down, the kites wheeled in the sky like angels of death, and Michael was buried quickly and without fuss, as if Caraday wanted the sad affair to be over and done with. There was no eulogy, no roll of drums, no sad note of bugle: only the thud of earth on the coffin, a muted cough or two, and a muffled sob from Maureen.

And that's it, David thought. Here on this hillside, just another cross among those already here, the white cross that marks the final footnote to a man's life, he will wait for whatever is the end of everything. I'll never come back here, and so the years that are to come will be just like those that have gone: half a world will separate us. But with one difference: for a moment we understood each other.

He felt someone take his elbow: it was Caraday. "I think he is happy now, David. You may not agree, but I'm sure it is the way he would have looked at it. When you love God as he did, there is no sadness in death."

"I can't argue, Charlie. Polemics are no substitute for a funeral oration. I'd rather have a drink."

Caraday looked at him out of a face dark with fatigue and sorrow. "I think our arguments are over, David. I'll be sorry to see you go. Just as sorry—" He looked back at the grave, now rapidly being filled up as the two men threw in the earth. "I mean that, David."

2

After the funeral David and Caraday took Maureen back to the hospital in the Land Rover. Maung Zan and the others had already gone straight from the graveside; Rose had walked quickly down to the hospital Land Rover and the others had followed her. Caraday had taken a step, as if to go after Rose, but he would have had to run to catch up with her and he had thought better of it. David had looked at him and Caraday had shrugged, then turned towards the bungalow. Twenty minutes later they, too, were driving down to the hospital.

Maureen was still upset by Michael's death, even though she had been waiting for it; her concern, and the lack of sleep last night, made her look pale and ill. When David left her and Caraday at the hospital, she said, "I'm going to bed for a couple of hours. You won't need me, will you?"

"No," David said. "I'll come down and see you tonight. There's nothing to keep us here now, so we may as well go back to Mandalay tomorrow with George."

Caraday, who had been as quiet as Maureen, looked up at that. "Of course. Somehow I'd forgotten that you'd have to be leaving now—I mean, not for another week at least—"

"There's no point in staying on, Charlie. Ask Zan about having dinner with the three of us tonight. You two can wish us bon voyage or whatever they say here in Burma. Then we'll push off in the morning."

He left them and drove on to the telegraph office in the centre of the town. He went in and wired the Embassy in Rangoon and the consulate in Mandalay that his father had died and had been buried in Sheromere. The clerk read the message and looked up sympathetically. "Colonel Breton was a very nice man, sir. I sometimes sent messages for him. Will you be taking his place, sir?"

David looked up, startled. "Eh? No, of course not." His voice sounded sharp in his own ears. He tried to soften its tone: "No, the British Government doesn't work that way, I'm afraid. Except in Parliament."

The clerk didn't understand the sarcasm. "I took over this window from my father," he said with pride; he held up his ink-stained fingers. "We have been writing messages for almost fifty years, my father and I."

"Congratulations," said David, paid for the telegram and went out of the office. He had no desire at all to succeed his father, least of all as Consul. He had come, belatedly, to love his father, but he had no wish to emulate him. Nor would Michael want him to. One of the successes of their reunion was that they had met as equals, as man to man.

He stepped down from the porch of the telegraph office and almost knocked Rose down as she came hurrying through the crowd. He grabbed her by the arm and saved her from falling headlong into the filth-littered gutter. "You should walk more sedately. *Cheong-sams* are not meant for running in. Nor shoes like that." She was dressed in a red *cheong-sam* and stilt-heeled shoes: she did not look like a girl who had just come from a funeral. "Are you on your way to a party?"

"Let me go, David, *please!*"

"No, I think it's time you and I had another talk, Rose." He kept his grip of her elbow. The crowd going by them hadn't stopped, but several people had slowed down and were looking back at them. "Don't make a scene, dear girl. Try and look as if you are glad to be with me. Where shall we go?"

For a moment it looked as if she might struggle to break away from him. She looked up at him, her dark eyes flashing with what could have been hate for him; then suddenly her eyes went dull, and she gently removed his hand from her elbow. "All right, David. There is a tea shop at the corner. It is not very elegant, but if you don't mind—"

They walked along the street, past the curious bystanders in the shop doorways, and went into the crowded Chinese tea shop on the corner of the street. The shop was wide open on two sides and as they took their place at a table, half a dozen children gathered on the street outside to stand and stare in at them. The other customers had also turned to look at them; and when the owner of the shop came to take their order, he smiled down at them with the same frank curiosity.

209

Till now, David had never realised the privacy there was in a Lyons tea shop in London. He had not been into a Lyons since his student days, but he had memories of its being a horribly public place. This was much worse.

"Welcome." The owner was a young Chinese, plump and happy. He gave them a golden smile, and David guessed he was probably one of Ho Sang's better customers. David had learned from Caraday that Ho Sang might no longer be strong enough in the wrists to be good at extractions, but he still made the best gold teeth in Sheromere. The young Chinese carried five of them, all shown to their best advantage. "Miss Churchill comes here often, but it is the first time we have had the pleasing to meet you, sir."

"Bring us some tea, Kung." It was evident that Rose knew the young Chinese well, and David wondered if he had been another of her boy friends. "And tell those children to go away."

Kung shouted at the children, who all laughed at him but took off at once. The customers at the other tables turned back to their cups of tea and their desultory conversation, and in a moment Kung came back with two cups of pale tea for Rose and David. "Special. I always serve you special tea, is not so, Miss Churchill?"

"Always," said Rose, but gave him no encouragement.

"Nothing but special for her, sir," Kung said to David, then ducked his head in a small bow and went away.

"He's talkative for a Chinese, isn't he?" David said.

"We're not all as inscrutable as you Westerners like to make out."

"Oh, so you're Chinese today? Are you going to be inscrutable or not?"

"Depends what you want to talk to me about." She sipped her tea. "I can be awfully inscrutable when I like."

"No doubt of that, dear girl." He sipped his own tea, wishing it were stronger. He had had no breakfast and now he was beginning to feel hungry. He looked towards the counter at the rice cakes there, but decided against them. He looked about him, then leaned forward, resting his arms on the table, his face only a foot or so from hers. He dropped his voice. "You spent Saturday night with Shero, am I right?" She did not look up, but continued to stare down into her cup. "You could save all these people." He nodded at the customers in the tea shop, at the crowd passing along the street outside. A woman went by, one arm holding a baby on her hip, the other arm just a useless stump. He nodded at her. "What tiger got at her? I wonder. Was it your tiger or the man-eater?"

Rose looked after the woman with flat interest. "She was run over by a police jeep. I helped Maung Zan take off her arm."

"All right," he said, smiling. "I picked the wrong one. But what about Moriarty?" he said, and stopped smiling.

She shook her head, looked around her as if about to get up and rush out of the shop, then abruptly looked back at him. "I told you, I had nothing to do with what happened to Moriarty. I knew about what happened to him, but it was *afterwards.*"

"Was it you who told them which was Moriarty's good eye?"

She looked away again. Someone waved to her from the street outside and she nodded back. Then she looked back at David and for the first time relaxed in her chair, as if she had decided to give up any idea of escaping and hear everything he had to say. "I told them. I didn't know what it was all about. We were just talking—"

"Who? You and Shero?"

She nodded. A radio had been turned on in the shop: a girl sang of love in a voice and melody that grated against David's ear. "How was I to know what they were going to do?"

"How well do you know Shero?"

"Not awfully well." She hesitated, then she said, "But well enough in a way, I suppose."

"He's your lover, is that what you mean?" She hesitated again, then she nodded. She looked up at the radio on the shelf behind the counter, as if the girl singer had just said something that had some significance. Then she looked back at David as he said, "Why, Rose? I mean, why pick a man like him?"

She fiddled with the heavy bracelet on her wrist. It consisted of tiny figurines and amulets strung together on a cheap rolled-gold chain, and he wondered what significance they had. Did she wear the bracelet as some sort of charm against evil or disaster? If she did, it had done her no good. "Remember I told you how I was treated down in Rangoon? I didn't tell you all of it. I went with an Englishman down there for a whole year. I was his mistress, if you like to call it that. I thought I was going to be his wife. In the end it turned out

211

he thought of me only as his concubine. There are a lot of words, aren't there, to describe what a woman can be to a man? Lady-love, mistress, inamorata, concubine, his wench, his bit of fluff—" Again he had the feeling that he was listening to a schoolgirl reciting: she knew all the words in the thesaurus of lust. He waited, but she stopped before she got to the filthy words. "He was working for the government as an engineering adviser. I thought he was going to take me back to England. He had left Burma before I even knew he was going. I got a letter from him, posted in Rome—it took him all that way to write half a dozen lines—saying he knew I would understand, that I would have been very unhappy if he had taken me back to St. Albans. What is St. Albans like?"

"Hardly the place for a concubine. The Romans had them there in the old days, but the practice died out when the middle class took over. I don't think you would have been very happy there, Rose."

"Even as his wife?"

"Do you think he ever intended marrying you?"

The girl on the radio finished her song with a thin reedy sob. Although David could not understand the words, he knew the song was cheap and banal: Tin Pan Alley now ran all the way round the world. "No, I suppose not," Rose said, and signalled to Kung for more tea. He came, took away their cups and was back in a moment with fresh tea.

"You are enjoying your little chat? This is more special tea. Nothing but special for Miss Churchill, sir."

"Yes," said David, thinking of the English engineer who had had other ideas about what was special for Miss Churchill. He waited till Kung had gone away again, then he said, "That doesn't explain why you picked on Shero."

"No, it doesn't, does it? And it would be awfully hard to explain. But you see, David, all I want now is money. And Shero has it, lots of it."

"Your grandfather isn't short of it, I'm told."

"He hasn't as much as Shero. And I can't ask him for it. Not if I want to use it to go away from him." She was selfish, but she was not heartless. She still knew the softer side of love. "No, some day I'm going to go away with Shero—"

"That's what he's told you?" She nodded. "Didn't your Englishman tell you the same thing?"

She tried to drink her tea, but it was too hot. She almost dropped the cup back in its saucer, spilling the tea. "It is going to be different with Shero. We're the same kind, don't

212

you see? Remember you said it was the outsiders who had to help each other? Shero and I are both outsiders—"

"What help are you to Shero?"

"He needs a woman, someone to love him—"

"Oh God Almighty!" he said, and knocked over his own cup of tea. Kung rushed to wipe up the mess, but David waved him away. Kung retreated, as if he knew now that something critical was happening between them, that they wanted to be alone. The other customers were huddled over their cups, but David was aware of them looking at him and Rose out of the corners of their almond eyes. "Why don't you grow up, Rose? Life isn't anything like those cheap romances you read. No man needs love," he said, and suddenly knew that was a lie. Argument died down in him like a fire doused by a sudden flood of water. His father had needed love. Why shouldn't Shero? He said weakly, "You'll be ditched again, Rose. If a harmless English engineer from St. Albans can ditch you, what's to stop a murderer like Shero doing the same?"

"I don't think of him as a murderer. He's not like that with me."

He was getting nowhere with her. "What man takes his trade into bed, except the gigolo? Do you think I act the plastic surgeon when I'm in bed with a woman?"

"I wouldn't know," she said without coquetry.

He stood up, put some money on the table. "Stay close to the cherry trees, Rose. Otherwise you're going to be hurt."

Kung came towards them as they made their way out of the shop. "Come again, sir. Bring Miss Churchill. Perhaps next time I can let you have a special private room. Just the place for a little chat—"

David nodded. He knew there would be no more little chats with Rose. She had talked to him today, but she might just as well have been inscrutable. He hadn't learned what he had wanted to know, the whereabouts of Shero. "So you won't tell me where we can find Shero?" She shook her head. "I could turn you over to the police, you know."

"Father Caraday and Ho Sang wouldn't let you do that."

"You'd use them, wouldn't you? You talk of love, Rose, but what about some love for those two men?"

"They don't need it. Grandfather is too old to care about it any more. And everyone loves Father Caraday. He doesn't need any love from me."

"You're a calculating little bit of fluff, aren't you?" He was tired now: he resorted to insult, the cheap weapon of which he had been a master.

"I had an awfully hard time growing up, David, I told you that."

The crowd flowed past them as they stood by the side of the road. There was the sound of a drum being banged, of cymbals clashing tinnily, and the *katein* procession came down the street. There were half a dozen carts drawn by skinny ponies: each cart bore a tall bamboo frame on which was hung the gifts for the monks: pots, pans, umbrellas, brooms: the procession looked like a mobile church bazaar. Youths wearing masks, some in fancy costume, pranced at the head of the long column that followed the carts. At the rear of the procession waddled the fattest man David had ever seen, clad only in a *longyi*, his bare upper torso, face and bald skull painted with a white solution. Breasts hung down on him as on a woman; he opened a toothless red mouth to scream some song. Obscene as a pornographic postcard, he undulated towards David. The latter stepped back to avoid him, and as he did so, Rose darted across the road through the procession. David saw the red *cheong-sam* melting away into the crowd on the other side of the street, but there was neither the opportunity nor the urge to chase after her. He stared at the mountainous creature quivering before him like a huge mound of white jelly, then he turned sharply on his heel, resisting the temptation to spit, and pushed his way through the crowd towards the Land Rover. He wondered what gifts, if any, Rose was sending to the *katein*. It was hardly likely she would be asking for prayers for release from Shero.

3

He drove back to the hospital, where Caraday and Maung Zan were waiting for him. "What kept you?" Caraday said. "I was just about to come looking for you. I thought maybe you'd gone walkabout."

"What's that?"

"The abos in Australia do it. They go off for long hikes in the bush when they want to get away from things."

"An admirable habit, except that I've never been a keen walker." He got out of the Land Rover. "I met Rose. We had a little chat over the tea cups."

"What did you learn?"

"Nothing." He decided that he owed Rose some loyalty, although he was not sure why he should. He was still angry with her for her unco-operative attitude, but he had also now begun to feel sorry for her.

"One never does learn anything from her," Maung Zan said bitterly. He sounded as if he had now lost all patience with her; he was more than just the disappointed lover. "I think we might all be better off if she went back to Rangoon."

"I think there is very little chance of that," said David, and left it at that. He knew the others would probably guess why she would not go back to Rangoon. He looked at Caraday. "Ready to go back to the mission?"

"Zan and I are going out to Arahzup. There's a bit of a mystery about this man who was taken by the tiger yesterday. He's a stranger to Arahzup."

"How do they know? How much of him did the tiger leave?"

"Enough. Tigers are much like humans—they always eat the best flesh first. They don't bother with the head."

David grimaced. "No more details. I haven't had breakfast yet."

"Do you want to come?" Caraday asked kindly.

"I'll come," he said, not wanting to go back to the mission, not wanting to sit there in the empty bungalow and have time to think. He was suddenly afraid that grief might catch up with him as a delayed reaction.

They drove back through Sheromere and down to the small ferry at the bottom of town. They crossed the river and turned east along the road that led to Arahzup. They passed a wide clearing in the forests where a dozen elephants, worked by their *oozies*, or drivers, were manoeuvring huge teak logs from a stack beside the road towards a muddy runway down which the logs slid into the river. Down on the river the logs were being bound together to make huge rafts, on which rough huts were being erected. The *oozies* on the elephants, the men down on the rafts, all shouted and waved to the Land Rover as it drove past, recognising Caraday and calling his name. He waved back, his dark face, which up till now had been closed up with sorrow, suddenly coming alight with friendliness. He pulled his head back inside the cabin.

"Those rafts go all the way down to Rangoon. I've been promising myself a trip on one of them one of these days. I'll probably never make it." He looked out the window again, at the river flowing by beyond the trees. "A man could get away from a lot of things on that river."

215

Then they were coming to Arahzup. The Mountain With No Name towered right above it; the village looked like something that might have slid down the slopes. It was one of the poorest villages David had seen since coming up here, a collection of rude huts built on high wooden piles that looked ready to collapse if someone should dance or jump in one of the dwellings. Ladders led up to the huts, and beneath were the livestock. The huts were built round a muddy square, and the whole of the village was surrounded by a fence of sharp stakes interlaced with thorn bushes. The villagers opened a gate as they saw the Land Rover approaching and David drove into the middle of the square.

"These people keep to themselves," Maung Zan said. "They will have nothing to do with us down in Sheromere." Caraday had got down from the Land Rover and the villagers came crowding round him, shaking his hand and smiling at him. "But Charlie is their darling. Isn't that the song we used to sing?"

"I'm surprised you remember, Zan."

"I remember a lot from those days, David. They were worth remembering." Maung Zan smiled and winked, but there was really no cheerfulness in his face. He spoke like a man who had only memories left, a middle-aged man who had no interest in the years ahead. "Well, shall we look at what the tiger has left of the dead stranger?"

"You and Charlie have the same macabre sense of humour as first-year students."

"You are too accustomed to Mayfair, old chap. Nothing is really macabre in these mountains."

He looked around at the villagers, who stood eyeing him suspiciously and without the welcome that had been accorded Caraday. Of course, David thought, he's a Burmese: in this village he is an outsider even in his own country. But Maung Zan seemed unaware of the hostility of the villagers; or perhaps he just did not care. He turned back to David. "When I first came back here from London, I was like you. But as Charlie says, the country grows on you."

The villagers led them to a buffalo cart that was piled high with thorn bushes. They pulled off the bushes and exposed what looked to be a mound of banana fronds.

"The thorn bushes would have put the tiger off if he'd had any ideas about coming back for his kill," Caraday said. "This crowd here are about the most superstitious mob around these parts. They wouldn't take the body of a stranger into

216

their huts, since they wouldn't know what evil spirits he had been carrying."

"No converts in this village?"

"Not a chance," said Caraday, and turned back as Maung Zan moved forward to take the banana fronds from the dead man. Before the frond that covered the man's head had been removed, David knew who he was: the suède shoes, muddy and scuffed though they were now, hanging from what was left of the man's legs, were easily recognisable. Caraday looked at David. "Those are your shoes, aren't they?"

David nodded and looked up at the dark shape of the mountain. "Where did the tiger jump on him?"

Caraday spoke to one of the villagers. "He says they found him on a path up there on that first ridge." He nodded towards the mountain, his face expressionless. "So now we know where both tigers are."

"The first thing to do is to have this man buried," Maung Zan said. "Then we'll think about hunting tigers." He spoke to the head man of the village, an old man whose face was so covered with wrinkles and scars that at first glance he seemed to be wearing a net over it. He answered Maung Zan out of a mouth that showed only one yellow tooth, hissing his words through withered gums. Maung Zan turned to David. "He wants to know if you want your shoes. I told him they were yours."

"Hardly, old boy." He looked down at the old man's feet; bony and calloused, they looked like the feet of some ancient lizard. "He's welcome to them if he wants them."

Maung Zan spoke again to the head man, who flashed a one-tooth grin at David and bowed in thanks. "He thanks you," said Maung Zan, "but says it is bad luck to walk in a dead man's shoes."

"Those shoes may be bad luck for Shero," David said. "Now we know where he is. I think it is time we got the Army in, Charlie."

"I think so, too," Maung Zan said.

Caraday looked as if he were going to argue, then he shrugged. "I wish we could do it without them, but I suppose you're right."

"Will these people help us?" David asked.

Caraday shook his head. "Not if Shero and his men are hidden out at the top of the mountain. That's where the *nats* are." David noticed that he always spoke of the *nats* in the same way as the villagers themselves must speak of them, as

217

if he actually acknowledged their existence. Perhaps that was the secret of his popularity with the local people: he succeeded in being one of them, even when his beliefs ran contrary to theirs. "We'd never get these people up beyond that first ridge."

"All right then, it's up to the Army. I don't think we should lose any time." As David got back into the Land Rover, he looked up at the mountain. "I'll bet Shero already knows we are here. Would he have any friends in this village?"

"He might have," Caraday said. "But no one here speaks English, so they won't know what we've got in mind." He and Maung Zan got into the Land Rover, the villagers crowded round outside. "But the less we say, the better. At least till we get to the D.C. You never know who's listening, even in Sheromere."

"Do you have to approach the D.C.?"

"Red tape, old chap," said Maung Zan. "You British taught us that."

When they got back to the hospital and pulled up in front of Maung Zan's office, Maureen came out of the ward and walked across towards them. "You didn't sleep long," David said, looking at his watch. "Not even a couple of hours."

"I couldn't sleep. My mind was too wide awake." She turned to Maung Zan. "To give myself something to keep me occupied, I went across to help in the wards. I think you should have another look at Moriarty, Maung Zan. I don't think he should have come to the funeral this morning. He appears to have pulled some stitches in his eye. I didn't touch the dressing, but he's complaining of the pain—"

"Damn!" said Caraday, and at once strode off towards the ward. "Come on, Zan, we'd better look at him at once."

Maung Zan followed him, leaving David with Maureen. She took a cigarette from a pack she took from her pocket, and he flicked his lighter for her. "I don't think I shall even be able to sleep tonight. My mind is like an ant heap." She made a gesture of busyness with her fingers.

"Mine will probably be the same tonight. Up till now I just haven't had time to think." He told her about his meeting with Rose and of the identity of the tiger victim out at Arahzup. "Have you seen Rose?"

"She's on duty in one of the wards. We've hardly spoken these last couple of days."

"Don't talk to her, then. At least not till this evening. By then the Army should be out after Shero, might even have caught him."

Maureen drew on her cigarette, then blew out the smoke in a long fan. She knew as well as Rose the unhappiness that lay in love. "I feel sorry for her, David."

"So do I," he admitted, and she was surprised at the tolerance in his voice. Their roles had been reversed: *he* was the one who was now full of surprises for *her*. "But she'll be better off if Shero is caught. She may not think so at first, but in the long run it will be best for her."

She was tired and strained, but she managed a smile. "No man should ever attempt to tell a girl what is best for her. She won't thank you for it."

"I know," he said with a grin. "She told me as much this morning." They began to walk towards the wards building. "Can you wait another day or two? I mean, about going back to Mandalay? I'd like to be in on the end of this, just to see how it finishes. It should all be over by tomorrow."

"I can wait. I'd like to see how it ends, too."

"We'll have to go back by bus. George will need to leave tomorrow morning with the Land Rover. Consulate work won't stop just because my father has died."

"Will it be safe in the bus? I don't think I could put up with another ambush, David." She dropped the cigarette on the path and trod on it. She looked up at him, and standing close to her, with the sun shining on her face, he saw her clearly again as he once used to see her clearly when lying beside her in bed. In those days there had been the bright shine of happiness or the black light of passion in her eyes; her skin had been clear and glowing, her lips wet from his kisses. Now her eyes were dull from lack of sleep, and there were faint circles under them, like fading bruises. The past couple of weeks of sun had brought out freckles; they stood out now against the paleness of her cheeks. She did not look old, but it seemed to him then that every year she had lived had suddenly come to the surface of her. She was lonely and frightened and she was turning to him for help. Not so long ago he would have been flattered. He was surprised now that he was humbled. He bent down and brushed his lips against her forehead.

"Once they catch Shero, there'll be no more ambushes."

"David—" She was too weak to go on alone: she surrendered. "Do you want me to go to the Mayo?"

His own surrender was as complete: "No. I want you to come back to London with me."

Chapter 12

1

"You will have to stay in bed, Moriarty," Maung Zan said. "You cannot go gallivanting around if it means you are going to keep tearing these stitches."

"Gallivanting?" Moriarty winced as Maung Zan began to re-apply the dressing. "What word is that?"

"It's an old aboriginal word," said David.

"I wonder when Father Caraday is going to teach me the Australian language. Perhaps I could learn now while I am in hospital."

"It would keep you from gallivanting," said David, and turned as Caraday came down the ward and into the dispensary. "Well?"

"Get rid of these dressings, Nurse," Maung Zan said, and the young nurse picked up the white enamel bucket with the discarded dressings and went out of the dispensary. Caraday waited till she had gone, then said, "The D.C. has gone to the *katein*."

"Then we'd better go to the *katein* and get him." David now was possessed by an urge to get something done; he was impatient, like a man who sees the end of a long operation at last in sight. "I'll go with you."

Caraday leaned wearily back against the wall. "Do we have to go for him now? Can't we wait till the *katein* is over? I'm too tired now to go chasing up mountains after tigers."

"Who said you had to go chasing up the mountain? That's why we're getting the Army. Let them do it."

"You can't keep putting it off, Charlie." Maung Zan had recognised Caraday's reluctance. The priest had reached the stage where he was like Moriarty, praying for a miracle to solve everything. "Have you forgotten what Shero did to Moriarty?"

"Of course not!" Caraday straightened up with anger; then looked at Moriarty as if for forgiveness. "That's why I'd like to get Shero myself!"

"There you go thinking of revenge again!" David wanted to shake the priest, to bring him to his senses. "God damn it, why have you always got to make this a personal war between you and Shero? Are you still intent on being the leader around here—" He was suddenly aware of Moriarty watching the two of them, one eye hidden behind its dressing but the other flickering brightly, missing nothing. He turned to the Indian. "We know where Shero is, Moriarty. He is on the Mountain With No Name. Tell Father Caraday that the best thing is to get the Army, tell him to let them do the job of capturing Shero!"

The single eye looked steadily at the three men in turn. Then it looked back at Caraday. "Let the Army capture him, Father. I would not want you to risk your life for me. I should be praying all the time that you were kept safe. Perhaps the Lord would not hear me—He has already granted me one miracle—"

He's overdoing it again, David thought. But Caraday all at once came forward and took the Indian's hand. The latter tried to sit up on the table where he lay, but Maung Zan pushed him gently back. "All right, Moriarty," Caraday said. "We'll get the Army."

"They will get him, Father." Moriarty reached into the pocket of his pyjamas, brought out his rosary beads. "I shall pray for the Army to shoot him down."

"Do that," said David, making for the door, certain now that Caraday would follow him. "A bullet for every bead."

Outside, as they got into the Land Rover, Caraday said, "You didn't have to get him to work on me."

"Why not? Wasn't he your excuse for not wanting the Army? Don't you see yourself as the man of vengeance, the lone wolf—" He slammed in the gears and started the Land Rover with a jerk.

"You're wrong, David." Caraday fell against the door as

the Land Rover swerved out of the gate into the road. The door swung open, but he nimbly saved himself from falling out. He had had plenty of practice in the old mission jeep; danger was familiar at every bend in the road. He slammed the door shut and settled back in the seat, staring straight ahead of him as David drove down the road at furious speed. "I can never tell you why, but you couldn't be more wrong."

They had no trouble finding the *katein*. It was being held in the town's largest temple, down by the river. People were converging on it, dressed in their best, some carrying their gifts that they had not managed to buy in time to have displayed in the procession last night. As David brought the Land Rover to a halt at the gates to the temple, they could hear the slow rhythmic beating of a gong. It was a deep sound that seemed to throb in the air; one could imagine its carrying down the river all the way to Mandalay. To David's ear it had a threatening note. The bells of English churches, as he remembered them, were gay and carefree against the sound of this gong.

They got out of the Land Rover. Caraday took off his boots and David followed suit. They left them among the jumble of shoes and sandals beside the two huge white *chinthes*, the legendary beasts that guarded the entrance to the temple. David glanced up at one of the *chinthes*: its cold blank eye seemed to be a warning not to enter the temple. But nothing could happen to him. He was not here to ask anything of Buddha or the monks, but only to ask the D.C. to make a phone call.

They followed the crowd into the temple. Several people looked curiously at Caraday, but most of them smiled in welcome: they seemed to see nothing strange in a Catholic priest's being here at a Buddhist *katein*. Then it struck David that nothing Caraday did would seem strange to these people; he was not an outsider, but one of them. Caraday spoke to a man, who nodded further into the temple. "Come on," Caraday said. "The D.C. is in one of the side rooms. They're feeding the *pongyis* before the gift-giving."

They pushed through the crowd of people standing outside the door of the side room, everyone making way for them without demur or resentment. The room was bare of furniture except for a score of low tables around which monks squatted in groups of six or seven. Light struck in from windows on the western wall and the room seemed to glow with the reflection from the dozens of saffron robes. The shaven heads of the monks gleamed like so many helmets, almost as if they had been oiled; David remembered the glisten of oil on his father's face, but these men were a long way from death. They ate wolfishly from the heaped bowls that the servers placed before them; they were not hungry, but greedy like children at a party. A tall monk moved among the tables, supervising the serving like a head waiter; he looked determined that everyone should have more than his fill. The food kept coming, brought in on big heaped trays; the room smelled of food, the sweat of the voracious eaters and something that resembled incense. There was no sound from the monks but the slurp and champ of eating; they left all the talking to the tall monk who was seeing they were kept well supplied with food. The scene was by Brueghel, painted over by some Buddhist artist. The day of the *katein*, David thought, was the day the monks forgot their asceticism and became men of the flesh. He had no doubt that it happened in monasteries of all faiths all over the world. He could never bring himself to believe that men could give up the animal pleasures for all time. He wondered what effect this scene was having on Caraday.

The priest was looking about the room. Suddenly he moved forward and spoke to a bald-headed man in a white suit who sat with his back against one of the walls, his feet in bright yellow socks stuck out in front of him. He wore dark glasses, of the type whose lenses were also mirrors: he raised his head as Caraday spoke to him, the whole of the room reflected in the sockets of his bony skull. He shook his head, gesturing at the room about him; but Caraday persisted, and after a moment the man rose and came towards David, standing by the door. He nodded curtly to David and walked out of the temple.

He searched among the shoes and sandals heaped by the base of the *chinthe*, found a pair of new bright tan shoes and pulled them on over his yellow socks, then straightened up irritably. "Why cannot it wait, Father Caraday? The *katein* is very important to us Buddhists. Do I come up and disturb you at your services at Christmas and Easter?" The Deputy Commissioner's voice was high and peevish: the voice of authority in Sheromere was a whine. He sounds like a man with a sore crotch from fence-sitting, David thought; this D.C. wanted to offend no one, not even a murderer like Shero. "Let it wait, Father."

"It can't wait," Caraday said. Now that he had taken the

step, had come here to find the D.C., there was no longer any reluctance to go ahead with the hunt for Shero. "You've got to ring up the Army now, get them here before Shero wakes up to what is happening."

"The Army?" The D.C. bobbed his head: the temple went up and down in the mirror of his glasses, like a building shaken by an earthquake. "Oh, we cannot have *them* up here not—the *Army*—"

"Yes, the Army. Or do you want me to ring through to Rangoon?"

The D.C. hesitated, then he began to lead the way towards the gates. "You priests, you are always interfering—" He looked at David. "You are not a priest, sir?"

"No, I am a doctor."

"Oh yes, they told me about you." He didn't say who "they" were. He had no air of authority, but like all people in authority, he had his spies. Even the weak ones can find someone to kow-tow to them, David thought.

They drove the D.C. back to his office and he got on the phone to the army commander in Myitkyina. He spoke in Kachin, but the whine was still in his voice: he didn't welcome the Army under any circumstances, already he could see his authority slipping away. He hung up and looked at Caraday. "There you are, Father Caraday. They will leave immediately. I hope you have done the right thing." He was not accepting the responsibility for anything. If the Army moved in, took over Sheromere and acted like conquerors, he would blame it all on Caraday.

"I hope so, too," said Caraday, and led David out to the Land Rover. As they got into the vehicle, he said, "They'll be an hour, maybe a bit more. We'd better go back to the mission."

"Why?"

"To get our guns."

"You're not going to join in the hunt with them!"

"There's that other tiger on the mountain, too. The man-eater."

"He won't stay there long when he hears the troops moving in."

"No. But he gives me a good excuse for being there."

"You're not thinking of going ahead of the Army, are you?"

"No, I'll wait." He looked at David and grinned. The eyes were still sad, but the mouth had some of the old friendly hu-

224

mour in it. "Don't worry, David. But do you think I could not be there, after the way I've felt about Shero for two years?"

"No, I suppose not." David slowed the Land Rover as he came up behind half a dozen buffalo ambling slowly down the road. He tooted the horn, but the buffalo ignored him. He swung the Land Rover over to the side of the road, bumped along in the shallow ditch there, then pulled back on to the road.

"You're learning patience," Caraday said. "That's one thing you need in this country. A week ago you would have cursed those beasts."

"Probably. About Shero—" He looked at Caraday. "I think I'd like to be on the mountain, too, when they take him."

"I was hoping you'd say that. You might even get your second shot at the man-eater."

They drove up to the mission and collected their guns. As they came out of the bungalow, George came round the corner. He looked older and smaller now, but there was no mark of grief on his brown scarred face: grief was a private torture. "George, I'm taking the Land Rover again for a while," David said. "Is that all right?"

"Of course, sir. I have nowhere to go." He looked about him as if lost, then looked back at David. "Not till tomorrow, sir. Then I must go back to Mandalay."

"Will you stay in Mandalay?"

The Gurkha shook his head. "I do not know, sir. It will not be the same. Perhaps I shall go home to Nepal." He looked to the north-west: after forty years' absence, he knew the exact direction in which home lay. "But it will not be the same there, either, sir."

"You could stay here, George," Caraday said suddenly, and David knew it was an impulsive gesture: charity burst out of the man as something that could never be contained.

"Thank you, sir." The Gurkha looked tempted, but David had the feeling he would not stay. His life was over, as finished as that of his colonel lying beneath the new white cross in the cemetery across the meadow. There was nothing to do but go home and die.

2

David and Caraday drove down to the hospital. As they reached there, Maung Zan and Maureen came out of the office and hurried towards them. "Did you see Rose?"

"What's the matter with her?" Over the last half-hour Caraday had begun to relax; now he was suddenly tense again. "Where is she?"

"We were working in the ward together," Maureen said. "She was putting Moriarty back to bed. Then all of a sudden she just left him and ran out of the ward. She even left Moriarty sitting on the side of his bed."

Caraday swore softly and began to hurry towards the ward. David stayed with Maung Zan and Maureen. "I can guess what's happened. We should have known that Moriarty would talk too much."

"Is the Army coming?" Maung Zan asked.

They had begun to walk towards the ward. "They'll be here in an hour or so. With a bit of luck this may be the end of Shero."

"I doubt it." The young boy, Karim Naung, ran past on some errand. He flashed a clumsy salute and Maung Zan nodded absently. "This isn't the first time they've come looking for him. They haven't had any luck so far. He's awfully cunning, old boy."

"They've got to catch him sooner or later," Maureen said. "None of these outlaws die in their beds."

"Shero is different from Jesse James and Billy the Kid," David said. "For one thing, he's got more men than they ever had. He's more like that other fellow—Cantrell?"

"Quantrill. Where did you learn about him?"

"I got trapped one night in front of a television set."

"You couldn't have seen the end of the show. Quantrill was killed by the Federal troops. That's what will happen to Shero. I've got a feeling it will be today."

"A woman's intuition," David said. "Invaluable assistance when fighting bandits."

"Don't underestimate us women. You've already underestimated Rose," Maureen said, and was almost knocked over as Caraday came out of the door in a rush and pushed past her, heading for the Land Rover. David grabbed Maureen to prevent her falling, then let her go and ran after Caraday. The latter was opening the door on the driver's side as David clutched his arm and swung him round.

"Let me go! I've got to go after her, David!"

"Not in the Land Rover. You've forgotten—this is British government property."

"Oh, for God's sake! Don't be so bloody stuffy—or are you being funny? This is serious, man!" He tried to pull away from David's grip, but David wouldn't let him go. "David, don't you understand? She's gone out to warn Sherol!"

"I guessed that. Let her go. Why should you risk your life or her now?"

"Oh God, you'll never understand!" Suddenly he twisted, at the same time pushing David away. The latter lost his grip on Caraday's arm and fell back. The priest swung open the door of the Land Rover and jumped in. He started up the engine and shot the vehicle forward, the tires squealing as they tried to bite into the gravel. Next moment there was a shriek of brakes as Caraday brought the Land Rover to a shuddering halt to avoid Karim Naung as the boy, still on the run, came out from behind a large clump of rhododendrons and skipped across the drive. In the moment that the Land Rover was halted David, regaining his balance, had reached the passenger's side and wrenched open the door. He leapt in, slamming the door behind him, as Caraday let in the gears again and hurled the vehicle forward.

"Slow down, you fool! We'll never get there at this rate!"

Caraday ignored him. He took the Land Rover out of the gates of the hospital at almost full speed, swung it recklessly round into the road and headed for the town and the ferry beyond. He said nothing, but his lips were moving: it was difficult to tell whether he was cursing or praying, his face was so dark with emotion. Whatever he was saying when they started, he was cursing by the time they reached the ferry.

"Come on!" He sat in the cab, bouncing his hands impatiently on the steering wheel as he waited for the ferry to come back across the river. "For God's sake, get a move on!"

"Relax, Charlie." David sat back in the corner of the seat, watching the distraught priest. He knew now he was going to get nothing out of Caraday by bullying him. "You won't get across any quicker than by the ferry. Unless you want to go Christ one better and try *driving* on water."

"Keep your cheap blasphemy to yourself," Caraday snapped.

"I'm not trying to be blasphemous, Charlie." His voice was patient, quiet. He had often talked like this to patients who had come to him for surgery; a plastic surgeon learned early in his career that he had to be as much psychologist as doctor if he was to be a success. Caraday needed some sort of mental surgery and he had to find out what it was. "I'm trying to help you. I didn't come along just for the ride, or to protect

227

British government property. I came because I think you need help."

Caraday bounced his hands once more on the wheel, then seemed to get a grip on himself. He drew in his breath, then let out a long sigh. He relaxed, letting his long thin body slump in the seat. An elephant went past, its *oozie* riding it and talking to it in a soft sing-song voice, and lumbered down to the river. He watched it go into the water without hesitation and begin to swim towards the other side. The *oozie* was kneeling on its back, holding tight to a surcingle and using a small stick instead of his feet to guide the elephant. Both the elephant and the *oozie* seemed to be enjoying the long swim and people had gathered along the bank to cheer them on. There was an air of gaiety along the river bank, almost a picnic atmosphere. The day of the *katein* was a holiday and the people were looking for any small amusement.

"I do need help, David. I've needed it for years."

"The ferry's in," David said quietly. "Tell me about it when we're aboard."

Caraday drove the Land Rover down the slope of the bank and up the ramp on to the ferry. People laughed and waved to him and he waved back, creasing his face into a smile. He stopped the vehicle and switched off the engine. He took out his pipe, filled it and lit it. He did everything deliberately and without hurry. He wanted to say something, but he was taking his time while he found the right words. The foul smoke of the pipe blew out the window on his side; the river breeze came through the window on David's side. David was thankful for that, but he would have said nothing even if the breeze had been blowing the other way. At last Caraday looked at him.

"Rose is my daughter," he said.

David had been prepared for a confession of some sort, but not for something as blunt and startling as this. But he contained his shock: he had also learned that a plastic surgeon had to be something of an actor. "Go on."

"I met her mother down in Rangoon during the war. I wasn't a priest then," he said defensively, as if David might have forgotten.

"I know. You don't have to excuse yourself to me, Charlie. I'm not the bishop."

"I never expected you to be my confessor." He grinned sadly and puffed on his pipe; the fumes of hell went out the window and down-river. The ferry began to move out into

228

the stream. "I knew her for only two days. And nights," he added. "It was the nights that did the damage."

"Did you love Rose's mother?"

"I haven't even that in my favour. It was lust pure and simple. There was another word we used for it in the army in those days. But you don't expect me to use it now." He grinned, but his attempt at humour was hollow and he knew it. The grin turned to a grimace and he blew another cloud of smoke out the window. "Maybe if there had been more time, I might have come to love her. I *liked* her. That's the truth at least."

He was silent for a while. The ferry eased its way across the river. Downstream from it the elephant, lunging along like a great rubber ball in the water, suddenly decided to submerge. It disappeared beneath the water, the *oozie* still clinging to its back; the people on the ferry gathered along the rail, laughing and shouting encouragement to the *oozie*. The elephant came to the surface, both it and the *oozie* took huge gulping breaths, and down it went again. It was a game that the elephant, the *oozie* and the people on the ferry seemed to enjoy hugely. Caraday and David sat in the Land Rover surrounded by merriment.

"But there wasn't time to find out if I might have loved her. The Japs came and we had to get out. I never saw her again."

Upriver David could see the dark mass of the Mountain With No Name wearing its nimbus of eagles. Rose would be almost at Arahzup now, hurrying to climb the mountain and warn her lover. Had she gone there out of love or lust? "When did you find out about Rose?"

"Years afterwards. When I came back to Burma as a missionary, I was posted up here to Sheromere. I put that down to one of the ironic acts of God—although I shouldn't accuse Him of irony."

"I think He is the greatest ironist of all. But that doesn't matter. Why did you think this particular posting was ironic?"

"Because Rose's mother—her name was Meng, not a very pretty name for a woman—had told me she came from Sheromere. That was about all I knew of her. When I was sent here, I thought I was being punished for my sin. I was right, except that it was only the beginning of the punishment."

The ferry bumped against the bank. Downstream the elephant had also reached the bank; almost exhausted, it clambered out of the water, the *oozie* still on its back. Caraday started up the engine and drove the Land Rover up the slope and on to the road. He turned east and headed for Arahzup. The road swung away from the river, the jungle closed in and they drove down a long green corridor.

Caraday said, "I got to know Ho Sang, but it was some time before I found out he was Meng's father."

"Did you tell him you'd known her?"

"Known her? Two nights in her bed, and I was half-drunk each time. How can you tell a father that about his daughter?"

"It seems to me that Meng was a bit of a harlot. Was she?"

"If you mean did she take money—no. She was—well, she was wild and pretty free and easy, if you like to call it that. That was why she had run away from home. There wasn't enough excitement in Sheromere for her."

"Like mother, like daughter."

"Don't twist the knife too much, David." He was driving fast, but less recklessly than when he had driven out of the hospital gates. Now that he had begun to talk to David, he seemed eager to go on talking; he looked almost relaxed, as if the mere act of confession were some sort of sedative. I wonder if it is like this in the confessional, David thought; and couldn't remember back that far, couldn't remember the burden of sin.

"Then Ho Sang told me of Meng, told me she'd been raped and killed by the Japs down in Rangoon. He told me at the same time about his granddaughter, the child he'd never seen. Meng had written him asking him for money. He'd gone down to Rangoon to find her, but he was too late. She was dead by the time he got there, and no one knew where the child was."

"Did you guess it was your child?"

"I *knew* it was mine. She'd told him its father was an Australian soldier, a doctor."

"Did you tell him it was you?"

"Not at once. I've never found confession an easy thing. That makes me a pretty poor priest, I suppose. Confession is good for the soul, I'm supposed to teach. I *do* teach it, but I find it hard to practise it. No, I didn't tell him right away. I managed to persuade the bishop to send me down to Rangoon. That was a job—I had to get him to do that without telling him any lies. I could have lied to him, but what's the point of lying to your confessor? Anyhow, he sent me down there for a rest. I didn't rest, of course. I began searching for Rose. That was what her mother had called her—Rose."

"How did she get the Churchill?"

"I don't know. Someone had given her that during the war. It was obvious that her father was a European, so they named her after the most famous European of them all. It happened quite a lot, you know. Old Winston has probably had more bastards named after him than any other man in history." ·

"Did you have much trouble finding Rose?"

"It wasn't easy. Meng had told Ho Sang what she had called the child. It wasn't much to go on, but it was something. A girl about fourteen or so, a Eurasian whose name was Rose. Except, of course, that her name by then could be anything. Rose, Jane, Betty, Lotus, What-have-you. Well, I found her. It was a miracle, if you like, but not one I'm ever likely to tell Moriarty about. She was in an orphanage, a Catholic one. The nuns had given her a saint's name, they didn't know her real one. They called her Elizabeth."

"How did you know it was her?"

"You know that Chinese bracelet she wears? I'd given that to her mother. It's not expensive, not worth stealing. Somehow or other, even when she was a baby, it had stayed with her. Maybe the people who had looked after her when she was young had thought it was some kind of charm. Anyhow, when the nuns brought this young Eurasian girl to me, the one they called Elizabeth, I knew who she was."

"How did you feel?"

"Terrible." Involuntarily he slowed the Land Rover. He reached up a hand as if to wipe the cobweb of a bitter memory from his face; it bumped against the pipe, which, now gone out and forgotten, was still clenched between his teeth. He took the pipe out of his mouth and dropped it on the seat between him and David. "Ashamed. It wasn't that I felt I was faced by my sin. I don't think I even thought of myself as a priest that first moment I saw her. I was her father and I'd neglected her for all those years. If it hadn't been for the charity of those nuns and the people who'd looked after her before that, she might have died."

"What happened then?" They passed the clearing where the teak logs were being rolled into the river. The rafts stood there waiting to make the long trip down to Rangoon. It had been a forlorn wish of Caraday's this morning that he could make the trip down the river: nowhere at all, not even on the rafts drifting down to Rangoon, could he get away from his tiger.

"I told the nuns I knew where her grandfather was. I came back to Sheromere and told Ho Sang I'd found her."

"What else did you tell him?"

"The truth. I'd learned by then that Ho Sang was a man who could be trusted to keep a confidence. And he has."

"How did he feel towards you?"

"More charitable than I deserved. All he asked was that I should help him look after Rose. We've tried to do that. We haven't succeeded as well as we'd have liked, but we've tried. Ho Sang went down to Rangoon and brought her back. She stayed here a year or so, then like her mother, she ran away to Rangoon again."

"She's told me about that." The Land Rover had come out of the jungle and now was speeding along the road as it skirted the river bank. The Mountain With No Name had begun to loom ahead of them. Clouds were building up behind it, promising rain; already the peak of the mountain was flying shredded pennants of cloud. David began to feel uneasy, began to hope that the Army would arrive ahead of time. He appreciated Caraday's concern and love for Rose, but privately he wondered if she were worth the risking of their lives to save her. Admittedly she knew nothing of her relationship to Caraday, and on the surface she owed him nothing. But she did owe something to Ho Sang, and she appeared to have had no consideration for him at all. "How long have you known she's been in contact with Shero?"

"About six months. There was nothing we could do about it. Ho Sang spoke to her about it and she just stared him in the face and told him he must have had an opium dream, that she knew no more about Shero than anyone else. She is a great little liar. So was her mother. Sometimes I wonder what there is of me in her."

"Why should there be any of you in her? You were only there at her conception. That didn't allow much time for influence or example."

"I've seen a lot of her in the last two years."

"As her father or as Father Caraday? Be reasonable, Charlie. I'm no authority on raising a family—" He smiled at the thought and was glad to see that Caraday also smiled: the priest was more relaxed now. He did not expect to be able to persuade Caraday not to go climbing the mountain in pursuit of Rose, but he hoped to be able to get Caraday to exercise some caution. "After all, you were a Wild Colonial Boy yourself before you became a priest. You told me so. And if you'll forgive my moralising, your behaviour with Rose's mother was not exactly exemplary. You may not be a congenital liar, Charlie, but somewhere in you is a streak of the sinner. Why should Rose have inherited only your virtues and not your vices?"

Then they were coming into Arahzup. The gates of the village stockade swung open as they came up the road, and Caraday had to brake sharply as a jeep came out of the gates. The Land Rover skidded in the dirt of the road, but Caraday kept it under control. He jerked it to a halt, jumped out and ran out in front of the jeep as it came towards him. The jeep driver slowed down and Caraday spoke to him. By the time David had collected their guns and got out of the Land Rover, the jeep had started up again and was heading back along the road towards Sheromere. Caraday came back and took his gun.

"That was a taxi driver. He brought Rose out here. We're only about five minutes behind her. Come on!"

David looked up at the mountain, its top now completely enshrouded by cloud. "You're risking your life for her, Charlie."

"Good God, man!" Caraday was no longer relaxed. He had made his confession: he hungered now for penance: "Don't you think I owe her that?"

Chapter 13

1

Three of the villagers went with them to show them the quickest way up the mountain. But at the top of the first ridge the villagers stopped. "This is as far as they'll come," Caraday said.

"They have more sense than we have," David murmured, but Caraday had turned back to listen to one of the men.

The man, his broken-nosed and scarred face relieved by a beautiful white-toothed smile, raised a hand that had only two fingers and pointed. He was a hunter, afraid neither of Shero nor the tiger; afraid only of the *nats* at the top of the mountain. He and his companions, armed with their crossbows, longed to be in the hunt. But superstition was too strong.

"He says that's where the man-eater is," Caraday said.

"I thought we'd come after—" Then David remembered the Springfield in his hand and their excuse for being here. He looked back down the ridge towards the ribbon of road that ran along beside the river. There was no sign of the Army, nothing in sight but a file of half a dozen elephants coming into sight out of a clump of forest half a mile downstream. "Oh, yes. Tell them we'll get the tiger."

Caraday spoke to the men and each of them shook hands with him and David in the Kachin fashion. Then the three villagers turned and went down the ridge, hurrying down the narrow path as if afraid that the *nats* were already on their

234

way down from the mountain top to avenge this invasion of their privacy. Caraday turned back to face the mountain. "Come on." He blessed himself, then suddenly faced David. "Why are you coming, David? This is no concern of yours—you don't have to risk *your* life for her—"

"I am not here for her sake," David said quietly. "But if we want to catch up with her, we'd better get cracking."

Caraday bit his lip. The sad eyes blinked, and the big wide mouth worked as if it were about to pour out a spate of words. But he said nothing. He turned quickly on his heel and began to lead the way up the mountain.

He moved fast and David, still not in good condition for life in these hills, was hard pressed to keep up with him. The open ridge where the hill rice grew was soon left behind; it was not long before they were clambering up through evergreen forest. The path was steep and slippery; the sun never got down below the trees to dry out the mud. Several times David slipped and fell flat; each time, without a word, Caraday turned back and helped him to his feet. The trees were huge, much bigger than David had expected to find on the side of a mountain, and the undergrowth between them was thick. Rhododendrons grew in large clumps; hollow logs held orchids in wild profusion; one wall of the path was a bank of magnolia trees. At times David had the feeling he was climbing through a vast botanical garden that had run amok, had taken over the world. There was no sign of life, but once or twice they heard the chatter of monkeys and then the deeper bark of gibbons. Moisture dripped continuously from the trees and David was soon soaked. He was sweating profusely and his boots were full of mud. Then inside his trouser legs he felt the suck of leeches, but there was no time to stop and knock them off.

What am I doing here? he wondered. What, in less than two weeks, has brought me to this lonely mountain, risking my life for a girl I care nothing about? But even as he asked himself the question, he knew he had the answer. He was not here because of Rose. Caraday was here because of Rose; and he was here because of Caraday. I'm involved with him, he thought angrily; and stopped for a moment on the path. How the hell did that happen, how did I become involved with him?

Caraday stopped and looked back. "Had it, David? Look, why don't you stay here?"

A good question. Why don't I? He could feel the shuddering in his legs, the breath tearing its way in and out of his lungs, the leeches robbing him of blood; he knew he was on the point of collapse, that he would be of no use at all to Caraday when the moment of crisis came. It would be like it had been on the mountain near Mali Ga; he would never be able to shoot, no matter which tiger crossed their path. But he looked up at the tall thin man standing on the path above him, at the dark face and the sad eyes that had forgotten how to laugh, and he said, "How have I become involved with you, Charlie?"

The slanting light of the sun struck through only the tops of the trees; it was reflected from the underpart of the tree crowns, came down as a golden-green light to the path. Against it, in his battered hat and ragged trousers, Caraday looked a scarecrow, a beggar on whom the world could have turned its back. "I don't know, David. But it was not one of the ironic acts of God. It was one of His good acts."

"You bring Him into everything."

"I can't help it. It's the way I think, the way I live."

"It'll never be the way I think, nor live."

"You never know. You say you're involved with me, that means you're concerned for me. And if for me, pretty soon it will be for others. Being concerned for mankind, David, is the first step towards God."

"You choose the strangest places for sermons."

"I didn't choose it. You asked the question."

"Well, anyway, you're stuck with me, Charlie."

Caraday reached back and put out his hand. "No, you're stuck with me. There's quite a difference. And don't think I don't appreciate it."

David grinned and took Caraday's hand. They were standing like that in the middle of the path, no sound about them but the gentle dripping of water from the trees and the haunting creaking of a cane clump, when they heard the tiger roar. Caraday wrenched his hand away and spun round. He went plunging up the path, once falling to his knees as his feet, trying to move too fast, slid away beneath him in the treacherous mud. He didn't look back to see if David had followed him, but the latter had also begun to scramble up the path. Fifty yards up, the forest suddenly opened out.

They came out from beneath the ceiling of trees and stopped suddenly on the edge of a steep drop down into a stony watercourse. A swift narrow stream plunged down the mountainside; its sound hadn't penetrated into the thick-walled cavern of the forest. On the other side of the stream the path, reached by a series of steppingstones that split the plunging water into long white scarves, went up through a thick brake of tall bamboo cane. The bamboo grew to a height of thirty feet or more and, except for where the path had been hacked through, looked almost impenetrable.

Caraday grabbed David's arm. "There she is!"

David saw Rose and the tiger in the same instant. Rose was in the canebrake, desperately trying to twist her way through the closely growing stalks; she was distinguishable only by her vivid red *cheong-sam*, so that she looked like some brightly plumaged bird trapped behind the bars of a cage. The tiger, not so easily distinguishable, yellow and black against the grey-yellow and black of the cane and its own shadows, was struggling to extricate itself from between two thick stalks, snarling in anger and frustration as it threshed its huge body. Rose looked safe enough for the moment, but there was no knowing when the tiger would break loose and crash its way through the bamboo after her. The canebrake had looked a good refuge for her, but it was only a temporary one. It was only a question of time before the tiger reached her.

Caraday checked the catch on the Mannlicher, then slid down the bank of the watercourse. David followed him, sliding on the mud like a skier. He lost his footing, crashed to the bottom of the slope, picked himself up and went running across the stones that bridged the stream and up the opposite bank. Caraday was already at the top of the bank. The tiger roared again, the sound echoing against the limestone cliff that rose sheer behind the bamboo brake. David climbed the bank, his heart pounding, his eyes blinded with sweat, knowing he would be nothing but a spectator to whatever was going to happen. He came up behind Caraday as the latter put the Mannlicher to his shoulder, aiming into the brake and the heaving, roaring yellow target that was the tiger.

The Mannlicher went off, the shot echoing back as the tiger's roar had done; but Caraday had fired too late, had missed. The tiger, with one last desperate heave, had plunged through the bamboo and reached Rose. She screamed, caught between the bamboo as the tiger had been. The tiger rose up, unable to spring but trying to strike down at Rose through the thickly growing stalks. Caraday ran along the top of the bank, now and again clutching at the wall of bamboo to prevent himself falling back down into the watercourse. He came opposite the spot where Rose and the tiger were. David, following, saw everything as if in slow motion. The tiger rose up, slashed down with one paw. Rose screamed, the Mannlicher thundered again, and the tiger spun round, dead but held upright by the bamboo into which it had fallen. The echo of the Mannlicher died away and there was only the loud hiss of the cascading stream and the low agonised moaning of Rose.

David dropped the Springfield and went into the bamboo. He had difficulty in squeezing himself between the stalks, but he followed the path the tiger had made. Jagged ends of cane ripped at him, but he hardly felt them. He pushed past the dead tiger, still savage and dangerous-looking in death, its yellow hide stained by its blood; he had to step on it, as on a rock, to get over it and through to Rose. She was sitting upright, held by the bamboo. She had fainted now, and he was glad of that. The whole left side of her face had taken the full weight of the tiger's paw; her head and face were as bright as her red *cheong-sam*. Race and beauty had been obliterated.

It was impossible to carry her out through the bamboo. He took her by the shoulders and slowly, carefully, dragged her out on to the path. Caraday dropped his gun and fell on his knees beside her. He blessed himself and took one of her hands between his and began to pray silently.

"Get up!" David said angrily. "She's not dead yet. There's still a chance."

Caraday looked up, his eyes blank and his face stiff with shock. He didn't appear to have heard David; his lips went on moving. David grabbed him by the shoulder and shook him furiously. "Stop being a priest for a moment! You'll be more use to her if you start thinking as a doctor again!"

Caraday's lips stopped moving. He stared at David uncomprehendingly; then abruptly understanding came back into his gaze. He shifted his hands on Rose's to feel her pulse with his finger. Then he looked up again at David. "We've got to stop that blood flow!"

David said nothing. He was always angry when prayers got in the way of medicine; prayers were for the dead, not the living. He pushed Caraday aside, picked up Rose and, sliding in the mud, carried her down to the stream. He tore off the shirt he wore, no longer white but streaked with mud and sweat now, and vigorously washed it in the swift waters of the stream. The shirt was none too clean when he had finished, but it would have to do. He ripped it into strips and turned back to Rose. Caraday, using a handkerchief, had already washed the blood away from Rose's face. But the wound, extending from above her left eye down to her jaw, the nose broken and the eye hidden by the peeled-back flesh, was still oozing blood. David began to bind up the wound.

The two shots and the roaring of the tiger had roused the forest. A troop of gibbons went scuttling across the watercourse further upstream like a family of panic-stricken midgets. Monkeys were now visible in the tops of the trees, urchinlike in their curiosity. Birds were exploding from the bushes along the bank: a streaked spider hunter, with its long thin curved beak, hung in the air as if pinned there, then shot away above the canebrake. The sun had sunk lower and the yellow light struck almost horizontally up the watercourse. Cloud had come down the mountain now, but there was still no rain. David wondered how much longer the Army would be getting here.

"There's nothing more we can do till we get her back to the hospital."

Caraday nodded, dumbly; he seemed to be in a state of shock. He stood up, turned away and picked up the guns. Then a voice, raised above the hissing rumble of the stream, said, "Drop the guns, Father Caraday!"

2

The birds and animals of the forest were not the only things that had been roused by the shots and the tiger's roar. It was difficult to believe that so many men could appear so silently and so suddenly. More than a hundred of them stood along the banks of the watercourse, all of them with their guns trained on the little group beside the stream. David looked up, saw the masked figure of Shero, then went back to finishing the rough dressing on Rose's wound. He was not being brave nor defiant. Exhausted from the climb up the mountain, sickened by what had happened to Rose, torn by pity for Caraday, he had reached the limit of his endurance. He might just as well die working at his trade as with his hands in the air. He had already failed as a man, but he had never failed as a doctor. Not when he put his mind to it.

"You, Englishman!" Shero's voice was muffled by his mask, but there was no mistaking the angry command in it. "Stand up! Put your hands up!"

Deliberately, unhurriedly, David tied the rough bandage. He lifted Rose's head, rolled a smooth rock under it as a pillow, then gently laid her head back on it. Then he stood up, raising his hands above his head. Caraday had dropped the guns and already stood with his hands raised. The stream plunged by beneath their feet, glittering and clean and free, mocking men for the danger and bonds that they could build for themselves with their free will. Pray for a miracle now, Charlie, thought David. Nothing less will get us out of this.

Shero slung his Sten gun over his shoulder by its strap and came sliding down the bank. He crossed the stream by the steppingstones, moving as gracefully as a ballet dancer, and came up to the two men and the unconscious Rose. He stood above Rose, covering her with his shadow, and for the first time seemed to realise how badly hurt she was. He looked down at her, at the bandages already beginning to show blood at the edges, then he looked up at Caraday. "Did you shoot her?"

"Why should I do that?" Caraday still looked shocked; his voice sounded puzzled. "Why should I try to kill her, Shero? What has she ever done to me? She is my—"

"The tiger got her," David said quickly, afraid now that Caraday was going to confess his secret to the world. He had kept it to himself for so long; what was the point in broadcasting it now? It was as if he had become infected with confession; he wanted to spread the word, like some parody of his priestly task. Shame, not faith, was his message; the hairshirt was to be his soutane. Not while I'm here, David thought. "Father Caraday shot the tiger, but not in time. It's up there in the bamboo."

The hooded head turned and shouted to one of the men on the bank close to the canebrake. The man disappeared, came back in a moment. He shouted something and Shero turned back to the two men. "You are fortunate. If you had done that to her—" He looked down at the still figure of Rose. "Is she badly hurt?"

"We'll have to get her to the hospital as quickly as possible." David was doing all the talking: he didn't trust Caraday to open his mouth.

Shero shook his head. It was frustrating not to know what expressions were passing across the face hidden beneath the green hood. David had spent hours of his life talking with men and women behind masks, other surgeons, anaesthetists, nurses; but their eyes had always been clearly visible, had been enough to show what they were thinking. But the slits in the green hood showed too little of Shero's eyes: occasionally one caught a gleam in a dark iris, but that was all. Behind the hood, even the voice seemed muffled of emotion. "No, you are not taking her down there."

Suddenly Caraday came out of his shock. "Don't talk bloody rot, Shero!" He was the old Caraday: his voice grated

240

with anger, scorn for the other's stupidity. "She'll die if we don't get her down there!"

"This Englishman is a doctor," Shero said. "And I have heard about you, too. From Rose. She told me how you helped them down at the hospital during the cholera epidemic. You know something about medicine, too."

"That's beside the point," Caraday snapped. "A doctor is no good without equipment, without drugs. A diagnosis is not what we need here."

"He's right, Shero." Later David would recall that he had been able to call this man by his name with less difficulty than he had been able to call his own father by his familial title. But then Shero was the enemy, and embarrassment was a handicap that never occurred when dealing with an enemy. Embarrassment implied some measure of respect for the other man's feelings: it was not just an exposure of one's own feelings. "A doctor is useless in a case like this unless he has some tools to work with. And the longer we stand here arguing with you, the less chance she has of surviving!"

"Don't lose your temper with me." Shero's voice was soft, but there was no mistaking the threat behind it. For the first time David noticed there was a faint lisping in the voice, a slight difficulty with the *r*'s. "Father Caraday is enough to put up with. I would have killed him long ago if it had not been for Rose. She asked me not to, did you know that, Father?"

Caraday blinked, and for a moment the sadness lifted from his eyes. He looked down at Rose, and David thought he was going to weep. "I owe her my life then."

"I'll send men down to raid the hospital," Shero said. "We'll get all the equipment you need. You shouldn't have had her ask for that box back, the one we took last week. If we still had that, there would be no need to raid the hospital. Someone may get killed. It might even be Maung Zan. Rose told me about him—"

Where was the Army? David wondered. If he and Caraday could only keep Shero here talking . . . But while they would be doing that, Rose's blood would be seeping out of her. "There won't be time, Shero! It will be quicker to take her down to the hospital—"

Suddenly Caraday bent down and swept Rose up in his arms. "I'm taking her down to the hospital, Shero. It's her life that needs saving now."

"No!" Shero's voice rose. The guns along the banks of the watercourse came up in the hands that held them. David was conscious of a hundred barrels that seemed to be pointed right at him. Sweat broke on him, but it was cold sweat: the chill of death ran down his spine: cloud came down over the sun, wiping out the long black shadow of his body. "We'll get all the equipment you need! She goes back with us—"

He was interrupted by a shout. A man came running up the path out of the forest. He pushed his way through the line of men at the top of the bank. He shouted down at Shero, then turned and pointed down the mountain with the barrel of his gun. There was a note of panic in his voice; it communicated itself to the line of men. They stirred restlessly, all their attention gone from the small tableau beside the stream. They looked down the mountain, the barrels of their guns turning to be lined up with the direction of their gaze. Then they looked back at Shero, waiting for his order. They were dacoits, murderers and robbers, but they were as disciplined as soldiers. Shero was not the leader of a rabble.

David looked at Caraday. "It's the Army," the priest said. "They're already on their way up the mountain."

Shero shouted an order and all but half a dozen of the men turned at once and disappeared into the forest on each side of the watercourse. Then Shero looked at David and Caraday. "Come with me." He unslung his gun and gestured at Caraday with it. "I'll have my men take over from you when you get tired."

"I'm not coming, Shero." Caraday's voice was quiet; it seemed that all his anger had gone. He looked down at the limp figure in his arms, then back at Shero. It had begun to rain now; water ran down his cheeks like tears. "I'm taking her down to the hospital. I owe her that in payment for my life. And for other things."

He walked steadily past Shero and out on to the stones that spanned the stream. He was halfway across the stream when Shero shot him in the legs. He fell, dropping Rose into the stream; she fell against a rock, the water breaking over her like a torn sheet. Caraday turned as he lay on his side in the water, looking back at Shero as if puzzled by what had happened. The puzzled look was still on the long dark face when he died, as Shero shot him again in the chest. From down the mountain came the sound of other shots, like a swift echoing and re-echoing of the shot that had killed Caraday. Shero turned towards David, his finger still on the trigger.

"You'd better kill me, too." David was too weary and sick now to be afraid. Death would be a relief; eternity held its promise. Was this how his father had felt in the last monents? He tried for a prayer, but could remember none and lidn't regret it: he had never been a hypocrite, one couldn't expect God to welcome the fear-driven penitent. "I haven't he strength even to pick her up."

He looked down the barrel, saw the finger tighten on the rigger, felt the bullet in his brain even before it had left the gun. Then the barrel dipped, swung away as Shero spun round and the men came running up the path out of the forest. They slid down the bank and plunged across the stream, hip-deep to the racing waters. Shero shouted at them, but hey raced past him and up the bank, disappearing up the path that led through the canebrake. Shero looked up at the opposite bank, but the troops had not yet appeared. He seemed to have forgotten David. He looked down at Rose, took a step towards her, then suddenly turned and went racing up the bank towards the canebrake, pulling off his hood as he ran.

Later David would marvel at how quickly and coolly he had acted. He dropped down on one knee, picked up the Springfield and, without rising, put the rifle to his shoulder. He sighted along the barrel, saw the slim green figure about to disappear into the bamboo, remembered the other tiger he had aimed at and missed, then squeezed the trigger. Shero halted as if a hand had reached out and grabbed him. He turned back, screamed something that David didn't catch, then plunged headlong down the bank, sliding face first down through the mud into the rushing torrent of the stream.

As the first of the soldiers came up the path out of the forest, David put down the rifle. He went into the stream, the rain as cold on his bare back as the water on his legs, picked up Caraday and brought him back to lay him on the gravel and mud of the bank. He went back into the water and brought out Rose and laid her beside Caraday. Then he moved to where Shero lay with his head buried beneath the water. He took the dacoit by the legs and pulled him out and turned him over on his back.

Without the hood, Shero was a stranger, a young Chinese who was handsome and, in death, even a little innocent-looking.

3

"It was a pleasure to watch you at work," Maung Zan said. "Although, perhaps, pleasure is the wrong word. There was no pleasure in knowing who was on the table—" For a moment he looked as if he were about to break down. He turned away, stripping off his gloves, and began to wash. He and David were alone in the small room off the theatre; Maureen and the other nurses were preparing to take Rose back to a ward. He dried his hands carefully before he spoke again. "What are her chances, David?"

David, too, had begun to wash. He was still sweating from the heat of the theatre; he would have to wait till he got back to the mission before he could relax in a bath. His head was aching, and he was weak from hunger; he realised only now that he had not eaten all day, but he knew he would not be able to eat anything now. He dried his hands. "She'll live, Zan. There's no worry there. She lost a lot of blood, but she'll get over that."

"I know that, David. I didn't mean that."

"Her looks, you mean?" He shrugged. "I can't tell at this stage. All I've done so far is to repair her face as close as I could to its original shape and planes. I didn't have much to work with, as you saw." At times during the operation he had thought that Maung Zan was going to collapse. When he had brought Rose back to the hospital, one look at Maung Zan had told him that the latter would not be able to operate on her. It was then that he had volunteered to operate himself and Maung Zan had been almost pathetic in his gratitude for the offer. Maung Zan had acted as anaesthetist; the other doctor had been on duty in the out-patients' clinic. Two nurses had been brought in as assistants, and David and Maureen had completed the team. It was a much smaller team than David had ever worked with before; at one point he had remembered drily the crowded theatre when other surgeons had come to watch him at work. There was an old doctors' saw that all that was needed for a good operation was a good surgeon; but David knew today's operation had been made easier for him by Maureen's help. Their teamwork had had all the smooth skill of their best days in London. He knew now how badly he would have missed her if she had gone to the Mayo.

"She was awfully vain about her looks." Maung Zan's tone was not unkind; he spoke as he might have of a child he loved very much. "When she is over the op., that is when we shall have the most worry with her. And now that Shero is dead—"

"Don't be so pessimistic, Zan. She's young, perhaps she has more resilience than you give her credit for." He looked out the window, saw the cherry trees beside the nurses' bunga low: Rose had wandered too far from their protection. "She's half-Chinese and she once told me the Chinese have a talent for survival."

"Perhaps." Maung Zan was not to be consoled so easily. This was the blackest day he had ever experienced: he had just lost two of his closest friends, and the girl he loved had been scarred into frightening ugliness. If he believes in the *nats*, David thought, they have certainly feasted on him today. "Could her face ever be rebuilt? I'd like to tell her so—"

"It's possible. I've rebuilt faces as badly damaged as hers. But it is a long job, Zan. It's not a matter of one operation—"

"I know that, David. I've read of some of the work you have done—" David was embarrassed at the tone of praise and pride in the other's voice. He had never given a thought to Maung Zan over the past ten years, not since the unanswered letters had stopped coming; but Maung Zan had followed his career, had bothered to read the detailed descriptions of a type of operation that he himself would never be called upon to attempt. Maung Zan had kept alive a one-sided friendship. "But I'd like to give her some hope—"

David wiped the sweat from his body with a towel and put the threatre gown back on: he had not had time to go up to the mission to get a clean shirt to replace the one he had torn up for bandages. "I'd like to help her, Zan. But I couldn't keep coming out here for the operations. I'd do the ops. for nothing, that would be no expense. But she would have to come to London, have to live there, perhaps for a year, two years, however long it took to do the job. It would cost money—"

"I don't think that would be a problem. Ho Sang has money. You saw how he was when you brought her in—he still loves her, David. As much as I do." It was his first confession of love. But there was no embarrassment; he told it to David as frankly as he might have admitted his own name. This is my day for the confessional, David thought, but I'm on the wrong side of the grille. "Ho would send her to London if she would go."

"That will be your problem. *If* she will go."

Rose had still to learn how badly she had been disfigured. She had recovered faint consciousness as two soldiers had been carrying her down the mountain on a stretcher. David, borrowing morphine from the medical aid orderly, had put her under sedation again. When they had arrived back at the hospital, she had at once been taken to the operating theatre.

It would be the middle of the night before she would be conscious enough to realise what had happened to her.

It had been a sad procession that had come down the mountain. There had been three stretchers, carrying Rose and the bodies of Caraday and Shero. The soldiers had been elated at the killing of Shero; the majority of his men had been captured once they knew their leader was dead. There would be no more trouble from dacoits in the Sheromere district; not till another leader rose up and collected another band of cutthroats. But the soldiers' elation had been dampened when they had come back from the chase of the dacoits and learned that Caraday was dead. He had been known and loved as far down the river as Myitkyina; one of the soldiers had sunk on his knees beside the body and wept openly. The captain in charge, a short muscular man with a high-pitched voice that sounded ridiculous when it shouted a command, yet seemed effective enough, judging by the way the men responded, had come down to David as the latter stood beside the three bodies he had laid out beside the stream. He stuck his pistol back into his holster.

"The priest is dead?" David had nodded, not trusting himself to speak. "He was a holy man. He had charity."

David remembered the remark his father had made in the dusk on the verandah of the consulate down in Mandalay: *He is a charitable man.* "Yes, he had that. Perhaps too much."

The captain looked down at the tall thin body of Caraday lying like that of a man asleep on the mud and gravel beside the stream. "Was it charity that brought him up here—to this?"

"Perhaps," said David. "If charity is another name for love."

"We Buddhists are taught that it is. Is that not so with Christians?"

"Yes," said David, who had learned the lesson here on this mountain. "It is so."

Then the stretcher-bearers had come up, and a few minutes later they had begun the descent to the bottom of the mountain. When they had come into Arahzup the villagers had rushed forward, then pulled up suddenly when they had seen who was on the first stretcher. The head man came forward and looked down at Caraday. When at last he looked up, tears were running down over the gullied cheeks. He gestured at the silent villagers standing round him, then he took David's hand and shook it, Kachin fashion: he was

246

offering the village's sympathy, telling David that he was not alone in his grief. David could say nothing, even if he had understood the language. The loss of his father during the night, the loss of Caraday this afternoon, had proved too much. Words had become stones in his throat.

The scene had been repeated when they had returned to the hospital. The body of Shero had been taken on by the Army to some unknown destination; David hadn't bothered to enquire where it was going, nor did he care. Shero meant nothing now; it was too late even to hate him for what he had done. At that moment David had wondered if he would ever hate again: hate required a certain strength and by the time he had reached the hospital he had had no strength at all. He had stood holding Maureen to him as she had wept, but he had been leaning on her as much as she on him.

At last her weeping had quietened and they had both turned to Ho Sang, standing quietly and impassively, like a withered tree, beside the door to Maung Zan's office. It was impossible to tell if he had been weeping. The thick-lensed glasses distorted his eyes: what looked like the glisten of tears could have been the refraction of light. "I hope Charlie died at once, without pain." He was concerned for Rose, the living, but he had not forgotten the dead. "He had enough pain while he was alive."

"It was quick," David said.

"I am glad of that." He was silent for a moment, an old man suddenly aware of loneliness and the imminence of his own death. "Am I going to lose Rose?"

"Not unless there are unexpected complications."

"Will you come and see me later, David? I should like to talk to you."

As the old man walked away Maureen said, "I wonder why he wants to see you."

"I don't know," said David, but he could guess. Ho Sang would ask him how much he knew, and he would tell him the truth. He would not dissipate the secret any further; that he could promise with certainty to Ho Sang and the dead Caraday. He would never tell Maureen nor Maung Zan nor even Rose herself. He had learned at an early age the value of a tight tongue; the habit would never leave him. Caraday would profit from Michael and Laura Breton's early desertion of their son: the boy in the school long ago had had his own secret: he had kept his loneliness to himself like a secret shame.

247

"It's time we were getting ready," Maureen then said. "But are you sure you're up to an op. right now?"

"Better me than Zan," he said, then saw Moriarty coming towards them, hurrying but stumbling a little, like a man who hadn't yet learned to trust one eye. He was dressed in pyjamas and was barefooted. His hands were clasped before him, manacled by his rosary beads. "You shouldn't be out of bed, Moriarty."

"They just told me, Mr. Breton!" David understood now why Moriarty had been stumbling like a blind man: the astigmatism of tears could trip a man as easily as could a lurking root. "Where is he? Where is Father Caraday?"

"It is best that you don't see him now." David was glad that the orderlies had come and taken away Caraday's body. He felt he could not cope with the hysteria of Moriarty's grief.

"It was my fault! They told me he went after Miss Rose—"

"Who's they?" Tongues were already beginning to crack like whips: wittingly or unwittingly, they would strip the hide from Moriarty, from Rose, perhaps from the dead Caraday.

Moriarty shook his head, moaning to himself in some dialect that David didn't understand: the tongue of his childhood spoke for him in his grief. He leaned against the wall of the office, his knees bent, looking ready to collapse. The dialect turned into English, still little more than a mumble: "I told her the Army was going after Shero. That was why she left me so suddenly. I thought she was sick. I killed him—"

"No, Moriarty. You didn't kill him." The tone of David's voice made the Indian look up. "Father Caraday made that appointment on that mountain many years ago."

"I don't understand, Mr. Breton." The one eye was blank with tears and puzzlement, unintelligent as a wet marble.

"Believe me, it is true, Moriarty. Call it fate, the hand of God, whatever you like, but Father Caraday understood why he was there." He lied, knowing it was a sin Caraday would forgive: "Before he died, he told me to say goodbye to you. There was no mention of blaming you, Moriarty. You know he was not the man ever to do that."

The Indian blinked away the tears: the eye shone. "Oh, I am so glad! I shall pray for his soul." He held up the beads.

"Do that," said David, and meant it.

Chapter 14

1

"David Alexander Breton!"

As he moved forward in answer to his name, David remembered with dry amusement the last time he had been called to court. Then he had been the respondent; now he was a witness for the prosecution. A lot had happened in the last three months. He had been subjected to surgery; not the sort that had been performed upon Elinor Beatty, but surgery that might have profited her more than a Breton nose. He realised now that he and Elinor Beatty had had more in common than they had known: selfishness had been a form of cancer with each of them. His own had been cut out, he had been cured; Elinor Beatty's, he guessed, was still with her. He wondered what effect Caraday would have had on her.

As the prosecutor rose to question him, David looked round the court. For political reasons, the trial of the captured dacoits was taking place in Rangoon. He hadn't queried the exact nature of the reasons, but he had guessed that Mandalay was too close to the Kachin and Shan States. The defendants were being charged as common criminals, guilty of murder and robbery; but in Mandalay there were troublemakers who would have had no difficulty in whipping up support for them as fighters for independence. Trucks could have brought people down from Lashio, Taunggyi and Myitkyina for demonstrations; but Rangoon was too far, the police would have thrown up roadblocks long before they got to the capital. Nonetheless, the court and the corridors outside were crowded with curious, and in some cases sympathetic, spectators. These men had led a life that had given them some escape from drudgery and poverty; adventure was still a banner that people saluted. As he had pushed his way through the crowd to enter the court, David had heard several people muttering against him.

It had been warm in the streets outside, but with the crush of people in the court buildings it was even warmer inside. David and Maung Zan had come into the court buildings together, and as soon as they had entered the front lobby the petition writers had descended on them, only to turn away as soon as they realised that these men were too educated to need their services. David and Maung Zan had pushed their way up the wide stairs, past the beggars interested neither in justice nor mercy, but only charity; past the relatives of defendants, weeping even before the verdicts were known; past the court clerks, superior in their clean white shirts and their knowledge of the law. A policeman, smart, in grey shirt, dark blue trousers and black slouch hat, looking more impressively representative of the law than the dirty lobbies with their peeling discoloured walls and the faded fly-specked photographs of Aung San and U Nu, had directed them to the room where witnesses were to wait. They had sat down on a bench against the wall, apart from the other witnesses, who had smiled shyly at them from the other side of the room.

"How is Maureen?" Maung Zan had said. David had arrived yesterday from London, but Maung Zan had come down only this morning from Sheromere. He had called for David at the latter's hotel and they had come straight to the court. "I should have asked about her sooner."

"She is well. Glad she came back to London with me."

"You are not married yet? Or shouldn't I ask that?" He smiled tentatively: even now he was never quite sure how much privacy Westerners insisted upon.

David returned the smile. "Not yet. I'm on a good-behaviour bond. Remember that time you and six or seven other overseas chaps put on that rag in Trafalgar Square? The police hauled you out from under the fountains and you pleaded you didn't realise you were under the fountains, you thought it was just the usual London weather? And the magistrate put you on a bond for six months?"

Maung Zan laughed, his eyes shining with happy memories

that he had almost forgotten. "You lent me the money for the bond, remember?"

"Did I?" David had forgotten, but now he was pleased to be reminded; perhaps he had been a better friend to Maung Zan in those days than he had remembered. "Well, anyway, Maureen has put me on a bond for six months. I think I'll come through it all right."

"I hope so, David. She would be good for you. And I don't mean just as your theatre sister."

David nodded. "My father would have been pleased. She was always a favourite of his." He hesitated, then he said, "I was sorry about Rose."

The shine died in Maung Zan's eyes. David had reopened a wound. "I had no idea she and Ho Sang were going. I used to see her every day. I was the only one she would let visit her—all her other boy friends, she wouldn't let them near her. She would come out occasionally with me for a drive, but she would always wear a veil—even when I visited her in the house, she wore the veil. I tried to tell her that her face could be repaired, but I couldn't make her believe me. Even the letters you and Maureen wrote, they made no difference. It was useless, David. Ho Sang said he would take her to London, have you work on her, but it was no use."

"How did she feel about Shero's being killed?"

"We never discussed him. I don't know whether she missed him or not. I didn't want to know." For a moment there was a flash of light in his eyes. Then it died away almost at once. "When Karim Naung brought me her letter, I couldn't believe it. I went up to Ho Sang's shop and searched right through it, as if I expected them to be hiding behind some screen. I wanted to wreck the place—all those teeth grinning at me as if some horrible joke had been played on me—but in the end I did nothing. I didn't even attempt to find out which route they had taken into China. They had gone and I knew they would never be back."

"Do you think it was Ho Sang who persuaded her to go back to China with him?"

Maung Zan shook his head. "Why should he want to go back there? Ho Sang was a wealthy man. There's no place for wealthy men in China today. No, I'm sure it was Rose's idea. I can't understand it, but then I never could understand her. I just loved her, that was all."

She was loved by three men, David thought: Maung Zan, Ho Sang and Caraday. But she had turned her back on them for the questionable love of a dacoit chief; no one, perhaps even Rose herself, would ever know if Shero had loved her. It was difficult to feel pity for her, yet David did; he felt pity for her for the way her life had begun, for the struggle she had had to come as far as she had. Her end, even though she had not yet reached it, was destined to be tragic; it would follow the pattern of her life. Caraday, with terrible accuracy, had predicted unhappiness for her. *The sins of the father . . .* David wondered if Caraday, in a mood of bitter penance, had ever preached such a sermon. Caraday's one sin had been visited upon his child with a vengeance; it was Caraday himself who had finally escaped. Rose would grow old and ugly in some hill village in China, and would never know why fate had treated her so cruelly. Or perhaps it was God and not fate; David would not debate that point even with himself. He had learned to love man, but he had not yet learned to love God. That might come later; but not now. He did not understand why a charitable God should have treated Rose as she had been for a sin that had been her father's. Perhaps even Caraday had not understood it, but as far as David knew, he had never queried it. One did not know God by His essence but by His effects, Caraday had once told him; and faith was needed to accept those effects without demur. He did not have that faith himself, but it might come. Over the past months he had come to know the vacuum in himself, a vacuum that could not be filled by belief in himself alone. Perhaps it was the need to fill just such a vacuum that had brought Michael back to God; he wished now that he had discussed it further with his father. But whether he found faith or not, he would never understand why Rose had been punished as she had been. And so his pity for her would always remain.

Then he had been called into court and now he was being questioned by the prosecutor. The judge, in white bib and black robes, but wearing a pink *gaung-baung* instead of a wig, fanned himself with a small bamboo fan. Short and round, his small fat face was as blank of expression as the clock without hands above him; this was the Eastern face of justice, inscrutable till the final moment. The public had crowded into the courtroom, spilling over into the main body of the court; many of them had brought food with them, eating from paper bags in their laps while the questioning droned on. The prisoners, some twenty of them, all that had been taken alive, were crowded together in a makeshift dock like cattle. They had no more expression on their faces than cattle bound for the abattoirs would have had. They knew their fate and they looked bored by all the rigmarole that had to be gone through before they reached their appointed date with the gaoler. They stared at David, but there was no animosity towards him.

The prosecutor shuffled his papers, then abruptly looked up. He was a small thin man with gold-rimmed glasses, and he had a trick of running his tongue round his lips, as if tasting each question before asking it. "Mr. Breton, you have described how you and Father Caraday went after Miss Churchill that day on the mountain. We know why Miss Churchill was there. Why were you there?"

"I was with Father Caraday," David replied carefully. "We had already been out to Arahzup earlier in the day, to see about hunting the man-eater I told you about."

"Was that your primary reason for going *back* to the village?"

"No." David had begun to sweat. He could feel it running down inside his shirt. He resisted the temptation to wipe his face with his handkerchief. He did not want to give the impression, especially at this moment, that he was disturbed by the questioning.

"Why did you go back?"

"I told you," David said irritably. "We went after Miss Churchill."

"She was going to warn Shero that the Army was coming?"

The question had been asked and answered once before. "Yes," David said, and tried to to sound patient. Why was the prosecutor pressing him like this? He was a witness for the prosecution, not for the defence.

"Did you think you could catch Miss Churchill before she got to Shero?"

"We hoped so."

"Mr. Breton, we have no suspicions about your part in this case." David couldn't help his look of surprise, but the prosecutor made no comment on it. He licked his lips, then said, "But we have to probe Father Caraday's part in this. He had lived in Sheromere for several years. He knew more people than a foreigner would normally come to know. He had influence."

So that's it, David thought. They aren't content to make this just a criminal case; they are playing politics, too. They suspect Caraday of having had Kachin and Shan sympathies and they are trying to discredit him. He was a foreigner and therefore he was suspect; it was the pattern in all the countries of the East today. They were getting back at the imperialists; any foreigner would do as a butt. They didn't know Caraday; but they had heard of his influence. They didn't know that he had sympathy for Kachins and Shans, for Burmese and Indians, for Chinese and Eurasians and Europeans, that he had sympathy for all mankind. They would never know that, nor were they interested in knowing.

"It was you who shot Shero, Mr. Breton. It was not Father Caraday, although he was the one with the reputation as a shot. Why was he on that mountain? Why couldn't he have waited for the Army? He knew it was on its way. The Army would have caught Shero and his men even if Miss Churchill had reached him to warn him."

That was debatable, David thought, but he said nothing. He was not here to question the efficiency of the Army. He was here, he realised now, to defend Caraday, to keep alive the image of the priest in the memories of the people of Sheromere. He was not going to commit perjury; but he was not going to speak the truth, not all of it. Truth never hurts the teller, that crass romantic Browning had said. But David was not here to defend himself.

"He was there to save Miss Churchill."

"Why save her? Oh, come, Mr. Breton. Why save a woman who was a traitor to her town, who was not even one of his parishioners? A woman who, by Buddhist or Christian standards, any standards you care to name, was a sinner. Why risk his life to save her?"

David hesitated, then he said, "He had the gift of true charity. The captain who led the soldiers up the mountain made that remark of Father Caraday, and I endorse it. His bishop endorsed it and so did the people of Sheromere. If you go up to Sheromere, look at the cross that marks his grave, you'll find that that is his epitaph, written in English, Kachin and Burmese. He would have gone up that mountain for anyone in Sheromere if he had known they were in danger." Now he knew he was speaking the full truth. "Ask the witnesses who are to follow me, ask the people of Sheromere. I am not a religious man, nor even a charitable one," he said, and his voice rose, "but I am a better man for having met Father Caraday! The pity of it is that he is not here today for you to meet!"

The prosecutor looked up at the judge, licking his lips to

ask to have the witness restrained. But the judge had stopped fanning himself, had leaned forward. He was not interested in politics; the law was his sole concern. He did not recognise imperialists, foreigners, intriguers; but he recognised an honest man, one who felt enough passion to defend the name of a dead friend. "Mr. Breton, it is not Father Caraday who is on trial here today. You do not have to defend him before this Bench." He looked down at the prosecutor. "Father Caraday rests in peace. Let him remain that way."

2

The hostess, smiling shyly, approached them. "Mr. Breton, it is time to go through the Customs."

"Coming," said David, and turned back to Maung Zan. "Do you think you'll ever be coming to London again?"

Maung Zan shook his head. "No, David. For better or worse, Burma is my home. I'd never be happy anywhere else."

You'll never be really happy here, David thought, not unless Rose comes back. "It would be an empty promise for me to say I'll come back here some day. There's reason enough—to visit you, to place wreaths on a couple of graves. But somehow—" He shrugged. "It took me twenty years to come out here to visit my father, even while he was alive. To be honest, I don't think I'll ever be back, Zan."

"You were always honest, David. Whatever your other faults, you were always honest. Sometimes too brutally so."

"Not always," said David, but said no more. Even now he would not tell Maung Zan of Caraday's secret. Let him rest in peace. "Goodbye, Zan. Each Christmas I'll toast you in lemonade. Vintage stuff."

"Jolly good. Well, goodbye, old chap."

"Zan, if there is ever anything you need in London—"

"Just write me, David," Maung Zan said, and the black eyes were uncommonly bright. "That's all."

"I'll do that," said David, and turned quickly and followed the tiny smiling hostess into the airport customs room.

Twenty minutes later when he walked out on to the tarmac to cross to the waiting plane, he saw Maung Zan standing at the door to the airport lounge. He raised his arm and waved, and Maung Zan waved back. The Burman, small and remote now, was still standing in the doorway when the plane turned and began to taxi down to the end of the runway. He stood there in his white suit, his arm still raised, unrecognisable now at a distance; then it was impossible to distinguish him at all, he was lost in the shadow of the doorway, he was part of the past. David sat back, aware of a sense of loss such as he had felt when his father and then Caraday had died. The sense of loss that only a knowledge of love can bring.

The plane began to climb. Maureen waited for him, six thousand miles and twelve hours to the west; he smiled at the thought, and the pain of loss was assuaged. The plane banked and he looked down on the brilliance, like a small hill of gold, of the Shwe Dagon pagoda. Antlike people went about their devotions as they had been doing for countless centuries. A saffron mite moved across a courtyard. A man stood in a tower and struck a soundless gong. Down a road between the rice fields a caravan of buffalo carts moved with the imperceptible progress of time itself. The tide of Burma flowed and ebbed, undisturbed by the comings and goings of individual men. It slumbered beneath the sun, still only half-awake in the middle of the twentieth century, still uninvolved in the convulsions of the world. But he knew that that uninvolvement could not last. He looked out of the window of the plane to the east and north, to the plains stretching away to the mountains, to the awakening giant that was China. Countries were like men: there was no longer any isolation.

Then the plane was passing over the Irrawaddy. Olive-green, pitted with small boats, it wound away to the north. Past Mandalay, past Bhamo, past Myitkyina to Sheromere and the mountains beyond. Past the town, the hospital and finally the mission. Past the two crosses in the cemetery below the tangled hill, past the remains of the two men who had helped him track the invisible tiger.